CHOKED UP

Maisie McGrane Mysteries by Janey Mack

Time's Up

Choked Up

Published by Kensington Publishing Corporation

CHOKED UP

Janey Mack

KENSINGTON BOOKS
www.kensingtonbooks.com

KENSINGTON BOOKS are published by

Kensington Publishing Corp.
119 West 40th Street
New York, NY 10018

All Kensington titles, imprints, and distributed lines are available at special quantity discounts for bulk purchases for sales promotion, premiums, fund-raising, educational, or institutional use.

Special book excerpts or customized printings can also be created to fit specific needs. For details, write or phone the office of the Kensington Sales Manager: Kensington Publishing Corp., 119 West 40th Street, New York, NY 10018. Attn. Sales Department. Phone: 1-800-221-2647.

Kensington and the K logo Reg. U.S. Pat. & TM Off.

eISBN-13: 978-1-61773-693-3
eISBN-10: 1-61773-693-7
First Kensington Electronic Edition: January 2016

ISBN-13: 978-1-61773-692-6
ISBN-10: 1-61773-692-9
First Kensington Trade Paperback Printing: January 2016

10 9 8 7 6 5 4 3 2 1

Printed in the United States of America

For David,
who chokes me up

Acknowledgments

Mom: *"All that I am, or hope to be, I owe to my angel mother."*

For every good and patient thing: Dad, Jameson, Hudson, and Grayson.

Dori Lucero, for her unending support and friendship.

My home team: Bob and Nicole, Bob and Char, Polly Ringdahl, Barb Pearse, Georgann Shiely, Cristin Clark, and Nancy Calico.

A deep and grateful thanks to Glen Schiffer, and my generous and extraordinary friends: Katherine Bohn, Jared Cagle, James H. Carroll, Andrew Cleghorn, Matt Dawson, James Dodger, Zack Dudek, Edward Dunne, Les Edgerton, Danny Fletcher, Mark Filter, Michael Fritz, John Gold, Nathan Goode, Carlos Grieco, Joshua Johnson, James Kennedy, Chris Keck, Jade Langley, Peter Brian MacDonald, Jon Mack, Mark Morrison, Matt Pettinger, Robert Pugh, Paul and Lori Renick, Mike R., A. J. Rodriguez, Steve Schoeneck, Jennifer Steager, David Sutton, Thomas Wilcox, Dr. Mike Williams, Terry Yant.

And, as always, agent Laura Bradford, editor Martin Biro, production editor Paula Reedy, and copy editor Christy Phillippe.

Chapter 1

I punched out at the Traffic Enforcement Bureau, the *ca-chunk* of the time stamp putting a bullet in the brain of yet another workday. I started the five-block hike to my car, feeling lighter with each step. Only three days and a wake-up until Hank returned.

By the time I hit Marston Avenue's squalid stretch of sidewalk, I was a heel away from skipping. Nothing makes a tomboy feel as deliciously girly as dating the ultimate alpha male. And with five older brothers carrying more machismo per square inch than The Wild Bunch, I'm pretty much an expert.

A teal Chevy Sonic swerved toward me, window down. "Fuck you, Meter Bitch!" A white ball flew out, bounced off the sidewalk, and nailed me in the shin.

The Sonic's tires squealed and it tore off up the street.

Gee, thanks, guy.

Rubbing my leg, I looked down at the cement. A rolled-up disposable diaper.

Who does that?

I picked up the stale diaper rock with two fingers and threw it in a street can, feeling nothing but lucky it hadn't hit me in the face. A typical Thursday.

Infatuation had me off my game. I was still wearing the "Loogie," the neon phlegm yellow-green reflective vest of a Chicago Parking Enforcement Agent. *Idiot.* I took it off and shoved it in my backpack as I rounded the corner onto Fourth Street.

No raining on my parade—it's Miller Time.

There may be blood, though, after I kick the ass of the bum sleeping on the hood of my—well, Hank's—perfectly restored Dodge Coronet.

The guy leaned against the windshield, head lolled back onto the roof.

"Hey. Buddy!" I called in my best law and order voice from across the street. "Off the car."

The guy didn't flinch. A couple steps closer and I saw and smelled why.

Oh jeez.

His throat was a gaping maw of red. And pink and white gristle. Slashed from ear to ear. "Holy mother of . . ." I averted my eyes to the car's grille. Thickening blood covered the air intakes while a slow trickle of red slid down the Coronet's glossy black fender wing and dripped into a puddle on the pavement.

I fumbled my iPhone out of my pocket and sent a dozen crime scene snaps to the Cloud. "Call Hank's office," I slurred into the mic, talking too fast, Siri unable to understand. I started again, "Call—"

"Step away from the car, ma'am," a man said over a loudspeaker.

I slipped my phone down the front of my shirt and glanced over my shoulder to see a blue and white CPD Tahoe, red lights flashing.

I raised my hands and backed up.

Officer Reynolds was about as nice as they came, but even with a blanket and a Hershey bar, the back of a police car was not a fun place to be. No amount of Febreze could eradicate the lingering stink of piss and puke that permeated the leather seats. Reynolds peered at me through silver-rimmed specs in the rearview mirror.

Please don't.

"Where'd you go to high school, Maisie?"

I sighed inwardly. "St. Ignatius."

"Nope. Not it." He shook his head. "Where do I know you from?"

"I just have one of those faces."

He kept staring. I rotated my fingers in a circle. "This is where you say I have the look of an Irish angel."

"Ha!" Officer Reynolds twisted awkwardly in his seat and jabbed a finger at me. "You're the meter maid. The one that threw up on Coles."

They never remember the car bomb I saved the mayor from. Only the puking.

A Crime Scene van parked in front of us and a couple of techs got out. One, a pal of my brother Rory's, spotted me in the back of the Tahoe and gave me the surprised-point-and-smile. I returned a halfhearted salute.

"How do you know—" The young cop's voice trailed off as the penny dropped. "Wait. Maisie McGrane as in one of the *McGrane* McGranes?"

I nodded.

"Man, your whole family's on the force."

"Half. The other half's defense attorneys, to keep it even."

"So why are you a meter maid?"

"Ouch. Don't pull any punches, do you?"

"I . . . erm." Reynolds's cheeks reddened. "Do you like it?"

About as much as teaching blind kids to use a band saw. "It's okay."

A couple of beat cops and a detective showed up and started working the scene. Reynolds drummed his fingers on the steering wheel. "Think your brothers'll show?"

I sure as hell hope not. "Maybe."

It was killing him to miss out on the action. And it was killing me to have him in the car. "Are you sure they don't need you out there?"

"Well . . ." He puffed out his cheeks in a show of consideration while his hand went straight to the door handle. "I probably should let 'em know I gotcha in the car."

I had my phone out of my shirt before he was all the way out of the Tahoe. He shut the door and I hit Call.

"Mr. Bannon's office," Hank's secretary answered in a voice so smoky-sexy I wanted to wipe my ear off. "How may I help you, Ms. McGrane?"

"I need to get a message to him."

"I'm afraid that won't be possible. Mr. Bannon is currently in-country and unable to receive messages for the next twenty-two hours and eight minutes."

"That's, um . . ." *Unfortunate.* I ran a hand through my hair. "We have kind of a . . . situation."

"Type?"

I blew out a slow breath. "I drove his car to work today. Now there's a dead guy lying on the hood and I'm calling you from the back of a police car."

"Will you be needing a ride home from the police station?"

Why the heck not? "Yes, please," I said and hung up as Officer Reynolds got back behind the wheel.

"How you feeling, Maisie?" His voice was light, but he'd gone a little green around the gills. "That was a pretty tough thing to see."

I suppose it would be if I hadn't spent my childhood playing Concentration with crime scene photos. "I'm okay."

Dispatch came in loud and clear over the Tahoe's radio. "Car 261, call in, please."

The young cop took his cell from the glove box and called in. "Officer Brian Reynolds reporting."

There was a short silence.

Reynolds shot upright in his seat. "Yessir, Captain Mc-Grane."

Aww for cripes' sake. Da.

"Yessir. She's in the patrol car." Officer Reynolds practically vibrated with excitement. "No sir. Detective Forman hasn't interviewed her yet."

A tiny window of hope opened before me.

"I'll bring her in myself, sir. Thank you, sir."

And slammed shut in my face.

Reynolds smiled at me in the rearview mirror. "You want me to light 'em up?"

Please don't.

I spent the next half hour ignoring the urge to check the crime scene photos and playing Zombie Gunship on my phone, cooling my heels in the frigid gray-on-gray interrogation room.

I figured I'd waited long enough and raised my phone to the two-way mirror. I shut it off, stowed it in my pocket, then folded my arms on the gray Formica table and put my head down.

That worked.

Detective Alan Forman came into the room, all pleasantries and platitudes, thinking I didn't know any better. He offered me a soda, which I declined, then took a seat, turned on a voice recorder and trolled through the usual questions.

No, I don't know the victim. No, Hank has been out of town for the last ten days. Yes, I currently reside in his home. Yes, I drive his vehicle on a regular basis. Blah blah blah.

"Hang on." The detective tapped his pen against his teeth. "I want to make sure I got this right. This Bannon guy restores a 1969 Dodge Super Bee 440 six-pack to cherry and says what— 'Hey girl, drive this to work instead of your Accord'?"

"Pretty much."

He gave me a quick once-over and scratched a note on his pad. "I see."

"What?" I was chilly, hungry, and getting tired. "You see *what?*"

The detective shrugged. "Golden handcuffs."

"Hardly," I said. "Hank believes material things are only that. Things."

"You'd know." He stifled a snort. "So what exactly is Mr. Bannon doing in Eastern Europe?"

I rubbed my eyes with the heels of my hands. "About that soda . . ."

A female uniformed officer entered the room and whispered something into the detective's ear. Whatever she said made my interrogator click off his recorder and close his notebook with a strained smile. "I think we've finished here, Miss McGrane. Officer Miller will show you out."

Officer Miller, however, did not return me to the main lobby. Instead she turned right and led me down a series of beige hallways to a tiny nondescript conference room. "Take a seat," she said and left.

I was moving up in the world. The room was warm, beige, and did not contain a two-way mirror. This would be Da or my brothers—Flynn and Rory or even Cash—jacking me around for the hell of it and, of course, for living in sin with my ex–Army Ranger boyfriend.

A soft knock at the door preceded a lightly tanned man in his early fifties wearing an expensive gray suit with a silver striped tie and brown John Lobb shoes. A heavy hitter. Good-looking in a polished, aristocratic way with a slim, foxy face and flaxen hair. "Do you have a moment, Miss McGrane?"

I straightened up. "Yes sir."

No matter where he was or what he was doing, Hank always had my six.

Hank's Law Number Twenty-One: Never confuse politeness with civility.

The man slid into the seat, folded his hands on the table, and took a good long look at me. His eyes, the color of cognac held to light, were fringed with thick gold lashes and left me feeling as exposed as a field mouse in a clearing. "My name is Walt Sawyer. I command the Bureau of Organized Crime's Special Unit."

Was the murder vic Mob connected? A thin layer of sweat broke out between my shoulder blades while my fingers turned to ice.

Easy now. Don't spin out.

My mother, "Hang 'Em High July Pruitt," was a former prosecutor. This wouldn't be my first or worst interrogation. "Nice to meet you, sir. I'm not sure what I'll be able to add to what I told Detective Forman."

"I have no interest in that case."

"Oh?"

"I am, however, interested in you."

This just kept getting better.

"May I ask why you turned down Mayor Coles's personal appointment to join the Chicago Police Department, Miss McGrane?"

Hello, left field. "Yes sir."

This was his dance. He could lead.

Sawyer's lips twitched. "Yes, as in I may ask but you won't tell?"

"I'm guessing as Special Unit commander, you have a pretty good idea already." Coles was as dirty as they came. Not even being a cop was worth working his private security detail.

He unbuttoned the button of his suit coat. "Have you ever considered applying to the BOC?"

"No sir, I haven't." *Gee, you're cute. I can be cute, too.* "I didn't imagine the Bureau of Organized Crime would have much use for a police academy washout turned meter maid."

"But you weren't really a washout, were you, Miss McGrane? A BS in Criminal Justice. Top cadet at the Academy." He gave me a vulpine smile and said lazily, "Until, of course, your father clipped your wings."

I took a slow breath, unclenched my teeth, and lied. "I don't know what you're referring to, sir."

"The pressure Homicide Captain Conn McGrane applied to the police academy psychologist to falsify your psych report, resulting in your subsequent expulsion."

Jaysus crimeny, he's been busy. "I'm afraid you're mistaken, sir."

"No matter." Sawyer leaned back in his chair and plucked invisible lint from his French cuff. "It's my preference to develop inexperienced high fliers in Special Unit." He reached inside his suit jacket, removed a tri-folded paper, and slid it across the table to me.

I opened it.

A letter. On Police Academy stationery.

> *Upon further review of Case #7M-23RC426
> re: Cadet Maisie McGrane, I rescind my
> previous diagnosis of borderline personality
> disorder.*
>   Ms. McGrane is fit for duty within the
> Chicago Police Department.
>   Dr. Tom Lucey

The bullshit Benghazi-style lack of reason and responsibility certified its legitimacy. My fingers trembled, rattling the paper.

"Miss McGrane, I want you to work for me as an undercover officer in Special Unit."

Blood pulsed in my ears. *Me? An undercover cop?*

"I find recruits infinitely more valuable without the indelible imprint of police work."

The cop look. The stance, the stride, the indefinable big-dog attitude. Eyes continually scanning for weapons while assessing threat level. Half my family walked around with it. I'd been hoping I'd acquired it through osmosis, but apparently not.

"As you can imagine," he said, "the least desirable action for an undercover officer is to react as a patrolman. My U.C.s aren't merely police working in plainclothes. No short-stint Vice stings. True undercover agents are infiltrators, going native for months, even years at a time. Identity on a need-to-know basis only."

I cleared my throat, trying hard to stay frosty in the face of serious Serpico action. I could keep my nerve and my mouth shut, sure. But a police spook? It wasn't the way I wanted to be a cop.

"Covert work is highly stressful and extremely dangerous." He held out his hand for the letter. "I wouldn't be here if I didn't think you were built for it."

I folded it up and handed it back to him, unable to look away as he returned it to his inside jacket pocket.

Sawyer cocked his head. "Reservations?"

"Maybe." It wasn't the criminals I was afraid of. It was my family.

"Rather tortured, aren't you?" His odd-colored eyes seemed

lit from within. "Shielding the father who betrayed you and dreaming of becoming a cop while sleeping with a mercenary."

My entire life summed up in one smooth sentence. It wasn't enough to make me swoon. "I won't go against Hank Bannon or my father. Not ever."

A whisper of irritation crossed his face. "Special Unit has little interest in an ex–Army Ranger operating primarily outside of the United States. Even less for a decorated police captain exerting his influence, which I assume he'll continue to do."

Yes, he will, goddammit.

Sawyer leaned forward. "This is your shot. Are you going to take it?"

"Yes," I said. *Hell, yes!*

He handed me a small white envelope.

"What's this?"

Sawyer's mouth quirked at the corner. "Your ticket to the show." He rose and walked to the door. "I'll be in touch."

Tiny sparks danced in front of my eyes.

Holy cat.

Where's a paper bag when you need one?

Chapter 2

I opened the envelope. Inside was a thick ivory business card engraved with navy ink and a small silver star, the words *Walt Sawyer, Commander, B.O.C. Special Unit* and a phone number. Definitely not standard issue. I had the feeling not much about Walt Sawyer was.

On the back were three lines in an elegant scrawl:

> DANNY KAPLAN
> SATURDAY, 6:45 A.M.
> 41466 W. 43RD AVE.

I put the card in my pocket, the envelope in the trash can, and wandered out into the lobby of the Chicago Police Department. Sawyer's words bounced around in my brain like a Super Ball dropped from a skyscraper.

I'm on the job. I'm finally on the goddamn job.

I floated past the reception desk, trying to find my feet. Two dark-eyed, dark-haired, square-jawed tough guys in jeans and sport coats loitered at the plate-glass entrance.

Da let slip the dogs of war.

My brothers, Flynn and Rory. Six-feet-one-inch and six feet of pure black-Irish charm, piss and vinegar. I walked toward them, praying my ride was already there.

"You find a body and you don't call?" Flynn said. "You don't write?"

Aww. Hurt feelings on top of everything. "I didn't want you to get your hopes up. You'd have to recuse yourself anyway."

Flynn's lip curled. "Sweet."

"Let's go, Snap." Rory grabbed me by the arm, none too gently.

"Thanks." I resisted the urge to pull away. "I have a ride."

"Yeah. Us."

Flynn half-closed his eyes in confirmation. "We sent your town car back." He pushed open the door for Rory and me. "What kind of brothers would we be, leaving you all on your own?"

Nice ones?

Rory frog-marched me to his Cadillac CTS sedan. Flynn stepped ahead and opened the back passenger door with a flourish.

"Gee, thanks." At least he didn't give me the perp head-duck as I got in and buckled up. "You guys need directions to Hank's?"

Rory glowered at me in the rearview mirror. "You feckin' kidding?" He started the car and pulled out.

"We know the way," Flynn said.

Since when?

Before I could press him, Rory tagged in. "How'd you know the vic?"

"I didn't," I said.

"You sure?" Rory juiced the car, weaving in and out of traffic at a sedate 20 mph over the city speed limit.

"She's too small-fry for that level of depravity." Flynn rubbed the back of his neck. "It's a message for Bannon. Or someone he works for."

Rory grabbed his phone off the dash and tossed it to Flynn. "Nancy's e-mailing the crime scene photos."

Flynn scrolled through the messages. "When did the 'Matchstick' become Nancy?"

"How the feck you think I'm getting the pictures?"

"Matchstick?" I said.

"Skinny redhead CSI tech," Flynn answered over his shoulder. "Has the shivering fits every time Rory walks by."

"Shut it." Rory merged onto the freeway and shifted into high gear.

"If you go any faster, I'm lighting it up," Flynn warned.

I curled toward the window. City lights streaked by in a blur as I traced the outline of Sawyer's business card in my cargo pants pocket. My heart thrummed.

Oh my god oh my god oh my god.

Not only am I going to be a cop, I'm going undercover. Squee!

This must be what Ecstasy feels like.

Built into the bluffs, Hank's house was a high-tech fortress of midcentury modern meets bomb shelter. Rory pulled into the driveway, igniting a stadium's worth of motion lights. I popped my seat belt before he put the car in Park.

"Thanks for the ride, guys." I grabbed the door handle. It didn't open.

Stupid child safety locks.

Rory smirked in the rearview mirror. "Let me get that for you."

"The least we can do is walk you to the door." Flynn got out, too.

Super.

They followed me into the portico tighter than ticks on a hound. The massive front door was surrounded by square opaque black glass tiles. I laid my hand on one and leaned into the one above it, right eye open. After the retinal and palm scan, an illuminated keypad appeared where I'd put my hand.

Rory spat on the sidewalk. "Fancy."

I typed in the ten-digit security code. The screen blinked green twice. No one had entered the premises since I'd left. The door unlocked with a soft *click.* I turned around. "Thanks again, guys. Have a safe trip home."

"Wouldn't send us off without a beer, now, would you?" Flynn said as they jostled past me, throwing open the heavy door.

"As a matter of fact—" I hustled after them.

"Jaysus." Rory whistled. "Get a load of this feckin' place. All cement and steel."

And sex appeal. It was a perfect extension of Hank: lean, rugged sophistication.

"An airplane hangar hijacked by Restoration Hardware."
Flynn took in the spectacular view of city lights with a skeptical
eye. "This didn't come cheap." He leaned on the granite bar
counter. "Want to tell me again what your boyfriend does for a
living?"

*Ah, the joy of having brothers who run in-depth background
checks.* "Not especially."

Rory went behind the wet bar like he owned it, opened the
fridge, and took out three Budweisers. He twisted off the tops
and set two on the bar. "Get your goddamn head on straight
and come home, Snap."

"Well, since you're asking so sweet . . ."

Flynn took his beer off the counter, left the living room, and
started walking down the hallway toward the east wing.

"Hey! Where do you think you're going?" I said, as he disappeared at the end of the hall.

Dammit. I started after him, feeling Rory move behind me in
the opposite direction. The old split 'em up. "Knock it off, you
guys." I rounded the corner after Flynn.

"What's this?" My brother smacked his hand against the
heavy steel door that led to the basement. It, too, was inset with
a black glass square. "The Batcave or the kill room?"

"Not my business." I stepped between Flynn and the door.
"Not yours, either."

"What's in there?"

"I don't know."

"Bullshit. Just because you're not going to be a cop doesn't
mean you'd turn a blind eye to criminal activity."

Not a cop, eh? "Oh, you'd be surprised at what I can ignore." I put my right hand and right eye to the scanner. A small
red light flashed with the words *Access Denied.* "See?"

The scan required my right eye, *left* hand, and a different ten-
digit code. Even though I had access, I'd never used it. Hank
asked me not to, and that was good enough for me.

Flynn spun on his heel and opened the door to the four-car
garage. Black Craftsman cabinets and toolboxes rode the rear
wall, the floor a spotless tan epoxy. The first two bays were

empty. Hank's G-Wagen was at the airport and the Super Bee in the police impound lot. My unused Honda Accord rested in the third stall while the fourth held an Indian motorcycle, a couple dirt bikes, and an ATV.

The garage made Flynn even angrier than the locked door.

Shaking his head, he returned to the main hall and entered the remaining room. The master bedroom. He glanced in the teak and white tile bathroom, purposely ignored the bed, and strode into the walk-in closet. Hank's things were on the right, mine on the left.

Most of the clothes on my side were brand-new. Flynn swiped his hand across a bunch of shirts and dresses, setting tags from Saks and Neiman Marcus fluttering.

"You let him *buy you* . . ." he asked haltingly, wanting it to sting, "all this?"

"Yeah. That's something boyfriends do. Buy presents for their girlfriends." I patted his chest. "You get one someday, you'll understand."

It wasn't the clothes that had Flynn grinding his teeth. Not really. As July Pruitt's—of the Georgia Pruitts—adopted children, we were each endowed with a trust fund. It was Da who'd tainted our brood with Irish-Catholic guilt and the ideal of the self-made man.

"Maybe I'll ask the Matchstick out," Flynn said.

Oh God . . . Rory.

I ran down the hall. The west wing held two bedrooms, two bathrooms, a home gym, and Hank's office.

Rory lounged behind Hank's airplane-wing desk, boots on the credenza, drinking his second beer, as evidenced by the empty bottle next to the keyboard.

"Nickel tour's over." I jerked my thumb toward the door. "Beat it."

Rory raised his palms. "Just wanted to check my e-mail."

"You can do that on your phone."

"I am."

Flynn came in with another beer and dropped down onto the charcoal leather couch. "Let's take a look."

I picked up the remote and turned on the giant LCD TV across from Hank's desk. "He's got AirPlay. Send your signal."

Rory tapped his phone, and the dead guy on Hank's car appeared on the monitor in all his macabre glory. "Like a lamb to the slaughter." He swiped through the photos.

"Weird," I squeaked and cleared my throat. "How'd the perp keep him on the car while he sliced him?"

"Go back one." Flynn squinted at the screen. "Close in on his hands."

Rory magnified the vic's hands. Clear plastic cable ties secured his wrists to his own belt loops. He zoomed out. "Not much arterial spray."

I sank down next to Flynn.

"See it yet?" he asked.

I shook my head.

"Take your time," Flynn said patiently. "How would you do it?"

I took a long swallow, the cold beer going directly to my temples. The answer appeared when I set the bottle down and saw what I should have seen from the start. The giant pool of blood between the vic's black denim–clad legs.

"I'm guessing the perp put the vic up onto the car, sliced his femoral artery, and waited a couple minutes until he was too weak to struggle against the final slash."

Flynn nodded. "That's my take, too."

"Perp's a feckin' asshole," Rory said. "Helluva message."

"Yeah?" I said. "How so?"

He chuckle-scoffed. "Snap, yeh do realize what he's done to the car. Piss and shite and blood in the vents and air intakes. Sludge coating half the engine by now." An unpleasant smile split his face. "Your lad's gonna have to have it rebuilt."

Cripes.

I wanted to tell them so very badly about Walt Sawyer and going undercover. I opened my mouth and a giant yawn of adrenaline release came out of nowhere, saving me from myself. I barely covered it with my hand. "Sorry," I said and yawned again.

What is wrong with me?

I stood up and clicked off the monitor. "That ol' highway's a callin', boys."

Flynn folded his arms across his chest. "You can't stay here, Maisie."

"I'm perfectly safe."

Flynn stood and laid his hand on my shoulder. "When he's around, maybe."

"And that's a big feckin' maybe." Rory got up.

Hank's Law Number Seventeen: De-escalate. The true fight is won without fighting.

I nodded. "I'm wrecked, guys. Meter maid duty and a dead body are pretty much all I can handle in one day." *And, of course, that tiny little life-changer—joining the BOC.*

A long look passed between them. "Okay," Flynn said. "We're gone."

They walked out, not liking it, but taking it just the same. I locked the door behind them and slumped against it, feeling like a bear with my head stuck in a hive.

A five-mile run, followed by a bath and a bag of Sour Patch Kids might induce a little Zen.

I changed, hopped on the tread, and put on my pink wireless Beats. In minutes I was sweating, running a straight and steady eight-minute mile, listening to Toby Stephens reading *From Russia with Love,* feeling about as secret-agent as I could get. Seven miles later I turned off the treadmill.

Look out Special Unit. Here I come.

At 3:00 in the morning, I shot up in bed, chest aching, unable to breathe, blood thundering in my ears. When I quit shaking, I went into the closet and dug one of Hank's dress shirts out of the dirty clothes bin.

I slipped it on, inhaling the faint smell of laundry soap, Paco Rabanne, and the indefinable pheromone magic that was Hank. Armoring up in his discipline and calm with each button I fastened, I let my thoughts drift.

I'd trained with Hank for over a year, flashing him the googly heart–eyes the entire time. He'd never shown me a flicker of interest until the worst day of my life, the day the Academy gave me the ax.

That night, he took me to Blackie's, a swanky private club.

Over martinis, the sharp humiliation dulled to a manageable haze as I gazed at him, mesmerized. It wasn't his eyes—so pale they were almost colorless—that held me immobile, it was his mouth. A thin, cruel upper lip with a full lower one. The same shaped mouth I'd seen in every Batman and Captain America comic book I've ever read.

He'd smiled at me then. An intimate, sexy superhero smile.

"You seem real broken up about my news," I said.

"I'm not." Hank put his hand over mine. "I don't date cops."

Whoa.

Even now, months later, just thinking about it gave me a happy shiver.

I climbed back in bed—his side this time—closed my eyes, and tried to cycle down. But I couldn't. Those four little words niggled and burrowed in my brain. "I don't date cops."

I rolled over and mashed the pillow into shape. That was months ago.

He couldn't possibly mean it now.

Chapter 3

I sprang out of bed like a kid with one more day until summer vacation. Tomorrow I'd meet Sawyer's mysterious Mr. Kaplan and finally get the iron albatross aka Parking Enforcement, off my back.

Sugar-free Amp in hand, I sped to work, the windows of my Accord down, heat cranked, singing along to songs I didn't know the words to.

I parked in the pay lot close to work, cheerfully taking the thirty-six-dollar scalp. It was entirely possible today could be my last day meter-maiding. Forever. Fingers crossed.

I swiped my key card through the security lock of the Traffic Enforcement Bureau's satellite office and traversed the gray hallway to the break room. I rounded the corner and was assaulted by the smell of old Chobani yogurt, maple syrup, and mildew. A couple dozen uniformed parking enforcement agents milled around the time card punch.

I got the walleye from a select few and was ignored by the rest.

Golly, how will I ever be able to leave such a friendly workplace?

"Hi there, Maisie," hummed Sylvia Owen's unmistakable Midwestern drone. "Can ya spare a minute?"

I nodded.

She glanced around the room. Naturally, not a soul was paying attention. "There's this group of, well . . ." She leaned forward and whispered, ". . . *vandals*. And they're *not normal*."

"Oh?" I couldn't give a flying squirrel. "What are they doing?"

"They're feeding the meters and washing off my chalk marks. I'm so far off quota, I'll be on probation faster 'n you can say Velveeta."

"And?"

Sylvia held up crossed fingers on both sides of her face. "Could we swap routes for a day?"

"Sure." I'd be undercover in a matter of hours. I could afford to be generous.

Thwack-pop!

It hit the windshield in a small explosion. I stomped on the brakes. The rear of the cart fishtailed left. I cycled the wheel to the right, counter-steering. "No. No!" The LTI gauge hit the red zone and I was on two wheels. Frozen in a split second of slomo eternity. "*Nonono!*"

The Interceptor wobbled and dropped its third wheel back on the unforgiving asphalt with a reverberating *thunk*. I goosed the gas. The cart shuddered and stalled.

In the middle of LaSalle.

I dropped my head onto the steering wheel, laugh-panting in relief. "Whoo-hoo!"

Nothing is as schadenfreudeily delicious to a Chicagoan as a meter maid tipping her cart.

Denied! Suck it, haters!

I looked at the windshield to see what had me panicking like a meth-head in a dentist's chair.

An egg.

Nice reflexes, Tex. Cripes. I almost deserved to tip over.

Thwack-pop!

Three men, each wearing green hoodies with a single long feather attached, surrounded my cart.

I guess Sylvia wasn't kidding about the "not normal" part.

One shouted, "Huzzah!" and the twentysomething basement dwellers opened fire. Eggs pinged the thin steel doors and windows of the cart. From the sound and coverage, I was guessing about three-dozen worth.

Jaysus. If Walt Sawyer could see me now . . . He'd rescind his offer faster than fur off a PETA model.

The Interceptor needed a minute to restart, so I sat there and took it, ignoring the itch to turn on the windshield wipers. Of course this had to happen here. Because the gods of comeuppance agreed that only one place in the entire city qualified for my maximum humiliation.

City Hall.

Ammo expended, the vandals ambled off, exchanging fist bumps with the few scattered pedestrians. I started the Interceptor and hit the wipers. Smear city. A Lava Lamp display of yolk, albumen, and wiper fluid, hardening with every squelch.

I wouldn't make it to the end of the block.

Wyckoff's Car Wash taunted me from a half mile away, even though the odds of me *not* getting stuck in the soap cycle for an hour were lower than a dyslexic winning a spelling bee.

With a groan, I crossed LaSalle to the City Hall side. Flexing his executive muscle, the illustrious Mayor Coles had rezoned the fire lane to a "special permit" standing zone. So now there was plenty of space for his select few. I pulled into the empty curb a good ten yards ahead of a gleaming navy Range Rover, popped my seat belt, and got out.

Rounding the cart, I glanced back at the SUV. The newspaper-reading driver waited patiently for whatever VIP slime Coles was courting. A small silver badge mounted next to the front door winked in the early afternoon sun, discreetly proclaiming the Range Rover was the ultimate elite model, an Autobiography Black.

I gave a low whistle. Coles's VIP may be a whale, but he was an orca. Sly enough to pay $230K for a car whose exterior was indistinguishable from its $85K counterpart. Except, of course, for the 7.8-inch longer wheel base and non-glare bulletproof windows.

I wasn't a car fanatic by nature, merely osmosis. Only two topics of discussion held center stage at McGrane family dinners. Bad guys and badass cars.

I popped the Interceptor's trunk and retrieved my standard emergency kit—Costco baby wipes and Hefty bags. I opened the passenger door, using the jamb as a step, and started swiping eggs off the roof into the garbage bag.

How does a parking enforcement agent handle the public's adoration?

A glob of egg slid down inside my shirtsleeve to the elbow.

Gingerly.

I hopped off, closed the door, and started wiping it down, ignoring the honks and howls of passersby. And people think New Yorkers are dinks.

At least the sidewalk in front of City Hall was a desert wasteland since it was after lunch hour.

I moved to the hood.

Perspiration misted my forehead. I reached across the hood, straining on tiptoe to scrub the tiny flecks of shell already stuck cement-style to the top of the windshield.

I can honestly say I'm not gonna miss this.

A heavy weight landed between my shoulder blades, pinning me to the hood. "Where's Bannon?" a man's voice demanded.

My tongue went thick in my mouth. "I don't know who you're talking about." The hand on my back crushed the breath from me. "Uhnngh."

"You sure about that?" he said.

Hank's Law Number Four: Keep your head.

"No sir," I lied. "I mean, yessir, I don't know any Bannon, sir." His right hand went between my legs. "How about now?"

"Please don't."

His hand grasped and twisted at my groin, fingers wrenching my heavy polyester cargo pants and underpants. "Stop!"

He didn't. "Hank and I, we used to share everything."

Not me, you sonuvabitch!

I went dead weight. He lost his grip as I dropped my full 116 pounds on the hand between my legs. When my chest hit the Interceptor's bumper, I blasted up from the ground, aiming for his chin with the top of my head.

Nothing. Just air.

He's fast.

I threw a high hard left elbow that didn't connect, using my body's rotation to unleash a vicious spinning kick that landed . . . back where I started. My foot slammed into the Interceptor's hood and I stumbled backward up onto the curb.

"Damn, you're slow." He shook his head. "Not quite as slow as the stringer I left on your car, but close." Caucasian, brown and brown, six feet tall, 180 pounds. The kind of man that was intentionally unremarkable in every way.

A killer wearing Levi's and a Gap tee. He leered. "Where is he, Maisie?"

He knows my name. My brain stalled.

The really horrible thing about learning hand-to-hand combat from an ex–Army Ranger is that you know when you're outmatched. Instantly.

Gap Tee was faster, stronger, and more experienced.

I was armed with . . . unpredictability. He was too close to my cart and City Hall was too far. If I could get the Range Rover between us, I could run circles around it until someone intervened or he gave up.

Gap Tee appeared immobile, but his weight was on the balls of his feet, arms loose at his sides, jonesing for me to make a move.

I glanced over my shoulder at City Hall. A group of dark suits converged on the steps an untenable thirty yards away. I let my eyes linger, hoping Gap Tee would turn his head or step left. He didn't.

Shit. Plan B.

I clicked the radio on my vest. "Code Blue, Code Blue." I took a step toward him. "City Hall. Felony Assault."

Gap Tee's eyebrows arched in disbelief.

I stepped closer. My radio buzzed with static. "Police notified," Dispatch replied. "ETA ten minutes."

I kept my hand on my radio trying to look terrified—which I was—and secretly unhooked it from the clip.

He snorted in amusement. "You think that's gonna help?"

"I was hoping—" I flung the radio at his face and sprinted toward the Range Rover. He caught me by the ponytail and yanked. My fingertips glanced off the hood.

He tightened his grip on my hair, walked me forward, and smacked my head down on the hood of the SUV.

The driver lowered the newspaper and raised it again.

I guess a rescue is out.

I kicked backward. My work boot glanced off his shin.

He let go of my hair and pinned me by the neck. His thumb ground into the soft tissue pressure point beneath my jaw. Involuntary tears poured from my eyes. He kicked my feet apart.

Oh Jesus.

I looked sideways up at him.

He drew back his arm, but he didn't make a fist. Instead his fingers curled into a tiger's claw. "Don't worry. I'll leave you recognizable."

I didn't flinch. Refused to close my eyes. I wouldn't give him the satisfaction.

A shadow crossed behind him. Gap Tee's head cracked off the Rover's steel windshield frame and disappeared from sight.

I rested there, ignoring the scuffling sounds, my cheek pressed to the cool metal hood, blinking, trying to stem the streaming sinus tears.

A pale, angular, close-shaven face with bright and wild blue eyes appeared next to mine. "He is gone."

I tried to smile. My lips trembled. I pressed myself upright and turned to face my savior. A lean and lithe five-nine in a Gieves and Hawkes suit, raven-haired, with an Eastern European accent.

Russian?

Three suit-wearing gorillas ringed a protective detail around him, each managing to look simultaneously detached and pissed off that Gap Tee had escaped.

"You wanted help, yes?" the man said.

"Yes." *I am an infant. Raised on a desert island by other infants.* I wiped my cheeks on my sleeve and held out my hand. "Thanks. Very much."

He took it in both of his. "You are welcome . . . ?"

"Maisie," I said. "Maisie McGrane."

"Stannis." He grinned and said something I couldn't understand to the men surrounding him. "You will tell me, Maisie." He nodded, still holding my hand. "My driver. He did not help you?"

A bodyguard went around to the driver's door, opened it, and dragged the driver over.

Uh-oh. "He wasn't—"

Stannis let go, took two quick steps, and backhanded the driver across the face. The man fell to one knee, head turned away as Stannis spoke in his ear. The driver's face went the color of green chalk.

I recognized a couple of swear words. Not Russian. *Serbian.* Watching grown men cry on FIFA World Cup Soccer has its perks after all.

Stannis returned to me, all smiles and nods. "He works for *me.*" He tapped his chest. "He represents *me.* You understand?"

Sure. The Serbian Mob has come to Chi-town. "Yes," I said.

Behind Stannis, the driver clutched his left hand to his chest, tripping over his feet in his haste to get back behind the wheel.

"Now you call police?"

Oh jeez. The police . . . Why the hell did I do that? "I did," I said. "On my radio."

Hank, all icy fury and efficiency, would want to handle Gap Tee his own way. Violently. The last thing I needed was my trio of cop brothers showing up, nosing around and getting curious. Or worse. Da.

Jaysus Criminey. I gotta shut this down. Now.

I scanned the sidewalk for the little black plastic box.

One of the gorillas handed it to Stannis, who offered it to me. I plugged the radio back into my vest and popped the button three times. "This is McGrane. Cancel Code Blue."

"You sure about that?" came Dispatch's scratchy reply.

"Positive. Cancel Code Blue. McGrane out."

Stannis frowned at me. "I would wait. Tell his likeness to police."

"No point. You chased him off." I looked up at him through my lashes and changed the subject. "Why did you do that?"

He bared his lower teeth, crooked and white. "Maybe one day you help Stannis."

"I owe you." *Super. Always fun to owe a criminal a favor.*

"So, my new friend. Tell me. Why no police?"

Out of the FryDaddy into the lava pit. "Um . . ."

Hmmm. How best to explain to a Serbian Mobster he's just rescued me from one of my dark horse boyfriend's enemies?

Don't even try. "He's a bad man."

Stannis's blue eyes were electric on mine. "So am I."

Chapter 4

After Stannis and his gorillas drove away, I got in the Interceptor, locked the doors, and forced myself to take two full minutes of deep breaths, trying to get the rusty gears of rational thought to mesh together for a tactical response.

What the hell was that?

On the plus side, I now knew what the killer looked like. Minus side, he was using me as leverage against Hank. And he was as brazen as a devil in the Delta.

I realized I wasn't going to get any calmer and called in.

"Mr. Bannon's office," the secretary answered in her languorous drawl. "How may I help you, Ms. McGrane?"

"I need to speak with him."

"I apologize. That's not possible. Mr. Bannon is still in-country. Two hours and three minutes until he's able to receive messages."

A bark of laughter escaped my throat. "Great."

"Level of urgency?"

For me? Off the freaking charts. For Hank? I was, after all, fine. "Low to moderate."

"Ms. McGrane, the vocal imprint system is detecting a significant amount of stress in your speech. Mr. Bannon has several assets on retainer I can make immediately available to you at this time."

Assets? More like associates. Cripes. This was getting worse by the second. "Um, no thanks."

"Your message?" Her soft lilt turned metallic. I'd be leaving one or else.

"Please tell Mr. Ba—er, Hank, I met the guy who left the message yesterday and I'm staying at my parents." I hung up before she smooth-talked me into more trouble.

I drove all the way back to the Traffic Enforcement Bureau lot, surfing the panic wave, head swiveling like an owl on Adderall. Inside the barbed-wire, camera-laden, armed-guarded parking enforcement lot, I started to relax. Slightly.

I hosed down the Interceptor, so the cart dogs wouldn't be scrubbing egg adhesive all night, then went inside the office, got a Coke from the vending machine, and sat down to write up my reports.

The pink Interceptor accident form was first. I wrote it up, tucked it in my pocket, and started on the incident report. But Gap Tee getting the jump on me was pretty much all I could think about. It took forever and an hour to fill in the short worksheet and describe the idiotic band of feathered hoodie wearers' egging.

A hand slapped down on the table across from me. "You wanna 'splain that Code Blue recall, McGrane?" I looked up. Leticia Jackson's four-eleven bulk loomed over me, an open sack of Cheetos clutched in her hand.

"I panicked."

"Bullshit." My stubby supervisor rolled her eyes in disbelief. "A Code Blue's a three-day mandatory leave. Why you go mess up an all-paid vaycay?"

"Because taking a ration of shit from my brothers for the rest of my life is definitely not worth it."

Leticia gave a musical titter and in a surprisingly deft motion pulled the chair back with her foot as she swept her hand across the table, snagged the report, and sat down. She tipped her head back and poured in a mouthful of Cheetos. Crunching, she scanned the form. "Don't see no mention of the B-A-D, McGrane."

"The what?"

"Big ass dent in the hood o' your Interceptor."

"Yeah. That's on me." *When my spin kick missed Gap Tee by a country mile.* I removed the pink accident form from my pocket and handed it across. "Dock me. It wasn't part of the egging. I did it."

She snickered. "With what? Your imagination? Your tiny white onion couldn't make a dent in a cardboard box."

"I . . . uh, kicked it."

"What, you take a ka-rah-tay class after work and now you think you some kinda Bruce Lee ninja?" Before I could answer she tore the pink form in half, took a pen from her shirt pocket and clicked it three times. "Get me a Kit Kat. Those hoodie motherfuckers are gonna take the heat on this."

I returned with a candy bar and a Dr Pepper. Leticia stood up and gathered the snacks and the incident report to her chest. "Go on home and rub a lil' Vaseline on your behind, Mc-Grane."

"Huh?"

She laughed. "Must be chappin' your ass not to pay for that dent."

I watched her strut to the locker room, wondering where the hell she got the idea that I was some kind of saint, seeing as I was about to lie like a legless dog to my entire family.

Still, $150 not docked from my soon-to-be final paycheck. Not everything about the day sucked monkey balls.

The iPhone chirped. A text from Hank's office.

Msg received. ET of contact: 0500.

An overwhelming sense of relief washed over me, leaving me loose-limbed and determined to prove to Hank I could play it smart and take care of myself. Which meant I had to leave the Accord, arm up, and never be alone.

I got my gear and called my youngest older brother Cash for a ride home. Because if a girl isn't safe in a house full of cops and lawyers with semiautomatic weapons, where is she really?

* * *

A bright yellow Ford Mustang pulled up in front of the Parking Enforcement office. Subterranean Ska blasted through the stereo, the bass shaking the windows. A younger, rowdier carbon copy of Flynn and Rory leaned out the window. "Cash's Taxi Service."

I got in. "Thanks."

"What's wrong with the wheels?"

"Something wasn't quite right!" I yelled, knowing better than to ask him to turn it down. "I didn't want to risk driving it!" *Mostly true.*

Cash lowered the volume. "Why? Was there a body on it, too?"

"Funny."

"'Fess up. You wanted an armed escort."

"What can I say?" I fastened my seat belt. "I think security guard and you're the first one to come to mind."

"Ba-da-bum. *Chshhh*." He hit my head at his cymbal clash. "So was it bad or really bad?"

"Moderate blood. Above-average gore. It wouldn't make the Top Twenty or anything."

"Didja recognize him?"

"No." I sighed and lied, "Neither would Hank. Just another random Chicago snuff that keeps us America's Murder Capital."

"I hear that's what Detective Forman thinks, anyway. So—" He tagged me in the shoulder with a playful punch. "Where to? James Bond's super-secret hideout?"

"Home, Jeeves."

He nodded, a self-satisfied look on his face. "About time."

"Don't."

"Don't what?"

I pinched the bridge of my nose. "Start on Hank."

"Christ, I wasn't about to. Last time I looked in the mirror I wasn't Da or Flynn or Rory pissing on your leg just because you got a boyfriend."

"Yeah, well—"

"Bannon's a stand-up guy. I'm cool with him."

Whoa. "Sorry."

"You should be." Cash's jaw edged forward. "You're killing Da, Maisie."

"Hardly."

He shook his head. "You gonna nurse this grudge into the ground or what?"

Great. Cash, once firmly on my side, was now sliding traitorously toward Team Family Unity. "I wouldn't get too cocky if I were you. Da waited until the last minute to stick the knife in my back. You're not wearing a SWAT uniform yet, cowboy."

"Wanna bet?" He grinned. "My transfer's official next week. The delay was all on Vice's end. They begged SWAT for one more month of Cash McGrane's patented mayhem arrest magic."

"That's terrific. I'm really happy for you."

He glanced at me, waiting for a punch line that didn't come. "Uh . . . thanks."

"You bet." I closed my eyes and chewed the insides of my cheeks. *My God, if he knew—hell, if they all knew—I was BOC, they'd explode like Roman candles dipped in kerosene.*

Cash, hoping I was considering forgiving Da, decided to keep his mouth shut. We drove the rest of the way home thinking our own thoughts.

He hit the clicker for our security gate and drove in.

No cars in the driveway. Which didn't mean much. With five older brothers, there were always a couple malingering about. Cash pulled into his stall. Mom's Jag, and Da's Mercedes were there, but their date-night Aston Martin was gone. The other stalls were empty.

My shoulders sagged in relief. For once, no one was home.

"You wanna put on a headset, knock back some beers, and play a lil' *Halo* or *MOH Warfighter?*"

"Rain check?"

Cash snorted in disgust. "Wuss. Whatevs."

We got out of the car. I left him monkeying with his gear and went inside. Mom had left a note on the kitchen counter.

> *Cash,*
> *Da and I are at an NRA fund-raising dinner*

with the twins. Thierry made roast chicken
with white bean tapenade. Apricot cakes for
dessert.
   Love,
   Mom
   P.S. Leave some for Flynn and Rory.

Thank God.
I bypassed dinner, snagged a tub of Häagen-Dazs Vanilla
Swiss Almond from the freezer, and went directly to bed.

The iPhone buzzed under my pillow. Instantly awake, I swiped
the screen. Hank was two hours and thirty-three minutes early.
   "Did he hurt you?" His voice was barely audible over the
whump-whump-whump of helicopter blades.
   "No." My heart started pumping double-time at the sound of
his voice. "But he was going to."
   "Appearance?"
   "White, brown and brown, six feet, one-eighty. Fit, fast. No
identifying marks."
   "Exact words?"
   " 'Hank and I used to share everything.' " My airway nar-
rowed. "And . . . 'I'll leave you recognizable.' "
   "Stay in the house until I come for you."
   "I can't."
   The rhythmic drone of the helicopter filled the silence. Hank
and I were walking the wire. Always. Da and my brothers were
just waiting for a slipup. Me staying home for no apparent rea-
son was raw meat in the tiger's cage.
   He cursed under his breath. "Two men will arrive within the
hour. One you'll see."
   And one I won't. "Okay."
   "And, Peaches? Wear your Glock."

Chapter 5

3:02 a.m., a faded blue, janky Ford pickup covered in duct tape parked under a streetlight across from our gated driveway.

Hello, one impossible to miss.

I pulled on some sweats and snuck downstairs into the kitchen. Nothing garners goodwill like a bribe. Into a paper grocery sack went a couple of Red Bulls, a Coke, a Gatorade, three PowerBars, a big bag of Fritos, and a turkey sandwich. I turned off the alarm and slipped outside to meet my new shadow.

I knocked on the bed of the pickup before approaching the driver's side.

An enormous man with shoulder-length blond hair cranked down the window. "Maisie McGrane."

"Yep."

He leaned his shaggy head out the window. A ragged scar ran down his cheek into a neck of shiny, puckered skin. "What's up?"

"Nothing." I held out the grocery bag. "I appreciate you being here."

He took it and threw me a two-finger salute. "Randolph Acrey. Everyone calls me—"

Thor?

"Ragnar."

I can see that.

He looked inside the bag and nodded. "Fuck me," he breathed. "Thanks!"

"How would you feel about giving me a ride around oh-five-thirty? I'll buy you brekkie."

Ragnar nodded. "Cool."

"Great. Thanks." With a wave, I scooted back into the house, reset the alarm, and went back to bed, patting myself on the back over the first step toward keeping my family as deep in the dark as a Russian sub in the Bering Strait.

Ragnar liked 7-Eleven breakfast burritos, country music, Descartes, lutefisk, Dana Perino, and dropping the f-bomb every third word. "You get up this early every fuckin' day?"

"Nope." I chugged down a third of my second sugar-free Amp. "Do you?"

He unwrapped another breakfast burrito. "Only for Bannon."

"Very often?"

Ragnar shook his finger. "Off-limits," he said around another mouthful of burrito.

My Viking companion had the wily skill set of a back-alley lawyer. Mom would adore him. In the hour we'd been sitting in the 7-Eleven parking lot, the only useful information I'd been able to glean was that he had no idea who Gap Tee was.

He gave me an appreciative glance. "You two pretty serious, huh?"

Forget flowers and candy. Nothing says I love you like a double tap. "What makes you say that?"

"I don't work cheap." Ragnar put the last of the burrito in his mouth. "You ready?"

"Sure."

He wiped his mouth on his sleeve, turned up Lynda Kay's "Jack & Coke," and started the truck.

The energy drinks had all the impact of warm milk. I closed my eyes, leaned back against the headrest, and dozed off.

"Hey." Ragnar shook my shoulder with a massive paw. "We're here." He put the truck in Park. I sat up, flipped down the passenger-side vanity mirror, daubed on some lip gloss, reached for the door, and stopped short. We were in the circular drive of an industrial building. A beige and white sign read *Silverthorn Estates Assisted Living. A Celebration of Senior Life.*

What the—? I snuck a peek at the back of Sawyer's business card. This was the place, all right.

"You carrying?" he said.

"Yeah." The Kimber Solo in my FlashBang bra holster, while undetectable beneath my navy Tahari suit coat, felt like it weighed thirty pounds. The holster was a birthday present from my brothers, who thought it was hilarious. They wouldn't be laughing now.

I hopped out. "My friend . . ." I jerked a thumb at the building and raised a shoulder. "I'm not sure how long I'll be."

"Fuck, kid." Ragnar ran a hand through his tangled blond hair. "I got nothing but time."

The inside of Silverthorn Estates was just like any other upscale Swedish-style medical facility. Light and airy with blond wood, stainless-steel railings, and terrazzo floors. Six thirty a.m. and the place was a bustling hive of activity. Staff members in solid jewel-tone scrubs with silver name badges wove in and out of groups of cheerful, well-coiffed seniors in various stages of decrepitude.

I waited in line at the reception desk. A woman in a bureaucratic gray suit greeted me. "Good morning."

"I have a six forty-five with Danny Kaplan."

"Yes." She gave me a practiced smile. "Welcome to Silverthorn Estates, Ms. McGrane." She typed rapidly into the computer. "I see the Kaplan estate has granted you unlimited family access. Please step this way."

I walked around the arc of the desk to a small alcove where a tan X had been painted on the floor. "Stand on the X please. Look up and smile."

I did. She snapped a picture and then spun the monitor in my direction. "Is this satisfactory?"

I nodded.

She returned to the computer and typed, talking nonstop. "Here at Silverthorn Estates, we strive to provide a high-security concierge experience for our guests. Our facility consists of five floors of ten wings of guests and a state-of-the-art in-house emergency operating room with helipad. Aside from providing a full physical rehabilitation center, we have a pool, spa, various outdoor courts, and we sponsor an ever-changing variety of off-campus activities."

I yawned discreetly into my fist.

She ran a plastic card through a couple of machines, continuing her recitation. "Each floor has its own recreational and dining facilities. Each wing is named after a precious stone and is color-coded both by door, floor tile, and staff uniform for ease of recognition. Ruby, sapphire, emerald, and so on. Each wing, as well as individual apartments, are accessible only by key card." She affixed my ID card to a lanyard, handed it to me, and smiled. "Danny Kaplan resides on the fifth floor in our Onyx wing."

I put the lanyard over my head.

"As today is your first day, floor nurse Erickson will arrive shortly and give you a tour of the facility. From then on, as long as the estate agrees, you may come and go as you please."

"Okay. Thanks very much."

"Our cappuccino coffee bar is complimentary." She pointed across the lobby with one hand and waved the next guest forward with the other. "You look a bit peaked, Ms. McGrane."

Gee, thanks. I stepped out of the way. More caffeine was the last thing I needed. My face was already itching from too many energy drinks. I snagged one of the few empty armchairs in a sunshine yellow grouping and waited.

And waited. Knee bouncing, fingers drumming.

This had to be one of the smartest "drops" ever. The perfect place for regular or sporadic visitors. Checking on an elderly relative was definitely low on the list of suspicious behaviors.

A well-dressed older woman sitting next to me gave me a sympathetic smile, reached over, and patted my arm. "Relax, dear. Remember them as they were, but accept them as they are today."

Is she on the game? "I beg your pardon?"

"Onyx." She pointed at the black square on my ID card. "The Alzheimer's and Dementia wing." She shook her head and *tsked*. "Black. Such an unfortunate choice of color."

"It certainly is." I picked up a pamphlet, putting an end to chatter. A new pal wasn't part of my cover. Not yet, at least.

I watched the rainbow of nurses and aides and tried to fall asleep. A petite, curvy, Italian-looking woman in solid black scrubs stopped next to my chair. "McGrane? You're up." She spun on her little rubberized clogs and took off.

I trotted after her into the southern elevator bay. "Onyx, huh? A little somber."

"It's all subliminal, you know? We chose it because the last color old bones want to be around is black. Reminds them of funeral homes and last rites." She walked to the farthest elevator. "This is ours." She waved her card past the elevator button. It opened instantly. "Move it."

I hustled after her, the doors closing almost before I was inside.

"Silverthorn general staff and patrons are unaware of our existence. Your ID has a microchip that activates this elevator and this one only." The nurse put a fist on her hip. "Every elevator car will get you to the fifth floor with your ID, but use only this one."

"Okay."

"You paying attention? This is important."

I nodded.

"Swipe your ID card and press the 4 and 5 buttons together. That means your car is not compromised and you go straight to the fifth floor. If you swipe and press only 5, we receive a message that your car is compromised and prepare accordingly. Understand?"

"Got it," I said.

"Yeah? 'Cause it's a real pain in the ass when you forget." She pointed to a tiny strip of lights in the corner. "See that blinking light?"

A tiny light near the ceiling blinked twice, then paused, then twice again. I nodded.

"The scanners picked up two weapons." She stared at me. "I know I'm carrying."

"Me, too."

"What and where?"

"Kimber. Bra holster."

"Yeah?" She squinted at my chest. "How do you like it?"

"Okay." I flipped my hand back and forth. "I haven't had a reason to justify getting my jackets recut." *Until now.* "You?"

"Ankle holster. Out of reach of the old bones. God knows the boobs aren't." She laughed and held out her hand. "Detective Anita Erickson, RN. Welcome to the BOC."

I shook it and the doors opened.

"Got your wits about you?" Anita waved her ID at the sensor in front of a pair of black steel doors and hit the round Door Open button with a hip. "Let's go see the Scorpion."

An elderly woman scooted past us, zipping for the door, propelling her wheelchair with fancy velvet-slippered feet. Anita caught one of the wheelchair handles just as the woman jammed her cane between the steel doors. "Not so fast, Lady Elaine." She jerked the chair around and gave Elaine, her cane, and her chair a shove toward the nurses' station.

"C'mon." Anita's clogs squeaked on the industrial flecked high-gloss linoleum. An old man in pajamas scolded an invisible truant.

Special Unit clearly preferred live window dressing.

We stopped at the end of the hall. She knocked and we waited a five-count until a small red light above the door turned white. She slid her card through the sensor and pushed open the door. "Look sharp, Grims! New blood walking."

Chapter 6

The Grims were a team of eight middle-aged men and women wearing black scrubs working glowing phones and computers inside tinted glass cubicles. A few looked up. No one smiled.

The semi-darkened room had been plucked from an *NCIS/CSI* television handbook of what secret law enforcement headquarters ought to look like. Mesh-paneled floors were interspersed with strips of textured carpet, LCD monitors and tables laden with electronic equipment were illuminated by high-powered micro task lights.

The farther I walked into the L-shaped room, the larger I realized it was. It spanned the entire end of the Onyx Alzheimer's wing. Six black steel doors, each about twenty feet apart, ran the length of the rear wall.

Anita stopped me in front of the fourth door, rapped twice, and left.

A mechanical *click* popped the door open a sliver. I pushed it wide and stepped inside. My feet sank into luxe carpet as I faced a floor-to-ceiling expanse of windows overlooking the Chicago skyline. The door closed and locked on its own behind me.

An insect-thin Japanese woman sat behind a scarlet lacquered desk the size of a Fiat Abarth. Her heavy dark hair stopped a precise inch above the shoulders of her celadon silk suit. "I'm your handler, Danny Kaplan."

"Excuse me?"

"For what?" She folded her arms across her chest. "Your surprise at my unisex name or the archaic mind-set that an American named Kaplan should be Caucasian?"

"Neither, ma'am," I said mildly. "I thought Mr. Sawyer was my handler."

"Walt Sawyer?" Her laugh was as harsh and sharp as the whine of wet birch through a wood chipper. "Lord, save me from yet another recruit as raw as steak tartare."

Hank's Law Number Ten: Keep your mouth shut.

I smiled politely and glanced around the room, letting her have her fun. Whoever had designed the outer office had pulled out all the stops. The remaining three walls were filled with black lacquer bookcases and file cabinets. The only break in the shiny ebony were six art-lit pottery pieces encased in glass boxes. I recognized one—an Oribe ware dish and lid that probably belonged in a museum.

"Special Unit is funded from a variety of private sources as well as federal and state. Our results are exemplary, and as Special Unit finds discretionary income to be the better part of valor, we are amply rewarded." Kaplan raised a chic pair of rim-free glasses and after a long and careful inspection of me, set them down with a sniff. She picked up a micro-digital recorder. "Maisie McGrane. Five-seven, one-twenty, natural redhead currently a bottle-blonde, eyes green, small frame, fit. Twenty-four. Could pass for nineteen. For now." She lowered her hand. "Fresh-faced naïveté doesn't last long in our business. Sit."

Sweet. My new boss is a praying mantis and I'm the baby bee.

A single straight-backed chair held several oversized black binders labeled O-S-T. I picked them up.

"Those are yours to memorize."

And sat down with the ten-pound homework assignment on my lap.

"Are you ready?"

"Yes, ma'am."

Ms. Kaplan tipped slightly back in her chair and tapped her pewter-polished nails together. "The Italians are outsourcing. They've green-lighted several of the Belgravian clans of the Srpska Mafija, the Serbian Mafia, throughout the United States. The Srp-

ska aims to become a leader in the lucrative world of arms traf-
ficking. And they're financing their expansion in part via car
theft. The Slajic Clan is working Chicago, Minneapolis, Kansas
City, Milwaukee, St. Louis."

A spark of excitement jumped in my chest. *Oh yeah. Welcome to the Majors.*

She continued, "Auto thefts are already up twenty-three percent from last year's watermark of shame. The ripple effect of
these thefts is hundreds of millions of dollars, hence insurance
companies are crawling all over the CPD, demanding federal in-
vestigations." Her dark red lips twisted in a cynical smirk. "Never
mind the body count, which, in the low teens, remains relatively
unnoticed."

Kaplan raised a remote control from a desk tray and pointed
it at the bank of windows. A large screen slid down. "The Srpska
are cloning, shopping, and chopping simultaneously."

She clicked through several slides. "Cloning. Thieves change
the VIN numbers, apply for title with fraudulent docs, and resell
them. Shopping means they steal an order of desired vehicles,
load them into containers, and ship them overseas. Chopping is
the process of completely dismantling and selling the parts, or
partially hijacking vehicles for high-dollar items such as air bags
and side panels." Danny Kaplan leaned forward, a smile just
shy of a sneer on her lips. "So why do you think the CPD's Auto
Theft Department is so incredibly inefficient?"

Neato. A pop quiz. "Three guys can strip a Honda Accord
down to frame in eight minutes." I shrugged. "You don't need an
operational base for eight minutes. Steal a car or truck, drive it a
couple of blocks away, and strip it in the back of an outfitted
semi or an abandoned building."

"That's . . . correct." She tapped the remote and the screen lit
up with the words *Operation Steal-Tow.* "The common denominator of all three methods is the theft itself. They're using tow
trucks—some rogue, some from legitimate companies."

She pressed the remote button and a photo of a gray-haired
man with a cruel and bloated face flashed on the screen. "Goran
Slajic." The picture had been taken through the window of a

Serbian restaurant. "Never leaves Serbia. His Chicago proxy is
his nephew, Stannislav 'The Bull' Renko." The pale face of the
man who rescued me from Gap Tee appeared on the screen.
"Cruel, capable, and competent. A triple threat."

"Stannis," I whispered.

"What?" Her voice snapped like a whip. "What did you say?"

"I know that man as Stannis."

"Enlighten me."

Heat crept up my neck. "I was working and some mope on
the street assaulted me. Stannis stopped him."

"Renko? Really?" Her fingers separated then intertwined.
"How unlike him . . ." Her eyes narrowed. "Are you pals now?"

"No. But you could say I owe him a favor."

"Which you'll repay, by showing him the error of his ways."
She took a folder from the desk drawer and opened it. "Ground
intelligence has been difficult to amass. We have enough evidence to arrest a few of the low-level members of Renko's crew,
but not enough to flip anyone. Yet." She scribbled a note as she
spoke. "Your assignment is to collect photographic evidence of
every possible illegal tow. Nothing more, nothing less. This is
not an infiltration."

Stakeout City, here I come!

"Let me make one thing perfectly clear to you, Miss Mc-
Grane. In the Bureau of Organized Crime, you are a rank-and-
file police officer. Within Special Unit, you're barely a grunt."

I nodded, itching to salute. "Yes, ma'am."

"If your aim is to become a specialist, investigator, detective,
or field agent, you earn it with years of proven service. There is
no room for grandstanders."

I kept nodding, feeling like a bobblehead on a dirt road.

"Don't think being hand-selected by Walt Sawyer makes you
special," Kaplan said. "Every one in Special Unit was."

I bit back a smile. If that was supposed to sting, it didn't.

"After some deliberation with Walt, I have decided the most
innocuous course of action is for you to maintain your present
employment with the Traffic Enforcement Bureau using your
own identity."

Something sucked the air from my lungs. "What?"

You've got to be kidding me.

Danny Kaplan's eyes glinted. "Maisie McGrane, you're still a meter maid."

I spent the next three hours in a glass cubicle, reviewing known crimes attributed to Slajic's and the other Belgravian clans, looking for patterns and commonality amidst torture, murder, rape, and assault. The Srpska Mafija liked to leave messages and preferred them gory. From what little information I could find on Stannislav Renko, the apple hadn't fallen far from the tree.

Why had he helped me?

I rubbed my eyes with the heels of my hands, trying to focus on Stannis and not the fact that I was still a goddamned meter maid, only now I was armed with a camera and a license to stalk.

Detective RN Anita rapped on my partition. "Lunchtime, Rook."

I pushed back from my desk. "Sure."

We returned to the main hallway of the Onyx wing, stopping short of the elevators, and entered the room labeled Dining Room off the nurses' center. It had the look of a well-to-do country club: damask-upholstered armchairs, cherrywood tables, even a short stocked bar at the far end of the room.

"Pretty deluxe cafeteria," I said.

"Special Unit is all about the perks." Anita nudged me with an elbow. "C'mon. Time to meet Uncle Edward."

A cherubic man in his late sixties with an infectious smile waved us over to the only occupied table in the room. He had thick alabaster-white hair and a matching goatee and wore a hunter green cardigan over a shirt and tie. "Thank you, Anita dear." Anita exited via what looked to be the kitchen doors at the end of the room.

He held out a hand. "Miss Maisie McGrane. Me-oh-my, if I had one like you at home, I'd never leave the house."

I'd heard that old line of blarney from the time I could walk, but from him, it sounded as though he'd composed it on the spot.

We shook hands. "Sir."

"It's a pleasure to make your acquaintance. I'm the CFO of the BOC, Edward Dunne. Take a load off."

I did. Edward smiled at me. "How are you finding your first day?"

Something about him loosened my tongue. "A bit anticlimactic, sir," I said wryly. "I'm still a meter maid."

"Ah, but you're an undercover officer *masquerading* as a meter maid." He chuckled. "The job is what you make of it."

"Yes sir." *Not like I haven't heard that one before.* "About that. How exactly does one become a field agent?"

"Not easily," Edward said thoughtfully. "Hard work and desire, naturally. And a leprechaun's worth of luck."

"That I've got." I grinned and raised my palms. "In spades."

"And how did you find Ms. Kaplan?"

"Er . . . intense, sir."

"Sweet saintly Jesus! Intense, you say." Edward chuckled. "She brings new meaning to the words 'bitch on wheels.' Don't take Danny's animosity too personally. Her promotion from field to desk, while physically necessitated—shot in the line of duty—has been a bitter pill. Not to mention"—he leaned forward and spoke confidentially—"you're Walt's sole female field recruit since he brought her on years ago. Poor thing must be as jealous as all get-out."

I tried unsuccessfully not to smile. "Thank you, sir."

"Enough with the formalities. You're forbidden to call me anything other than Edward."

A stocky waiter with a laden tray emerged from the door Anita had disappeared into. "Tomato bisque soup with sourdough brie and fig paninis." He placed two plates in front of us and two bottles of Pellegrino. "I'm Frank. Kitchen staff and floor security. Welcome aboard, Maisie."

"Thanks. Nice to meet you, Frank."

Frank left and Edward took a bite of grilled cheese. He closed his eyes, savoring it. "Glorious. One of the reasons half of Special Unit resides here."

My sandwich stopped halfway to my mouth. "Really?"

"Oh yes." Edward nestled back in his chair and nibbled away at the panini triangle. "Most of us are, well . . . unable to leave the job alone anyway, so it proved prudent to have our headquarters where we don't need to leave, don't open ourselves up to exposure."

Did I just wake up in a James Bond movie?

"It's rather like living in an extremely secure hotel. Laundry, food, gym, medical. No one is ever caught in traffic. Work is ten months on, two months off. Makes for lovely vacations."

Holy cat. My knee started bouncing. "How did this come about?"

"Walt Sawyer's brainchild. Of course, he was well-heeled enough to fund it. And a hard enough bastard to secure our unusual system of quid pro quo when it comes to busts." He reached into his shirt pocket, pulled out a stack of $100 prepaid Visa cards, and set them at my elbow. "Every girl needs a bit of walking-around money. Never mind receipts. An e-mailed summary of how it was spent is all that's required."

His fingers strayed to his goatee. His tone grew serious. "You may not feel this is an important assignment, Maisie, but everything that comes out of Special Unit has been carefully considered."

I nodded. I had the eerie feeling that I was wading neck-deep near a drop-off. Maybe meter maiding would make for a successful transition.

"Are you ready to ground and pound, Officer McGrane?"

"Yessir." *Am I ever.*

Chapter 7

Ragnar's faded blue pickup, still in the Silverthorn Estates drop-off circle, started as I approached it. The Norse guardian was observant.

I'd crammed a week's worth of learning into eight hours. I had the faces down, the names, and the rest of it. After my meeting with Edward Dunne, I now had an unregistered, untraceable Remington R51 9mm pistol in the waistband of my pants, fifteen $100 Visa prepaid cards, and a second preloaded retrofitted iPhone chock-full of little tricks.

Ragnar reached across and pushed open the passenger door. I climbed in. "Sorry I took so long. You must be starving. And bored."

"Nah. This is light duty."

"Guy, you've spent over thirteen straight hours in a truck. When's your guard duty shift over?"

"When I see Bannon's fucking mug."

"And when will that be?"

"Hell if I know," Ragnar said. "How's your friend?"

"Okay."

He put the truck in Drive. "Where to?"

"Wherever you want to get something to eat."

"Kid." He ran a hand through his shaggy blond hair. "I'm not the goddamn problem you need to be fretting over."

I know.

"So?" he said. "Where to?"

"My parents' house. Please."

A half hour later, Ragnar turned onto my street. Daicen's silver Audi gleamed in the driveway. Which meant Mom and probably Declan were there, as well. "Argh. Keep going," I said. "The legal eagles have landed."

He drove to the end of the block and turned the car off. "What the hell?"

"I live in that house with four cops and three attorneys. None of whom are stupid or blind." I raised my palms. "Decision time, Ragnar. You are cordially invited to dinner as my buddy from the gym or, unlike last night, you find a way to keep you and your truck out of sight."

He frowned. "I don't like this."

"I know." I got out of the truck. "You're more than welcome for dinner if you change your mind. Just ring the bell."

"Hang on." He hopped out of the truck and pointed his index and middle fingers at his eyes. "I'll watch you in."

I let myself in through the front door. Mom's voice, then Declan's and Daicen's, went around and around in their usual sort of muted argument. A case. Probably a big one. I slipped upstairs and into my bedroom, where I stashed my new gear and the Kimber Solo in the nightstand and changed into yoga pants and an old Jameson Whiskey T-shirt.

I felt fuzzy and hot. I flopped down on the bed and closed my eyes.

Stress reliever number one: Avoidance Nap.

A car door slammed and I jerked awake. The digital clock read 6:00 p.m. I got to the window in time to see the twins pull out of the driveway in Daicen's car. Two less people to lie to. I took a shower, dried my hair, and spent an inordinate amount of time applying war paint. I hadn't seen my father in almost three months.

I stared at my reflection and said, "Today I am a police officer." And my traitorous dark side snarked, *Maybe, but you're still not a member of the Table Club.*

Comical, in a sick way. My whole life I wanted to be a part of my da and brothers' world, and now that I was, I still couldn't say a goddamn thing.

Whatever.

I marched into the walk-in closet and looked for something edgy and still girly enough to make Da feel guilty. As if that was possible. I stepped out wearing leggings, a Marc Jacobs tunic, and knee-high Frye boots.

I went downstairs. Toots Thielemans's "Old Friend" played through the sound system. Which meant one thing: Belgian night. I followed the music into the kitchen.

"'Allo, Maisie!" Thierry, our French housekeeper, stood at the sink, noisily washing mussels. One of my all-time favorites.

"How'd you know I'd be home?"

He pointed a paring knife at a dark wooden crate on the opposite end of the granite counter. Burned into the wood were the words *Normandy, France.* I unlatched and opened the lid. A small brown envelope with *Maisie* on the front lay across two cloth-wrapped bottles surrounded by excelsior. I freed one from its gray cotton sackcloth. A 1972 Christian Drouin Dom *coeur de lion millesime.* Calvados brandy.

"Very good," Thierry said. "Very hard to get, Maisie."

I set the bottle of French brandy on the counter. "Moules and frites from this?"

"Half of Belgium is displaced French," Mom said, coming into the kitchen. She hugged me tight. "Read the card, baby. Give us some joy."

I opened it and read aloud,

"The roof might fall in; anything could happen."
H.

"Dashiell Hammett," I said, missing Hank like hell.

Mom's café-au-lait fingers plucked the card from my hand, and she fanned herself in mock swoon. "Mmm-mm-mmm. If the man's taste in fiction wasn't enough to love him, his propensity to quote it sure is."

"He's sweet that way."

She raised a delicately winged brow. *Uh-oh*. I shook my head to clear away the love haze.

Mom tapped the card on the counter. "Clever, too. Bribing you to come home to us now."

"The vic on the car was a random killing."

She poured herself a large glass of chardonnay. "Tell that to your father."

"Maybe I would if we were speaking."

She closed her eyes for a moment. "It's exhausting and unproductive to be angry all the time, Maisie. Not to mention you're the one coming up short."

She had a point. Da scuttled me and yet I was the one who lost the family. And while living with Hank pretty much mitigated any loss ever, I missed them terribly.

I tried to clear the fist-sized lump in my throat. "Forgive and forget, is that it?"

"Nothing so simplistic. What your father did was wrong." Mom laid a hand on my cheek. "But carrying around anger and hurt as a shield isn't nearly as effective as wielding it like a straight razor, slicing at will when the moment presents itself."

Thierry waved a mussel at me. "Your mother, Maisie. She has the Corsican heart."

Mom laughed, but her eyes were serious. "How about we try to find a way to live with this?"

I nodded.

"Let's start with you staying here whenever Hank's out of town."

"Yeah," I said. "I'd like that."

Mom and I crossed the hall and walked into the dining room. Da, Flynn, and Rory sat at one end of the long walnut table, drinking whiskey, wearing expressions hotter and blacker than liquid tar. Cash, his chair balanced on two legs, was texting, oblivious. Mom and I sat down on either side of Cash.

"How do, Snap?" Flynn said. "The roughneck let you out of the kennel, huh?"

I suppose "roughneck" is marginally better than "merce-nary."

"Careful . . ." Mom lifted her wineglass in caution.

Da shot me a small smile I couldn't return.

Flynn reached over and ruffled my hair in apology, which he knew I hated. "Sorry, Snap. It was like goddamn *Deliverance* today."

Thierry came in bearing crusty French bread, herbed butter, spinach salads, and serenity. Cash returned the front legs of his chair to the floor. "You can't believe what they're trying to do in Vice. On Friday—"

"What makes you think we give a good goddamn?" Rory said.

Da raised a palm. "Easy, now."

"The bloody BOC," Rory muttered and threw back his whiskey.

My ears swiveled like a NSA tracking dish. "What?"

"Bureau of Organized Crime," Flynn said. "We've been working four homicides. All mutts with records from here to eternity, all iced in different ways. But each one had things . . . missing."

Rory sloshed another three fingers of Jameson into his glass. "And they all traded in wheels."

Mom tapped a fingernail on the rim of her glass, interested now, the former prosecutor in her never far from the surface. "What were they missing?"

"Fingers, for one thing," Flynn said. "But the other pieces were different. One without toes, another an ear, and one poor bastard had an ice cream–sized scoop of flesh carved out of his ass."

Rory gave a mirthless bark of laughter. "Goddamned Sawyer tells us we don't know what the feck we're doing and he's got it now and it's all VICAP and coordinating with the Feds, that sanctimonious son of a—"

"Sawyer?" My brain pinged inside my skull like Speedy Gonzales on nitrous.

"Aye," Da scoffed, sliding into heavy Irish, "Walt the-black-hearted-bastard Sawyer."

"That's enough, Conn." Mom sucked in her cheeks. "Walt is a good friend."

Da circled the whiskey in his glass. "He was a helluva lot more than that to yeh."

Wow. What you don't hear at the dinner table. The nasty little part of me, the cruel vengeful bit I pretend doesn't really exist, whispered, *Talk about taking a straight razor when the time is right.*

Flynn and Rory went still. Cash quit texting.

Mom took a measured sip of wine. "I think marrying a widower and adopting his six small children is testament enough to my preference."

Da laughed. "That it is, darlin'. That it is."

Thierry removed the salad plates and returned with plates of moules, frites in paper cones, and icy Stella Artois.

I dipped a frite into spiced mayonnaise, and took a bite. "Best ever."

"You say that every time." Cash flipped one into the air and caught it in his mouth. "But when you're right, you're right."

"Jaysus, Mom," Rory groused, unable to let it go. "Do you've any idea how hard we've worked these cases?" He stabbed a mussel out of its shell.

"Ultimately, it's four less for you to clear, isn't it?" she asked.

"A feckin' comfort, eh?" Rory's dark eyes blazed. "You know as well as I do, the BOC's in bed with every lowlife skell and politician in Chicago."

"Yeah," Flynn said. "They've got all the objectivity of the IRS at a Tea Party rally."

Mom gave a snort of laughter into her wine. Which set Da to chuckling and Rory to smile. A tiny, relieved giggle burst from my chest.

No matter what, we were still a family.

The doorbell rang.

Oh jeez. Ragnar.

"I got it." I stood up so fast I almost knocked over my chair. Great. Just when things were calming down.

Chapter 8

I opened the front door. A hulking shadow just outside the door light caught my wrist and jerked me to him. My breath caught in my throat, but my lips curved in a smile as Hank's mouth came down on mine.

Behind my closed eyes, the vivid pulsing of my blood bloomed like fireworks.

It could have been hours. It could have been days.

Hank raised his head, his voice husky in my ear. "You opened the door blind."

Yeah, that wasn't so smart. I splayed my fingers across his chest. "I thought you were Ragnar."

"Cute," he said, and the smile in his voice cracked something inside of me.

"Do you want to come in for dinner?"

"What do you think?"

The tease was worse than the smile. I blinked fast. His hand went to the nape of my neck and we went inside.

Thierry had Hank seated and plated before we had the chance to opt out gracefully. I couldn't stop smiling.

Hank's black cargo shirtsleeves were rolled back on his muscled forearms. An errant comma of dark hair creased his forehead. The low light of the chandelier and close shave exacerbated the slight pallor and the lines around his mouth. He looked exhausted and dangerous and hyper-aware.

The middle of a McGrane family skirmish was the last place he ought to be.

"So, Bannon," Da said, "how hails the conquering hero?"

"Well. Thank you." Hank took a swallow of beer. "Although Belarus isn't the paradise it once was."

Mom laughed and flashed a dead-eye warning at my brothers and Da, who knuckled under. A superficially pleasant conversation flowed through dinner.

Until dessert.

"Funny you should show up tonight, Bannon," Rory said. "It's about time we had some answers."

Hank said nothing.

"The murdered man on your car." Rory flexed his fingers into a fist. "What do you know about it?"

"I know Maisie had the misfortune to find him," Hank said. "And she handled it like a champ."

"You wouldn't be knowin' the vic, now, would you?" Da asked, angling for trouble, his brogue showing.

"My car is in the police impound lot," Hank said. "I have a meet with Detective Forman next week." He leaned his forearms on the table and looked from Da to Rory. "If it'll make you feel better, I'll take a look at the crime scene photos."

I clapped a hand over my mouth. A smile from me would be like handing a lit torch to a couple of gasoline-soaked baboons. I bent my head toward Hank and noticed a small dark stain on the side of his shirt, high up on his rib cage, under his arm.

"They're joking." Mom bestowed an arctic smile on Rory and Da. "Why, it's not even their case."

"I don't mind," Hank said.

Something wasn't right. The purple-blue shadows beneath Hank's pale eyes were more than exhaustion, the slight hitch as he leaned forward . . .

The slowly growing spot on his shirt was blood.

"Gosh, it's getting late." I tossed my napkin on my plate and stood up. "Hank hasn't been home in weeks and he's too polite to say he's wrecked."

Mom was on her feet before Hank was. "Oh baby, do you really have to go?"

"Yeah. We do."

Hank checked the rearview when we hit the freeway. Ragnar's faded blue Ford followed a couple of car lengths behind.

I sank into the black leather seat of the Mercedes. Hank was home and, depending on what was beneath his shirt, mostly all right. He turned on the radio. Chet Baker's bittersweet satin tenor enveloped the SUV, and the tension bled out of me like a slow tire leak.

July McGrane's Rules of Engagement Number Two: Let him go first.

The single rule of my mother's I excelled at. Because lawyers talk about nothing and cops don't talk at all.

When he finally spoke, Hank's voice was hoarse. "I'm sorry to Christ that happened, Maisie."

"It's not on you."

"Like hell it's not." He adjusted his grip on the steering wheel. "The vic's a stringer. One of Vi's."

"Vi" was Violetta Veteratti. They had, as Hank so eloquently put it, "a history." Her twin, Eddie, was a made guy and a mad dog. He ran Chicago's Labor Union. Ran it exactly like Tony Lombardo did for Capone in the 1920s.

"I don't follow. How'd I rate a shadow?"

"You don't. Vi doesn't take precautions." Hank's jaw went tight. "Especially not useless ones."

The stringer's death, apparently proof positive of his incompetence to Hank.

He stared straight ahead. "What did Mant do to you?"

"Man?"

"Jeff *Mant*. Former paratrooper. Drug runner. Sociopath."

"Seriously? My Gap tee–wearing assailant's name is *Jeff*? God, that's so . . . lame." I really, really didn't want to talk about it.

Hank took a deep breath in through his nose and let it out slowly. "Maisie."

"He got the drop on me. Threatened me." I rubbed my hands on my thighs. "You know."

"No. I don't." A tiny tic began to pulse at the base of his jaw.

"He pulled my hair, held me down." I blinked fast and kept talking. "Felt me up over my clothes . . . That was it."

"And he let you go?" Hank asked, eerily nonchalant.

"Pretty much," I hedged. "It was the middle of the day in front of the mayor's office. Some guy came over for a closer look and Mant took off."

"Who?"

"Never seen him before." *Accurate but not honest.*

"Are you sure?"

"I got lucky. Mant was going to hurt me." My shoulders gave a spastic jerk.

"Not anymore. His number's up." Hank cracked his neck and shot me a sideways glance, mouth quirked up at the corner. "Why'd we leave the party, Angel Face?"

"Forced interrogation is one thing. Bleeding on the dining room chair during it, is something else entirely."

He swore and reached across to his left side. The pads of his fingers came away red. "Couple of pulled stitches. Nothing a Band-Aid won't fix."

I sat on the wide white quartz counter of the master bathroom next to a first-aid spread that would put a third world hospital to shame. I peeled the sodden red-stained gauze off and felt a little woozy. "I don't think a Band-Aid's gonna cut it."

Hank sat on a stool, left arm bent behind his head. "Don't go soft on me now, Slim."

I fingered one of the intact stitches on the built-up ridge of tissue. "How many?"

"Not bad. A dozen or so inside," Hank said, "a half-dozen to close the outside."

"Actually, you have fourteen exterior stitches." *Which means how many?* "Six of them are not just pulled apart, but ripped clear through."

"Any of the interiors open?"

"No. I mean . . . I don't think so. I can't really tell." I laid the fourth piece of stitch tape across the gaping oval slit on his left lat—latissimus dorsi—the thick muscle beneath his arm that gave him his perfect vee-shaped torso.

"A good place to take a hit, if you have to." He craned his neck to see it in the mirror. "Full mobility, no bleed out."

I squinched my eyes shut, trying to halt the gears of my brain from processing the injury in front of me. The oval profile of his wound told me the knife was smooth-bladed with a single cutting edge. A C-shaped black bruise had formed beneath one end of the wound. *Too late.* The bright bathroom lights flickered.

Jesus Criminey. He'd been stabbed up to the hilt.

The room started to spin. Saliva ran down the back of my throat.

"Getting a little green, Sport Shake." Hank laid a heavy hand on my shoulder. "How 'bout you make us a drink and let me finish up."

"You can't reach." I swallowed fast a couple times. "Just talk," I rasped, "okay?"

He sifted his fingers through the ends of my hair. "I was running a deep clean on a building. Below my pay grade."

Oh God. I adhered another piece of stitch tape across the slow-bleeding hole in his flesh. "W-why?"

"A final test before my new assignment. The crime lord has me run it with his son, Drago. A goddamned squirrel. And raw, too." He blew out a breath. "Kid misses a hallway, and before you can blink, we're boxed in by four guys slinging blades, aiming to keep it on the QT. I take three and let Drago cut his teeth on one."

Well, that was nice of you.

"I hit the first one fast, he's over. I engage Number Two and Three rushes my blind side. Three's blade glances off my vest and into me. Two's done by then. I drop my arm and pivot. Three can't hang on to the knife. I end Three, and argue with Drago the goddamn squirrel for the next fifteen because he can't stand me walking around with the blade in. Kid's practically eating his own hand to get me to pull it out."

I affixed the tenth and final strip of stitch tape, careful to keep breathing through my mouth. This was not what I had in mind when I asked him to talk. I crumpled up the stitch tape wrappers and opened a gauze pad.

"First rule when taking damage?" Hank asked.

"Keep a level head. Act quick." I taped the gauze pad over the stitches.

"So." Hank stared at me in the mirror. "Why did I leave the knife in?"

Trust Captain Alpha-Male to make this a teachable moment.

"Um . . . Basic displacement theory. You'll bleed more once you remove the blade."

He dropped his arm and grinned at me in the mirror. "Right. I apply pressure on either side *toward* the blade so it doesn't slide out, and wait another twenty while Drago reports in and lines up a decent tailor."

"Gee," I said, not knowing what I could possibly add to that.

He lowered his forehead to mine. "Gee, you're pretty." His hands went to my waist, fingers spanning the small of my back.

He nuzzled my neck and gave my throat a soft bite, a move that normally made me go softer than Arizona asphalt. But I was a mannequin, plastic and hollow.

Hank leaned back. A shadow flickered across his pale eyes. "I'm gonna make you a drink." He kissed me. Searing and primal and strangely different from any kiss he'd given me before. "Hell, I'll make you two."

Hank had a road map of scars. Cruel, thin ones, raised and white with age. Others, dark and sunken. The most disconcerting weal was a perfect square, horrifying in its man-made shape.

This was just one more.

I flipped the lid of the very large, very battered red first-aid tool kit, opened the cantilever shelves inside, and started putting the supplies away. Betadine swab sticks, two unused packages of stitch tape, scissors, alcohol pads, gauze, tape. I returned an unused—*thank God*—sterile package labeled "suture 2-0 nylon armed with cutting needle" into a half-full twelve-count box.

Next to the sutures were unopened syringes and several thin cartons with rubber-stopped vials visible through cellophane windows. I tipped my head to read the labels. *Nalbuphine, promethazine, naloxone, morphine.*

Nothing the average joe could acquire even *with* a prescription. I reached back for the incongruous and unnecessary box of Band-Aids and knocked it off the counter.

Adhesive strips rained onto the floor. I dropped to my knees and tried to pick the slick paper wrappers off the smooth limestone. My fingers were trembling. "Dammit." I swept them into a pile, crumpled them into my fists, and stood up.

I caught sight of myself in the mirror. My reflection stared back at me, white-faced and shaking, mouth moving silently, swearing to God.

What he does is who he is. Being scared and worrying and weak is on me. He can take care of himself and he's a pro and for chrissakes, it's just one more scar.

Of how many?

My eyes went soft, and so did the rest of me. For the first time, I understood exactly how Da had done what he did to me. And why.

A moment of clarity that was . . . less than pleasant.

I put the last bits of the first-aid kit away, barely noticing that one of the Israeli Battle Dressing kits had an old bloody fingerprint on the wrapper. Oblivious even, to the 60cc Demerol vial with only 15cc left. I shut the kit and smacked the metal locks home, stinging my palms.

I had a call to make.

Da answered his cell on the third ring. "Maisie? What's wrong?"

I choked, unable to force any sound out. I laid my head down on Hank's desk.

"Are you there, luv?"

I sat up and let out a choppy breath. "I get it," I said, my voice squeezed and tight. "Why you did what you did to me. I wanted you to know that today, I understand."

But I don't forgive.

There was more. So much that needed to be said. But the words compounded like quick-dry cement. Each one harder to release than the one before.

And he knew it.

"I miss you." He was silent for a moment. "More than there are stars in the sky."

My childhood good-night. "Sands in the desert," I filled in my line.

"Tears in the ocean." He sighed. "I love you."

"Me, too." I disconnected and drifted back into the bedroom, feeling like a soap bubble in a cactus patch.

Hank was waiting with two Stolis on the rocks. He handed me one and raised his glass. "You know what's great about you?"

"Thrill me."

"You don't fuss." He clinked his glass against mine.

I took a long swallow. The vodka sent an icy shiver to the back of my neck. I set my glass down with a *click* on the night-stand. I raised my chin. "God, you're a cagey son of a gun."

He pulled me to him with a smirk. "Do you have a problem with that?"

I bit my lip, worrying it between my teeth to stop from saying something pathetic like *"Are you sure you should be doing this?"* And then he was chewing it for me.

It was smoky, serious sex. The kind that says *I missed you and this is how much*. It ended as always, with Hank on his back and me lying across his chest, while his fingers grazed across my bare back.

I floated in the twilight between sleep and relaxation. Cool tears slipped down my cheeks.

"Maisie?" he said. "Are you crying?"

"Yeah." I sniffled and wiped my eyes with my fingers. "Transcendent sex has that effect on me."

"I know," he murmured into my hair. Chin against my temple, he fell asleep.

Chapter 9

Monday morning at 0500, I came out of the closet buttoning my navy blue poly-blend Parking Enforcement Agent uniform over my bra holster. Hank lay propped up against the pillows reading the *Wall Street Journal* on an iPad, sheet crumpled at his waist. Even at ease, the muscles of his abdomen and chest were sculpted from stone. "Call in sick."

His lazy order released a fleet of butterflies in my chest. *I would have if I hadn't joined the BOC.* "I . . . I can't." I scooted back into the closet and dropped down onto the teak bench. "Does it ever bother you that I'm a meter maid?" I asked in a rush to distract him.

"No."

"Really?" I started lacing my work boots.

"Maisie, what you do doesn't define you as much as how you do it."

"What does that mean?"

"If you're happy, I'm happy. Besides," he teased, "at least you're not a cop."

He's kidding. He's got to be kidding. I stared at myself in the mirror. *Cripes. Keep it together.* I took a deep breath and stepped out of the closet.

Hank crooked a finger at me. I trotted over and dropped a kiss on his forehead. "Can't be late—" I turned away. His fingers snagged the waistband of my pants. He jerked me back, kissed me hard and fast, and let go.

He picked up the tablet.

What was that? "Um . . . The Super Bee's in impound, and my Honda's racking up a small fortune in the ramp . . . Can I take the G-Wagen?"

"Won't need it."

Huh?

The doorbell rang.

"Your ride's here." He looked up from the iPad, a gleam in his cement-gray eyes. "Serve 'em hell, Bluebell."

Ragnar, my chauffeur and shadow, informed me we'd be leaving my Honda in the lot until after work. And he was going to tail me. The entire day. And every day after until Mant's number was up.

"Gee," I said. "That'll be . . . cozy."

"Ever vigilant, kid. I got the heads-up on Mant. That dude is one sick fuck. You carrying?"

"Yep." I opened the door.

"Where are you going?"

"To stow my gear, clock in, and get my ticket gun."

Ragnar's eyes narrowed.

"Wanna check in with Hank?" I asked sweetly.

"Hurry up."

I closed the door on him, jogged up to the gate, and waved at Chen in the bulletproof guardhouse. The gate raised and I loped across the barbed-wire enclosed lot. I entered the office from the rear, bypassed the break room, and pulled my ticket gun from the charger. A hot pink Post-it was affixed to the butt.

> *McGrane—*
> *Sanchez is out sick. You're up.*
> *Leticia*

Happy Monday. Crap.

My first day of undercover work and I had to hit quota on a route I didn't know. Ability to gather photographic evidence on as many tow trucks as possible? Nonexistent.

Sanchez's route was Ashland and Belmont. The hippie hippie shake. Vegan restaurants, head shops, hookah bars, and fetish stores. Zero parking and tie-dyed muumuu-clad bitch-'n'-moaners. Groovy.

I spent most of the morning cruising the outskirts of the route, feeling more than a little conspicuous with Ragnar tailing me. Still, I managed to lay a decent number of tickets before getting to what had to be Sanchez's sweet spot, because parking offenders don't stack up in front of establishments that don't open before ten. But they do at 11:07 a.m. I turned on to Belmont.

Ahh, nothing like the fragrant combination of patchouli and piss.

I tagged a couple of fish taking more than their allotted time inside The Hookah Hub. I hadn't seen one tow truck. Not one. Not even driving by. In four hours and forty-three minutes.

Of course, ancient Buick Skylarks and rusted-out Chevy Aeros probably weren't real high on the Serbian shopping list. I cracked my neck, and out of sheer boredom, typed the plate of a custom-painted flesh-colored Prius parked in front of The Vinyl Frontier into my ticket gun.

Jackpot. $734 in unpaids.

I pulled the Interceptor up tight to the curb, out of sight of the fetish store's display window filled with everything from rubber suits to ball gags. I popped the trunk and lugged out a thirty-five-pound, bright orange Wolverine spiked parking boot. I slid it up under the rear tire of the Prius, secured and tightened the plate over the hubcap.

Anchored in less than forty seconds. Not nearly my best, but respectable. I glanced behind me.

Ragnar flipped me a thumbs-up from behind the wheel. I waved and forced myself not to jog back to the Interceptor. Quota hit, the rest of the day was mine to devote to my new job. I tapped my fingers against my forehead. Lunch hour.

Where would I go to steal an upscale car?

I zipped up to Rise Sushi at Roscoe and Southport. The only

parking was residential permit, and with Rise's steady take-out trade, there were always expensive cars double-parked.

I glanced in the rearview. Ragnar was still tight on my tail. I dropped a few obvious tickets so he wouldn't get suspicious, but as for tow trucks . . . Zip. Nada. Nil. And I had the niggling sensation that my new "hell on wheels" boss, Danny Kaplan, wouldn't exactly be disappointed at my lack of results.

I cycled around the block to kill some time before cruising Rise Sushi again. The back street was a combination of small offices, apartments, and nose-to-nose parallel parking. I crept past, looking for the tiny yellow resident permit stuck in the upper left corner of the windshield that allowed them to pay to park on the street where they lived.

I passed a properly parked and stickered brand-new maroon Lexus E300H with a vinyl cling in the rear window—*Stick it to your liberal parents. Become "The Man."* One of the few fish Leticia would ever cut a break. Heck, she would've taken a photo of the cling.

I got to the end of the block, turned around, and parked in the fire lane. Ragnar pulled in behind me. My eager-beaver attitude was rapidly devolving into anxiety-beaver.

How in the hell am I ever going to get the evidence Special Unit was looking for?

A fluorescent pink tow truck, with *Drag Queen* in mirrored letters on the door, slowed at the Lexus. And drove on.

Cripes. I hadn't even pulled my super-spy iPhone from the damn cargo pocket. I took it out, lined up the camera, and took a couple shots of the Lexus for practice. Even through the spotted Interceptor windshield the photos were crystal crisp.

This assignment was an exercise in futility. I tossed the phone on the dash, dug a warm sugar-free Red Bull out of my backpack, and popped the top. Definitely better cold.

I glanced in the rearview. Ragnar's head scanned from side to side, constantly checking the street. Maybe I should ask him if he wanted a PowerBar. I took another sip and straightened up in my seat.

The Drag Queen was back.

I slammed the can into the cup holder, the liquid splashing out over my hand. I grabbed the iPhone and started recording.

The Drag Queen turned on its emergency lights and pulled in perpendicular to the Lexus. The tow truck driver wore a black blinged-out ball cap and black tank top with glittery lettering.

The whine of hydraulics echoed inside my cart, as the blue winch—a T-shaped bar—lowered automatically. The crossbar of the *T* rotated around the rear of the tires. Another hiss of the hydraulics and the arms on each side of the T-bar closed securely around each tire. The boom raised the rear of the Lexus. The Drag Queen drove forward, pulling the Lexus neatly from the spot and off down the block.

According to the video recorder on the iPhone, the entire operation had taken thirty-six seconds and the driver hadn't even left the cab.

Holy cat. This was going to be harder than finding common sense in Common Core.

I got out of the cart and took a couple more shots to orient the crime scene for Ms. Kaplan.

"Excuse me."

I turned.

An East Indian man with liquid brown eyes, in blue scrubs, trotted up to me. "Did you just tow my car?"

"No sir."

He frowned. "Then where is it?"

I took a breath. "What I meant to say is that the City of Chicago did not tow your car."

"I have the current city parking permit."

"Yes sir. The City did not ticket or tow your car. It's been privately towed. By either the neighborhood or the building organization . . ." No matter how crummy I felt about it, I couldn't tip him off that his car had almost certainly been stolen.

He stepped closer to me and bent his head so we were at eye level. "I'm improperly and illegally towed, while city employees feed like hogs at the trough of my taxes?"

I flashed him the *Don't Tread on Me* snake sticker on the bottom of my ticket gun. Leticia had put them on all the guns in our office. The majority of the parking agents believed it was a warning to parking offenders à la *No, Chicago, we will not take your shit.*

The doctor winced and nodded. "I apologize. I am very upset."

"No problem. Good luck to you."

And as I left the poor bastard standing at the empty space, dialing his cell phone, I had a terribly marvelous idea.

I knocked on Leticia's open office door.

"What?" she barked without looking up.

"Have a minute?"

Leticia looked up and eyed me speculatively. "McGrane." She jerked her head at a chair in front of her desk. "Plant yourself."

I sat down in a wobbly chair with stained gold fabric and waited to exploit my brothers and my boss for the BOC's gain. Next to an American flag in the corner was a giant framed poster of Ronald Reagan. On her desk, next to a giant jar of jelly beans, stood a picture of her and Sean Hannity.

"I got a problem," she said. "The PEAs be dropping like flies from a bug zapper. Lost three this month. Those goddamn Robin McHoodie bastards ain't helping. You're the touchy-feely kind, McGrane. You think maybe we need a motto or somethin'?"

"Like what? Parking Enforcement: The toughest job you'll never like?"

"Now you're talking." She hooted. "We could get some T-shirts made an' shit. So, what you want?"

Once upon a time . . . "You know how some of my brothers are cops, right?"

"Yeah."

"Well, one of them has been getting some complaints. Weird ones. People getting towed for no reason."

"Same ol', same ol'."

"Except," I set the trap, "there seems to be an unusually high percentage of these people who had stickers on their cars that lean to the right of the political spectrum."

The idea of conservative repression was irresistible bait.

Leticia snapped it up faster than the last beer at a NASCAR race. She jabbed a finger at me. "I been tellin' you. The struggle is real, girl."

"Yeah." I nodded in agreement. "It got me thinking. What if we had a couple of PEAs taking cell phone pictures of tow trucks and cars towed? My brother could check those cars against the stolen car list and police impound."

She scooped a handful of jelly beans from the jar and chewed, considering. "How you planning on talking our crew into helping the Blues?"

"Ten dollars cash for each set of pictures—one of the tow truck, one of the towed car. Gotta have readable license plates in both pictures, time and date stamped or no deal."

Leticia stroked the furrow between her brows with a sparkle-encrusted lemon yellow fingernail. "What happens afterwards?"

"Huh?"

She rolled her eyes to the ceiling. "McGrane, this is prime TV shit. This story could blow the fuck up! You hearin' what I'm thinking? I could be on *The Kelly File*."

Sweet Jesus on a saltine. The stars in her eyes were blinding.

"Leticia," I cautioned, "this is a cop's hunch. And a secret one at that. He has to be able to prove it before anything can happen."

"True 'dat. True 'dat." She puffed out her cheeks.

"So?" I said. "What do you think?"

"I think you solved my morale problem. I'm gonna go rile the PEAs about their new incentive opportunity." Leticia leaned an elbow on the desk and put her other hand on her ample hip. "Then we let them get froggy and jump."

"What took so long in there?" Ragnar asked as he drove into the parking ramp that held my Accord.

"My turn to get cussed out by the boss."

His blue eyes widened in surprise. "Really?"

"No. You have to dump the info from the ticket guns. It takes a while."

Ragnar drove past my car and stopped the pickup at the farthest corner away. "Stay in the truck."

"Okay."

He got out and grabbed a duffel from the aluminum truck box.

I watched him pull out a sort of stick with a mirror and an up light. He made three slow passes beneath the car. Next, he rummaged in the bag and came out with a needle-nose pliers. In under a minute, he had popped the hood. He raised it slowly and ran a flashlight over the engine.

Ragnar went back to the duffel and removed a small black box with three nubby antennas on top. He set the device on the roof of the Accord.

A cell phone jammer. Just in case Jeff Mant felt the need to blow me up remotely.

After a cursory search of the interior, the blond giant set the cell phone jammer on the passenger seat and waved me over.

"It's clean," he said. "Where we headed?"

"Hank's."

He waited until I got inside the car and closed the door. I waved and he started for the truck.

My key jammed partway in the ignition. I pulled it out. A small piece of wire stuck out of the starter.

My vision dimmed at the edges, hand shot to the door handle.

Hank's Law Number Three: Don't let your lizard brain go rogue.

I flared my fingers and slowly returned my left hand to the steering wheel. With my right, I thumbed the flashlight app on my phone and took a closer look.

A piece of paper was wrapped around the wire protruding from the starter. A message on a semi-straightened paper clip. My chest inflated as I sucked in a deep breath of relief. If the Gap tee–wearing Jeff Mant wanted to kill me, he wouldn't have left a note.

I pressed my head against the headrest, wriggled the wire from the ignition, and unrolled the note. Handwritten on a scrap of newsprint with the day's date was the warning, *I don't like women in black underwear.*

What the . . . *what?*

Chapter 10

Ragnar followed me out of the parking lot. I drove home, a patch of greasy fear-sweat slicking between my shoulder blades. "I don't like women in black underwear," I mimicked in a whiny voice. "Like that's supposed to be scary? Choose a color every woman in America wears and say 'don't'? Why not nude? Why not white? Whatev."

It took two miles until I peeked inside my shirt to see what color bra I was wearing. Black. *Great.* The fear-sweat oozed down my spine.

The longer I drove, the more I saw the brilliance of Mant's threat. A poetic storm of pervy promise and violent undertones.

I needed a shower. Desperately.

No way was I going to mention this to Hank, who, I was certain, had already taken steps far beyond Ragnar to corral Jeff Mant. Even so, he'd put me under house arrest. And that couldn't happen. I could just imagine the conversation: *"Um, Ms. Kaplan? Mr. Sawyer? One of my mercenary boyfriend's ex-partners is trying to kill me to screw with him, so I'm gonna take a few days off the case. Please promote me to field agent."*

What was I really getting so wound and bound about, anyway? A note in my ignition? Mant had had all day to break into my car. Hell, you could score the *Tribune* at 4:00 a.m. from any newsstand. He probably got up early, planted it, and lay around watching soaps all day, letting his creep factor do all the heavy lifting.

Unfortunately, true sociopaths were always jonesing for calculated violence. They thrive on premeditated crimes with controllable risks.

Sometimes it sucks knowing what I know.

I pulled into Hank's driveway and stopped. A thick-muscled white guy held up a hand. Five-foot-nine, 185 pounds, he had fierce tatts, a pair of night vision goggles around his neck, side arm, and a black Belgian Malinois on a leash.

I glanced back at Ragnar, who threw me a salute and drove off.

Apparently Man-with-a-Dog was A-okay. I rolled down the window. "Hiya."

"Miss McGrane? I'm Chris Ledoux. This is Havoc. We came on duty before Mr. Bannon left this evening. If you have any . . . ah . . . trouble—"

"Just part my lips and scream?"

Chris frowned. "I was going to say flash the lights." He scanned the area behind me. "But that'll work. Close the garage door, please, before you get out of the car."

He and Havoc stepped out of the way. I pulled in the garage and breathed a sigh of relief as the door lowered behind me.

Alone time.

I went in the house. Stoli beckoned from the bar freezer. I threw a couple ice cubes into a lowball glass and didn't stop pouring until it hit the rim. My first hefty slug went down like water. I wiped my mouth on the back of my hand and saw the note on the counter.

M
I'll wake you.
H

I took another swallow, pulled out my juiced-up iPhone, and sent Danny Kaplan the video and stills of the Drag Queen stealing the Lexus.

Vodka can do a lot of wonderful things, but erasing the stink of your own fear isn't one of them. I finished my drink, stripped down, and took a shower.

I spent twenty minutes under the stream trying not to think about Jeff Mant. Which was actually far more pleasant than thinking about all the things I wasn't telling Hank.

Afterward, wrapped up in a fluffy white bamboo-cotton towel, I went into my closet, put on one of Hank's T-shirts and opened the dresser drawer for some underpants. A third of my underwear was black.

"You sick fuck," I said out loud, "it's my underwear." But my voice sounded scared to my own ears, and that set my freak off. In a spastic frenzy, I separated all my black underwear and buried it in the bottom drawer under a couple of Hank's old sweatshirts.

My BOC iPhone buzzed with an incoming text. I ran into the bedroom to answer it.

Danny Kaplan: *Is that all the evidence you collected today?*
Yes.
Danny Kaplan: *One tow truck?*
Yes. But I'm almost certain it was stolen.
Danny Kaplan: *I see. No need to send in piecemeal. Bring what you have to debrief Thursday 5:00 p.m. sharp.*

I shut off the phone. *Gee, Danny. There's this guy named Jeff I'd love to set you up with.*

The sound of the garage door woke me at 2:15 a.m. I listened further and heard nothing, which was normal. Hank moved with the stealth of a big cat. I rolled onto my stomach and dozed off.

Hank slid in next to me and pulled me into his chest. I nestled into the hard warmth of him. "Mmm."

"Rough road ahead," he said.

"Oh? I'll make sure to buckle up."

"Mant's a killer, Maisie. He's contacted a pal, looking for a fast money job. He knows I'm back now." Hank tightened his hold. "I'm not taking any chances. You'll have a shadow for the next few days." He gently nipped my ear, his warm breath sending a shiver through me. "I'll be working nights."

Hunting.

* * *

Thursday after work I was as skittish as a toy poodle in the rain. Ragnar drove me to the BOC's super-spy headquarters at Silverthorn Estates. At 4:59 p.m. I knocked twice on Kaplan's office door. It clicked open and I entered the room.

Walt Sawyer and Danny Kaplan sat across the sleek conference table, piles of files stacked between them and one open chair for me. "Maisie." Sawyer stood and held out a hand. "How are you finding the BOC?"

Uh-oh. I shook his hand and took a seat. "Very fine, sir."

As always, the pair of them were dressed to the nines. Which made my navy poly-blend uniform feel a little itchier. Kaplan picked up a folder and handed it across to him. "This is one of Ms. McGrane's pieces of evidence."

"The Lexus was stolen?" he said.

"Yes." Kaplan nodded. "Have you any more to share with us, Maisie?"

"Yes, ma'am." I pulled a black binder from my bag. "I'm afraid I didn't realize the debrief was with you, as well, sir, so I only made one copy." I handed the binder across to him. He flipped through the photos in plastic sleeves. "Of the thirty-seven photographed tows," I said, "I think it's safe to assume forty percent have been stolen."

Kaplan leaned back in her chair. "Assumption is the mother of all fuckups." Sawyer handed her the binder. She flipped through it, set it down, and folded her thin arms across her chest. "How?"

"How what?" I said.

"How did you manage this? In three days?"

I cleared my throat. *Time to fly with the eagles or scratch with the chickens.* "I told my supervisor that my police officer brother believed cars were being towed illegally."

"You did what?" Kaplan's cheeks went taut. "On whose authority?"

"Uh . . . my own?" I turned to Sawyer. His cognac-colored eyes gave away nothing. "She in turn offered it as an incentive program to the rest of the Parking Enforcement Agents."

"Go on," Danny said.

"Each PEA who turns in a time and date-stamped set of photos receives ten dollars cash. I figured we could pull the city impound records and immediately remove legal tows, and whatever is left is potentially part of the stolen car ring."

"How are you paying for this?" Kaplan snapped.

"Mr. Dunne gave me fifteen hundred dollars of petty cash."

"You see, Danny?" Sawyer said. "She's done what we've asked. And better and more efficiently than we could have wished." A slow, sly smile spread across his face. "Maisie, you've shown the initiative of an A player. Maintain this level of intensity and you'll be a field agent in no time."

I blushed in the glow of his praise. He had that charisma, the kind that gets someone twenty years younger wondering how he'd be in the sack. No wonder Mom liked him. And from the daggers my new boss was shooting at me, maybe Kaplan did, too.

Her nostrils pinched white in irritation. "What happens when your supervisor confronts your brother? What then?"

"He'll cover for me."

"Allowing for that possibility, which is a stretch—"

"Oh Danny." Sawyer chuckled. "What you don't know about the Irish!"

"Allowing for that possibility," she continued, "what do you plan on telling your brother when he confronts you?"

"Since I can't find a way onto the force, I've decided to become an investigative journalist." I blinked in surprise. The lie came out of my mouth so smoothly it felt as though I'd planned it months in advance.

"She's a natural, Danny."

"I'll defer to your judgment." Kaplan slid a stack of files in front of me. "The latest on rakija-drinking cowboys of the Slajic Clan and Stannislav 'The Bull' Renko. Have you seen him again?"

"Stannis?" I asked. "No, ma'am."

"Good," she said. "The last thing we need is for Renko to get caught up in some bullshit two-bit bust."

"Isn't it better if he has a record?"

"Not in Chicago." Sawyer shook his head. "That's the rub

for Special Unit. Corruption is rampant and pervasive within the CPD. A flag, or 'leader,' in the system alerts the opportunists within." He smiled coldly. "The BOC, you see, is in the unpleasant position of needing our criminals to be clever enough to fly below the radar, and yet rash enough to get caught."

I nodded, feeling like a minor leaguer.

Sawyer glanced at his watch. "Get whatever you need from Edward Dunne, Maisie. And keep up the good work."

I left Kaplan's office with a whopper-sized smile on my face. I took the file back to my glass cube desk and called Leticia.

"Yo, McGrane. I'll be outta cash by the end of the day. Six more in my e-mail already."

"No sweat. I'll drop off a dozen cards tomorrow."

"Twelve hundred bucks? Where's the CPD getting the drink to piss away that kind of scratch?"

"They're prepared to pay you, too."

"Fuck you, McGrane." She chortled. "This my civic duty. You got a timeline on when I can break my story?"

Time to put the brakes on. "Leticia, it's going to take several months of these pictures to compile definitive proof."

"Harumph." She tapped her nails on the phone. "Well, if you ain't callin' to give me congratulatory greetings an' the green light, then what you want?"

"To switch to night shift."

"Slow your roll, McGrane. You transfer to night, you ain't never gettin' back on days."

"I don't mean permanently." *But I will if I have to. Once Walt Sawyer sees what I can really do, I'll burn this goddamn uniform in effigy.* "Isn't someone short on vacation or anything?" I prodded. "My guy's working nights for the next couple of weeks. It'd make my life a helluva lot easier to work the same hours, you know?"

"I hear you. God gave 'em a snake so they gotta act the worm." She heaved a sigh. "You're gonna lose a day of pay. Night shift works extended hours. Four days on and four off."

That was even better than I could have hoped. "So, is it a go?"

"I'll have you up tomorrow night."

"Thanks." I hung up.

Initiative taken. I pulled Stannislav Renko's file and went through the case notes again. The guy brought new meaning to the word *clubber.* The only area he avoided was Boystown. No surprise there. Eastern Europeans were about as pro-gay as the average Muslim mullah.

The trick would be finding him.

"You switched shifts?" Hank's face went completely blank.

"Yeah," I said. "I thought it'd be nice for us to have the days together."

He rubbed the back of his head. A sure sign he wasn't thrilled. Instead he said, "Sounds fun." The phone in his office started ringing. He got up, pulled his cell from his pocket, and slid it across the counter. "Call Ragnar, let him know."

Wow. That was way easier than I thought it would be. I called my shadow.

"Are you outta your fucking mind?" Ragnar said. "Night shift? Jesus-fucking-Christ, why does Bannon let you do this fucking job anyway?"

"Excuse me?"

"Mant's a goddamn menace. You know that. And now you're gonna just serve yourself up?" He scoffed. "It takes weeks to get into the rhythm of working nights. Which means you'll be tired and making bad fucking decisions every goddamn minute."

Oookay. "Look—"

"I'll pick you up tomorrow night." He hung up.

Early Friday evening, I swung by Leticia's office, dropped off more of Edward's cash cards, grabbed my route and ticket gun, and hustled to my cart. Hank may be on the hunt for Mant, but I wasn't taking any chances. My gear was coming with me.

I started up my cart and reviewed my route. The near North Side nightlife district aka the Viagra Triangle. Rich old men, Botoxed cougars, and beautiful young ones looking for a free ride—no matter how temporary.

I punched the air with my fists. "I could kiss you, Letitia!"

I went straight to Gibson's Bar and Steakhouse. The unofficial headquarters of the V.T.

And there like a rat in a humane trap, was a double-parked Aegean blue metallic Bentley W-12 Mulliner. I typed the ticket into my gun, grinning. This was the stuff that legends were made of at the Traffic Enforcement Bureau.

My ticket gun blinked.

Holy mother of God. A boot.

In thirty-two seconds, I booted my first Flying Spur. A $200K four-door sedan that pretty much resembled an über-posh Buick. I took a couple of photos for the girls in the break room and got the hell out of there.

Green Day started playing "Basket Case" on my phone. "Hey, Cash," I answered.

"Whatcha doing?"

"I just dropped a boot on a Flying Spur."

"Christ, you need a hobby." He laughed. "Heard you're working graveyard. Tonight's my last night on Vice."

"Look out, SWAT."

"My CO's finally letting us bust this douchebag drug club, Swag. It's gonna be off the feckin' hook! Wanna swing by, watch me bust some heads?"

"Yeah, sounds fun," I said and meant it.

"Go time's ten after one. We're celebrating afterward at Hud's and I'm buying."

I felt like celebrating myself. Walt Sawyer approved of my initiative. As soon as I got my three days off, I'd stake out Stannis, and Walt Sawyer would come to believe I was the sun and the stars. "I'll be there." I hung up.

I drove the block and a half over to Swag, scanning for offenders but not really caring. I'd laid a prize boot and was looking forward to playing hooky. I parked across from the gentlemen's club and got out.

My devoted shadow, Ragnar, idled in front of a hydrant. I jogged over to the pickup.

He had the window down before I got there. "What's up?"

"I'm gonna stay here for the next hour or so. My brother's meeting me."

"There?" He pointed at Swag.

"Yeah," I said, razzing him. "You know what hounds cops are. But when my brother's buying, I gotta drink."

"You?" His face twisted in disbelief. "Drinking on the job?"

"Rags, as a meter maid, I'm legally allowed to drive on the sidewalk." I dug my nails into my palms to keep a straight face. "Besides. The cart can't go over twenty-eight miles per hour."

He tucked his chin in disapproval and rolled up the window.

I turned and walked down the block, shoulders shaking with laughter. *The bigger they are, the harder they fall for it.*

I glanced at my watch. Plenty of time before the show. I walked down the block, ran a ticket on an Audi and another on a Nissan. As I slid the offender's orange envelope beneath the wiper, I froze at the sight of the car behind it.

A navy Range Rover, Autobiography Black, complete with cowardly newspaper-reading driver behind the wheel.

Holy cat.

Stannislav Renko. I'd bet my shirt on it.

Chapter 11

"No flags in the system." Walt Sawyer's words echoed in my head. A Vice bust would light up Stannis brighter than an emergency flare.

I looked at my watch. Forty minutes until the bust.

This wasn't opportunity knocking, these were the thundering hooves of a gift horse. And I was going to ride this bow-wearing Secretariat until its legs fell off.

I dumped my gun under the seat, grabbed my backpack, got out of the cart, and signaled to Ragnar I was going inside. He shook his head in disgust. I trotted up to the black- and gold-striped awning, trying to piece together a generic yet believable meter-maidesque reason as to why the two bouncers should let me in.

The wide black guy stopped me with a fleshy palm to the chest. "Gentlemen's club. No dykes."

"I'm . . . er . . . trying out," I said.

"Shit, kid." The white bouncer with a Jack Daniels nose shook his head. "Lemme save you the trouble. Firstly, ain't no one gonna think a meter maid is hot. Secondly, especially not one with no tits and less ass."

"Yeah?" I patted the ticket gun on my hip. "You oughta see what I can do with this."

The black guy laughed and opened the door for me. "Good luck."

Swag was an uncomfortable mutation of a seventies disco

movie and a bad Nike commercial. The strobe-lit music made it even worse, but the slavering patrons—a sea of shiny suit coats and satin sweat suits—seemed to like it just fine.

A sweeping staircase led to a series of curtained private rooms. Stannis's gorillas all present and accounted for. The biggest stood in front of the first black-curtained room. One waited midway on the stairs while the last stood guard on the bottom step.

No possible way I was going to get past the velvet ropes and his men without looking like I belonged here.

A girl in cowboy boots, denim thong, and Confederate flag push-up bra brushed by me. A sliver of light glowed from the darkened door she'd just exited.

The bathroom.

I went inside and looked at my watch. Thirty-one minutes before Vice hit.

You can do this.

I took off my cargo pants and my shirt. Thanks to Jeff the sociopath, I was wearing a Simone Perele lace bra and matching hi-rise bikinis in boring white.

Oh well. Can't be helped.

I pulled my hair into two high pigtails, tightened my bra to the last closure, shortened the straps, and stuffed a bunch of Kleenex in each cup. *Voilà. Boobage overflow.*

I put on the neon PEA vest, holster, and ticket gun. Pretty tame, but the clock was ticking. I smeared on a thick coat of lip gloss, grabbed a couple prepaid Visas, and finished my costume with mirrored sunglasses. I lifted the half-empty plastic liner out of the garbage can, stashed my bag at the bottom of the can, and repositioned the garbage bag over the top.

Here goes nothing.

I sauntered over to the bar and stopped at the waitress station. On the way, a clammy hand grabbed my ass. *Nice.* I passed muster with the low-level drunks, at least.

A bartender in a skimpy bikini and stiletto heels that had her balancing in pointe position motioned for me to order.

"A bottle of rakija and two glasses, please." I tossed $200 on the counter.

She tiptoed over, mincing through the treacherous honey-comb of rubber floor mat. "You new?"

"Yeah."

"Dick and balls management never tells me when we hire someone." She rolled her eyes, then bent beneath the bar, still talking. "Serbs. You ever had this shit?"

"No."

She slammed a bottle of Žuta Osa and a couple of lowball glasses on a tray. "It means Yellow Wasp." She rang it up at the register and gave me back $30. "Worst headache you'll ever have."

I left her $10. "Thanks."

"Keep it. You tip out at the end of the night."

I shoved the ten and twenty down my bra and picked up the tray.

A waitress in a black corset, thigh-high black boots, kitty-cat ears, and a feather boa tail strutted to the staircase with a bottle of champagne in one hand and two glasses in the other. I fell in step behind her, as one of Stannis's bodyguards, ever the gentleman, unhooked the velvet rope for us to go up.

The bodyguard on the stairs didn't notice me. Cat-girl was working it enough for both of us. That left the last and biggest ape in front of the cordoned room. When we got to the top step, I reached over and gave Cat-girl's tail a sharp yank. She spun, wielding the bottle at the gorilla's head. He raised his hands as she swore at him.

I stepped behind him and passed between the curtains.

Renko was straddling some flavor of the month. His hands gripped the back of the couch. *Of all the times to interrupt.*

Great. He's getting a hummer.

"Um . . . Stannis?" I took off my sunglasses.

No response. The music blasted from the dance floor below.

"Excuse me," I said louder. "Stannis?"

He waved his hand without looking back. "Get out."

"Not without you," I said.

With one hand still on the back of the couch, he swung his

head toward me. The irritation in his face changed to confusion as he recognized and then tried to place me. "You?"

"I owe you a favor."

A funny, sad sort of smile spread across his face. "No, no." He pushed himself upright from the couch and turned and came toward me. His open shirt and pants exposed a harsh, sinewy torso and obvious arousal.

My jaw sagged open as I saw who was on the couch beneath him.

Whoa!

"You!" Mayor Talbott Cottle Coles reared up from the couch.

"No." Stannis raised a palm to him. "Is okey. She—"

"What the fuck are you doing here?" Coles glared at me in pure hate.

"Interrupting boys' night, apparently," I said.

Coles launched himself at me. His fist cracked across my chin like a two-by-four. I wobbled and dropped like a sack full of kittens onto my bare knees.

Sucker-punching sonuvabitch.

Stannis grabbed Coles around the waist and shoved him backward. "Stop!" He pointed at me. "You. What you want?"

"Vithe," I slurred, blood flooding my teeth and tongue.

Goddamn, that hurt.

I wasn't about to give him the satisfaction. I stood up, spat out a red mouthful, and cocked a brow at Coles. "Vice is busting the joint in"—I glanced at my watch—"sixteen minutes."

Coles tucked in his shirt and jabbed a finger at me. "This better not be a fucking setup!"

I shrugged at Stannis. "It's not."

"You! You better keep your cunt mouth shut. And you"—he pointed at Stannis—"you make sure she does." Coles stormed past us and through the curtains.

You're welcome, sir. Say hi to the wife and the kids for me, you two-timing closeted sack of shit.

Stannis walked to the table, opened the bottle of rakija, and poured some in a glass. He handed it to me. "Is good."

I took a swig. It tasted like Manischewitz and Everclear, and man, did it burn the inside of my shredded mouth. I finished it.

He fastened his pants, not bothering to button his shirt. "You work here?" He took a drink straight from the bottle.

"No."

He rubbed the bridge of his nose. "How do you come to be here?"

"It's a long story." I tapped the face of my watch. "And you don't have time to hear it."

Stannis stood there staring at me for a full minute. "Okey." He put an arm around my waist. "Now we go. Together."

We slipped out the curtains and down the stairs.

"My gear—" I jerked away from him and took a step toward the bathroom. One of his men blocked my way.

"You come talk to me outside," Stannis's blue eyes burned into mine. "*Maisie.*"

Great. He remembers my name. "Uh, yeah. You bet." At his nod, the man stepped aside and I sprinted to the bathroom.

I grabbed the liner out of the garbage can, kicked off my work boots, and pulled on my cargo pants. No time for the shirt, but I still had the vest on. I managed to yank the pigtails out and stow the glasses and ticket gun in my bag before I shot out the front door.

A gorilla waited next to the bouncers. "Come now," he said. *Shit. Ragnar.*

"You really don't want me to do that," I said, scanning the block. "Uh . . . Tell Stannis I'll be one block north, at T.G.I. Friday's. In the bar."

"No," said Stannis's head gorilla.

"Hey, guys?" I raised my palms in appeal to the bouncers. "A lil' help here?"

One of the bouncers laid a hand on the gorilla and things went south as I sprinted to my cart and got in. Vice started rolling in just as I finished buttoning up my shirt. I started the Interceptor and took off for Friday's, equal parts relieved and dismayed as Ragnar followed.

* * *

I chose a booth in the darkened bar. The generically pleasant T.G.I. Friday's was as safe a place as any to meet one of the top dogs of the Srpska Mafija.

My lip was swelling. Even with the metallic tang of blood in my mouth, I could still taste Yellow Wasp.

Goddamn Coles. A bit of a shocker, actually, to discover he bats both ways.

Clever cover, having a gay affair in a straight strip club.

I dropped my head back onto the padded seat of the high red leather booth, and closed my eyes. The first misgivings of the spontaneous rescue churned in my stomach. Walt Sawyer didn't want Renko in the system, but he hadn't authorized contact, either.

And I was up to my neck in contact.

"Can I help you?" asked a waitress.

"Stoli. Double. On the rocks," I said without opening my eyes.

"Can I see some ID, honey?"

"Sure." Without moving, I dug my wallet out of my purse, and flipped it open on the table.

"Could you look my way, please?"

I turned my head.

She pursed her lips in a silent whistle. "Need anything else?"

"Ice and a napkin?"

"I'll do you one better." She returned with the vodka and one of those insta–ice packs that you crack against a counter to start working. She wrapped it in a clean bar towel and handed it to me.

"Thanks."

"No one has the right to hit you."

The mayor of Chicago sure thinks he does. I nodded. She left.

I held the ice pack to my mouth, ramping up my inner Tony Robbins. *Sawyer hired me to be an undercover, right? He'd applauded my initiative with the photos. High fliers belong in the field, right?*

I sipped the Stoli. Slowly.

Halfway through, I started to worry I'd overplayed Renko.

He slid into the booth. A sleek navy suit jacket now covered his pale blue Kitsuné shirt, open at the throat. "I don't like to chase."

"I find that hard to believe."

His eyes went shark-flat.

I swallowed convulsively. "That wasn't a good place to talk."

The waitress returned, ready to give my assumed abuser the what for. But she got a look at a real live killer and deflated. "Can I get you something, sir?"

Stannis's eyes never left mine.

I pointed at my glass and she scurried away.

He didn't speak, just stared unnervingly at me until he'd been served. "Explain tonight."

Hank's Law Number Twenty-Three: The strongest lies are built on truth.

"I was almost off shift. My brother, a Vice cop, asked me to go out for drinks after they busted Swag." I raised a shoulder. "I went there to meet him and saw your car."

"Ah. Fast to think." He tapped a finger against his temple. "Too fast, maybe?" A shadow of doubt crossed his face. "You betray your brother for a stranger?"

"A friend, I thought." I switched the ice pack to my other hand. "You saved me from . . ." For a split second, I felt Mant's hands on me and twitched.

Hello, PTSD.

I picked up my drink. My hand shook hard enough to set the ice rattling. Blood rushed to my cheeks and I downed the rest of it in one go. I set the glass down with a sharp *click* and cleared my throat. "Anyway, nobody likes to get arrested."

Stannis tipped his head to one side and nodded. "This is so."

I sat back, waiting. But apparently the ball was still in my court. "Why'd you help me?"

"I see you fighting. Good, but not pro. I see in your face you know this." He rapped his knuckles on the table. "Still you try. You show no fear." He gave a wistful smile. "I know someone else like this, one time ago."

"Thank you." I tucked my hair behind my ears. According to

Mom and the twins, small confessions build confidence with a subject. "I'm the black sheep of my family. Do you know what that is?"

"Yes." Stannis squinted and tapped his chest. "I also."

"Most of my family are police."

"Is that why you do this work?" He gestured to my uniform. "To anger them?"

"Maybe."

"What is Coles to you?"

"I saved his life once," I said. "He can't get past it."

"He is significant man. Connected."

"I'm not looking for trouble, Stannis."

His lip raised at the corner. "You don't need to look when you wear it on your person as a dress."

You're not the first guy to tell me that.

"May I?" He reached toward my chin.

I lowered the ice pack. Before I could flinch, he took my lower lip between his thumb and forefinger, gently pulled it out and surveyed the damage. "Is not bad." He let go. "Still . . ." He shook his head and his fingers curled into a fist. "A man should not hit woman with closed hand."

"Gee, thanks," I dead-panned. "Remind him a little sooner next time."

Stannis pointed at me and laughed. A deceptively humanizing sound, charming and boyish. "Is funny."

I grinned.

He ran his thumb across his lower lip, thinking. "You interest me, Maisie."

I sure hope so, because I'm about to press my luck. "So, you and Coles?"

Stannis squinted at me. "Coles? He likes to be in love. Me? I like to fuck." Stannis leaned across the table and grinned. "And there's nothing better than to fuck significant one in love."

I can see that. My phone buzzed. Incoming text. "Excuse me, please?"

Stannis raised his drink. "Yes."
It was from Cash.

WTH RU?! On way to Hud's.

I flipped the phone around. "My brother. Want to come?"
He caught my wrist and pulled me in close. His electric eyes intense, forehead inches from mine. "What is this game you play?"
"I could ask you the same thing."
Stannis thought that over. So close to me I could see the faint blue veins and heavy black whiskers just beneath his pale skin.
I forced out a tinkling laugh. "I guess a date's out of the question."
His black brows met in a momentary frown.
I was about to pull my hand away when he turned it over and raised the underside of my wrist to his lips, eyes glinting. "Is it?"
Uh-oh.
He stood up. "One must be in darkness for another to experience light, Maisie." And then he was gone.

Chapter 12

Jaysus, Mary and Joseph.

I drove the Interceptor back to the Traffic Enforcement Bureau, riding the roller coaster of simultaneous nausea and exhilaration. I clocked out, cuted up, and yawned, trying to release some of the ache in my jaw.

Asshat Coles.

The passenger door swung open as I approached Ragnar's truck. I tossed my bag on the floor and hopped up into the cab.

He waited until I latched my seat belt. He twisted in his seat and leaned in until we were nose to nose. "Are you fuckin' kidding me?"

"Easy now." I kept my voice gentle. "No problem here."

"Yeah? What the hell am I supposed to tell Bannon?"

"Whatever you want."

"You sure 'bout that?" The pink puckered scar on his cheek twisted in a mirthless smile. "So you coming out of a strip club with no shirt on is A-okay?"

"I may be your responsibility, but you're working for Hank," I said, neatly laying the dilemma back in his lap.

"And that's it?"

"That's it."

"Ergh." He ran a rough hand through his hair. "Christ." He flopped back against the driver's seat. "Where to?"

"Hud's."

The drive was short and strained, barely long enough for

Dwight Yoakam to cover "I Want You to Want Me." The park-ing lot of Chicago's top cop bar boasted a show of security as impressive as the Traffic Bureau's. Because you don't become the ultimate cop hangout if police cars are vandalized or worse, stolen. Ragnar weaved his pickup between rows of plain-wrappeds—un-marked Tauruses, Crown Vics, and Mustangs and the usual blue and white Explorers and Impalas. A security guard patrolled with a German shepherd.

"It's been a lousy night, Rags. My brother Cash and his best buddy, Koji, finally made SWAT. C'mon. Let's go, let them buy us a beer or three."

For the barest instant his face softened. If I'd have blinked, I'd have missed it. "Go ahead," he said. "But do me a favor, will ya?"

"Sure. Name it."

"Keep your goddamn shirt on."

Even at a quarter to three in the morning, Hud's was packed. Smoky as hell because John Wayne cowboys don't cotton to no e-cigs and the CPD is above the law, baby. The entire floor be-tween the tables and the bar had been taken over by a badge bunny rendition of a high school dance. Drunken groping and swaying; the only things missing were cheap carnation corsages.

I spied Cash in a corner booth in the back of the bar, a crowd of über-fit tough guys on his left. His new team members. I started threading my way through woozy, slow dancers. A hand circled my wrist, then slid down to grip my fingers before rais-ing my arm and tugging me backward.

Koji Hattoro. Cash's partner and the only cop in Chicago who could dance. Really dance.

I let him twirl me backward, to the awe and dismay of the zombie-treading badge bunnies. I grinned and relaxed as he dropped me into a floor-sweeping dip. Only the face I smiled up into wasn't Koji's. It was the sharply planed cheekbones and white tiger teeth of SWAT commander Lee Sharpe.

"Maisie McGrane," he said. "Looking worse for wear and hotter than hell, as per." He raised me upright.

Whoa.

"Hi, Lee." Sharpe was a charismatic, happy-go-lucky badass and an also-ran in the anorexic love diary of Maisie McGrane. His hand moved to the small of my back as he led me back to the SWAT team corner.

"Here she is, lads!" Cash yelled in delight, hoisting himself up onto unsteady feet before kissing my cheek. "Me wee baby sister."

Sweet Jesus, the drunken brogue.

"Sit the feck down." Rory landed a heavy hand on Cash's shoulder and forced him back into his seat.

Bad cop's here. Good cop can't be far behind.

"Christ," Flynn said from behind me, carrying three bottles of beer in each hand. "He's so bad he makes Paltrow's Brit sound authentic."

Even Rory smiled at that one. Aside from Da, Rory was the sole McGrane with the legitimate call of the Celts. He'd spent his childhood summers in Ireland on our grandparents' farm.

"The twins coming?" I asked.

Cash shook his head. "Defense attorneys are only slightly less welcome at Hud's than meter maids."

"Ha-ha. Very funny." I elbowed him. "Shove over." He scooted. I slid into the booth, Lee behind me, throwing his arm across the back of the seat. A move that was met with approval by all three of my brothers as well as Koji, who arrived at the table with a tray full of Jager shots.

"Look who's rejoined the land of the living." An impish smirk curled on Koji's thin, pointed face. "*Wolfenstein*'s not the same without Cash and me stepping over your dead body every thirty seconds."

"Ha!" Cash popped Koji in the chest.

"Aww." I tapped my watch. "Almost fourteen seconds without a video game reference. Our little Koji's growing up."

"You're vibrating," Lee said into my ear.

"Huh?"

"Your leg."

I reached between us and dug the pulsing BOC iPhone out of my cargo pants pocket, opting to turn away from Cash and toward Lee to read my incoming text from Danny Kaplan.

Thursday. 5:00 p.m. sharp.

Cripes. What kind of boss sends a 3:00 a.m. weekend reminder for a weekday meeting? The buzz-killing kind.

I'll be there, I typed, wondering if she'd be as irritated by my instant response text as I was to receive hers.

I ran a hand over my face. *Dammit.* I hadn't even considered my debrief might not include Walt Sawyer.

"Who's Danny?" Lee said. "I thought his name was Hank."

"And I thought SWAT guys weren't as nosy as regular cops."

"So much to learn . . ." Lee gave the ends of my hair a playful tug. "But I'm willing to teach. How about dinner? Wednesday night."

I secured the phone back in my pants pocket and said archly, "I'd rather kiss a puppy with the flu."

Lee laughed and leaned forward, drumming his hands bongo-style on the table. "Hey, Cash. Your sister shot me down. Again. Come Monday training, you're gonna find payback's a warrior princess bitch."

"Chill, *sir.*" Koji slid a Jager shot to Lee and another in front of me. "A couple more of these and she'll think you *are* Hank."

"Lee"—I pointed at my brother and his best pal—"I'll take it as a personal affront if you *don't* ride these mutts harder than everyone else."

Cash, Koji, and Lee kept ribbing each other. I picked up my shot and surreptitiously handed it off behind Lee to Rory, who sat glaring off into space.

"I hate this shite." He drank it and made a face. "If we're going to get drunk, let's do it properly." He pushed away from the table and stomped off toward the bar.

"What's eating him?" I asked Flynn.

"He's still pissed over the BOC swooping in and snatching our pod of connected homicide cases." Flynn moved over onto Rory's chair.

Lee's hands went around my waist. "Hey," I said.

"Allow me." He dragged me across his lap, careful not to bang my knees on the table, and set me down on the other side.

"My, how chivalrous," I said.

"Can't have you talking behind my back." Lee winked and returned to Cash and Koji.

"Jaysus." Flynn rolled his eyes. "You through?" He motioned for me to lean in.

I did. "Spill."

"Rory hit pay dirt with some mook—this Serb kid who says he knows who capped two of our four vics."

Holy cat. "And?"

Flynn rubbed his eye with the heel of his hand. "Rory and I aren't so sure Walt Sawyer's all he's cracked up to be."

My spine stiffened. *Stay casual.* "Meaning?"

"We don't feel like sharing. This isn't the first time the BOC preempted us. Last time, *poof.*" He blew across his fingertips. "Never again did those cases see the light of day."

"Seriously?" I said. "The CPD's *cleared* murder case rate is at a gutterific twenty-five percent and you guys want to hang on to four more?"

That hit Flynn where it hurt. "The force is down three hundred officers. And those were real cases, not din't-see-nuthin gangbangs."

"Yeah, well. Only a matter of time until Chicago's the new Detroit, right?"

Rory returned with a bottle of Jameson and three glasses. Getting properly drunk didn't include Cash, Koji, or SWAT. He filled one glass all the way to the rim, set the bottle down, raised the glass, and threw back the entire contents.

Flynn and I exchanged raised brows. Rory sloshed too much into our glasses before filling his own again. "Drink."

Rory slugged down the whiskey and wiped his mouth on the back of his hand. He reached for the bottle. I got there first. "Don't feck with me, Snap," he said.

I let go. "Awfully thirsty, aren't you?"

"Mebbe you'd be, as well," he scoffed, eyes shining, "if you'd found the poor bastard with not a feckin' finger left on his hand."

Flynn's jaw tightened. "What?"

"The goddamn idiot called me. For help." Rory poured another. "Stupid feck almost bled to death"—fury scalded his voice—"tryin' to fashion a tourniquet from a tube sock."

"Where's the kid now?" Flynn said.

Rory cracked his neck. "Safe."

Flynn frowned. "For how long?"

"Shut it," Rory said.

We drank in silence, ignoring the merry end of the table.

At the rate Rory was putting it away, he'd be unconscious before I'd be able to get anything out of him. He'd drunk more than a fifth already and showed no sign of stopping, his temper increasing exponentially.

There was only one way this night was going to end.

Bloody.

Lee nudged me with an elbow. "Hang on," I said.

"Your five o'clock." He jerked his head toward the door. "Why do I think he belongs to you?"

I turned. A familiar six-foot-seven, 340-pound hulk pushed his way through the bar and stopped at our table. "Let's go, Maisie," Ragnar said.

Uh-oh. "Hey, guys," I said. "This is my friend—"

Rory kicked back his chair and stood up, a slight sway in his stance, a dangerous light in his eyes. The table went quiet. "Me sister won't be goin' anywhere with the likes of yeh."

And here we go again.

Drunk, Rory had the devil's share of anger and half the common sense of a capuchin monkey.

The Viking squinted at him, taking in the half-empty bottle of whiskey and the resignation in my face. "Outside, then?"

"Why for?" Rory said.

Flynn got to his feet. "You want to brawl? Take it outside." He tossed a wad of twenties onto the table. "The rest of you, stay inside and chill the feck out. Please."

Cash raised a beer in acquiescence. "Don't let him hurt that pretty face of yours, Rory."

"Best of luck," Koji said.

"Maisie?" Lee said.

"Gotta go." I flipped him a salute. "Keep an eye on Cash, will you?"

He leaned back hard in the booth, frowning, not liking it. "Sure thing."

Ragnar was already outside, Rory close behind, taking overly deliberate steps. Flynn grabbed me by the arm as we hustled out of the bar. "Who's the giant?"

"I told you. A friend."

"Can't say I'm disappointed." Flynn gave a bark of laughter. "At least it won't end with me, Cash, or SWAT mixing it up with Rory."

Rory would be taking my medicine. No doubt Ragnar felt the need to beat the crap out of somebody after tonight's strip club adventure.

They faced off in the gravel secondary parking lot, under the weird orange-yellow lights. Ragnar's fists went up.

An unholy smile of glee crossed Rory's face. But his eyes had gone glassy, his sway more pronounced. The whiskey was taking over. He took a lurching hop forward, and his jab glanced off Ragnar's chin. He followed with a gut shot, hard and heavy.

The Viking returned a combo of his own. And another.

Rory's sluggish right nicked the Viking's nose. Ragnar flinched in surprise and with a speed I hadn't seen yet, shoved Rory hard in the chest.

Rory stumbled backwards, tripped over a parking block, and landed hard on his back, knocking the wind out of himself. He rolled onto all fours, stood up, and wiped his hands on his pants, laughing.

Ragnar started laughing, too.

Rory rushed him, tackling him around the waist. The Viking brought his fists down hard between his shoulder blades. Rory hit the gravel in a cloud of dust.

"Stay down." Flynn dragged a hand over his face and muttered, "For the love of Christ, stay down."

But our brother, the human bobber, popped up on his feet.

They stood there hammering it out like Godzilla and Mothra.

Taking and inflicting damage points. Something to see, maybe, if Rory'd been sober.

Only he wasn't.

Idiots.

"I'm tired, Rags," I said, giving him the nod to end it.

He nodded and threw two short jabs to Rory's face. Bright red blood spurted from his nose like something from a viral video. Ragnar followed up with a pair of heavy body blows that doubled Rory over. My brother swayed in place, panting and spitting, smearing and dripping blood on his shirtsleeves.

Flynn put a hand on his back. "Towel's in."

"Ssss not broke," Rory said, swiping at his nose. "Jes gimme a feckin' minute."

"He can't go home like this," I said. "One look and Da won't rest until . . ."

Flynn rubbed his forehead. "Well, what the hell am I gonna do with him?"

"I'll take him," I said. "Let him sober up in Hank's guest room."

Flynn jerked a thumb at Ragnar. "You think your *friend* will be okay with that?"

"Absolutely."

He laid a hand on my head and mussed my hair. "Sometimes I think I don't know you at all anymore."

Ragnar was positively jovial after kicking Rory's ass. And Rory, skunk-drunk and fury spent, was as happy to have taken his licks, as dished them out. They were fast friends by the time we hit the freeway, comparing fight stories.

Fine by me. I had plenty to think about.

Rory's snitch. What was urgent enough for Rags to roust me from Hud's but not so important that he could make time for a bar fight? And how exactly were we going to slip past Hank's night sentry, Chris, without Rory getting wise?

I took the easy one first. "Uh, Rags?" I interrupted. "Got a number for that *pal* of yours, Chris Ledoux? I'm thinking about scoring his extra Sox tickets."

"Er . . ." It took him a few seconds to catch on. "You bet." He handed me his cell phone. Rory, blissfully unaware, blarneyed on.

I scrolled through his contacts, clicked on Ledoux, and typed.

Arriving with overnight guest. Please stay out of sight.
Maisie

Minutes later, Ragnar drove into Hank's driveway. Sentry and dog, nowhere to be seen.

Perfect.

Rory opened the door and slowly climbed out.

I hung back. "Why'd you come into the bar tonight, Ragnar?"

"Mant's ghosted. Got the call to bring you here and tell you Bannon won't be back 'til morning."

The dashboard clock read 4:05 a.m. "Does that qualify?"

"Fuck if I know." Ragnar shrugged.

"Okay," I said. "Thanks for not breaking Rory's nose."

"What can I say? I'm a classy guy."

Rory slung a heavy arm across my shoulders. I grabbed him around the middle, and we stumble-walked up the sidewalk.

"Thanks, Snap." He leaned against the door while I typed in the security code.

"Anytime." I pushed open the door. "All this over a snitch, huh?"

Rory sagged forward into the foyer. "Thass the feckin' thing of it. Kid's only fifteen. A cripple for the rest o' his life now, yeah?"

Political correctness was never your forte. "Where'd you take him? Lurie Children's?"

"Nah," he said with surprising frankness. "I called Joy."

Dr. Joy Schaffer was a pediatric surgeon and Rory's ex-girlfriend. A slinky brunette with an easy smile and the unflappable cool of a frozen lake. No matter how hard he tried—and he tried damn hard—Rory couldn't quite get over her.

I led him to the guest room. He flopped down on the bed.

I pulled the blinds and went into the en suite bath and got towels, spare toothbrush and toothpaste out of the cabinet. "So. You set a juvie snitch up in a private hospital? That's—"

"Safe as I could make it and get him treated. Joy's stretching to gimme three days. After that, I dunno." He shook his head.

I leaned against the guest bath doorjamb. "Quite a luxury, then, for you to nurse a two-day hangover."

"Aww, feck." He threw an arm over his face and groaned. "Bring me a glass of salt water."

I returned with the salt water, aspirin, and three bottles of Gatorade.

"Thanks." Rory took the glass and went into the bathroom. He started retching before I made it to the door.

I took a shower and sluiced the stink of smoke and wired-up monkey grease from my skin. Afterward, wrapped in a towel, the night's tension melted away beneath the blow-dryer's somnolent heat until I caught my reflection and a brutal dose of conscience in the mirror.

Even the smattering of freckles across my nose was accusatory.

All I ever wanted to do was to make the table club, to be one of them. And now that I was on the job, I was using my brothers for my own ambition. Tonight, I stole Cash's righteous collar and was scheming to heist a maimed teenage snitch from under Flynn and Rory.

God, I suck.

It was after four o'clock and Hank still wasn't home. I put on underpants and an Army T-shirt, not letting myself think about his hunt for a psychotic hit man.

"Your worrying," he said once, after an assignment, while I was lying across his chest in bed, "means you don't trust me or my ability."

"No." Tears of frustration blurred my vision. "I don't trust other people."

He flipped me onto my back, looming over me. "Situational awareness, Peaches."

"But—"

He pinned my arms over my head, holding me by the wrists. There was nothing better than lying powerless beneath him.

"Trust me." He nuzzled, his scruffy chin into my collarbone. "Promise me you'll never worry."

I did.

"I take it back," I said aloud to the empty room. "Where are you, Hank?"

I crawled into bed, missing him like hell, certain that no matter how tired I was, sleep would never come.

I was wrong.

Chapter 13

Face mashed into the pillow, arms over my head, I slept dead to the world.

Rush Limbaugh's theme song blared. I fumbled across the nightstand for my phone. "Leticia?"

"Do you know what goddamn time it is?" she squawked.

"Uh . . ." I rolled over onto my back and looked blearily at the clock. "6:04 a.m.?"

Hank isn't home yet.

"And what goddamn day it is?"

"Saturday?"

"Since you're all coherent an' shit, enlighten me as to why I'm calling you at the crack of dawn on my day off?"

Oh shit. Cutting my shift. I got up and started pacing, trying to force blood to my brain. "I'm sorry. I didn't think—"

"Hell right, you din't. Booting a Bentley? This is Chicago. Someone own a car like that, they so connected you think three times before you write the ticket, then you hold up and think again."

The blood drained from my head into my stomach and roiled. "Whose was it?"

"The Honorable Mrs. Coles," she said.

Fuck. Me.

"You boot the mayor's wife's car outside a bunch of hoochie clubs? Whee! You kicked the proverbial hell outta that tatted girl's hornets' nest."

My brain, encased in Jell-O, could form no response.

"McGrane? You there?"

"Yeah."

"Lemme tell you how this is gonna play out. You gonna bust your tiny white onion down to my desk. In the bottom drawer in a file labeled *Hillsdale College* you're gonna find the North Impound ID swipe cards and keys."

"Yes, ma'am."

"Then you're gonna get your sorry and subservient self to North Impound by 7:00 a.m. sharp so one o' the mayor's crew can pick his Bentley up and erase all goddamn traces of your stupidity."

"Got it."

"No, what you got is a temporary suspension. I'll see you in my office first thing Monday morning." She disconnected.

From bad to worse faster than IRS hard drives spontaneously combusting.

Grinding on two hours' sleep, I raided Hank's medicine cabinet, searching through the go pills and no-go pills. Amphetamines and sleeping pills. Dexedrine and beta-blockers. Modafinil.

"Less speed, more focus," was how Hank described them. I shook out a couple of tablets, washed them down with water straight from the tap, and put on jeans, a black tee, and a blazer, and armed up with the Kimber Solo, boot knife, and pepper spray.

I went into the kitchen and scribbled a note.

> *Hank,*
> *I stepped in something at work. Rory's*
> *sleeping it off in the guest room.*
> *Home in time for lunch.*
> *Xoxo*
> *Maisie*

I popped the tab on a Xenergy Cherry Lime and chugged it on the way to the garage. And stopped short. My Accord was at my house. Hank took the G-Wagen and the Super Bee was getting detailed after the stringer and spending the week in the police impound. Which left . . . I looked at the key rack and grinned.

The Indian.

Which came with the added benefit that Chris the sentry wouldn't be faced with the dilemma of staying on duty or chasing me down. He'd never catch me.

I grabbed the keys and a helmet and started the motorcycle before I hit the garage door clicker.

Hank's Modafinil kicked in somewhere on the freeway. I was flying at a steady 85 mph, at one with the bike. Everything seemed to have slowed down. Become clearer. Colors brighter. I felt calm, full of focus, and perfectly alert.

By the time I recovered the keys from Leticia's desk, I had a plan and ten minutes to make it to North Impound.

Piece of cake.

I parked Hank's bike in front of the office door, cracked my knuckles, and sent my sole ally at Special Unit, Edward Dunne, a text.

I have a lead, but I'm not ready to take it to Kaplan yet.
Edward Dunne: *What do you need?*
Photos of "The Bull" and his crew.
Edward Dunne: *For how long?*
3 hrs.
Edward Dunne: *You'll have them in twenty minutes. Coded to erase by noon.*
Thanks! ☺

I hung up the phone. Quarter after and still no mayoral lackey had shown up. It'd be just like that jerkoff Coles to make me wait until noon.

Come on. Come on. The clock was ticking.

And so was my Tag Heuer. *Holy cat, it's loud.*

I bounced in place, shadow boxing, killing time. It was dying a slow death. I needed to interview Rory's Serb before my brother sobered up, talked to Da, and they dumped the kid into Witness Protection.

Seven thirty. A black-armored limo drove up and parked across three handicapped spots. The door swung open and out stepped an enormous black man wearing the 1920s Hollywood's ideal of a proper driver's ensemble. Cap, double-breasted jacket with brass buttons, jodphurs, and high boots. The whole nine yards. Embarrassing and intimidating at the same time. "Holy shit!" He tipped down his mirrored sunglasses. "Maisie-save-my-ass-McGrane. Who'd you piss off to get this detail?"

"Coles."

"Oh no. No!" He started laughing. Howling, actually. Covering his mouth, he pointed at me and slapped his leg. "Damn, girl. Thought you'd learned your lesson after you booted his ass the first time."

"You'd think." I smiled. "How you been, Dozen?"

"Same ol', new day."

A chunky Korean mini-me version of Poppa Dozen popped out of the limo's still open driver's door.

Dozen tipped his glasses back up. "Did I tell you to get out of the car?" He snapped twice and pointed at the car. The little man got back in and closed the door.

"Jesus." Dozen shook his head. "What the hell kind of driver is that?"

He sat down on the hood of the limo and took a crumpled pack of unfiltered Camels from inside his jacket. He lit up while I watched, momentarily entranced by the acrid smell and the slow curl of smoke from his exhale, the diamond studs in his ears, the nick on his cheek from shaving. "You know you gonna lose your job, right?" he said.

"Nah."

"The hell you ain't."

"I didn't know it was his car. And I did manage to get his mayoral butt out of Swag before Vice busted him for . . . ah . . ."

"Not a word. Not ever." Dozen whipped off his glasses, his yellowish whites a bloodshot road map. "You best cut throat right now, a'fore I mop you."

"Okay, okay." I forgot how scary Dozen could be. "I get it."

"The hell you do. Coles hates you so bad, if you was on fire and he had water, the mutherfucker'd drink it, then go piss in the corner."

Hank's Law Number Two: Respond to threats with complete confidence.

I gave a rough chuckle. "Can't we all just get along?"

"You a cold piece, McGrane. You get up in the man's union business, red-face him on TV, then save his skinny-ass neck. Right there you in the shit. But do you want to climb out? Hell no. You dive in like some crunking Jacks Cousteau. Coles offers you a job and you tell him to suck his own dick?" Dozen shook his head and slid the mirrored shades back on. "The man don't want you down, girl. He wants you dead."

"Gee, when you put it that way . . ."

"Shit." He flicked his glowing cigarette over my shoulder and stood up. "Where the car at?"

"Come on." He followed me into the North Impound office. I found the gate keys and the car on the computer, and after an exercise in massive irritation—unlocking and locking and card swiping through three separate gates—got both the Bentley and Poppa Dozen out of Impound.

The Bentley's window slid down and Dozen leaned out. "Coles is a ruthless mutherfucker, McGrane. Watch your back, hear?"

You betcha.

He drove off, followed by the armored limo, and I hustled back into the office. North Impound opened at nine. Assuming a twenty-minute bumper for the early-to-work-ers, which granted, were in short supply at the Traffic Enforcement Bureau, I had a nine-and-a-half-minute window to find the paperwork and delete the files from the computer. Highly illegal and the real reason I suspected Leticia drafted me for this mission.

I cleared all traces in six.

Modafinil rocks.

Chapter 14

Halstad's posh private hospital had less security than the average elementary school. Still, finding Rory's informant wasn't going to be a slam dunk. An eighty-five-dollar flower arrangement with a bear and balloons and some chipper small talk was all it took to discover the children's ward was on the seventh floor and that Dr. Schaffer wasn't expected in for rounds until 1:30 p.m.

I spent a solid fifteen pretending to be on my cell in the waiting room, hanging around for a patsy. A ditzy blonde came toward me in white scrubs with a bright red-and-white-striped apron and a fist-sized explosion of ribbons pinned to her hair. She pushed a beige metal cart loaded with inexpensive toys, magazines, coloring books, and crayons.

Perfect.

I held the flowers in front of my face, took three quick steps, and crashed right into her cart.

"Omigod! I'm so sorry. Are you okay?" she gushed. "I soo didn't see you."

I rubbed my leg, pouring it on. I winced. "No, no. My fault."

"Is there anything I can do to help you? I could, like, deliver your flowers."

"I wish," I said. "I was supposed to bring these to some kid except I wrote down who they were from not who they're for. And if I don't deliver them, I'm totally fired."

"I really shouldn't . . ." she said, even as she pulled a clipboard from the cart. "Um, what do you know about the patient?"

I tapped the balloon with a car on it. "Male. Teenager maybe? My boss wasn't sure if he'd be in the children's or adult wing." I could tell by her face that wasn't enough. I stammered, "The sender's name has those weird letters, like Russian? Any patients with those?"

She flipped through the pages rapidly. "A bunch of boys over twelve. None with strange letters."

"If I could just take a look—"

"Sorry, but that's soo not allowed." With a sympathetic frown, she put the clipboard back in the cart pocket and moved away.

I rapped my knuckle against my forehead. *Think, Maisie. What would Rory—*

"Miss! Wait." I trotted after her down the hall.

She stopped.

"Is there a Seán Ó Rudaí on the list?"

The candy striper flipped through her clipboard and nodded vigorously, happy to be of service. "Room 714. How'd you ever remember?"

It's Irish for John Doe. "The cart must've jarred it loose."

I entered 714. The kid lay in the bed, sleeping. His arm was suspended in a sling, up and away from his body. Fifteen he might be, but with a man's growth of beard. Dr. Joy would be hard-pressed to keep him under wraps in Pediatrics for three days.

I set the flowers on the dresser, walked over to the bed, moved his Call button out of reach, and shook his leg.

His eyes flew open. With a spastic jerk he reached for the Call button, turning gray when he realized it was gone.

I raised a finger to my lips.

He nodded, eyes dull.

Mom called them "commodity eyes." The look people get when they realize they can be bought and sold and for exactly how little.

"I am here to help you," I said quietly. "But you must help me first."

He nodded, not believing. "Are you police?"

"No. There are other people who want them brought to justice. Could you look at some pictures?"

He gave a twisted grimace and a head tic I interpreted as a nod. I pulled out my BOC iPhone. "Are any of these men the killers you told Detective McGrane about?"

"Detective McGrane saved me," he said.

"I know." I smiled. "He's one of the good guys. So am I." I opened each of Edward's eleven photos separately. The kid identified Lukic Kraljić and Nicola Svetozar, two known hitters from Renko's gang. I showed him the remaining three photos and he picked out Stannis's lead gorilla, Nebojsa Ivanović, as a witness.

Rory said the kid could ID two. I was done.

The only photo I hadn't shown him was Stannis's. I didn't want to.

"Can you show me who hurt you?"

He glanced at his hand in the sling. "No." Eyes wet, he rubbed at them with his good hand. "I did not see. Blindfold."

"Okay," I said as though I believed his elephantine lie and stood up. "Oh, one more." I clicked on Stannis's photo and turned the phone to him.

The kid cringed and whipped his head wildly across the pillow. "No! Not him. Is not him! No!"

The unmistakable reek of urine filled the room.

His face crumpled in a combination of fear and humiliation. Tears rolled down his cheeks.

"We're done." I put the phone away and laid a hand on his shoulder. "You are very brave. Thank you."

I rode the elevator down to the lobby wearing the prickly undershirt of a guilty conscience. Poor kid. I went back to the hospital gift shop. The woman behind the register smiled at me. "Can I help you?"

"Yeah. Got anything for a teenager?"

I left ten minutes and two $150 cash cards later, while a loaded Kindle Fire, headphones, and app card were en route to Seán Ó Rudaí in room 714.

I didn't feel any better.

I texted Edward from the bike.

Thanks. Witness legit.
Edward: *Pass it on to Danny straightaway.*

I called.

She answered immediately. "Danny Kaplan, go ahead."

"I have a witness to at least two of the four homicide cases the BOC appropriated from Homicide."

"Oh?"

"A kid. He's hurt. In Halstad Hospital under a fake name."
Crickets.

"Seán Ó Rudaí. Room 714," I said. "He'll be there a day or two at most."

"Bring it along to Thursday's debrief."

"But he'll be gone by Monday. Don't you want eyes on him?"

"Thursday debrief." She hung up.

Well, hell. Not nearly the "good work" pat-on-the-head response I was expecting. At all.

I jabbed my phone off, crammed on my helmet, and jumped on the kick-starter, twisting the throttle. The beast growled to life. I drove back to Hank's far too fast, upset and dissatisfied.

Chapter 15

Hank and Rory were eating pizza in the great room. A Sox game played on the big screen. The cement coffee table was covered in empty bottles of Coors and cane sugar Coke. "Hey, Snap," Rory called, "where yeh been?"

"Hi," I said to Hank, who winked. "Man"—I shot my brother a sideways look—"Thor sure took a hammer to your face last night. Oh wait, that was just his hand."

"Very funny, Florence Nightingale." Rory tossed a pizza crust into the box. "An ice pack never crossed your mind?"

"Looks like she could have used one herself," Hank said, in a horribly nonchalant voice.

My hand flew to my chin. *Shoot!*

"Yeah, about that . . ." Rory cracked open another Coors. "An out-of-uniform misdemeanor battery or an in-uniform felony?"

"Ran into a door. Just another day in the life of a parking enforcement agent." I took a slice of pepperoni and perched on the couch arm next to Hank. "How's *your* uniform, Rory?" My brother was wearing a pair of Hank's sweatpants and a T-shirt.

"Jaysus." Rory shook his head. "My shirt's fecked. I bled out like a stuck pig."

"A dirty shirt's not all you've got to worry about." I circled my hand in the direction of his face.

"Ha! Me battered mug'll give hope to the Homicide rooks that something excitin' can happen on the job."

A faint mechanical hum started. It sounded like a furnace/AC fan, but was actually a setting on Hank's alarm system. He hit the remote and a small corner on the TV screen showed the front gate. Flynn's red Ford F-150. Hank tapped the remote. The gate started to open, the picture disappearing off the screen.

Rory stood up and drained his beer. "Thanks for letting me sleep it off, yeh?"

"Sure." Hank stood and walked him out.

Still sitting on the broad arm of the couch, I laid my head on the back, face to the ceiling, eyes closed. The door opened and closed. I felt Hank's face over mine. "I'm beat," I said.

Silence.

I opened my eyes and stared into his, upside down. It didn't make him look any less angry. "You took the Indian," he said softly. "Unescorted."

"Work. It was crazy . . ." The words died in my throat.

"No. Mant is crazy. Understand?"

I nodded.

He ran an index finger across my bruised chin. "I don't like you getting knocked around, Slim."

"That makes two of us." I didn't think Ragnar ratted me out. Still, Hank gave away less than a professional magician.

"Time to quit." He let that sink in, coming around to loom over me properly. "Open a gym. Raise Rottweilers. Go to law school."

The law school crack nettled. My family's continual rant, it was enough to pop my lower lip like a sullen teenager, just like he knew it would. His mouth hovered an inch above mine. "Or stay home." He slid a hand up my T-shirt. "Housewife by day . . ."

Ooh. The w word . . . "Mercenary's moll by night?"

He raised his head and looked at me, fingers drumming against my ribs. When he finally spoke, his voice was easy, silky with promise. "Rest up. We're going out tonight."

I took a final look in the closet mirror and dropped my robe. My hair was styled in a high teased-twist with thick side-swept bangs. Flawless makeup with a double set of fake lashes. I shimmied into a midnight blue Herve Leger long-sleeved bandage dress with a flared hem and stepped into nude satin mules. I felt a rush of coltish, flirtatious energy as I walked into the bedroom.

Shirtless, wearing black dress pants and Bally loafers, Hank came out of the bathroom rubbing aftershave into his throat. He hadn't shaved. His two-day full-face scruff had ramped into day three, at odds with his close-cropped dark hair.

"Going for the 'hot Jesus' look, are we?"

He came in close. "Don't like it?"

There's nothing about you I don't like. "I wouldn't say that."

He laughed and nuzzled his chin up underneath my jaw. "Vi prefers I look a little less . . . military."

"And more Mobster? Maybe if you gained thirty pounds and didn't shower for a month."

"Cute. Keep a lid on it tonight." He pressed his fingers against my lips. "Vi doesn't have a sense of humor." He dropped his hand and walked into the closet.

I stared after him. *What?*

Hank had taken harsh and exacting measures to ensure I was not part of his working life. Jeff Mant was an anomaly that was eating him alive. But introducing me to Violetta Veteratti?

My stomach flip-flopped. *Really?*

This was a more serious step in our relationship than the night he brought me home and asked me to stay.

He returned in a slim-fitting silvery Givenchy shirt, pulling on a black sports coat.

"What?" I said, "No matching shiny tie to complete the *Goodfellas* ensemble?"

"That"—he dropped an index finger on the tip of my nose—"is exactly what I'm talking about."

Giorgio's was a rat hole in an alley wall. Inside, the décor wasn't throwback, it just hadn't changed in seventy years. The sharp tang of garlic was mellowed slightly by cigar smoke.

Only two tables in the tiny restaurant were occupied. Three men in cheap dark suits sat at the small square closest to the door drinking Sambuca.

A powerhouse of a guy with short, slicked-back hair and Satan's goatee got to his feet.

"Jimmy the Wolf," Hank said out of the side of his mouth. He stepped out to meet him palms-up.

The Wolf frisked him, not shying away from the groin, not missing the ankles. Finished, he moved toward me.

"Not a chance, Jimmy," Hank said. "Give him your bag, doll."

I handed the Wolf my clutch and watched him paw through its meager contents. BOC iPhone, headphones, lipstick, compact, and wallet. He handed it back. "She's not going back."

"Okay." Hank shrugged and without a look at me, strode toward the only other occupied table in Giorgio's.

Something's up.

Hank's Law Number Ten: Keep your mouth shut.

The six men at the rear corner round turned as Hank approached, and I got a good long look at the woman at the center of the action.

Violetta Veteratti. Attractive in a callous, mannish way. Her thick shoulder-length hair, colored an expensive shade of blond, her only nod to femininity.

"Over there." Jimmy the Wolf bump-walked me to an empty table. I sat down and pulled out my iPhone.

He snapped his fingers in my face. "No calls. No texts. No pictures."

"Music okay?"

He grunted and took the chair across from me.

I put on my earbuds. *Let's see how high-tech the BOC really is.* I monkeyed with the headphone jack and activated the enhanced surveillance microphone so I could hear Hank's conversation. I set the phone on the table and smiled at Jimmy the Wolf, whose eyes never left my chest.

I tried not to jump as Vi's nasal purr reverberated in my ears. "Look who's here, fellas. Tall, dark, and sonuvabitch." She gave a sly yip of laughter. "How you doin', Bannon?"

"Hullo, Vi."

"What's with the tagalong?" she said. "Fuck your way through models and movie stars to end up banging angel bait?" The men at the table laughed. "Bring her over."

"Later." Hank held out his hand and tipped his head toward the opposite corner. "Shall we?"

"You wanna talk?" Vi leaned back in her chair and made a show of crossing her legs. "Talk."

The Wolf's hand shot out over my phone. He tipped it, read the screen: Gorillaz "To Binge." He shrugged and set it down.

This guy wasn't messing around.

I closed my eyes and swayed from side to side in my chair.

"I'm out," Hank said.

The temperature of the room dropped to freezing.

Incredulity popped Vi's voice into the stratosphere. "What?"

The Wolf glanced back over a broad shoulder.

Eyes on the table, Maisie.

"You said the contract was sewn up tight," Hank said.

"It was. It is!"

"Your stringer bled out on my goddamn Dodge and your brother, Eddie, let Mant out of the cage." His voice turned to ice. "So, tell me again how we're cool."

"Who the fuck do you think you are?" Vi said, loud enough to hear without the headphones.

"Not the sap running interference for you."

"Like hell you're not." She kicked back her chair and stood up. Vi's cheeks went scarlet. "You're out when I say so." Her hand cracked across his cheek like a whip.

Hank caught her wrist and jerked her forward. He reached down, grabbed a knife off a plate, and slapped it into her palm. "Try this next time, sister. It's faster."

He let go. Vi stumbled backward into her seat. "Goddamn you, Bannon."

Hank turned and walked away.

Vi shouted at his back. "This isn't over!"

The Wolf was on his feet, moving to intercept him, me tight on his heels.

Hank shook his head. "Not today, Jimmy."

The Wolf hesitated, considering, and let him pass.

Hank took me by the elbow. "Let's bounce."

Firmly ensconced in a booth at Blackie's, I waited as long as I could. Until the waiter deposited the second round of Stoli martinis. "Kind of not what I thought you had in mind when you said I'd meet Vi."

"Turned on a dime, tonight. Christ. Jimmy?" Hank shook his head in disbelief. "Playing the muscle?"

Talk about a perfect typecast . . . The guy was a monster.

Then again, Hank's Law Number Eleven: Heavy hitters don't advertise.

He grazed my cheek with the back of his hand. "You were perfect."

I tried not to grin like an idiot and failed. "Big-picture time, then? Broad strokes?"

"Why not?" Hank ran a hand over his mouth and cursed softly. "Vi and Eddie were tight. Real tight. Until Eddie started 'chasing the dragon.' "

So my brothers were right. Eddie V. had gone from recreational drug user to balls-out Scarface-*level addict.*

Hank bent over his drink, a lank of dark hair fell across his forehead. "Vi pitched me the contract. Said whether he knew it or not, Eddie needed a cool head to represent New York." He shrugged. "I got the blessing."

From the Don. The hair raised on the back of my neck. *Jaysus crimeny. And I'm in bed with the Bureau of Organized Crime.*

"Belarus?" I guessed. "Is that the contract?"

Hank's gray eyes narrowed slightly. "Yes."

I rubbed my arms. For once, I didn't want to hear any more. "Chilly?"

"No. A little tired, is all."

But Hank wanted to talk. "Eddie didn't like Vi going around him or me getting the nod, so he let Mant off the leash." Hank's eyes turned to steel. "Mant signed his own warrant the day he laid hands on you."

"And Vi?"

"She's trying to protect Eddie or take his place. Doesn't matter. The stringer's proof she wasn't straight with me." He leaned back and raised his glass. "I'm out."

"Just like that? The contract's over?"

"What?" He laughed, deep and warm. "Sugar Pop, my contract's not with Vi, and it sure as hell isn't with Eddie."

Cripes. You're working for the fucking Don. "So when does it end?"

"When it ends." Something changed in his face. The lines eased at the corner of his mouth. A strange light glinted in his pale eyes. "Everything's gonna be fine." He grinned.

And it would be.

Because he could tell me the moon was a flashlight, and I'd run out for batteries.

Chapter 16

After a Sunday of sex, guns, and PT, I was back to invincible. Hank insisted Ragnar drive me to work, which suited me fine. The creep factor of Mant's note in the starter of my Honda gnawed at the back of my brain. I felt like a prize-class weasel not telling Hank, but it wasn't like I had a wide range of options.

A butterfly gave a halfhearted flutter across my stomach as I neared the Traffic Enforcement Bureau.

The last PEA to mess up Leticia's weekend became her personal gal Friday and spent two weeks of "in office" detention fetching Leticia's dry cleaning, lunch, banking, snacks, even putting money on her layaway account at Kmart . . . pretty much anything she could think of.

Ragnar pulled up to the rear gate. Chen, the front gate guard, shoved open his window and thrust out his dried-apple face. "No. No, no. Authorized vehicles only."

I leaned across Ragnar so Chen could see me. "I have a meeting with Leticia."

"You getting fiii-red!" he crowed. "You getting fiii-red!"

"Transferred," I fibbed and sprinkled a little sand in his salad, "so I can see your happy face every day."

"Geh!" He slammed the window shut, raised the gate, and gave us the good morning bird as we drove through.

It was shaping up to be a delightful morning.

* * *

Leticia, clad in a neon yellow blouse and an orange infinity scarf, was on the phone. She saw me leaning on the doorjamb and waved me into her office. I took the chair in front of her desk and smiled back at Glenn Beck and Mark Levin in the double-sided picture frames. Which meant Sean Hannity and Rush Limbaugh were facing her.

Righteous indignation was her mood this morning.

Leticia's hot pink leopard-patterned nails gripped the handset so tightly it made a wrenching squeak. "Oh, I hear you, aight." Her nostrils flared in annoyance. "Yeah. Yeah. I'll keep that in mind." She slammed down the phone, yanked the lid off her candy jar, and scooped out a handful of jelly beans. "That was the vice president of the Traffic Enforcement Bureau. Seems Mrs. Coles's Bentley's been scratched to hell." She tossed the candy into her mouth, chewing around it as she spoke. "Jesum M. Crow, McGrane. Do you even know how much trouble you in?"

I cleared every trace at the impound lot. "How bad?"

"You spit-roasted. Screwed at both ends." She massaged her temples, fingers splayed. "You got two choices. The file room or West Englewood. Night shift."

West Englewood's claim to fame was running a victim of violent crime ratio somewhere around one-in-thirteen.

Leticia scooped out another handful of candy. "I figured they'd banish you to the suburbials or some such. But Englewood? Damn. Even I won't go there."

Neither would the Srpska Mafija.

The blood drained from my head to my gut, which clenched accordingly.

I am officially off the street. Shit.

She shook her head and held out the jelly bean jar. "You don't look so good, McGrane."

"Screw this." I got up. "I need a cinnamon-pretzel donut from Stan's and a Mexican Coke."

"Now you're talkin'. Bring me back a couple o' them pieces o' legalized X-TC. And a Fanta."

* * *

There is something decadent about having a driver. I trotted in and out of Stan's, bringing Ragnar a sizeable snack and oversized coffee. Back in Leticia's office, I felt markedly better. Virtuous, even. We both did, gorging ourselves on the salty, melty goodness while Dennis Prager's chipper tirade echoed throughout her office.

Leticia dabbed her hot pink lips with a napkin. "At least you kiss a girl before you slip her the crippl'er."

"What's that supposed to mean?" I brushed cinnamon-salt off my pants.

"Your beef with Coles. That crap don't hurt only you." She tossed a file my way. "I got PEAs dropping faster than Ebola victims. And now you in the office? Our numbers can only pray to be wormshit."

Things are tough all over. "I'm sorrier than you—"

"Save it." She swept the breakfast wrappers off her desk into the trash can. "We square. Your secret incentivizing program is keeping the rest of 'em around." She stood and cracked her back. "C'mon. Let's go see your twentieth circle o' hell."

"Gee, how can I resist?" *Filing. Almost as exciting as a glass of club soda.*

My fearless supervisor led me down the hall into a dank, musty room. She flipped the light switch. Droning fluorescents cast a dismal glow over dusty paperwork and hills of collapsing cardboard boxes.

More like caustic soda. "Ugh," I said, walking into the room. "Turn them off."

"Pew-ee." Leticia fanned the air in front of her face. "Smells worse than a cat box in here."

"They can't be serious." I lifted a few papers. Gritty and slightly moist at the same time. *Ergh. Where's the hazard pay for working at Mold Central?*

"It gets worse." She left the doorway and returned with an industrial paper shredder.

"Safer to incinerate the stuff."

"You're gonna shred all the shit in the boxes. Then, you file all the loose papers into the same empty boxes."

"But they're wet."

"You don't get it, do you?"

"Huh?"

"The mayor has you riding a two-wheeled trike on a tread-mill."

A tiny groan escaped me. *Talbott Cottle Coles sure knows how to hurt a girl.*

"Well, let's not hang around gettin' all morose an' shit. It's lunchtime, and Monday is pizza day."

"Wouldn't miss it."

Leticia clattered away on her stilettos, while I took a final look at my new and dismal future. I shut off the lights, closed the door, and hit the break room.

There was a reason why I never, ever came back to the office during the day. The employee lunchroom was as friendly and accepting of multicultural diversity as your average prison yard.

Sanchez and her mini La Raza crew held the tables at the vending machines while the Betty Bruisers—a squad of fifty-something hefty white women who weighed more than a Mack Truck—staked out the fridge and microwave. The Bella Donnas, hair-hopping Mafia wannabes, drifted between the break room and the locker room, the fruity, floral stink of cheap body spray delineating their territory. Leticia, generally found sitting with the 'Hood Sistas, was the only one able to cross gang lines with no fear of retribution.

That left me, a couple of Asians, some random no-loads, and a chubby white guy with a mullet hovering at the edges of the pizza party, waiting to snatch a couple of greasy slices without drawing attention.

"Aww, jeez. They always order Marie's," Mullet whined and thumped his heart with his fist. "Are they trying to gimme a grabber?"

"One of the Bettys'll spot you some nitro." I reached around him and shifted a slab of Marie's Special—sausage, green peppers, onions, and mushrooms—onto a flimsy paper plate. I backed away to the neutral corner—the one farthest from the time clock—and dug in.

"Yo! Not so fast, *culo*."

I looked up to see hotheaded Sanchez step in front of a huge Eastern European in a suit and tie. I recognized the dark hair, the broad, rounded shoulders and the scarred, lumpy Neanderthal forehead.

Stannis's head gorilla.

He was there for me, I knew, but the chance of seeing Sanchez get knocked down a peg or two had me superglued to my seat.

The break room went dead quiet, everyone crossing their fingers for bloodshed.

"Where you think you going? This a private building and you ain't got no clearance." Sanchez rolled her shoulders. La Raza got to their feet behind her.

"I look for girl," he said.

"Ain't no *girls* here, Holmes. Fuck off."

The gorilla didn't like that. "I help you understand, *Frijolero*."

The tips of Sanchez's ears went brick red.

He scratched his chin, his Spanish stilted and slow, "*Te voy a meter una leche*. Yes?"

Sanchez rocked back and forth on her heels, furious with an edge of fear.

Leticia stood up, hiked down her skimpy optic yellow print skirt, and jumped in. "Simmer down," she said to Sanchez and La Raza. "The man obviously don't speak no Spanish."

Yeah, instead of "I'll beat the fuck out of you" maybe he meant shit.

Sanchez weighed her chances, spat on the floor, and went back to the vending machines.

Another charming display of PEA manners.

Leticia sauntered up to the gorilla, hips undulating like a cobra on LSD. "I'm Traffic Enforcement Supervisor Leticia Jackson." She thrust out her chest. "How can I help you?"

The gorilla gave her an appreciative eye. "I seek Maisie McGrane."

"And what would a fine man like yourself want with her?"

I raised my hand in a halfhearted wave. The gorilla saw me, pressed the headset at his ear, and said something into his wrist.

One of the Betty Bruisers whispered loudly, "Forget it, Leticia. You're too fat for him." Which was along the lines of a blimp telling a hot air balloon they were overinflated.

Leticia smoothed a hand down the side of her body. "This ain't fat. This is sexy overflow."

A second suited Serbian entered the break room, carrying a colossal cut-crystal vase of pink roses.

Yikes.

The gorilla led him through the ocean of my slack-jawed hill-people coworkers and gestured to my table. The man set the flowers down.

The gorilla said in a low voice, "Stannislav Renko sends his regards." He gave me a short nod and the two men left.

"Who you fucking now, *puta?*" Sanchez sneered from across the room.

The mini La Razas started heckling rapid-fire. Thankfully, I couldn't understand the bulk of what they said.

They had Leticia chuckling, though, as she came over to in-spect the bounty. She reached out and squeezed a rose where the petals met the stem. "Firm. Some damn fine flowers," she mu-mured absently. "You oughtta toss in a couple o' aspirin in the vase, keep 'em fresh."

"Yeah. Thanks."

She eyed me, brow puckered in consternation. "What is this, McGrane?"

Six dozen, from the looks of it.

"A marriage proposal?" She elbowed me in the ribs. "Or a 'please, baby, take my sorry ass back'?"

"I have no idea."

I officed the day in the break room in front of the ocean of pink flowers. Amidst the occasional hissing slur, I filled out the paperwork for my new position, made a list of the hazmat gear I needed from Home Depot, and chewed over Stannis's inten-tions.

Are the flowers a thank-you, or God forbid, an overture to a date?

I'd never cheat on Hank. Not for the Bureau of Organized Crime's Special Unit. Not ever. But even in an alternate universe where Hank didn't exist, I don't think I could get past what I walked in on at the strip club.

I blew out a breath, ruffling some rose petals.

Danny and Walt will have to be told about my office demotion. And the strip club. And Mayor Coles. And T.G.I. Friday's. And the flowers.

When exactly had my proactive-initiative-taking turned into job-jeopardizing-insanity?

Dammit.

I pushed away from the table and left the break room to rummage in my locker. Beneath my gym bag, poly-blend uniforms, and a stash of PowerBars, lay half a package of personally engraved Connor stationery from Barney's. Because when your mother is July Pruitt of the Georgia Pruitts, a handwritten thank-you card for any gift received will be thoughtfully penned on personal stationery and sent the following day or the earth will come to a screeching halt upon its axis, condemning all enlightened society to utter darkness.

It took four drafts to get the right tone.

> *Dear Stannis,*
> *I am overwhelmed by your generosity. You*
> *are a kind and thoughtful friend.*
> *Maisie*

I sealed the letter and put it in the front pouch of my rucksack. I had no address for Stannislav Renko. Not yet.

Ragnar was waiting in the truck. He drove me home in a cocoon of country music and confusion. I didn't need to be clairvoyant to know something was about to happen with Stannis. And, just like Mant's note, I couldn't say a damn thing about it.

Hank protected me from his gray world. Locked it away in a

box of silence so I never had to lie to my family. Or even myself. I just had to leave the box alone.

No sweat. Being with Hank was more important than any secret.

He'd marveled once at the blind faith I had in him. "I could never be okay with not knowing," he said, voice so gravelly I could feel it in my chest.

I looked down at my hands in my lap. My arms felt like they weighed a thousand pounds. Almost as heavy as my conscience.

I didn't have the guts to tell Hank I was a cop. Because . . . well, I had more reasons than I could count, and "coward" pretty much topped the list.

Ragnar pulled into the driveway. Hank was leaning against the garage door, arms folded, superhero mouth in a laconic grin.

Time to find out if I have the chops to keep my own box of silence.

Ragnar honked his horn twice and drove away.

"Hi," I said to Hank.

"Hi, yourself." He held out his fists. "Choose."

I tapped his right hand. He opened it. Car keys.

He took the garage door opener from his pants pocket. "Number two."

I pressed the middle button. The door opened on a pitch-black Dodge Challenger SRT Hellcat. "Whoa. Did a little shopping today, I see."

"Like it?"

"What's not to love?" The V-8 alone was a big F.U. to the carbon footprint wussies who wouldn't recognize exhilaration if it put them in a headlock and ground its knuckles into their skulls. "Where's the Super Bee?"

"In storage. Try number one."

An obsidian Ford Mustang Shelby GT500. Another modern-day muscle car. I gave a low whistle. "Are you planning a race?"

"If you'd rather drive the Shelby—"

"What?"

Hank squinted at me. "*What* what?"

I held up the keys. "You're letting me choose your new car?"

"No. Yours." He slung his arm over my shoulders.

"Hank—"

He gave me a playful swat. "Let's tear it up." He trotted to the passenger side of the Hellcat and reached for the door.

My vision blurred. *I hate myself.* "Hank, it's one thing to let me drive your cars, but this is something else entirely."

"No," he said. "But I realize you think it is. Get in."

I did, feeling like a heel. I put my hands on the wheel, breathing in the new car smell. "An automatic?" I said, unable to disguise the happy in my voice.

"Tested faster than manual."

"How'd you know I'd pick that hand?"

"I didn't. Top of the bluffs?"

I smiled and started the car. And it was glorious. I touched the gas and it leapt into life as though it had been stung. Flying around the hairpin curves, the steering was, as my brothers would say, talkative. The Hellcat was a heavy, road-gripping beast.

There was no way I would accept a $68K muscle car. As much as I coveted it. But that was a talk for another day.

"We'll hit the track," Hank promised as I came to a stop. "Soon."

I parked and we got out of the car. Hank leaned his forearms on the roof and stared across at me, his face strangely vulnerable, the hard lines of his jaw blurred by his thick scruff. "I need to be in Central America for the next five days."

Oookay. "I'll miss you."

"I need you to take the week off. Stay protected."

I tapped the hood of the car. "This a carrot?"

"No. You can't drive it until I come home."

I sighed. "Hank . . ."

"Mant's a threat. You will be safe."

Wow. That was pretty final. "You let me go to work with Ragnar—"

"Because Mant would come for me first. And I won't be here."

I walked around to his side of the car. "I need to go to work. I'll lose my mind if I don't."

His jaw tightened.

I put my hand on his arm. "Besides, I promised my mom I'd go home the next time you went out of town."

"No."

A breathy laugh slipped from my mouth. "I'll be in a house with four cops. And you can surround me with Ragnar and Chris—heck, hire a small army for all I care."

He stared at me until I couldn't bear it a second longer.

"Okay, okay," I said. "I'll stay the week at your place. Let Ragnar drive me to work every day. Spend Friday and Saturday at my house. Everyone's home on the weekend. You can pick me up on the way home from the airport."

"I don't like this," he said. But he lumped it. And left that night.

Tuesday, at the office, same time, same way, the gorilla oversaw delivery of a massive tower of fruit and nuts. Wednesday, bricks of Belgian chocolate. Stannis's gifts were giving my social status a leg up. I now had a temporary seat at the Bettys' table, and a creeping sense of dread of what today would bring.

The gifts were equally disconcerting and disturbing. So much so, I was almost looking forward to my debrief with Danny Kaplan after work.

The break room was filled to capacity. At 12:40, the gorilla sat down across from me. He glared at the Bettys, who after twenty long seconds got the hint, gathered their lunches, and lumbered off to gather at the microwave.

"Mr. Renko would like to see you."

"When?"

"Friday night. Dinner. Nine. He will send car. Address?"

"Uh, I'm not sure I can make it."

The gorilla stared at me, unblinking. "Address?"

Oookay. I scrambled around for a napkin and pen, scribbled my parents' address, and handed it to him. He removed a small red leather box from his suit coat pocket and placed it on the table. It was decorated with an unmistakable pattern in gold leaf.

Cartier.

He pushed it in front of me with two thick fingers.

I flipped the lid.

Diamond earrings. Not little ones, either. Danglers, exquisite and delicate. Each a strand of five alternating pear and round-cut diamonds suspended in white gold.

Cripes.

I tried to clear my throat, but I couldn't get any air to or from my lungs.

The gorilla leaned forward and slapped me on the back. I started coughing.

"Dress pretty," he said. "Mr. Renko likes pretty things."

Chapter 17

I rode up the fourth elevator at Silverthorn Estates Assisted Living for my debrief with the insect-waisted, wasp-vicious Danny Kaplan, careful to push both the fourth and fifth buttons at the same time. Two tiny lights went on in the upper right-hand corner. The Kimber Solo and Swiss Army knife in my backpack had been detected.

I swiped my way into Special Unit and ran into Officer/Nurse Anita Erickson. "Heads up, Rook. Kaplan's spitting nails. A word to the wise, get in and get out as fast as you can."

Terrific. "Anything in particular?"

She grimaced. "We seem to have misplaced a field agent."

Is that a euphemism for clipped or was the agent actually missing?

I knocked and entered Ms. Kaplan's office. There were no chairs in front of her shiny red desk today. Instead they were tucked in tight to the conference table. She didn't look up from her laptop.

No Walt. No chairs. I get it. Grunts stand.

She was wearing a navy suit coat over a white shirt with cuffs so sharp I checked her wrists to see if they were bleeding.

I stood at full attention in front of her desk, concentrating on keeping my breathing even. There'd be no riding the next-level-bullshit train of prerehearsed excuses. Not today.

Four minutes later, Ms. Kaplan closed the laptop with a snap.

"Ahh, Miss McGrane." She rolled back her chair ever so slightly and snarled, "Seán Ó Rudaí. What the hell were you thinking?"

Whoa. My eyes popped. *Don't hold back.*

"You joined the Special Unit of the Bureau of Organized Crime, not a secret spy club with a password and a magic decoder ring. Everything within Special Unit is classified on a need-to-know basis. Young Mr. Ó Rudaí far exceeded your clearance level on Operation Steal-Tow."

Initiative taken not appreciated. Check.

"Your existence in the BOC is contingent upon my assessment, your grandstanding for Walt Sawyer notwithstanding. Do I make myself clear?"

"Yes, ma'am." I winced inwardly. *She's gonna love what's coming.*

"Your report?"

I handed her the binder containing my summary, spreadsheet, GPS marked and labeled map, along with individual sets of photos taken by the Parking Enforcement Agents that week. "I've been transferred," I blurted my shame. "Desk duty."

"Brilliant." Her smile could have cut glass. "How could you possibly have let this happen?"

"Well . . . uh . . ."

A funny thing happened on the way to the strip club . . .

She tossed the report onto a corner of the desk and folded her thin arms across her chest. "You're still able to collect data from the other meter maids, correct?"

I nodded.

"Continue on, then." She opened the laptop and began typing rapid-fire. "That'll be all."

Hardly.

I sucked up my guts and said calmly, "No, ma'am, I'm afraid it won't. Friday night, I helped Stannislav Renko elude a VICE bust at a strip club. I've received a gift from him every day this week, culminating in these." I opened the Cartier box and set it on her desk.

I had her attention now. Or at least the earrings did.

"Go on," she said.

"He wants to see me tomorrow night at nine o'clock."

"Pull up a chair."

I brought back a chair, sat down, and explained what happened Friday night.

"So Stannislav Renko wants a girlfriend." She sounded amused.

"Not exactly. When I went in to warn him, I found the mayor of Chicago performing . . . er . . . fellatio on him."

She went quite still. "Coerced?"

"Uh, no. Consensual. So, I'm not sure why he's sending me presents."

"I knew you were Catholic. I didn't realize you were raised in a nunnery." Kaplan scoffed. "A blow job doesn't necessarily delineate a definitive sexual preference."

Gee thanks. I think I prefer stupid to stupid and naïve.

"Your unauthorized interview and feckless rescue to keep Renko off the radar has jeopardized this entire operation."

My face turned to stone. *I may have to lie here and take it, but I wasn't gonna smile about it.* "Do you want me to cancel the meet with Renko, ma'am?"

Kaplan fingered the thick strand of Mikimoto pearls at her throat. "It's clear Renko is wooing you on the pretext that you can provide inside police information. That's not something I can or will facilitate."

Guess I'll be scuttling my brothers' police work all by myself. "I'll manage."

Wow. Thanks for the helping hand.

"If Renko is after more than police information, your Mr. Bannon may become a liability."

"He won't."

"If he does, I will request the necessary assistance to remove him from the situation. Special Unit has a long-standing relationship with the NSA. They appreciate our tip-offs on mercenaries and other undesirables."

My hands went numb. *Now you're just getting nasty.* I flexed my fingers, careful not to let them curl into fists, as I might lean over and punch her in the face.

Don't let the baby face fool you, sister. I'm as full of acid and ire as an IRA enforcer.

"Don't you want to be a field agent, Miss McGrane?"

No. Not like this. Not one goddamn bit.

"You're free to resign, of course."

Like hell. "No, thank you, ma'am."

"Well, then. Let's hope you possess the necessary intellect to stay alive in this job. All signs point to the contrary, although I expect we'll find out soon enough." Kaplan raised her shoulders in a shrug so tight it could have broken her back. "Enjoy your date with Mr. Renko, Special Agent McGrane."

I must have been wearing my distress on my sleeve, because when I went to Edward Dunne's office to requisition more Visa cards, he took one look at me and whisked me off into his private quarters at the end of the Onyx wing for green tea and ginger snaps.

Nestled into two chintz overstuffed armchairs with a spindly-legged mahogany table between us, he poured the tea and I poured out what went down with Danny Kaplan.

"You're convenient and far closer to the Steal-Tow epicenter than anyone else we have, which is why Danny leapt on you like a two-dollar tart." Edward shook his head. "Of all the times for Walt to go on holiday. You're a wee bit *unseasoned,* shall we say, to go up against one of the best of the Slajic clan." He took a sip from his china cup. "Walt will pitch a ruddy fit when he finds out."

"Sawyer wouldn't have recruited me if he thought I couldn't handle it."

Edward gave a doubtful chuckle. "You don't *handle* evil, my dear. You kill it."

Maybe I was in over my head. "Swiping intelligence from my brothers isn't what bothers me. Roles reversed, they'd do it themselves." I leaned forward. "Danny threatened to go to the NSA about Bannon if this doesn't play out."

"Aye. A Class-A bitch, Danny is. The only cork in the bottle'd be Walt tellin' her not to."

"Will he?"

"I don't know." Edward clucked his tongue in sympathy. "Mightn't matter if he did."

Chapter 18

Ragnar kindly carried the two heavy bags Hank had insisted I take. Because living in a mansion with a state-of-the-art security system and four police officers armed to the teeth apparently wasn't enough. I faithfully promised to set up a perimeter defense in my room as well as the hallway with the gear. Which, when I opened the bags, looked like it would take the entire weekend to set up.

I had two backpacks, one full of dirty PEA uniforms, the other an overnighter. Dumping it all in the hallway, I went upstairs. It wouldn't take long to get ready, but what in the Sam Hill was I going to wear?

Hours later a heaping pile of discarded separates lay on the bed. I moved onto dresses. Next on the pile was a pink Rickie Freeman, too frock-ish. Then an über-conservative black hit the pile, followed by a deep-V short red Jovani dress. Way too sexy.

I wriggled out of a beige Calvin Klein sheath dress that needed to be shortened. Which I'd told myself to do about a thousand times and hadn't. "Aigh!"

Clothes lock: that horrible paralyzing moment when you've tried on everything you own and it all sucks.

Back to the closet.

I mean, really, how hard can it be to find an outfit to wear on a date with a bisexual, Serbian Mobster with a penchant for torture?

I surveyed my walk-in closet in my bra and underpants, completely stumped.

"Why ssso sseriousss, Sisss?" Cash asked in a passable Joker, lounging against the doorjamb.

"Jeez!" I yanked a T-shirt off a hanger and put it on. "What do you want?"

"Your crap is everywhere." He pushed himself off the door frame and started bouncing from foot to foot, shaking out his arms. It was physically impossible for him to remain still. "You moving back home?"

"For a couple days. So beat it, will you? I gotta get ready."

"You and Bannon splitting up?"

"No. He's out of town."

"Oh yeah?" He snorted. He threw a couple of jabs in my direction. "Wouldn't have anything to do with Thor hanging around in that rickety blue pickup?"

I winced and started flipping through skirts. *Oh God. Ragnar. I hadn't even begun to consider how to get rid of him.* "Maybe."

Cash's brows disappeared beneath his bangs. "You're cheating with him?"

"No! And for God's sake, will you quit jumping around? He's a pal of Hank's . . . It's complicated."

He waved a hand at the scattered clothes. "What's all this for, then?"

"A friend asked me to dinner, that's all."

"Sure." He nodded. "Not to judge or anything but . . ." He tugged his ear. "A relationship's pretty much fecked if you put a tail on your girl."

Supes Awesome. Dating advice from the clown who'd put baby powder in my blow-dryer, frozen marbles in my bed, and still regularly strung plastic wrap across the doorway.

Hold up.

If anyone could help me lose Ragnar for the night, it'd be Cash.

I heaved a world-weary sigh and put on the sad face. "Hand me the phone, will you?"

"Why?"

"I'm not going. Thor will follow me and the whole thing will end in a raging hassle. I'm just not up for it."

"When's your date?"

"Nine-ish."

Cash's eyes lit up. "Leave it to me. I gotta call Koji!" He sprinted out of my room. Then popped his head back in. "The red. Definitely wear the red."

At 8:55 p.m. Ragnar moved his surveillance to the east end of the house, Cash was nowhere to be found, and Stannislav Renko's Land Rover idled in the driveway. At 8:59, the driver came to fetch me from the door. It was the newspaper reader. He was wearing a dark suit and driving gloves.

I opened the door. He smelled like raw chicken and looked like he wanted to tear my throat out.

Guess he's still a little miffed over Stannis's backhand.

My text alert went off. Cash. "Excuse me."

"No. Leave now." The driver moved forward.

Hands off, buddy. I slipped past him and trotted to the car, trying to put some distance between us. Raw Chicken followed a little too close behind me, his palpable dislike starting to make me more uneasy than uncomfortable.

I checked the text from Cash.

In position. Rt out of driveway & rt again

The driver opened the door with a jerk and I got into the empty car, pulling my foot in a frog's hair before he slammed the door on my ankle. *Jerk.* I waited until he started the ignition. "Please turn right out of the driveway. And take the first right after that."

Raw Chicken glared at me from the rearview. "Do not tell me how to drive."

This one wasn't up for debate. "Mr. Renko would prefer it."

He made a sound as though he was about to spit, but exited the driveway as instructed. Ragnar let us get to the end of the street before following. It was dark. Too dark to see what Cash and Koji had planned.

I tucked my legs up beneath me, twisted in my seat, and watched through the rear window.

Waiting.

Ragnar's headlights followed us onto the street. He got about sixty yards. A loud *bang* followed by the grating mechanical screech of the truck seizing up.

Oh shite. I hope they didn't wreck his truck. . . .

A new backpack of guilt to look forward to carrying. Jaysus.

I blew out a breath and turned around, quick enough to catch Raw Chicken's pervy ogle in the rearview.

Thank God I hadn't worn the red dress.

Raw Chicken popped the brakes in an abrupt stop in front of a dark glass building. My first real undercover op and I was going in cold, armed only with lipstick, my own phone, ID, and a hundred dollar bill. No Kimber, no sap, not even a Swiss Army knife.

A tuxedoed valet opened my door.

I got out. The valet escorted me up the steps to the door of the club, where I was met by a beauty in an emerald dress. "Good evening, Ms. McGrane. This way, please."

Whoa. Stannis is running with the big dogs.

We traversed a dark, narrow hallway. The only decoration, a lit easel with a black and white poster in an ornate gilt frame. *Bobby Blaze—Live Tonite.* Very 1940s. Very swank.

"Eddie Veteratti's pet project," Beauty said. "To bring the glamour of old New York's The Stork Club to Chicago."

She swung open the padded black leather doors to the lounge. "Welcome to The Storkling."

Game time.

I smoothed down my prudish black Tadashi Shoji dress and scanned the darkened lounge for my . . . *date?*

Stannislav Renko was standing in the corner, surrounded by a handful of goombahs. He had one arm folded across his chest, the other elbow resting on it, fist at his mouth. The ultimate Eurotrash model, if you didn't count the missing ennui in his electric blue eyes. He saw me, and with a predatory smile, came to me, hands extended, and kissed me on each cheek. "Maisie. Come, have drink."

I followed him through the darkened lounge to the bar. He held up two fingers, and before I could blink, a tuxedoed bartender presented two shots of rakija.

I surveyed the room and got that sinking feeling. I looked like an accountant who'd wandered into the Golden Globes.

Cash was right. I should have worn the red.

Stannis frowned. "What is wrong?"

"Uh . . ." Just to help me fit in, a nearby pair of twentysomethings in skintight satin mini-dresses whispered behind their hands and erupted into snorting giggles. I gave him a tight smile. "I might have worn something a little more—"

"No. You are beautiful. Restrained." He cast a scornful eye at the women in the mini-dresses. "Not whore."

Jaysus Criminey. Say it a little louder, why don't you.

The women glared at us, turned tail, and left.

"Now, we drink." He handed me a shot and raised his glass. "To many enemies. For a man without enemies is worthless."

I can see that. We drank. "That's a fantastic toast."

"Yes."

I trailed a finger behind my earring. "And these are fantastic, too." I took the final thank-you card from my clutch and set it on the bar.

Stannis picked it up and tapped it against his palm. "Thank-you letters. Pretty dress. Brave. Good breed."

"Well-bred," I said gently. "Thank you."

"Well-bred." Stannis slipped the card into the inside pocket of his suit coat, his blue-black hair gleamed beneath the pendant lights. "Why do you come?"

"Why did you ask me?"

He wagged a finger at me.

"You interest me," I said. *And the BOC.*

Stannis gestured at our empty glasses. "Another? Or too much?"

I hesitated. "I might get a little silly." *Talk about a whopper.*

McGranes were born with the alcohol tolerance of a rectory of recently defrocked priests.

"Is okey—silly." He signaled the bartender for another round. "How do I interest?"

My mind flashed on Jeff Mant and a rush of gratitude flooded my head. "I feel a sort of . . . *simpatico*." *Even though I know what you are.*

"What is *simpatico?*"

"A like-mindedness. Black sheep from the same herd."

Stannis cocked his head and hit his hand over his heart. "I also. That is why I ask you."

He handed me the shot of rakija, raised his glass just as before, and waited.

"Here's mud in your eye." I clinked my glass against his and we drank.

A chunky guy with black hair turning white in a skunk stripe came over and whispered something in Stannis's ear. Irritation crossed his face. I couldn't tell if it was the man's request, the fact that he'd interrupted us, or both.

Stannis pulled out a bar stool for me. "Please sit. You will not mind if I speak to this man?"

"Of course not."

The bartender rushed in and set a glass of ice water with lemon in front of me. I watched Renko back in the corner with the goombahs. He looked mulish. At the five-minute mark, I decided to take a powder.

I entered the ladies', a posh affair with a separate lounge that contained dark red walls, red leather furniture, and lacquered tables. At the opposite end was a short wall separating the sinks and stalls. As I approached, I heard a loud adenoidal Jersey accent, "Still, a good-looking asshole. Gotta luv them little skinny guys. They're like rabbits. They go all night."

I hovered at one side of the entry, trying to get a look at the voice's reflection before entering. Red Dress with Purple Dress at her elbow.

Lovely. The girls Stannis called whores.

Purple Dress seemed somehow familiar.

Oh crap.

My stomach sank. She was Tony "Big Tuna" LoGrasso's "niece."

Niece said, "Don't botha, cuz not only is he a total jerk, but Tony says he's freakin' qu-ee-r."

Ah, the contemptuous slur that only an East Coaster can draw into three syllables. What a sweetheart.

Jersey shrieked with laughter. "That explains the nun he brung. Wanna a line?"

"Stalls only," hissed Niece. They scuttled into a single stall and slid the lock home. "Can you keep a secret?"

Giggles from Jersey. "Abso-friggin'-lutely."

A giggle then a long concentrated sniff, and exhale. "Anyways, Tony's gonna tell Eddie that Renko's a queer. And they'll send him right back to Russia."

Jaysus crimeny.

Another line went up someone's nose.

Which was exactly like what would happen to Operation Steal-Tow. Blown.

"I mean, us?" Niece said. "We look like whores? Who the friggin' fuck does he think he is?"

Hank's Law Number Twelve: Improvise, adapt, and overcome.

How do I prove Stannis is straight in this super-prude dress?

Lowest, common-est denominator.

I scooted into the bathroom while they were still in the stall. I grabbed a handful of paper towels and ran them under the tap. *Here goes nothing.* I hiked up my skirt and pressed a wad of damp paper towels to my inner thigh.

"Ooh." I groaned in relief.

The girls came out of the stall. I looked up at them in the mirror and gave a little shriek of embarrassment. "Whisker burn. My thighs are on fire." I shook my head and rolled my eyes. "He only shaves once a day."

Their eyes bulged. Jersey slapped Tony's "niece" in the arm. "I tole you, short guys . . ."

I threw the paper towels away. "I'm sorry Renko was so rude. Europeans, you know?"

"He's an asshole."

"Tell me about it." I gave them a covetous glance. "I'd die to wear what you have on. You look amazing."

Mollified, they opened their evening bags and began applying lipstick.

"I mean, I'm wearin' a funeral dress for chrissakes," I said, trying to match their East Coast inflection. "But what Renko wants, Renko gets. You know what I'm sayin'?"

They nodded.

"You won't tell anyone, will you?" I begged, certain they would. "I'd die of embarrassment."

"Sure thing." They smiled at me, exchanged a look, and sauntered off.

Now to warn Stannis.

Stannis met me as I came back into the lounge. He was buzzing with a combination of vitality and aggression.

"Could we chat for a moment?" I asked.

Stannis gave a short shake of his head. "Forgive me, Maisie. Not at this time." He took my arm and with only the barest pressure on my elbow, led me through a sea of gold velvet curtains into the 1940s. The Storkling was pure allure. Intimate high-backed booths broke up landing strips of tables where glitterati were meant to be seen. On stage at the far end, a flame-haired torcher in a red sequined gown warbled "Black Coffee" in front of a tuxedoed twelve-piece band.

The maître d' gave us a short bow and raised a palm toward a table at a large elevated platform in the back. Four men in dark suits surrounded a stout man with fading dark hair and olive skin. He was exquisitely packaged in a creamy white dinner jacket over a white shirt and black tie. They were all smoking cigars.

We walked up the stairs. While the men all rose, only the man in the white jacket came around the table. Eddie Veteratti. Vi's twin and head of the Chicago Syndicate. "Renko."

"Eddie."

They shook hands, Stannis finished with a shoulder grip. The Mobster's smile went waxy.

Uh-oh.

"So, who's this?" Eddie's quick eyes gave me a halfhearted once-over. "Your secretary?"

I gazed up at Stannis in a look of pure adoration and then genteelly extended my hand. "Maisie McGrane." When Eddie took my hand, I leaned in, cupped my left hand to my cheek, and whispered in his ear, "Stannis prefers a prude in public and a bunny in the bedroom."

Eddie's eyes widened.

I left my hand in his. "It's a pleasure to make your acquaintance, Mr. Veteratti."

"Is she for real?" he asked Stannis. Eddie leaned in, exhaling smoke in my face. "Where'd you learn to talk so sweet?"

"The Sisters at St. Ignatius, sir."

"Oh my fuckin' God. *Sir,* she said." He called over his shoulder to one of the guys at the table. "Benny. Order the kid a champagne cocktail." He waved his cigar at Stannis. "Let's go."

Stannis pulled out a chair for me, I spun, took him firmly by the lapels, and kissed him. His mouth went stiff with surprise. Then he kissed me back.

Holy cat!

His fingers slid up the back of my neck and he bent me slightly backward.

He let go suddenly, leaving me gasping in shock. He raised his hands in apology to Eddie. "Like drug, she is." He winked at me and they left.

The four men smoked and stared at me. Cheeks burning, I took a seat at the table. I turned my chair slightly and focused on the singer. A waiter placed a drink in front of me. "Your champagne cocktail."

Anyone happen to catch the plate of the truck that just hit me?

What the what?

A tall Tom Collins glass held ice, lemon peel, and a dark tawny liquid filled to the brim. I raised a brow.

"Krug champagne and Martell Cordon Bleu Cognac." The waiter smiled politely. "Exactly like the original Stork Club made them for Gloria Swanson."

I took a taste. It was a champagne cocktail, all right. A damn good one.

Who was rescuing who here, anyway?

After another couple of sips, I leaned back in my chair and tried to relax.

Bobby Blaze purred a throaty "Bye Bye Blackbird," the band riding the edge of subdued swing. Ear candy. The likes of which I'd never heard live before.

I scanned the room, getting a feel for the clientele. A couple of television stars who'd never make it on the big screen cozying up to a couple of sports stars who had. Mobsters serenaded by a glut of city politicians ready to pick up the hammer and sickle.

The oozing froth of Chicagoland's who's who.

The only way I could have been happier was if Hank was sitting next to me.

Chapter 19

The torcher finished on a long low note. Her spot went dark. Colored lights flared and the band ramped into Gillespie-style jazz.

Eddie returned to the table with Renko, arm slung around his shoulder.

Stannis was in.

The waiter flittered around the table like an anxious bee, as Eddie V. pulled out the chair next to me. He took the seat on my right, leaned forward, and pointed at my near empty glass. "You like?"

"Very much, thank you." I smiled. "Heavenly."

He turned to the waiter. "A Manhattan for me and another cocktail for the kid."

"Mr. Renko?" the waiter asked.

"Rakija."

"Hustle it up," Eddie said. The waiter nodded and fled. Eddie turned to me. "So you and Renko. How'd that happen?"

"He's my white knight," I said. "He stopped a guy from mugging me."

"Yeah?" Eddie leaned back in his chair, bored and twitchy. "Sounds exciting."

"It was awful." I shuddered and let my voice go husky. "But, oh so wonderful when Stannis smashed his head into the windshield."

Eddie blinked.

Yeah, that's right, Scarface Junior. You don't know me at all.

"You see why Maisie is like drug to me?" Renko's slim hand covered mine and squeezed. "She understands the violence of men."

Eddie's lips bent in a thoughtful frown. He nodded and said over my head to Stannis, "Maybe you wanna let her"—his hands gestured vaguely in my direction—"look a little hotter, you know?"

"Maisie represents me." He tapped his chest. "She will not dress like whore."

"That may be, but she ain't gonna be happy coming along and not fitting in." Eddie leaned close to me. "Ain't that right, sweetheart?"

I glanced up at Stannis from beneath my lashes. "Well, I wouldn't say no to a new dress, Mr. Veteratti."

"Bastard," Stannis said, eyes twinkling.

Eddie laughed, eyes roaming the dining room. The chuckle died in his throat as Zara Coles, version 2.0, walked into the room.

The mayor's wife had dropped twenty pounds, joined Team Botox, and traded up her pedantic version of Jackie O. for the *House of Cards'* Claire Underwood. Her caramel-colored hair was short and chic, and her sternly tailored sheath dress fit her like a second skin.

Eddie was on his feet the second he clapped eyes on her. We watched as she approached our table. Stannis stood. I didn't see the point in staying seated and got up.

"Sweetheart." Eddie wrapped the mayor's wife in a warm embrace, kissing her on each cheek and finishing with one right on the mouth. "I didn't expect to see you here."

"Oh, Eddie. I've had the most dreadful week."

"Lay it on me, baby." He held out his opened palms. "I'm all ears."

"I haven't seen Talbott in ages. The children are convinced their father is a television character. I've attended a dozen events in the last five days, and to top it off, my brand-new Bentley looks like Br'er Rabbit drove it through the briar patch. Scratched to bits. I simply had to get out of the house."

"Lemme take care of you, Zu." Eddie snapped his fingers at the waiter and pointed at his Manhattan. "I'll have one of the boys come 'round for the car tomorrow. I got a body work guy'll have it better than new."

"That would be wonderful." Zara Coles gave him a sweet smile and a gentle head tip in our direction.

"Oh yeah," Eddie said. "This is Stannislav Renko. Zara Coles." Stannis shook her proffered hand. "Is nice to meet you."

The mayor's wife turned to me. "Zara Coles. But please, call me Zuzu." She rolled her eyes and moued. "It's one of those awful East Coast-y kind of nicknames, I know, but I've grown impossibly accustomed." She shrugged her shoulders. "And you are?"

"Maisie," Eddie said.

She jerked as if she were on the end of a puppet string. A tiny crease appeared on her forehead. "Maisie . . . McGrane?"

Yeah. The one who booted your car and is at least partly to blame for the scratches. I tried not to wince.

"Oh, thank you!" She gave a short almost-sob of breath and clutched my wrists. "I never got the chance to thank you. Thank you." She smiled at Eddie. "This is the girl. The one who saved Talbott's life."

"Oh yeah?" He glared at me. "Kid's a regular saint, ain't she."

Zuzu pressed her lips tight together, blinking fast. "I've wanted to express our family's gratitude so very many times. What you did was everything to me . . . to my family." She let go of my hands to wring her own. "Talbott was adamant you wouldn't welcome a gift or token of appreciation."

"He was right, ma'am." A grub worm of guilt twisted inside my stomach. Zuzu Coles was a nice lady. Her husband was a switch-hitting cheater. She didn't deserve that. Nobody did.

"But look at you," Zuzu chided. "You're gorgeous. You could have tied your wagon to his star. Made a career out of it."

"I'm kind of a private person."

"I wish I could be." She fingered the sapphire collar at her throat. "One of the perils of falling in love with a politician." A tiny pucker appeared on Zuzu's brow. "Didn't Talbott offer to make you a police officer? Like the rest of your family?"

On his extra-dirty security detail. "Yes. I turned him down."

"Why's that?" Eddie folded his arms across his chest.

"Half of my family are defense attorneys, Mr. Veteratti. The other half are cops."

"Eddie," Zuzu warned, laying a hand on his forearm.

I smiled. "Neither is a team I want to play for."

Instead of placating Eddie, my answer pissed him off. "You bring a fuckin' cop's kid in my club, Renko?"

Stannis bared his bottom teeth in amusement. "Maisie, Mrs. Coles, you excuse us, yes?"

We nodded and stood uncomfortably for a moment as the two men left the table. Zuzu turned and started chattering with the other men at the table.

Now might be an opportune time to get some air.

My heels tripped lightly down the stairs. The valet approached me. I waved him off and put some yardage between me and his station.

Jaysus Criminey.

All that and now I'm fingered as a narc. Supes terrif. I pinched the bridge of my nose and rocked back and forth on my heels.

Now what? Aside from the fact I was terrified Stannis actually wanted to date me, the idea that I'd compromised him with my family connections after all the evening's efforts, frankly, sucked.

My, it's going to be a lovely debrief with Danny.

A blurry clear film came down over my face. I gasped and plastic filled my nose and mouth. Choking me.

A plastic bag.

A heavy arm grabbed me across the chest, dragging me backward into the alley. Forcing the last bubble of oxygen from my throat.

Don't breathe don't breathe don't breathe.

I tried to rip at the thick plastic. My lungs were on fire, body heaving. Fingers slipping as I tried to rip a hole at my mouth.

The edges of my vision went black. Lungs tearing, chest bucking for air.

My hands fell away.

The bag was jerked from my face. Colors and lights burst in my eyes. I was pinned up against a brick wall, choking and coughing, trying to stop the world from spinning.

"Miss me?" Jeff Mant pulled out a gravity knife and popped the lever, letting the blade fall and lock slowly into the hilt. Savoring the moment.

I was dizzy, shuddering, sucking in air. Oxygen burning as much coming in as it had going without.

He jabbed the knife just below my breasts. The tip cut into me with each involuntary, heaving gasp.

Oh, please, no.

Mant leaned back and with a quick flip of the wrist, slit my bra and dress up to the base of my throat. I barely felt the hot slice of the blade over the fire in my lungs.

His nostrils flared. "I specifically told you not to wear black."

Another set of stars went off in my head. I saw a dark shape across the street.

A man. Moving toward me.

Hank?

"*Dalji ruke!*" Stannis's gruff Serbian rang in my ears as he shot out of the darkness and punched Jeff Mant in the soft cartilage of his throat.

Mant stumbled backward, clutching at his neck, dropping the knife.

Stannis was on the blade in a flash. He weighed it in his hand, bouncing on the balls of his feet. "Come." He gestured at Mant with the knife. "You bleed now."

Wheezing, I slid slowly down the side of the wall, the back of my dress riding up, snagging on the rough brick.

Mant's eyes slid from the man on the other side of the street to Stannis. They went flat. "Later," he rasped and turned and ran off down the alley, disappearing into the night.

I vaguely remember Stannis throwing his jacket around me, rescuing a shoe I didn't remember losing, and bundling me into his waiting car. Tucked into the backseat, I shivered with cold and tried to focus on what was happening in front of The Storkling.

The valet was a twentysomething kid who didn't deserve the sound and the fury Stannis was raining down on him. Eddie Veteratti and a couple of his men started down the stairs to see about the ruckus.

But my eyelids had turned to lead. I gave up and let them close.

Chapter 20

Stannis gently shook me awake. My head was in his lap. "Maisie? We are here."

I sat up, blinking and woozy, trying to find my feet. The driver had parked in front of a midrise industrial rehabbed building in the trendy West Loop.

"Stannis, I need to go home."

"No."

The driver opened the door, Stannis leapt out ahead and helped me into the building.

He swiped a key card in front of the electronic eye in the elevator. The top button labeled PH lit up.

Penthouse.

Huddled inside his suit coat, I tried to pull the front of my dress together. I took a tiny peek. I hissed as the fabric, sticky with blood, scraped and rubbed against the open cut that ran from right beneath my breasts to the base of my throat.

Gee thanks, Jeff. Half an autopsy cut.

My stomach roiled and I started mouth-breathing. The elevator doors opened and we stepped into an empty black granite foyer. "Stannis, I need to go home."

"No." He led me into a Spartan living room. Ebony hardwood floors, stone gray walls, and everything else, a pristine and brilliant white. He sat me down on a white linen sofa. "Three minutes."

You're the boss. A round of the chills passed through me. I laid my head down on the sofa arm.

And there he was, waking me up again. I opened an eye, a pouty frown on my face. He took me by the hand into the bathroom.

A white two-person soaking tub was steaming, filled with masses of bubbles. Fluffy white towels and a thick terry-cloth robe waited at one end.

He left without a word. I slipped out of my clothes, twisted my hair into a topknot, and got in. At first the shaking was so bad, small splashes of water erupted around me. When it slowed, I eased lower, the soapy water making the cut on my chest sting like hell. After a bit, I sat up and steeled myself to take a good look.

A fine, slowly oozing line about eight inches long ran from my breastbone to the base of my throat.

A devil's paper cut.

Delicate strains of Chopin's mournful "Prelude #4 in E Minor" filtered into the bathroom. I closed my eyes and sank back down to my chin.

After a bit, there was a soft knock at the door. It swung open and Stannis entered with a tea tray. White bone china cups and pot and several gaudily wrapped candy bars. He set the tray on a raw steel bench next to the tub, poured the tea, and handed me a cup.

It was warm and sweet. A London Fog—Earl Grey, steamed milk, and vanilla syrup.

Stannis sat down on the bench and poured his own cup. "We have much to discuss."

"Oh?"

"We will speak of what happened at the club."

"I'd rather not."

He shook his head. "Who is he?"

I took another sip and looked longingly at a bright red Clark Bar. Stannis took the cup from my hands, opened the candy bar, and handed it to me.

I need to call Hank. But how in the hell am I gonna explain how and why I lost Ragnar and . . .

I took a small bite, savoring the chocolate and honeycomb flake, and told him the truth. "His name is Jeff Mant. He's a sociopath and contract killer."

"How much?"

I squinted at him.

Stannis rubbed his fingers together.

"Oh, it's not about money." I took another bite of candy, stalling. "I don't know, really. He's somehow fixated on me."

"This, I understand." Stannis put his hand over mine. "I am not drawn to women. But I am drawn to you."

Uh-oh. "I like you, too."

He leaned back and ran a hand through his hair. "Can you do again what you did this night?"

Get choked out by Jeff Mant? I blinked.

"Kiss me," he said. "Be my woman."

My brain lagged like *Call of Duty* on dial-up. "Uh—"

His face creased with amusement. "Oh. No!" He laughed in delight. "Not always. Certain times." He put his hands on his knees. "A make-believe woman."

"Girlfriend," I said automatically, mind reeling.

He nodded. "I prefer only men."

Stannis wants me as his beard.

The BOC is gonna love this. Field Agent McGrane at your service.

"Yes?" He smiled. "You work as girlfriend. We have fun. I pay you."

I held out my hand to shake on it. "Yes."

As before, he raised it to his mouth, turned it gently, and kissed the underside of my wrist. "Now, I fix you."

He left the bathroom with the tea tray. I got out of the tub and slipped into the robe.

He returned with a gray T-shirt and thin cotton pajama pants. And a small brown bottle that read *Merthiolate.*

He took a Q-tip from a drawer. "Sit." He opened my robe.

"Is not bad at all." He dunked the Q-tip in the bottle. It came out bright red. He pinched his fingers together. "Little sting, yes?"

I swallowed and nodded. He stroked the Q-tip down in a light swipe over the first three inches of my cut.

Holy mother of—"Gah!" A small shriek split my lips.

He leaned forward and blew on my chest. "You are baby." He flipped the Q-tip, dunked again, and, ignoring my whimpers, swabbed the remaining five inches. Then blew.

A Serbian enforcer platonically blowing on disinfectant between my naked breasts in a penthouse bathroom. Not at all the way I'd thought the evening would turn out.

He handed the T-shirt to me. "If makes stain, is okey. You come." He picked up my torn dress and broken bra and left me in the bathroom.

I scrambled into my underpants and the pajamas.

What could possibly happen next?

Stannis was waiting for me as I came into the living room. His finely chiseled features gave him the look of a warring Adonis. He nodded for me to sit on the sofa, then picked up a real fox fur throw, lined with cream satin, and laid it over my lap.

He tipped his head toward the replenished tea tray on the coffee table. "You would like more?"

"No, thank you."

Stannis's eyes went to a closed door across the hall. "To sleep, then?"

Here? Sweet Jayus.

"Stannis, you've been absolutely lovely and I can't wait until our next adventure, but I have to go home."

"No. You stay night here."

"Not an option. I live with four police officers." I held up four fingers. "Four. Not a good idea."

Stannis scowled. "But your clothes. I buy you new dress tomorrow. Repair this one."

"No." I shook my head. "Please don't. It was an ugly dress, anyway."

"Yes." His eyes danced. "Very ugly. Okey, I call driver to take you home."

I couldn't bear the thought of Raw Chicken the chauffeur escorting me home alone. A nervous giggle sprang from my lips. "Please, can you come, too?"

He looked at me like I'd lost my mind.

God, could I be any more juvenile? I pressed my hands to my cheeks.

"You are frightened?" His eyes went flat, face grave.

"Too tired, I think." *But I still don't want to be in the car alone with that guy.* "Why does your driver dislike me so?"

"He was discourteous?"

"Yes. Er . . . no. Not horribly, but—"

Stannis spun sharply on his heel and went to the house phone. He tapped in a number and said something sharp and unpleasant in Serbian. He hung up the phone, came back, and knelt in front of me. "There is much you do not know about me, *mali anđeo.* My angel." He took my hands in his. "But we are the *simpatico,* yes?"

"Yes."

"In the village where I grow up, there is much terror. Much death."

I nodded.

"One learns one must burn a candle for the devil now and again."

Gee, that doesn't sound ominous at all.

He pulled me to my feet. "Come, I show you."

Oookay. We walked down a hallway. Stannis swung open a pair of white enameled French doors. Inside was a large office with a charcoal area rug so plush it was almost obscene. The walls were wood and stained a misty pewter. A black leather seating area surrounded a granite fireplace. At one end, a desk fashioned from raw steel held a large clear glass jar half full of ivory pieces.

At the opposite corner of the room, a large dark glass aquarium sat atop a granite pillar. I moved toward it, but Stannis caught my wrist and walked me over to his desk and pulled out his chair for me. "You sit."

I sat.

Oh God, please don't tell me anything horrible. I don't have the chops left for it.

There was a knock at the door. I looked up to see the chauffeur in the doorway, shifting slightly to and fro.

Stannis stood behind me, hands on either side of my shoulders. "Approach."

The driver came to the desk. "Sir."

"Show her," Stannis said pleasantly.

The driver's fingers began to tremble as he removed his leather driving glove. He set his left hand on the desk. A pulpy raw scar where the little finger had been suggested it had only recently gone missing.

Stannis put his cheek next to mine. "I think he forgets. He represents me."

Raw Chicken's eye twitched. "No. Sir."

"Let us see, shall we come?"

I followed Stannis and we crossed en masse to the opposite end of the office to the darkened aquarium. Stannis pressed a switch on the pillar and the smoke-tinted glass lit up to reveal . . . *beetles on a piece of dried fruit?*

"Staphylinidae. Rove beetles. Difficult to keep alive," Stannis said to me. He turned to the driver. "Look closely," he urged. "They haven't finished with your offering."

Eyes squeezed shut, the driver lowered his face to the glass, opened them, and shuddered.

I looked again. The beetles weren't on a piece of old banana.

They were on a human finger.

The driver's finger.

I fought the urge to back away. "You understand, yes?" Stannis reached over and tucked a lock of my hair behind my ear. "Is okey."

We went back to the desk, Stannis pulled out the chair for me. He opened the lower desk drawer and removed a battered wooden box scarred with deep cuts.

He set it on the desk with a *thud,* took an old iron key from his pocket, and set it in front of me. The dark grooves cut into the wood box ran perpendicular to the edges. Too workmanlike and uneven for intentional design.

A small whistle of panic escaped Raw Chicken.

"This wo—girlfriend of mine," Stannis said softly, "she thinks you do not like her."

The chauffeur's fingers plucked at the hem of his suit coat.

Stannis laid his hand atop the box. "It is said Pandora loosed all evils upon the world but trapped hope in the box for the benefit of men." He nodded at me.

I picked up the key, fit it in the well-oiled lock, and twisted.

"But you, Maisie, I think, know this to be wrong." Stannis lifted the lid and took out a strange-shaped iron blade with a battered walnut handle. Vicious and hoary, a sort of cleaver with two cutting edges. "For no evil is as cruel as hope."

Stannis closed the box and slid it in front of his driver. "Choose."

The driver raised his left hand and laid his ring finger on top of the box.

Oh Jaysus.

I am too tired for this shite.

The driver tapped the gold band on his finger. "Cannot take off."

Stannis cocked his head cavalierly and raised the blade. "Will hurt more."

"Wait!" My voice went croaky. "Stannis, please. Don't do this."

He frowned at me. "Why not?"

"He will respect me for my forgiveness."

Stannis turned to the driver. "Is this so?"

The driver nodded and bowed, scraping toward me.

"As you wish." Stannis raised his left palm. "I will pay the blood debt." Without a second thought he sliced his hand with the cleaver and winked at me.

He wiped the blade off on the driver's sports coat and replaced the cleaver. A rivulet of red trickled down his wrist.

I glanced wildly around me for a cloth and almost stood up. Almost. Instead, I barked, "Get him a towel."

The driver fled the room.

"You are right." Stannis nodded in approval. "Much respect now."

I slumped in the chair and swiped the thin layer of chilled perspiration from my forehead, wanting a drink but not wanting to stay a second longer. My eyes fell on the heavy glass jar half-filled with ivory pieces at the corner of his desk.

I leaned in.

It can't be. It just can't.

He put his uninjured hand on the jar and gently, reverently, moved it in front of me.

Aww, for chrissakes.

The ivory pieces were finger bones.

"My legacy," Stannis said.

Chapter 21

I slept the sleep of the comatose in my own bed in my own room at home until I turned on my side and woke myself up groaning. The cut hurt like a jellyfish sting on an open blister.

Stupid Jeff Mant.

Stupid stupid me.

I sat up and rubbed my eyes with the heels of my hands.

Stannis.

The fingers. Sweet Jaysus, the fingers.

My ears filled with pressure.

Hank.

Calling him was gonna make a trip to hell seem like Disney-land. Might as well eat breakfast before tying a knot in Lucifer's tail. I disappeared into my closet, pulled on a v-neck Black-hawks tee and some yoga pants, and caught sight of myself in the full-length mirror.

Where the heck is my head?

Stannis's antiseptic monkey-blood dye made me look like I'd had open-heart surgery. A condition only slightly more accept-able at the McGrane family breakfast table than a neck full of hickeys.

Cripes.

I rummaged in my closet for a tee to cover Mant's handi-work, then threw on a camouflage Under Armour logo hoodie and went downstairs to get something to eat.

Thierry was in the kitchen. Pulling out all the stops this morning. Steel bowls and whisks and food everywhere. "*Bonjour,* Maisie. *Chocolat* in the dining room. *Tartine Mistral* for you?"

"Ooh. Yes, please."

From the decadent bits of ingredients I recognized on the counters, Mom and Da were not only home for breakfast, but in a damn good mood and ready to shred their self-imposed caloric restrictions this Saturday morning.

I walked into the dining room and froze at the sight of enormous shoulders straining against a watch-plaid flannel shirt and thick blond hair tied into a low ponytail.

Ragnar, head bent in serious conversation with my mother over the dining room table.

Oh shite. With a capital S.

"Ragnar?"

"Randolph," Mom corrected and smiled at me. "Come sit, baby, I've hardly seen you."

I could feel his eyes burning into my back as I crossed to the sideboard and poured myself a steaming cup of *chocolat*.

"I can't tell you how happy I was to find your Mr. Acrey knocking on the door at six o'clock this morning." She beamed at the Viking.

Hank's Viking.

Ragnar bared his teeth, letting me know exactly how pissed off he was. "Your mother's a beautiful and fascinating woman."

"Oh, stop." Mom tagged him playfully on the arm. "With his instincts, interpersonal skills, and practical life experience, he'd make an excellent defense attorney." She raised a finger at him. "I'm never wrong about potential attorneys."

My shoulders sagged. *Oh God.* "No, she's not."

Thierry entered with a silver tray. He set a plate laden with gingerbread pancakes and poached pears in front of Ragnar, followed by a dinner plate of glazed ham and chicken apple sausages at his elbow.

He served my mother a minute portion. "As I was saying, Randolph, securing you a spot in Loyola would be a *snap*," Mom said, barely able to contain a shimmy of joy. "Maisie already has an open seat."

With a wink, Thierry set my favorite breakfast in front of me—half a toasted baguette with goat cheese and roasted peppers—and exited, presumably to go barbeque a sheep for our Nordic visitor.

Ragnar closed his eyes as he chewed. "This is fuc—er, I mean, fantastic."

Mom prattled right on, "And since my daughter has long since outgrown her current employ as a parking enforcement agent, I see no reason why you two pals couldn't start together in the spring."

Any port in a storm. I let her have her moment and took a bite of my breakfast.

Ragnar put half a sausage in his mouth and winked at me. "Sounds like a goddaaa—rn plan."

His chest must be full to bursting holding in unsaid swear words.

Da walked into the dining room. "Good morning, everyone." He made the rounds, kissed my mother, me, and put out a hand to the Viking. "Conn McGrane."

"Randolph Acrey," he said as they shook.

"Quite a car out there." Da jerked his head toward the window before sitting between my mother and me.

Ragnar's eyes never left my face as he answered, "A goddamn beaut, ain't she?"

"A lot of muscle for city driving," Da said, sizing him up and, unlike Mom, finding him lacking. "Car like that belongs on the track."

"Hell, yeah. Tell me about it."

Uh-oh.

I leaned forward and looked out the window. Instead of Ragnar's old blue pickup, the black Dodge Hellcat took center stage in the driveway.

Eff. Me.

"I suppose a firecracker like Maisie needs the muscle," Ragnar said around a mouthful of food, his baby blues sending me his telepathic message—*Payback's a bitch.*

Dad's smile went from cool to chilling. "And just what the hell do yeh mean by that, laddie?"

Ragnar drank half a glass of orange juice in one swallow before answering. "It's her car."

You son of a—

"Is that true, Maisie?"

"Of course not," I said. "It's Hank's."

"Something wrong with your car?"

I shook my head. "Nope."

"Discretion is the better part of valor," Mom muttered at her breakfast.

"My sins are my own, Maisie." His jaw slid forward. "You won't be riding them to perdition."

Hank's Law Number Three: Don't let your lizard brain go rogue.

Too late.

"Really, Da?" Flames shot up my throat. "Because I'm pretty sure Parking Enforcement is hell on earth and you put me there."

"You're rolling around in the ashes and muck because you choose to." Da's eyes went black with anger. "There's no ring on your finger."

Are you fecking kidding me? "So, I marry Hank, I can drive what I want. Do what I want? Is that it?"

He gave a harsh bark of laughter. "What makes you think I'd let you marry the bloody bastard?"

"Maisie. Conn. Desist," Mom said. "You're making our guest uncomfortable."

Da glared at Ragnar. "Who the feck are you, anyway? Ex-service—" He gestured at the pink puckered burn on his neck. "Afghanistan?"

"Yemen."

"And now you're just another demmed gun on Bannon's retainer."

Ragnar blinked. "No sir," he lied. "I met Maisie at Joe's Gym. We play paintball together."

"That's why he's here, Da. We have a game." I stood up. "Let's go, Rags, we don't want to let *the team* down."

I slid into the passenger seat of the Challenger.

"Oh Jesus, you fuckin' deserved that." Ragnar scowled at me as he folded himself behind the wheel. "And a hell of a lot more."

I latched my seat belt. "I'm sorry about last night. Really. It was a gag, that's all. I'll pay for any damage."

He shook his head. "You're outta your goddamned pea-brained mind if you think you can *fix* jacking me up in front of Bannon."

"Look. Hank and I—"

His entire face went ruddy. He gunned the engine, taking care not to leave tread until he hit the street. "I covered for you and your half-naked ass and you stab me in the back."

Whoa. "Hey, I never asked you to . . ."

His lip raised as his voice went high and mocked, "Hey, I'm not an asshole." He punched on the radio. Classic rock. Led Zeppelin. "Kashmir."

"I'm sorry. That was really decent of you."

He turned the volume up. I listened until he got close to the freeway. "Where we going?"

"Bannon's."

"No dice. Hank's picking me up at my parents' tomorrow."

"Where, then?"

"Silverthorn Estates. I may as well go make someone happy since everyone I know is ticked off at me. Thanks for ratting me out on the car, by the way."

" 'Least I could do." We drove on, rock music blaring. "Man, your dad's a scary sumbitch, I'll give you that."

After a while the red finally left his ears. He shot me a sideways glance. "Alright. I got a question for you."

"Shoot."

"How in fuck are you so goddamn skinny?" He shook his head. "That was the best goddamn breakfast I've ever had."

Chapter 22

I swished my card through the reader of the Onyx ward. RN/BOC guard Anita Erickson met me at the door. "Welcome, Maisie."

I frowned. "I hit both buttons."

"Always on alert. First time you've come in unarmed." She looked me over. "You doin' okay? You seem kinda . . . wired."

"Yeah. I'm great." And I was up. Crazy up. I made a beeline for the offices. "Kaplan around?"

"Yeah," Anita said to my back and something else I couldn't hear as I swiped through the door into the office.

A couple of Grims looked up from their desks but most didn't. The office was in full swing on a Saturday morning. Kaplan's door was ajar. I knocked and walked in.

Her dark head was almost touching Sawyer's flaxen one at the conference table.

Kaplan glanced up in irritation at my entrance. "What is it, McGrane?"

The aristocratic, debonair Mr. Sawyer, however, rose with a smile, came over, and shook my hand. "Your fieldwork has been outstanding."

My shoulders straightened. "Thank you, sir."

"Ahem," Kaplan coughed.

"I thought you would prefer the debrief from my date with Stannislav Renko as soon as possible, ma'am."

Sawyer tipped his foxy face to one side. "I beg your pardon?"

"So, it actually happened?" Kaplan said.

"Yes, ma'am."

"Close the door, Danny," Sawyer said flatly. "Maisie, please." He gestured to the table. "Begin at the beginning."

I waited until Kaplan had joined us. Her face was pinched and wan. More worried than angry.

Good enough for her.

I walked Sawyer through Stannis saving me from the assault followed by my returning the favor at the strip club. I told him about Stannis's sexual relationship with Coles, our conversation at T.G.I. Friday's, and his week of extravagant gifts.

Sawyer got up and went to the sideboard. "Cartier, hmm?" He poured a glass of ice water from a crystal pitcher and brought it to me. "You authorized this 'date,' Danny?"

"Yes, sir."

"Despite the fact that Maisie's a raw recruit with no field training? Rather rash."

"You yourself said she showed initiative beyond her age and experience," Kaplan said quietly. "Her Academy scores—"

"High scores don't measure field competence, do they, Danny?"

Kaplan's hand flew to her collarbone. She caught herself and finished by straightening her shirt. "No, sir. They don't."

So that's what Edward meant. Shot on the job. Kaplan took one in the chest and now she's behind a desk.

Sawyer returned to his seat. "Please continue, Maisie."

I told him about The Storkling and the gossip and kissing Stannis. And all about Eddie Veteratti.

Then I told him about Stannis's offer.

Walt Sawyer went perfectly still for a long moment.

The smile he gave Kaplan was brutal. "It would be prudent to bring in Edward at this juncture. Kindly brief him along the way."

She got up and marched stiffly to the door, closing it behind her.

I considered bringing up the fingerless boy in the hospital but decided against it. Kaplan was my handler, after all.

"I apologize for Agent Kaplan's lack of judgment in allowing you to default to a deep cover operative position. Stannislav

'The Bull' Renko . . ." Sawyer tapped the bridge of his nose and muttered under his breath, "Good Lord, July will have my head."

I've got an in with the biggest Serbian gangster in town, and you're worried about what my mom will think?

Sawyer folded his hands on the table. "You need to consider carefully what is being asked of you, Maisie. Your confirmation of Renko's relationship with Eddie V. affirms they are functioning proxies for Goran Slajic and Don Constantino."

I nodded.

"I'm sure you've reckoned by now that Special Unit operates beyond the boundaries of the CPD. I created Operation Steal-Tow as a sort of Midwestern canopy working independently with the many agencies that are affected. Our goal is to combat the multimillion-dollar economic ripple, which affects everything from insurance companies to consumers to unions to American auto exports."

"Yessir."

"These are ruthless and dangerous men, Maisie. Five days ago, we lost contact with our second field agent working with Slajic. Before he disappeared, we received a transmission that Slajic has successfully made inroads into the illegal arms market. Which elevates this situation to an entirely new level."

Edward Dunne and Kaplan entered the room. Edward clicked his black brogues together and threw me a sharp salute. "Congratulations, Field Agent Maisie McGrane. A regular up-and-comer. Why, you're Special Unit's youngest undercover."

My breath came in quick pants. *I'm in. I'm really in.*

They joined us at the table.

Kaplan nodded toward Edward. "Outfit her with the usual gear."

"No," Sawyer said. "I'm allowing this. With limits. She's going in cold. No spy tech. Live drops only, I want her protected."

Edward and Kaplan exchanged a look.

Sawyer pointed at me. "You're out at the first hint of anything untoward."

"Yessir."

He gave me a small nod, stood, and said to Edward, "Fill her in."

We watched him stride out the door and close it behind him.

"Okay, lassie." Edward smiled. "Let's discuss our objective."

The change in Kaplan was instantaneous, ball-buster back in charge. "Renko's leveraging Mob channels. And he's clever. He's getting cars, intact as well as chopped, out of Chicago by every possible method. Air, sea, train, and truck. Goran Slajic's primary funding is derived from Renko's proceeds of auto theft within the five-state area."

Edward nodded. "What we do know is that a large percentage of Renko's cars are eventually held in Honduras, before shipping to South America, the Middle East, and occasionally Eastern Europe."

"Our directive has increased from crippling Renko's organization to knocking Constantino's operation down a peg or two, as well." Kaplan sat back in her chair. "We want you to find out how, when, and where."

Gee. Piece of cake.

"Gear her up, Edward."

His elfin face darkened. "Walt said—"

"Give her the tools. Let her decide when and if to use them." Kaplan smiled at me. "You want to be a real live field agent, McGrane?"

I nodded.

She leaned forward on the table. "Then do the goddamn job."

I walked slowly out of the office and rode down the elevator to Silverthorn Estates's cheerful lobby. My hoodie was laden with $6K of prepaid Visa cards, a micro bug kit, a tiny cell phone jammer, a signal-detecting watch, and a document scanner pen. Real James Bond gear.

Which brought me back around again as to how exactly the Bureau of Organized Crime's Special Unit operated. Sawyer was well-heeled and well-connected, pulling together funding from all sorts of sources. The real mystery was how he was able to operate within and separately from the Chicago Police Department.

The distraction didn't last long. Mostly because I didn't really care how Walt Sawyer gave me my badge or where he was getting the money to pay my salary. I was a genuine bona fide field agent for Special Unit.

Someday, when I can speak, I will own the Table Club. Someday.

I trotted up the sidewalk to Ragnar in the Challenger, unable to shake the guilt rat from gnawing away at my brain.

Why, exactly, had I failed to mention the jar of finger bones in Stannis's office?

Chapter 23

Sunday afternoon, Hank still hadn't called or come by. And I was too chicken to call his office and talk to his sultry-voiced secretary.

Ragnar's blue pickup pulled into the driveway.

Might as well face the music.

I leaned against the front door, took a couple of deep exhales, and went out to meet the Viking.

What the—?

Lee Sharpe got out from behind the wheel. "Hey, baby." He opened his arms for a hug.

I stepped in and gave him one. "Hiya. Where'd you get the wheels?"

He laughed. "Cash thought your pal Thor might want 'em back."

"Ragnar."

"Whatever." He threw his arm around my shoulders. "Cash promised me beer and a ride home. How 'bout you take me?"

"Rain check."

He put me in a mock headlock and mussed my hair. "You're killing me."

We went into the great room. "What's your pleasure?"

"Anything American."

I got a couple of Coors bottles from the wet bar. He reached over and took one from my hand. He clinked his bottle against mine, eyes dancing. "To rain checks."

"How'd they stop the car, anyway?"

Lee leaned on the counter. "ESA S.Q.U.I.D. Blaster X-Net. Safe Quick Undercarriage Immobilization Device." He mimed a 1.5-foot circle about six inches high with his hands. "I hit the remote and masses of webbed belts shoot up into the undercarriage, get twisted in the axles, and stop the wheels from turning."

I frowned. "*You* hit the remote?"

"Well, sure." He licked his top lip. "SWAT just got 'em in, so when Cash called and said he had a practical application opportunity, I said, why not?"

I'll bet you did.

He crossed his muscular arms. "You're really not going to drive me home, are you?"

"Nope." I smiled.

"What if I sweeten the deal with dinner at Everest?"

"Ooh. Swanky." I pretended to think about it, then gave him the dead eye. "No dice."

He liked that. A lot. In a player's perverse way where a "no" is more interesting than a "yes."

Cash came in through the garage. "Hey, Lee, Maisie. Am I interrupting?"

Lee answered, "Yes." At the same time I said, "No."

Cash grabbed a beer. "Thanks for bringing the truck back, man."

"No sweat. Took the grease monkeys a while to get the belts out, but damage free." Lee shook his head. "Thirty mph and it locked him up before the end of the block. A winner."

"Yeah." Cash grinned at me. "Aw, man. You shoulda seen his face, Snap. Cripes, I never seen a guy so pissed."

"Snap?" Lee gave me a quizzical look.

"As in *ginger* snap," Cash supplied helpfully. "As in under all that blond she's a redhead."

Lee pursed his lips in a silent whistle.

"What?" I said.

"You're hot as a blonde, but you'd *scorch* as a spitfire."

Behind Lee's back, Cash pointed at him and gave me a thumbs-up.

Whatever.

Sunday night and everyone was out. The legal eagles stayed downtown, my parents were at another fund-raiser, Flynn and Rory were working, and Cash, Lee, and Koji opted for bar hopping. That left me, alone, watching *Once Upon a Time in the West,* unable to decide who I'd pick if I were Claudia Cardinale, Charles Bronson or Jason Robards.

The doorbell rang at 9:13 p.m. *Hank.*

I turned off the TV, then went and opened the door.

He leaned against a post, not moving toward me, face a blank. "Wanna hit the cage?"

Batting cages? "Uh . . . sure?"

"Hustle up."

I trotted up the stairs to my bedroom, feeling like a whipped puppy. *No kiss, no hug, no smile, no nothing.*

Hank was angry.

I swapped nude heels for black Keen tennis shoes and my Akris sleeveless leather tunic for an Angels jersey and hustled downstairs. Hank was waiting on the porch. He walked me to the G-Wagen and opened my door, closing it behind me.

No music. No talking.

No fun.

He merged onto the freeway and his phone chirped. He hit a button on the steering wheel. Speakerphone. "Yes?"

A heavy Italian accent asked, "Dis d'electrician?"

"Yes."

"Eddie wants to know 'bout da problem."

"No more destructive arcing," Hank said.

"Whaddafuck you sayin'?"

"The choke coil. Tell him the choke's been clipped." Hank disconnected.

I had so many questions that the different muscles in my face ticked independently.

He shot me a sideways glance. "Let it settle."

Hank worked for Don Constantino. He'd cut ties with Vi and now he was working for Eddie V.? It wasn't much of a leap that Scarface Junior would want Hank on his team if only to mess with his sister. But why would Hank agree?

"Fire away, Sport Shake."

"You're not working for Eddie V.," I said.

"No." Hank adjusted his grip on the steering wheel. "Notice anything?"

"Nooo," I said slowly, once again proving I have the situational awareness of a dead bird.

"Your bodyguards retired this afternoon."

Internal forehead slap.

Electric connections zapped through my synapses. *Mant is dead.*

It was settled.

Hank took the job from Eddie at Constantino's bidding. To end Mant. Because Eddie couldn't control him. And the Don doesn't like loose cannons.

"Feel better?" Hank said.

My breath came out in a half-laugh, half-sigh. "Lots." The innate cop in my DNA knew some mutts were meant to be put down. The only difference between me and my family? I honestly didn't care how it was done.

Hank drove the rest of the way to Scotty Jerome's Batting Cages. We listened to Cake while my mind kept spinning.

The parking lot was empty except for a single car. Hank parked in the far end, popped his seat belt, and turned in his seat. My mouth went dry.

"Wanna neck?" He grinned and pulled me to him.

He slid his hand up beneath my hair, fingers on the nape of my neck. He tugged me close and started kissing me. I went light-headed. The want, the black hot need for him, always just beneath the surface.

A lift and a jerk and I was in his lap, his hand sliding up my shirt, my back arching involuntarily. His fingers brushed across the devil's paper cut.

I sucked in my breath.

He lifted my shirt.

"What's this?"

"Jeff Mant's parting gift."

He eased my shirt back down and cupped my face in his hands. "Let's go."

"Can you still hit?" Hank asked, giving a nod to Scotty, who went and unlocked the door to the cages.

"My swing wasn't much before, so I doubt it'll be worse than usual."

There are some sports you take to naturally, instinctively. And others, where no matter how long and hard you try, you'll never top mediocre. As far as baseball went, I was doomed to stat-geek—memorizing batting averages, RBIs, and box scores and eating hot dogs.

Hank went first. Swinging loose and easy, taking ten pitches at a time, ramping up from 50 to 85 in 5 mph increments.

I watched him from outside the fence, fingers twined in the chain link, forehead on the cool steel.

Over and over, his shoulders bunched, body tensed as he hit launch position, the millisecond just before the bat began to move forward.

His swing was smooth, consistent, powerful. The stride and rotation of his hips, the ultimate mastery of repeatable motion. Each ball seemed to warp on his bat as he hit the sweet spot again and again.

I could have watched him all night.

"Your turn."

I entered the cage and took the bat. Hank set the articulated arm in motion at 45 mph and joined me. "Okay, Slugger. Eye on the ball."

I *ting*-ed the first one up into the ceiling netting. *Damn.*

It's all in the eyes. Almost all professional athletes have substantially better vision than the average population. They have a wider peripheral field, have better depth perception, can change focus faster, and have greater contrast sensitivity. Hank had the vision and the hand-eye coordination of a professional athlete.

Graced with the peepers of a mere mortal, I, however, whiffed and whiffed often. I choked up on the bat.

Hank said from behind the plate, "I want you to quit."

"Quit what?" I said and actually connected, knocking out a second-rate line drive.

"Everything."

I glanced back at him, then back to the pitching machine, just in time to *ting* the next pitch off the end of my bat into the ground three feet in front of me. "What?"

"Quit."

I swung and missed. "And do what?"

"Nothing."

What is he playing at?

I squared up my stance and took a good look at the machine. "Why?"

"Would a ring and a license help?"

Another ball whizzed past my shoulder. My mouth dropped open. The bat fell from my nerveless fingers as I spun to face him, stars in my eyes.

Oh my god, are you asking me to marry you?

"Doesn't matter either way," he said.

Huh?

He bolted at me, shot his hand out, and caught the ball zooming toward the back of my head with a *smack*.

I goggled at him.

"Situational awareness, Peaches." Hank tugged me by the front of my shirt across the plate.

"Thanks." I tried to blink the haze away. "Does it sting?"

"No." His mouth quirked up at the corner.

And as I looked up into the face of the man I loved beyond all reason, I realized he hadn't actually asked me to marry him. He'd asked if a ring and a license *would help*.

The fact that Hank would marry me to fulfill my need—that he didn't care one way or another—wasn't wonderful.

It was a baseball bat to the chest.

A ball smacked against the netting.

I needed him to *want* to marry me.

And he didn't.

I tucked my hair behind my ears. I was the only team member the BOC had in place with Stannislav Renko. And this was my shot. My chance to prove to my family, Hank, and most of all myself, that I had what it took to be a cop.

"Maisie?" Hank said.

I shook my head. "No. I don't think it'd help right now."

Hank drove us home to his house, completely unaffected by the shooting down of his potential marriage vow.

The pain of telling him "no," however, had turned my rib cage into a NuWave infrared oven, roasting my heart from the inside out.

We entered the house. "Drink?" he said. "Or Vanilla Swiss Almond?"

"Ice cream, definitely."

He got a fork, a spoon, and a tub of Häagen-Dazs. But instead of heading toward me and the couch, he disappeared down the hallway toward his bedroom. "C'mere."

I trotted after him into the bathroom. He started kissing me, backing me slowly into the cabinets. When I bumped up short, his hands slid to my waist and without stopping, set me up on the counter.

He broke away to hand me a fork—because the part I like best are the chocolate-covered almonds—and opened the ice cream.

In between bites and deliciously chilly kisses, I wound my legs around his hips. He slid my shirt up. I raised my arms and he tugged it over my head.

He undid my bra with one hand and eased it off. He ate another spoon of ice cream, twisting the spoon so it rested against the roof of his mouth, and bent his head to get a closer look at the stubborn monkey-blood dye that stained my skin. He set the spoon on the counter. "Is that . . . Mercurochrome?"

"Merthiolate," I said.

"They quit selling that in the States, Angel Face, about the time you were born."

"Oh?"

"Contains mercury."

Nifty. Naturally, the EPA cares more about a bluefin tuna than a Serbian.

"Who's the doc?" His mouth turned in a wry smile. "Not many prefer merthiolate over bacitracin."

Yeah. Tell me about it.

I tried to smile but couldn't. He was so close, I couldn't think . . .

"Cat got your tongue?" Hank growled into my ear before nipping the shell. "Maybe I'll just suck the name right out of your mouth."

Wow.

He kissed me then. Expertly, ruthlessly, and I thought I might drown. I wanted him to want me with the same aching desperation. "Hank—"

"Shhh." He laid a finger across my lips. "You're allowed a secret or two."

His pale, almost colorless eyes had gone steely and cold. The faintest hint of gray-blue washed to nothing. I tried to swallow and couldn't.

"It was painful," he said in a reassuring voice.

I cocked my head, face scrunched up in a squint.

Hank rasped his scruffy chin down my bare shoulder. Shivers cascaded down my spine. "He took a good long while to die."

Jeff Mant.

Chapter 24

I woke up at five o'clock. Just because Leticia transferred me to desk duty didn't mean my body knew it. Hank was already out of bed. I took a shower, taking extra time getting ready for work. I put on my uniform. I'd rather trash it than my street clothes in the Mold Central file room. Not to mention I'd be a constant reminder to Leticia of her lost quota, as well as a not-so-subtle irritation to the PEAs that I was still one of them.

Three hours before I had to be at work. And I had plenty to do with the time.

Like figure out how to fake-date Stannis while I really dated Hank.

I walked down the hall and heard him in his office, talking on the phone.

Opting for what military camouflage experts call "maximum disruptive contrast," I unbuttoned the top three buttons of my uniform shirt. Underneath I was wearing a La Perla robin's egg–blue lace push-up bra and matching hi-rise bikini panties. Courtesy of Hank, as I myself would not shell out three bills for any two pieces of underwear that didn't actively transform me into a size 00, big-breasted Playmate.

I lounged provocatively against the door frame to the office.

His voice was discordant and deep. "*Devushka beda. I beda ne prikhodit odna.*"

Beda was Russian for trouble. The only word I'd learned from our cleaning lady. Hank'd said it twice.

"*Da . . . khorosho.*" He hung up and winked at me. "C'mere, you."

"Russian, huh?" I sidled around the desk. "What I don't know about you could fill a Kindle."

"*Vy znayete vse, chto imeyet znacheniye, Persiki.*"

I hiked a hip onto the desk. "Enlighten?"

"You know everything that matters, Peaches," Hank translated. He put his hands on my thighs. "Sleep well?"

"Funny you should ask." I picked up the sugar-free Amp on his desk and took a sip. "I was having the most amazing dream about unicorns and candy mountains and . . . suddenly I was being mauled by a bear."

"Yeah?" His mouth quirked at the corner.

I grinned back. "Then it got really good."

He pushed my left leg wide, opened the desk drawer, and removed a black binder–clipped sheaf of papers and handed them to me.

"What's this?"

Hank smiled, teeth optic white against his morning shadow. I went light-headed at the sight. "Wilhelm."

Wilhelm was one of Hank's spoils of war. He'd found his butler chained up in a cellar during a cartel "cleaning" expedition in Colombia. Savaged by his imprisonment, Wilhelm had a pathological fear of human company. Hank was the only person he could bear.

And because Hank was cooler than liquid nitrogen at Ice Station Zebra, he gave Wilhelm the run of his property down to every last minute detail.

I'd never met him.

I flipped through ten pages of the single-spaced questionnaire. It started with food allergies, preferred vegetables, meats, styles of cuisine . . .

Jeez, I don't think this much about food even when I go out to dinner.

I paged through fill-in-the-blank personal preferences from soap to pens to makeup to political affiliations and sports teams. Investigative journalists had nothing on this guy.

It would take hours to fill it out.

Which meant . . . Hank was serious, in his own way.

My mouth went as dry as if I'd swallowed a handful of silica gel. I tipped my head and batted my eyelashes, trying to beat back the rising flood. *How exactly am I supposed to hide the fact that I'm an undercover cop from the dark horse love of my life?* "This is . . . wow."

"I don't want a housewife. I want you at hand."

The BOC needed me. And to operate, I needed alone time. But . . .

I tapped the questionnaire against my palm. "Hank, I—I need to go home."

"You live here," he said, pleasantly.

Yes and not exactly.

"Darlin'," I said, feeling my voice twang into the McGrane brothers' patented "let you down easy" Western drawl. "I need to make things right with Da. I had less than two days when you were in Honduras. And I couldn't think straight with Mant on the loose. I need to suck it up and see what I can salvage, for my family's sake."

"Okay." Hank shrugged. "One month."

"Huh?" *What the what?* "Wait—"

"One month to square things. Then you quit and live here."

The polar bear plunge had nothing on Hank.

He glanced at his watch. "Still early. Stella's Diner?" He jerked me forward to the edge of the desk. "Or a good morning mauling?"

I opted for maul.

My new Challenger Hellcat sure pissed off Chen. "You think you *Breaking Bad*, now, *Sanlu?* With your fancy muscle car?"

"I'm one hundred percent bad*ass*, Chen."

"Heh!" He spat out the window and hit the gate.

Another glorious day at the Traffic Enforcement Bureau.

I clocked in and trotted down to Leticia's office. Her door was closed. Muffled but raucous laughter came from inside. I knocked.

"C'mon in."

I opened the door. Leticia, squeezed into a blue mini-dress so tight it looked like a giant blood pressure cuff, sat behind her desk. Cozied up at one end was Stannis's head gorilla.

Uh-oh.

"Good morning?" I said cautiously.

"And a damn fine one it is, too, McGrane. Sit your lily white onion down." She gestured toward me with a croissant. "Told you, Renko. Kid's always early."

Stannis stepped from behind the door, closing it behind me. "Good morning, *mali anđeo.*" He kissed my cheek.

Wow. So not equipped to see you here this morning.

"Come." We took the two seats opposite Leticia and Gorilla.

The three of them were eating chocolate croissants on thick white napkins and drinking coffee out of white cardboard cups with the distinctive dark brown and gold logo of HendrickX Belgian Bread Crafter.

Stannis handed me a cup.

"Oh no—" Before I could say I didn't drink coffee, he said, "Is chocolate."

I took the cup, flattered and uneasy at the same time. "Thank you."

"See? I told you." Leticia gave a flirtatious shimmy to Gorilla. "Girl don't drink coffee." She waved an airbrushed rainbow nail in an S shape at me. "Show the man your brekkie, McGrane."

Stannis set his cup down on the end table. I pulled a Quest protein bar from my cargo pants pocket and handed it to him. He turned it over in his hands. "This?"

"Yes."

He opened the wrapper and took a bite. At the second chew he snapped his fingers. Gorilla picked up Leticia's trash can and held it in front of him. To Leticia's whoop of delight, Stannis spat the mouthful into the can. The rest of the bar followed. "No. This for animal."

Funny, I thought I was your new puppy.

"Go on, now." Leticia folded her arms beneath her breasts, giving Gorilla an eye-popping view. "I'm waitin'."

"A woman in love does many things she say she will never do." Stannis raised his chocolate-cherry croissant to my mouth.

Aww. Puppy gets a treat.

I took a bite. It was, as I knew from experience, decadently delicious. Bready and dark with a tang of cherry. It was almost impossible not to inhale the rest of it out of his hand.

Great. Now I'll dream about these for a month.

Leticia grunted in disgust. "You got it bad, kid."

Stannis handed me a croissant and a napkin. Then he took two tickets to the Oriental Theatre out of his suit coat pocket and set them on the desk.

"No way, no how. A bet's a bet." Leticia fanned herself with a napkin. "Can't take that."

"But you win two. I win only one." Stannis looked askance at me. "No opera for her."

"Now that, I believe. McGrane wouldn't know music if it crawled up her shoulder and spat in her ear." The tickets disappeared into the top drawer of her desk.

"You are desirable woman, Miss Jackson," Stannis said. "You know love, yes?"

She leaned back in her chair, cast the Gorilla with an appraising once-over before half-closing her brown eyes in suspicion. "I've known some fine men."

"I am not always in your country. I want Maisie all times when I am here." He gave her a 150-watt smile.

Leticia nodded slowly, sucking in her cheeks. "You after vacay for McGrane."

Oh no. No. We absolutely do not want that.

My brain felt like ice in a blender. If Stannis cut me from the herd of daily life, how could I report to the BOC, keep the parking enforcement agent evidence-gathering program going, and most importantly, maintain my cover story for Hank and the clan?

"I don't have any vacation time," I chirped up.

"No. You don't." Leticia carefully repositioned Rush Limbaugh's photograph on the corner of her desk. "You been shining me on all morning, Renko. And thass just a hundred kinds of wrong."

"No." Stannis gestured to me, rotated his fingers. "What is for not pay?"

"Unpaid leave of absence?" I said hoarsely.

"Yes." Stannis straightened the crease on his suit pants. "That."

A dark chortle burst from Leticia's bright red lips. "You're outta your goddamn mind."

Gorilla reached over and put his hand over hers. "Miss Jackson, is far better to be friend of Mr. Renko than enemy."

Leticia yanked her hand away. "Hands off the merchandise."

Gorilla showed his hands, leaned back, and undid the button of his suit coat. It fell open, exposing the butt of the handgun in his shoulder holster.

"What the hell, McGrane?" Leticia scooted her desk chair forward and gestured at the men with her left hand. "Runnin' with these jaw-jappin' mofos." With her right, she pulled her own piece from beneath her seat in one well-practiced motion. She pointed the S&W .38 Special at Stannis's chest.

"You surprise me, Miss Jackson." His eyes crinkled in delight. "Lady John Wayne."

"I'm goddamn Dirty Harriet, boy."

Stannis was unperturbed. "Ivanović is bodyguard. Has conceal carry permit. You, I think, do not."

That's right, Stannis. Let's see if you can get her to pull the trigger.

Leticia's head and shoulders began a slow cobra sway. "You in my office, askin' a favor by threatening me?"

"No. That choice you make." Stannis's promise was as crude as pig iron.

Her hand trembled ever so slightly.

Shite. "Leticia?" I said, giving her an almost-imperceptible head shake and an out. "I'm sure Stannis has no idea what he's asking."

"You think I click my heels and she's on unpaid leave?" She

sniffed and set the gun down. "Hell no. Girl needs doctor's agreement and TEB authorization."

Gorilla removed a paper from his jacket and set it in front of Leticia. "Medical excuse."

Ouch. They came prepared.

"Best of luck with the authorization. Ain't no way, no how that's ever gonna happen. Kid's on office duty because she booted the mayor's car. Shit rolls downhill, my friend."

Stannis was on his phone before she even finished. "Call Talbott," he commanded his iPhone. He moved around behind my chair, leaned down, and put the phone between our ears.

Leticia's eyes narrowed. She couldn't hear it, but she trusted me.

A buzz, then, "Mayor Coles's office. How may I help you?"

"Stannislav Renko."

The polite voice stiffened into immediate deference. "One moment please, sir."

"Stannis!" Talbott Cottle Coles's voice boomed through the phone. "What an unexpected surprise."

"Are you alone?" Stannis said.

"No. Hang on." The muffled sound of a hand over the receiver, followed by Coles's shout, "All of you, get the fuck outta my office. Yesterday!" Commotion. Then, in an oozing throb, he was back on. "Hey there, guy."

"I need favor."

"Name it."

"I was getting parking tick—"

"Those fucking meter maids! I swear to Christ—Just have one of your boys drop it off at City Hall."

"No." Stannis's mouth tipped in a clever smirk. "I call because I'm getting ticket and woman in uniform stops the ticket. You know why?"

Coles laughed. "Absolutely not."

"She knows my car from outside City Hall."

"It's not there as often as I'd like it," Coles said.

I gave a slight shudder.

"The midnight blue, she says." Stannis tipped his head against mine. "You are right. Is more distinctive than black."

"Goes better with your eyes, too."

Oh, for puke's sake!

I had no beef with Stannis's lifestyle. Just who he was life-styling it with—the Slime King of Corruption.

"So," Coles said, "what kind of favor would you like?"

Stannis ignored the flirt. "Letter for woman and supervisor. To show you appreciate public worker using mind."

"Sure, whatever you want. Are we still on for tonight? Atlantis at eleven o'clock?"

"Yes."

"Great. I'll send you back to Julie. She'll type up whatever you like."

"But letters are from you."

"Julie signs my name better than I do." Coles laughed. "Tonight. Can't wait."

Stannis stood up, hit speaker on his phone, and dictated two letters to Julie with assistance from Leticia. One for supervisory excellence for her file and an open-ended extended-leave letter for mine. They would be delivered to the TEB within the hour.

It's official.

The pooch was 100 percent screwed every which way to Sunday.

"Your keys?" Stannis asked. I gave him the Hellcat's black key fob. He tossed it to Gorilla. "Bring car to penthouse. No damage," he warned.

Gorilla shot Leticia a lusty ogle that she wasn't too offended to preen under. "May I call you?" he asked.

"You can try."

Gorilla left. I got up and stood next to Stannis.

Leticia's lip raised. "McGrane still needs to come in once a week."

Stannis weighed that over. "As favor?"

"Only if you wanna keep it all good to the gracious."

Stannis held out his hand. "I do." She shook it.

As we left the office, I paused at the door. "Hey, Chen called me *Sanlu* this morning."

Leticia snort-coughed.

"What is it?"

"Tainted milk." She slapped the table and chortled. "Damn, that's a good one."

Stannis frowned. "Who is this Chen?"

I laid a hand on his chest. "No one. It's a joke."

He pulled me in for a hug. "Come," Stannis said against my hair. "We go buy you pretty dress."

Chapter 25

Shopping with Stannis was more fun than I ever thought possible. We hit the Magnificent Mile on Michigan Avenue. He dropped a positively indecent sum on me at Gucci and Max Mara before having his driver take us to Blake.

His aesthetic was second only to his charisma.

But as I came out in the stellar dress he insisted I try on, his face was pinched, attention drifting. Something was bothering him and it wasn't the money.

With five older brothers, I recognized the symptoms immediately. Too much time had passed since the croissant carb overload.

A man with low blood sugar is as useless as dehydrated water.

I dialed Mom's office in the dressing room. It took less than a minute for her assistant, Anna Suchowian, to get us in at Anthony Martin's Tru for lunch. The Scottish salmon with winter radish and chive sauce was beyond exquisite. I could tell by the glow of Stannis's electric blue eyes he was pleased by my choice.

"This morning, I make you unhappy," he said. "But now you work for me."

"Yes." I laid my knife and fork across my plate. "About that. You need to let me keep my job, Stannis. Half of my family are cops. The other half are attorneys."

"Is no trouble. I am clean. In America. In Europe."

"Well, it's trouble for me. They don't like Eddie V. And they really don't like Coles."

"Maisie. Do not have concern." Stannis sat back in his chair and rested his elbow off the back. "The McGranes. They will like me."

Jaysus, Mary, and Joseph. They'll take to you like a Clinton to a congressional hearing.

I turned the conversation to old movies, and we took our time savoring dark Valrhona chocolates for dessert. When we finished, the hostess approached our table and asked if we cared to have our picture taken.

"Yes." Stannis slid over in the booth and put his arm around me. We smiled on cue.

"May I have your names?" she asked. "We print one for you here and post to Facebook."

"Stannislav Renko and Maisie McGrane," he answered.

Super. My brothers were gonna be on this faster than a pod of orcas on a bloody seal.

Well, I'll cross that rotting indigenous rain forest rope bridge when I come to it.

"Miss?" Stannis said. "You take one more, please?"

"Certainly." The hostess beamed, camera at the ready.

Stannis caught me by the chin and put his mouth to mine. The digital whir of the photo hummed. "This one," he said with a wink, "is better, I think."

Aww. Shoot.

Riding up in the elevator to Stannis's penthouse, I slipped my arm through his. "You look tired, Stannis."

"Yes." He waited for me to enter the foyer. We crossed into the great room. "I am weary." He blew out a heavy breath and moved his palms a few inches apart. "What is the short sleep?"

"Nap?"

"Yes. Come. Nap with me."

The physicality between us was as easy as it was between me and my brothers.

I followed him into his bedroom, a jaw-dropping masculine room of ebony wood and charcoal accented in army green. The bed, a king, was covered in a dark linen duvet cover and mounded with pillows. Stannis pointed at the left side. "Always, I sleep near to door."

I slipped off my new heels and climbed onto the right side of the bed. I reclined against the pillows. Stannis bounced down on the bed next to me. He threw an arm high over my rib cage and laid his dark head on my lower abdomen. "You see inside me like I am man of glass." He let out a heavy breath. "My heart is hot with anger."

Angry? Within the last eight hours, he'd scared the iridescent panties off Leticia, got me unlimited unpaid leave, dropped ten grand on clothes, and had a stellar meal. The very last emotion I'd have considered was anger. I reached down and very gently put my hand on his head. He nestled into me and I stroked his hair. He gave a quiet groan of pleasure.

I traced my fingers over his skull and the nape of his neck, feeling his muscles slacken. "Why are you angry?"

"Your nails too short. I fix tomorrow." He sighed. "*Chyornyj yastreb* ended what was not meant to be stopped."

"Cheeronee yah-streb?" I said. "What's that?"

Stannis chuckled. "*Chyornyj yastreb* is Black Hawk. Russian. Goran Slajic chooses him for operation. But now *Chyornyj yastreb* is friend. Good friend."

I traced a line around his ear. *A new player. Did the BOC know?* "What did he stop?"

"Me." He put his hand over mine, pressing it to his cheek. "But now I have you, *mali anđeo*. My angel. So, perhaps the devil does not deserve my anger at Black Hawk."

"Perhaps not," I said, smiling. He let go of my hand and I smoothed the lines on his forehead, waiting.

"I was born with the veil, yes?"

Born with the amniotic membrane intact. "Sure."

"A sign of bad magic in my village." He gave a bark of bitter laughter. "Perhaps true. Sandžaklije filth murder our parents. My sister and me, we are alone. Is difficult.

"A year later, the Sandžaklije return for my sister." His voice grew hard. "The men on the farm . . . They could have saved her. Kill the Muslim filth. Yet, they are cowards. They do nothing."

"Oh, Stannis. I'm so sorry."

"She fight very hard." He shook his head against my stomach. "Her blood is on all things."

A bubble of a sob rose in my throat.

"Head severed. The Sandžaklije leave bayonet between her legs."

Sweet Jesus. The evil of this world . . .

"Later . . . I take bayonet." Stannis stilled for a long moment. "Barefoot, wearing blanket, I go to farm. But I am boy. I know these men. Is no good. They will kill me before I can kill more than one. They are laughing and drinking, searching for courage to sleep as they had none to fight the Sandžaklije for my sister."

Tears tracked down my cheeks and dripped onto my collarbone.

"Superstitious peasants." He gave a harsh bark of laughter. "I see the great bull sleeping in field. And I know what I must do. I throw blanket over the beast's head. Cut its throat. I open its belly, take innards out, and climb inside. The men find me with the sunrise. I am reborn from the bull. Baptized in the devil's blood. And my sister is with me."

He sounded so victorious it broke my heart.

"The men fear me and call me *Bik*. The Bull. They did not yet know I will come for them one by one. Next I kill the Sandžaklije. I take very special time with each."

And who could blame you?

Hank's Law Number Eighteen: Even savage actions have explanations.

He leaned back, looked up at me, and frowned. "Do not cry, *mali anđeo*."

"But—"

"No." He reached up and brushed my wet cheek with his knuckles. "Each life has a path. Uncle Goran hears I am Bik. He brings me to his world, makes me important man."

"Is that what they call you? *Bik?* The Bull?"

"No." He yawned and nestled his arm under my body, hugging me to him. "Not since I was boy. As man, I am called *mesar*. The Butcher. Is not elegant but is truth."

*   *   *

I lay with his head on my lap for a solid ten minutes. Trying without success not to let the horror of his life sink as far into my heart as it had into my brain. Eventually, Stannis rolled off me and onto his stomach. His back rose and fell. Steady, even.

If I didn't go now, I knew I'd never find the courage.

I felt slimy and traitorous just thinking about it.

I slid off the bed and tucked a chenille throw around him. He didn't move.

Time to strike.

I got the document scanner pen out of my purse and stuck it down my bra. On tiptoe, I made my way to his office. At the doorway, I clicked the watch button three times and waited. The display lit up. Basic Wi-Fi signal, no devices transmitting from inside.

Don't look at the aquarium. Jaysus Criminey, don't look, don't look . . .

I went straight to the desk, pulling the scanner from my bra. A thin pile of papers lay atop it. Invoices from the CEC Intermodal Transport Company. Commercial descriptions of goods, quantities and estimated worth. Weight and lading bills. Shipment and container numbers.

Holy cat. Talk about taking candy from the devil's reborn baby . . .

My fingers were frozen, numb as I tried to activate the document scanner. Adrenaline overload messing with my fine motor functions.

Come on, Maisie. Put your Donnie Brasco pants on and do this.

I slid the top paper off, copied it, and hit the next one. My ears pulsed with Stannis's voice, *"The Butcher. The Butcher. The Butcher."* I scanned the next and the next.

Halfway through the pile I got the yips.

Bad.

Hank's Law Number Twenty-Four: Never ever ignore your gut.

I replaced the papers exactly as they were and slipped the document pen back down my dress.

"Maisie? *Mali andeo?*" Stannis called from the hallway.

Cripes.

I stepped away from the desk and popped into the armchair nearest the aquarium, tucking my feet up beneath me.

"Maisie?" Stannis padded into the room on bare feet. He flipped on the dim recessed lighting over the fireplace, a confused smile on his face. "Why are you here?"

"I wanted to . . . see." I dropped my face in my hands. "But then, I just couldn't."

Stannis walked over and dropped to one knee. He peeled one hand from my face and clasped it in his. "Is good. Curiosity feeds cat, yes?" He pressed his lips to my knuckles. "Mmm. Cold fingers." He smiled and tugged me to my feet. "Do not fear."

We walked to the granite plinth holding the darkened glass cage. He leaned forward and hesitated. "Is different inside now. Yes?"

The beetles have cleaned Raw Chicken's finger up shiny and new? I raised my shoulders in accord.

"Black Hawk stopped me but not at first. You know this. Yes?"

I nodded, having no idea what he was talking about and not really wanting to know.

Stannis flipped the light.

My free hand flew to my mouth.

In the case were six fingers, five far fresher than the driver's. But it was the fingerless man's hand, severed at the wrist, that had me biting the insides of my cheeks to keep from screaming.

Chapter 26

Stannis and I spent the early evening playing backgammon and watching *The Quiet Man*. "The Butcher" liked John Wayne and cuddling, which was especially disconcerting, as I couldn't stop thinking about the hand in the aquarium.

"I go out tonight," he said.

"Yes." To Atlantis for another strip club rendezvous with Coles. "I should go home."

"I call driver?" His eyes searched mine.

I gave him a big smile I didn't feel in the slightest. "Yeah. It's copacetic."

The driver, Raw Chicken, was no less repellent. But at least his skeevie glare had been replaced with a perma-frown.

When we arrived home, the Dodge Hellcat was parked on the street in front of my house.

The sickest, coolest muscle car ever.

Hank.

Six-feet-three-inches of steel and sex appeal ready to marry me, and yet, I spend the day with a guy into carrion beetles and severed fingers.

Because I'm a selfish idiot.

I wanted it all, everything, wrapped up in brown paper and tied with string. For Hank to love me as fiercely and desperately as I loved him. And a place at the Table Club.

Raw Chicken pulled up next to the Dodge, hit the hazards, got out, and opened the door for me. I stepped out and he held out his gloved hand, the key on his palm. I took it, pretending I didn't notice the little finger of his glove was empty, and walked slowly up the drive to the gate.

Thankfully, he saw no need to wait. The Range Rover receded into the night, and I turned around and trotted back down the driveway, got in the car, and sped to Silverthorn Estates.

I pulled into a visitor's spot, collected my gear, and went in to see who was around to debrief me. Anita met me at the elevators. "Looking sharp, Rook. What gives?"

"Thanks." I was still wearing the exquisite black Gucci dress and heels Stannis had bought me that morning. "Walt, Danny, or Edward around?"

"Sawyer's out." Anita jerked her head down the hall. "Kaplan and Dunne are in the dining room."

I found them in the empty room in the corner, whiskies at the elbow, papers and laptops covering the table. "Me-oh-my, look at this fine bit o' stuff." Edward stood up, hands out. "Hullo, Maisie, me gel." I put my hands in his and he kissed me on each cheek. "To what do we owe this unexpected pleasure?"

"Debrief?"

"Take a seat, McGrane," Kaplan said.

I took a seat in the club chair between them and took the document scanner pen from my purse and handed it to her. She plugged it into her laptop and pushed it slightly away from her so both Edward and I could see the screen.

"Where did you get these?" Kaplan scrolled through the invoices and bills of lading.

"From the desk in his office."

Ever the skeptic, Kaplan gave me a bitter smile. "Renko just let you in?"

"He fell asleep. I took the chance."

"And won the lottery." Edward whistled, reading the screen over the tops of his glasses. "The lad's brazen, I'll give him that. Christmas came early, Danny. A paper trail." He grinned and held out his hand. "Give it over."

Kaplan removed the scanner and handed it to Edward, who plugged it in and downloaded the contents.

"Ready for a lesson in shipping?"

"You bet," I said.

"Trains move billions of tons of freight annually. Every possible thing you can think of is shipped by rail." He waggled his brows and pulled up an invoice from ShipCEC. "This is a service schedule, representing the CEC portion of the trip."

He pointed to the screen. "CEC is an intermodal transport company. Intermodal freight containers are the lifeblood of business. They're the same cars on trains, which are then pulled by semitrucks. You want to sell car parts, you need to ship them across the country. Using only semitrucks, the cost would be so exorbitant, you'd be out of business before your parts arrived at their destination. Instead, you load your container at the warehouse and have a semi transport it the short distance to CEC."

I nodded, listening hard.

Edward continued, "At CEC, a crane picks up the container or your semi's entire trailer—wheels and all—and loads it onto a railroad car. A few days later, it arrives at the destination, where another crane takes the freight container off the train and puts it on your other semi, which transports it the short distance to the freight's final destination." He clasped his hands across his stomach.

Kaplan nodded. "The system works just as well for criminals transporting stolen goods. With so many cars, only the smallest fraction are ever inspected. And of that fraction, even fewer have a reason to be checked." She brought up a bill of lading on her computer. "Renko is using standard transmodal shipping containers."

"Those are twenty feet long, eight and a half feet wide and high," Edward said. "The space per load is twelve hundred cubic feet and could weigh fifty-five thousand pounds. So, lass, how are you as a single inspector going to check the freight of even a single car in one day?"

"It's impossible," I said. "The containers have only one opening, so you'd have to unpack the entire thing. For one person to unload even a fifth of the car—"

Edward tapped the side of his nose. "Exactly. So a smart chancer would . . ."

"Pack a false front." I drummed my fingers on the table. "Load the first two or three feet with what you said you were shipping and then fill the rest with whatever you wanted."

"Precisely." Danny nodded. "If the load was inspected, the odds of even the most dedicated inspector going deeper than three feet would be nonexistent."

"The railroads have crack teams of bomb and drug dogs, as well as thermal detectors." Edward raised his glass and took a sip. "But for stolen goods? Without a tip-off from law enforcement, it's a drop of water in the whiskey."

"But what about CEC or the other intermodal companies?" I asked.

"Any monkey with a computer can open an account. All they have to do is pay the transport and arrange for container drop-off and pickup." Kaplan clicked onto a separate ShipCEC invoice. "Renko's upcoming shipment."

Edward opened the same document and turned his laptop to me. "Five cars, carrying ten twenty-foot containers."

I pointed at a code to the left. "What is q300?"

"A sly dog, our Renko." Edward chuckled. "That's the freight code for slow ship. Kind of like the bulk rate at the post office. Low insurance rates. Even lower inspection rate."

"And that number there?" I asked.

"STCC: 8066602," Edward read aloud. "That's code for *Company Material-Misc. Car Parts*. It means scrap metal."

"The simplicity of it is pure cunning," Kaplan said. "Why, even if he didn't preload it with scrap, all the inspector will see are chopped car parts."

"Cocksure, as well, this one. Do you see"—Edward tapped at a coding on the bottom of the bill—"he's insured his five cars are locked. Traveling together in a 'five packer.' Taking no chance that one load of his freight ends up somewhere else."

"Makes sense," I said. "Pay a little extra for the assurance you'll be treated better."

"And that'll be his fall from grace, me gels." Edward rubbed his hands together. "I've the perfect plan."

"Not so fast," Kaplan said. "There is a very real possibility The Bull is setting her up."

Hardly. He'd seen me half-naked, took me shopping, showed me his legacy, messed up my meter maid cover, and is a massive cuddler.

Instead I said, "The nickname 'The Bull' is from his child-hood. They call him *mesar* now."

"Oh?" Danny said. "*Mesar?*"

It took a lot to keep the smirk from my mouth. "The Butcher."

"Lamb of the Lord Jesus. I don't care for that. Not a wee bit." Edward slipped his hands in his cardigan pockets. "Sawyer needs to know."

Kaplan gave him an impatient wave. "If this is legitimate, and that's a very big 'if,' this is the best intel we've had to date." Her bony fingers flew across the laptop's keys. "From a cursory glance, Renko's running a shell game with the company owner-ship, but it's been properly recorded."

"Exposing his operation? For a test?" Edward snorted and shook his head. "May the cat eat you, and the devil eat the cat. The ten trailers he's shipping to Newark are chopped parts." He collected his papers and laptop. "Well, I'm off to track down Walt. According to this, Renko's containers begin their journey tomorrow."

Edward gave a pleasant good night and left the dining room. Kaplan and I were alone.

"What happened to the boy from the hospital?" I asked. "The kid with no fingers on his left hand who was an eyewitness to two murders?"

"WITSEC." Danny rolled her eyes. "Again, not your con-cern."

"Why? We could have arrested two murderers."

"Frankly, McGrane, I find your naïveté tiresome." She closed her laptop. "Aside from the fact that they're killing thieves and other killers, we can close those murder cases whenever we wish.

Special Unit's priority is and will always be Operation Steal-Tow. We cannot afford to jeopardize our objectives."

I'd had my fill of runaround. "Which are?"

"To cripple Goran Slajic's chop-shop operation, to remove as many of Don Constantino's men as possible, and lastly and per- haps most importantly, to stop Renko from starting a small arms trading empire in Chicago." She pulled a pile of folders in front of her and opened one. "Your direct orders are to uncover and relay the maximum amount of information possible."

I smoothed a wrinkle from the skirt of my dress. "Are you going to stop the train cars?"

"We'll see."

Are you feckin' kidding me, lady?

She glanced at my face. "If you know, you'll show." Her lips split in a frosty smile. "The idea of working undercover is to re- main seamless in the face of surprise."

Chapter 27

I dreamed of trains and dead bodies until 6:15 a.m. I dressed in an Akris punto lace, snap-front shirtdress, with ankle boots. Conservative and very feminine, it showed only the tiniest fraction of my almost-healed devil's paper cut. I put on Stannis's Cartier earrings and went downstairs.

Frank Sinatra's "Brazil" blared through the kitchen speakers. Thierry rumba-ed his way around the kitchen island while Mom, perched at a bar stool in the kitchen, tapped her pen in time to the music while poring over a stack of legal docs. Flynn and Rory sat on either side of her devouring poached eggs, English muffins, and bacon.

Rory saw me first. "What the hell are yeh wearin', Snap?"

"Good morning, honey." Mom threw him an elbow. "You look very . . . feminine."

He snorted. "Stepford Wives on the cover of *Vogue* this month?"

"Summer Wind" came on. Thierry swept over and took my hand. "What would you like?"

"Green tea."

He danced me over to the Keurig machine, reached over and spun the cartridge holder. Laughing, I let go and got out a cup from the cupboard.

"And to eat?" Thierry pressed.

"Zip. Breakfast date," I fibbed. Stannis's driver was going to pick me up on the hour and my guts were too knotted up to eat.

"Oh?" Mom asked, all innocence. "I haven't seen Hank since the night you gave him the bum's rush in the middle of dinner. Perhaps I'll go late to the office."

"Uh . . ."

"You'll have a helluva wait, Mom." Flynn folded his arms across his chest. "Her brekkie date is with some Serbian named Stannislav Renko."

Uh-oh.

I took my tea and the stool next to Rory at the enormous granite bar that ringed the kitchen. *Sometimes the best defense is the truth.* "Exactly right, Flynn."

"What'd you tell the roughneck? You're perfect in every way, just not for me?"

"Cute," I said. "Hank and I are still together."

Rory gave a bark of laughter and flipped his dark hair out of his eyes. "Poor bastard ain't seen this yet, eh?" He flashed his iPhone at all of us, the picture of Stannis kissing me on the mouth at Tru full-screen.

Fecking Facebook.

I leaned back on the stool and threw my arm behind my head in a pinup pose. "Any press is good press, baby."

"Maisie?" Mom asked.

"A mistimed photo of a European greeting."

Mom cocked a brow and dropped her bomb. "The online snaps of you at The Storkling on ChicagoMag belie a certain sense of intimacy."

Flynn and Rory started typing and swiping on their phones to see what they'd missed.

Lovely.

"And what on earth possessed you to wear that disaster of a dress to The Storkling?" Mom dropped her chin and shrugged. "A shock they put you online in that awful rag."

"Gee, thanks, Mom. You bought it for me."

"Hmm." She tapped the pen against her mouth in mock thought. "I'm afraid I don't recall . . ."

"Jaysus." Rory held his phone out to me. On ChicagoMag

was a picture of me, Stannis, and Eddie Veteratti. "Is that feckin' Eddie V.?"

"He owns the club," I pointed out.

Flynn dragged a hand over his face and said to Mom, "I know the year's been shite for the kid, but don't you think it's time for ROP?"

Restriction of privileges.

You have got to be kidding me.

Mom sighed and rolled her eyes heavenward. "Flynn, dear. Consider this—if you were to marry and have a child of your own, you could ROP at will."

Rory laugh-gagged on his mouthful of orange juice.

The *Predator* theme played on my phone. *Hank.* "I need to take this." I shot out of the kitchen into the hallway. "Hello?"

"Hey, Sugar Pop."

Stay cool. "It's so good to hear your voice." *Aig. Not cool at all.*

"Yours, too."

Love-haze fragged the connection between my brain and mouth. "I miss you, Hank."

Nice. Lovelorn and lame at the same time.

"I'm out of reach for the next forty-eight."

"Oh. Okay."

"Call the office if you need anything. Stay safe." He disconnected.

I banged my forehead against the wall.

I'd have an easier time finding a frozen Coke in the sands of Death Valley than an ounce of cool for Hank.

Pasting on a happy face, I went back into the kitchen. The music was off and all the boys were gone. Mom's files were closed up and she was sitting at the table, her hands clasped loosely together. "I think it's time for a little 'Come to Jesus,' baby."

Terrific.

I slid into a chair next to her. "What's up?"

"Tell me about Mr. Renko."

I blew out a breath. I'd left my tea on the counter. The lack of caffeine had my brain rattling in my skull like a BB in a boxcar. "He's a friend. A very good friend."

"How did you meet?"

"He, um . . ." I rubbed my forehead. "Some mutt was hassling me on my route and Stannis helped me."

"A felony assault and you didn't report it?"

I opened my mouth to argue, but it was pointless.

Mom reached over and tapped the top of Jeff Mant's handiwork. "You really think you did the right thing not reporting that?"

Whew.

I sat up straighter to prevent my shoulders from sagging in relief. "That mutt won't be bothering anyone anytime soon."

Wrong answer.

The corner of her mouth turned up in dissent. "While I'm sure you have your reasons, not pressing charges was ill-advised, irresponsible, and frankly, disappointing."

I sighed. "Until you walk a day in my parking enforcement agent boots—"

"About that," she said, "awfully dressed up and late for work today."

Aiiigh. "I'm taking a personal day."

"To spend with Mr. Renko? What does Hank think of him?"

I raised my palms. "They haven't met yet."

There was a knock at the door.

Saved by the non-doorbell user.

"Invite Mr. Renko in, please."

"That's his driver, Mom. I gotta go." I gave her a hug, then grabbed my purse off the counter in the back hall and opened the door to the waiting Mr. Raw Chicken. I slipped past him and down the stairs to the driveway.

I could feel Mom watching me from the window. Refusing to look back, I waited at the car for him to open and close it for me.

Inside, I sank into the deep leather seat, feeling like I'd just been strafed by a fleet of Luftwaffe Stukas.

Must. Have. Sugar-free. Amp.

"Hey," I said as we neared Stannis's penthouse. "Stop at the Circle K."

Raw Chicken glared at me, but did as he was told.

A girl could get used to ordering people around.

He pulled up next to the air machines, the nose of the car pointing at the street, tail at the open alley. Raw Chicken was welltrained.

And because he still really gave me the creeps, I let him get out and open my door.

My heels clicked smartly across the cement as I passed the gas pumps and entered the convenience store. I made a beeline for the refrigerated glass wall and walked the walk of the eternally hopeful.

Hopeful they carried it. Hopeful it was in stock. Hopeful it was cold.

And the gods and the angels smiled down upon me and said, "Let there be sugar-free Amp!"

I cleaned out the row. By the time I got to the checkout, my arms were shivering from the nine frosty cans. I virtuously resisted the siren's call of a sleeve of powdered-sugar Donettes, swiped my credit card, and replied, "Yes, I'd like a bag," to the semiliterate, e-cig–smoking lottery ticket seller who believed a single plastic bag thinner than a fly's wing would sufficiently transport 144 ounces of liquid gold.

I clutched the bag to my chest, weaving my way out of the crowded store's glass doors.

A minivan full of children didn't have time to let me cross and pulled in front of the pumps.

Patience, Maisie.

I trotted on the toes of my Weitzman booties toward the Range Rover, stutter-stepping around an oil puddle.

Bits of concrete leapt up and stung my ankle.

A split second later the sound.

Rifle shot.

Dropping the bag I threw myself behind an old Mercury. Gravel shredded my palms. Blood thundered in my ears so loudly,

I couldn't hear the cans of Amp clattering and rolling across the parking lot.

"Get down!" I shouted at the full parking lot. "Gun! Everybody down on the ground!"

Everyone froze and looked at me blankly.

The first reaction to evil is confusion.

A bullet nailed the bumper of the Mercury. Followed again by the echo of the gunshot.

Idiots. "Police! Everyone get down!"

That seemed to work. Everyone moved. A little, at least.

Raw Chicken pulled the SUV up tight to the back end of the Mercury. He reached back and swung the rear door open. I crab-ran to the car, managing to snag an energy drink as I threw myself into the back of the car.

"Get down!" he shouted.

I hit the floor as he backed down the alleyway, tires squealing, and whipped a reverse U at the next block. He took a one-way the wrong way before peeling onto Lake Street. He drove us in a figure eight for the next ten minutes.

Holy cat. What the hell was that?

There was only one person I knew of who wanted to kill me. And Hank had neutralized him.

Right?

"You are unhurt?" the driver asked gruffly.

"Yeah." My hands stung and my shoes were thrashed. *Dammit.* I popped the top of the Amp and took a heavy swallow. The carbonation burned my throat and nose, but it felt good in a "glad to be alive" sort of way.

Confident we weren't being followed, Raw Chicken pulled over and called Stannis. "She is unhurt. Shot at, but unhurt."

I couldn't hear Stannis's reply, nor did I want to. *Jaysus Criminey.*

"Rifle. Two hundred, two hundred fifty meters. No silencer." Raw Chicken switched to Serbian. He said a few more things, then listened for a long while. "Yes, sir. My life."

Chapter 28

Stannis was waiting in front of the penthouse with a man a few years younger and a few inches taller than him. Swarthy, with a buzz cut, deep-chested with wide shoulders and a military bearing. He held a suit bag by the hanger.

Stannis opened the rear door of the Range Rover himself and climbed in the car. "Maisie, you are unhurt, yes?" He took my hands.

I sucked in my breath as I jerked them from his. "Scraped."

He cupped my face in his hands and leaned in close. His blue eyes burned into mine. "I will kill who fired at you."

The muscular man with the suit bag got into the front passenger seat.

"Who's this?" I asked.

"He is Kontrolyor."

"I beg your pardon?"

"Is Russian nickname." The man twisted in his seat to smile at me. "Ticket Checker. I am the one that comes at the end. To make sure everyone is dead." He pointed his fingers in the shape of a gun and pointed at the ground. "*Bap. Bap.*"

"Ticket Checker." I smiled, a little stiffly, but a smile all the same. "How about Kon for short?"

He looked at Stannis, who nodded, before grinning at me. "Kon is good."

Raw Chicken pulled up in front of the Ritz-Carlton. Kon got

out, opened my door, and escorted me around the end of the car to the sidewalk.

"Shall we?" Stannis offered his arm, I took it, and we entered the hotel. Kon followed with the suit bag.

Too wound up over the shooting, I hadn't paid more than the vaguest attention to where we were going. Counting down the seconds until I could run to the restroom and call Hank, I assumed we were there for a meet.

I couldn't have been more wrong.

"Welcome to the Spa at the Ritz-Carlton," said a woman in a black jacket with a gold name tag. "Mr. Renko, Ms. McGrane, we're so pleased you've chosen to spend your day with us."

Kon handed the attendant the suit bag and took a seat in the lobby.

We started with side-by-side pedicures. Bourbon scrub and vinotherapy, respectively. Stannis selected a fire engine red for my toes. Exactly the color I would have chosen myself. It was an unusual and interesting feeling—being "kept."

In a sick Scientologist sort of way, I could see how pleasant it was to release all autonomy and make no decisions.

Sheepy was a surprisingly comfortable state of being.

"I am very sorry for what occurred this morning," Stannis said in a low voice.

"It's not your fault." My words were automatic, but the thought behind them wasn't. *If Hank said Mant was dead, he was dead. But what if Mant had someone working for him?*

Stannis squeezed my hand. "This was to be a happy day for you. For us."

"A good scare reminds you that you are alive." I squeezed back. "And a spa day is always a happy day."

We chatted about music, eerily matching up on everything from LCD Soundsystem to Chet Baker. The more I knew him, the more I liked him.

The attendants quietly asked us to follow them to the manicure tables. I sat while Stannis confirmed the length of my new gel nails and selected a traditional French tip polish.

A private sanctuary, serene and seductive. There was no chance to leave a message for Hank between collagen masks and a bamboo and black sesame body scrub.

By the time we were escorted into the couples massage room, lit in low amber light, the shooting had taken on an ethereal, surreal quality. The clean scent of eucalyptus eased the pressure I hadn't realized I had in my sinuses.

I slipped out of my terry robe first, Stannis politely turning his back while I slid between the crisp linens on the heated bed of a massage table.

The music wasn't awful new age drums, but delicate classical. Two male masseurs clad in all white entered and introduced themselves. Mine asked, "Would you care for a cap for your hair?"

"No," Stannis answered for me. "Would you mind?" He held out his phone to the masseur with one hand and his other hand to me.

"Not at all, sir." Stannis's masseur took a picture of us holding hands and slipped the phone into Stannis's suit coat.

The masseur's hands on me were strong and capable. He started with firm, even pressure, working up to the knots in my shoulders. He laid into them with such pressure, my arms and fingers twitched and spasmed. "Hurt so good" took on an entirely new meaning.

I wasn't sure when exactly I started crying, but I couldn't stop. The masseur kept working and I cried harder, silently soaking the towel that surrounded my face. I turned my head and opened my eyes.

Stannis's electric blues stared back at me. "Is good," he mouthed and winked.

Stannis gave me twenty minutes to shower and dress. Which sucked, because I could have easily spent an hour or two in the posh locker room in my zombified state of relaxation. With only the tiniest window to try to contact Hank, I decided to skip washing my hair and took a fast four in the shower.

I called his office. "Mr. Bannon is not available," said his secretary in a sensual purr.

"I need two minutes from him. Now!" I hung up and prayed. Then I opened the suit bag.

Oh shite.

The ombre Halston Heritage strapless dress with a sweetheart neckline. High-heeled sandals in bags at the bottom. Stannis had packed for me. Which, while it was a lovely thought—as the last thing I wanted to see was a reminder of that morning—it meant we were going out. And I hadn't done my hair. I looked in the mirror. A complete and total nightmare. Slicked with massage oil, the best I could manage was a fast French twist.

I zipped the cocktail dress back in the bag, put on my shirt-dress and evening sandals, and tossed the Weitzman ankle boots in the garbage.

I had to ask for more time.

"C'mon, Hank," I muttered under my breath in the empty locker room. "Please."

Predator sounded on my iPhone. "Hank?"

"What's the scrape, Scotch Tape?"

"That choke coil . . . It's been extinguished, right?"

"Hold." He disappeared for thirty seconds, then came back as if he'd never left. "Clipped. No longer live. Hold."

I put makeup on with one hand for a minute before he returned and said, "Why?"

"No chance it was . . . er . . . connected to another . . . sparker?" *Cripes. I need a course in basic electricity.*

"No." His voice turned to ice. "Report."

"Nothing," I said too quickly. "A crow walked over my grave."

"Hold."

Four minutes later, makeup finished, phone at my ear, I collected my things and moved toward the door of the locker room.

Hank came back on. "You okay?"

"Yes. I'm sorry. I didn't mean—"

"You need anything, call Ragnar. He's ready and waiting."

"Everything's fine."

"Sure. Keep your head down." He hung up.

I slipped the phone into my jacket pocket and went out to the lobby to beg Stannis for more time. He was on the phone. Speaking Russian. I caught the words *Chyornyj Yastreb*. Black Hawk.

Stannis looked up to see me, gave me the finger and thumb "okay" sign, and said into the phone. "*Da. Ty pravy. Beda v moyom dome dolzhna zhit.*" He turned and walked a few steps down the hallway.

I sat down next to Kon. "Russian, right? What did he say?"

He shrugged. "The trouble must live in his home."

Well, that was about as useful as a Daisy razor to a feminist.

A new attendant in a black dress stopped in front of me. "Miss McGrane? This way, please."

"Uh, look, I came out because I need time to wash my hair."

"That won't be necessary, Ms. McGrane. Mr. Renko has arranged for a special service."

I stood, handed Kon the suit bag, and followed the attendant into a private salon room.

"Would you care for a glass of champagne?" She held out a thin black cotton robe for me to put on over the shirtdress.

"Sure." *Why the heck not?*

She opened the bottle in the room. Bollinger. A good year, too.

I sat down and she fixed a nylon gown at my neck. I sat, drinking champagne and feeling pretty damn terrific. Hearing Hank's voice was the capper. I was utterly relaxed, my nails looked pristine, and my hair was about to be blown out and straight-ironed.

Hard to feel the yips when you look like a million bucks.

The attendant was letting me take my time, apparently. A few moments later Stannis and a man with a shaggy mane of dark hair entered the room. I blinked in recognition. Jo' Paris, the famous stylist.

He came over and shook my hand. "Ready to be the best version of you?"

"Yes?" I said warily.

Jo' ran his hands through my hair, examined several strands before speaking in French to the attendant, who disappeared into another room. Jo' followed her.

Stannis came up behind me, smiling at me in the mirror. He put his hands on my shoulders and said softly into my ear, "My sister . . . Her hair was melted copper."

Sweet Jiminey Christmas.

That explains a helluva lot.

"You are my *Vatra Andeo*," he said. "My fire angel."

I smiled weakly. "Yes. I am."

The BOC is going to owe me triple.

Chapter 29

My hair might have been the color of flames, but Stannis was the one on fire. After dinner at Deca at the Ritz, we hit SUB 51. Filled to the gills with champagne and Yellow Wasp rakija, I sagged in inebriated relief at the 2 a.m. last call.

We pulled up to Stannis's penthouse. *Arrrgh.* He had no intention of letting me go home for the night.

Goody. A sleepover.

Kon glanced at me over his shoulder, a half wince on his face. He knew I was blitzed.

I wanted to ask him to carry me upstairs, but I couldn't feel my teeth.

Kon and Raw Chicken rode up in the elevator with us. We stepped into the foyer to Gorilla and nine other Eastern European men wearing suits in a grim-faced and badass reception line.

Oh, for feck's sake.

Stannis marched me down the line, introducing me to each man. Too hammered to remember a face or a name, I concentrated on not falling over.

The next thing I remember was Kon helping me step up onto the raised stone fireplace hearth in the great room.

Stannis stood in front of me. Every man had a water glass full of rakija. He raised his glass, "My *Vatra Anđeo,* Maisie! She will live here with me."

Uh-oh.

The men cheered and threw back their drinks. And then the party started in earnest.

Stannis helped me step down and pulled me in close. "Black Hawk tells me you must live with me. I see this is so. My men will keep you safe."

God help me.

The day I meet you, I'm gonna punch you in the face, Black Hawk. You interfering son of a gun.

I swayed in place, a glassy grin on my face, waiting while Stannis zigged and zagged around the room, pouring drinks, back-slapping, and talking.

After a while, nodding and barely stumbling at all, I edged toward the guest bedroom offered a scant few days ago. Gorilla caught me by the arm. "Mr. Renko!" he shouted across the room.

Stannis bounced over, all excitement. "We take picture. For Black Hawk."

Gorilla held his smartphone at the ready, so ridiculously small in his hands I started to giggle. Stannis put his arm around me and with his other hand, raised my chin. We smiled and Gorilla took several pictures.

"Always"—I yawned—"pictures."

"It is special day for us."

I tried to say, "Yes, we're celebrating my red-haired return to the nickname Ginger Snap." What came out was, "Yeshhhnap."

"Maisie . . ." Stannis squinted at me in surprise. "You are drunk."

"Very."

He took me into his room. "When the men are here, you sleep with me, yes?" He disappeared into the closet.

I sank down on the bed.

He came out with cotton pants and a T-shirt. "For you."

Inspiration clicked. Also known in the McGrane clan as *The Drunken Master Flash of Brilliance.* "I need your shirt," I said. "Right now."

A frown creased his brow as he searched his shirt for a stain and found none. He slipped off his suit coat and unbuttoned his shirt.

"Your shoes and socks, too."

Able to decipher my orders through the slurring, he did as requested. Which meant he had to be at least half in the bag himself.

He planted himself before me, palms up.

I reached out, undid his belt, then stood and mussed his hair. "Jacket back on." He looked at me like a dog on a bicycle, but he put it on over his v-neck undershirt.

Something wasn't quite right. I tapped a finger against my lips, thinking. It was still tacky with lip gloss. "Don't move." I held his face in my hands and smeared my mouth across his. I stepped back to admire my handiwork, bumped up hard against the bed, tripped, and landed on it in a heap.

Perfect. I rolled on my side and gave him a thumbs-up. "Go get 'em, tiger."

Stannis threw his head back and laughed. "I take longer time."

Just leave me alone so I can sleep. I nodded and dragged my foot up toward my hip, fingers fumbling at the thin ankle strap.

Stannis shook his head, pushed my hands away, then unfastened and took off my shoes. He leaned over and unzipped my dress.

I sat up on one elbow. His wrinkled dress shirt hit me in the face.

"You make good trouble," he said. "I like it."

The supersonic whine of a dentist's drill shredded my eardrums. *Oh God. Make it stop.*

It stopped.

Then it started again. I groaned in agony and opened gluey eyes.

Stannis's phone. Goddammit!

I sat up too fast and grabbed my head before the halves of my skull came apart. His phone was on the dresser.

Phone. So. Far. Away.

I hauled my roadkill carcass the four steps to the dresser. My mouth tasted like a dirt sandwich. I fumbled with the phone. "Hello?"

"Who the fuck is this?" said a strident and creepily familiar voice.

Saliva streamed down the back of my throat. "Who're you?"

"I'm the goddamn motherfucking mayor of Chicago."

"Please hold." *Oh God.* I staggered my way out into the great room and threw my hand in front of my eyes. *Too. Bright. Eyes. Melting.*

Stannis was at the table with four men playing cards and eating breakfast. Wearing the same clothes he'd had on last night and showing no ill effects from the massive amount of alcohol he'd consumed, the bloody bastard. "*Vatra Anđeo.*"

I held out the phone to him. "Coles."

He grabbed my arm and pulled me onto his lap. "Renko," he said into the phone. "Yes. You know this, Talbott. You know this very well."

Don't throw up don't throw up don't throw up.

I couldn't hear what Coles was saying, but he was angry. Stannis looked bored.

Gorilla's eyes drifted up my legs.

Stannis snapped his fingers. Gorilla looked away. "No," he said into the phone. "No more, Talbott. I talk later." He turned off the phone and tossed it onto the table with a clatter. He handed me his glass of orange juice. "Drink."

As I put the glass to my mouth, he nodded at Kontrolyor, standing in the kitchen. "Make *anđeo* some eggs." His lips curved. "And sardines. With the oil."

Gee, you're a honey.

I took a swig of the juice and gagged. *A screwdriver.* I slapped a hand over my mouth and sprinted for the bathroom, bare feet drumming on the hardwood, the men's laughter echoing in my ears.

Gorilla maneuvered the Range Rover into position in Cicero. A low-rent, mostly Hispanic neighborhood overlooking the CEC

Intermodal train yard. It was a crisscross of train tracks and buildings and enormous metal bridge structures.

"Time for work," Stannis said.

Gorilla and Kon got out of the car and went to the trunk. I forced myself not to turn around, to ignore the sounds of them opening cases and the sound of metal hitting metal.

Hank's Law Number Eleven: Heavy hitters don't advertise.

And I sure as hell aspired to be one.

Stannis removed a laptop from beneath the seat and opened it.

Sweet. I can make-up text my family and Hank. I pulled out my phone.

"No," Stannis said without so much as a glance away from the screen. "Shut down phone."

I did and slipped it back in my purse. *What would Hank do?* The master of silence and stillness would have put his head back against the seat and slept.

So I did.

"*Anđeo.* Is time." Stannis nudged me awake. "Come, outside."

We got out of the car. Kon was watching the train yard through a black Swarovski HD ATS 80 spotting scope on a tripod, cell phone at his ear.

Gorilla had a notebook, pen and a pair of binocs around his neck. He was on his phone, speaking in Serbian.

Stannis set the laptop on the hood of the car and picked up the second pair of Steiner Predator 8x50 binoculars. He spoke in Russian to Kon, who nodded in assent.

"Come, see." Stannis put his arm around my shoulders and the binocs in my hand. "We wait for my trucks." We looked down onto the yard. The activity was organized and frenetic, as though someone had split open a beehive.

Semis carrying all shapes and sizes of containers drove in and out of the transmodal station, some parking and unloading cargo, others driving beneath giant cranes that raised the cargo off the trucks and onto the flatbed railroad cars.

Gorilla and Kon murmured into their phones and kept a loose watch on the entrance to the Intermodal train yard.

"They aren't speaking the same language," I half-asked, half-stated.

"No. Kontrolyor is Russian. Former ODON. Russian is of more use, more speak Russian. But Serbian has many dialects. Difficult to replicate. Useful." He smiled. "English is the bridge."

Gorilla grunted. "Approaching inbound checkpoint."

Five semitrucks carrying multicolored double twenty-foot trailers arrived at the inbound point.

Gorilla checked his watch. "On time."

Kon began reading the stenciled numbers aloud off the containers. Gorilla scribbled them into his notebook, while Stannis checked it against the computers. "As is on the shipping instructions."

"May I?" I picked up Stannis's pair of binocs.

"Of course."

Stannis's trucks pulled into a single-file line. One at a time they drove beneath the open-sided roofed structure, halted at the checkpoint stop sign, while an inspector stopped at the driver's window, checked paperwork, and affixed a CEC Intermodal seal across the door of each container.

"The seal," I said. "He didn't check the cargo."

"Is not his interest. Does UPS or FedEx look in your package before they send it? A train container is same but larger."

I looked at the thousands of containers on the CEC Intermodal train yard and felt the enormity of what Edward and Danny had tried to explain to me. Trucks and trains. And no one except the shipper had any idea of what was inside.

Unable to help myself, I peeked over Stannis's shoulder at the laptop. "Why, you can see everything on the remote cameras."

"Yes," he said. "But dependency on electronics is weakness. I do not leave my business to others."

If you want something done right . . .

"Why are your trucks all in the same line?"

"I request all train cars locked together." He wove his fingers together. "They call this 'five-packer.' My containers arrive together. Do not get lost."

I nodded. If someone would have told me a train car could get lost, I'd have laughed in their face. But after seeing the thousands of containers, trains, and trucks moving in and out, loading and unloading cars, it was beyond belief that the vast majority of it got to its intended destination on time.

Through the binoculars, I watched Stannislav's trucks go through the checkpoints onto Lot D. A crane that resembled a portable bridge lifted each container off the semis and placed them, two apiece, atop five empty railcars.

When the railcars were hauled from view, Kon put the spotting scope away while Gorilla removed and snapped the SIM cards from their phones, put away the binocs, and disrupted the gravel, erasing any traces the tripod might have left.

Stannis's phone vibrated. "*Da,*" he answered. "*Chyornyj Yastreb . . .*"

At Black Hawk's name, Gorilla and Kon exchanged a glance and quickly got in the car.

A river of Russian poured out of Stannis as I surveyed the CEC Intermodal yard and felt more than a little sick at about just how simple it was to transport illegal goods within the United States.

Stannis hung up, walked over, and draped an arm over my shoulders. "A good day."

It was. Sunny with a soft breeze and a front-row seat to transportation of chop-shop parts. "I'm glad."

"Is good you are quiet," he said. "Make no fuss."

A copper-colored strand of hair blew in front of my face.

Jaysus. I'm a redhead.

I tucked it behind my ear. "What's he like, Black Hawk?"

"Soldier. Clever. Good friend."

"Handsome?"

"Yes." Stannis moued. "Why you ask this?"

"You seem happy when you talk to him."

Stannis began to laugh. "You are like little girl." He ruffled my hair. "*Chyornyj Yastreb* is right hand." He jerked his head at the car. "My soldiers. Eddie V. is business. Coles is . . . useful. Always all things must be separate."

"And me?"

He smiled, eyes crinkling at the corners. "You are little sister. Family."

Who is going to destroy you.

I returned a watery smile.

The phone buzzed again, and he answered without looking at it. "Yes?" He turned his face away from the phone and exhaled in irritation. "No." His voice was sharp. "Not possible . . ." He listened for a short while. "No." He disconnected and slid the phone into his pocket. "Talbott." He swore under his breath in Serbian.

I bumped my shoulder into his. "Aww," I teased. "He's just worried I make you happier than he does."

"You, I like." He shrugged. "Him, I fuck."

Chapter 30

The next day, Stannis came into the great room wearing a smart charcoal Hugo Boss suit and open-necked shirt in deep marine. "I have appointment."

"Okay." I started to get off the couch.

"No." He dropped a heavy hand on my shoulder. "Kontrolyor stay with you."

He pointed at Kon. "Make her happy. Make her safe."

The bodyguard nodded solemnly. As I heard the elevator doors close behind Stannislav, I slumped on the couch, finally free of my 165-pound Serbian straitjacket.

Kon was happily chopping vegetables in the kitchen. Open to the hallway, there was no way I was getting into the office unnoticed. I rubbed my eyes with the heels of my hands. I needed to call in to the BOC, check in with Leticia, and figure out what exactly I was going to say to my family and Hank.

I went into my room, closed the door, and took the BOC iPhone from my purse. As I brought it up to dial, I stopped at the sight of the BOC's electronic signal detector wristwatch.

Stannis wouldn't have . . . He liked me now more than before.

I pushed the buttons.

He had.

The watch glowed. Any electronic signals leaving my room would be captured. And specially encrypted texts and phone calls from my BOC iPhone would set off an alarm that would make an air-raid siren sound like a party horn.

Apparently the L in my luck has been replaced with F.

I changed into jeans, boots, and an old Sabo Cruz T-shirt and went into the kitchen to rattle Kon's cage. "Let's go," I said with my happiest face.

Panic flashed across his face. "We stay here."

"Mr. Renko wanted you to keep me happy, right?"

Kon gave a slow nod.

"It will make me happy to get my things from my parents' house." I offered him my phone. "Would you like to call *Stannis?*"

He chewed on the inside of his lip for a moment, dark eyes appraising. "Okey." Kon took off his apron, picked his Glock off the counter, and stowed it in his shoulder holster. He gave me a sideways glance as he slipped his suit coat on and got the keys from the drawer. "We go."

We traveled in Renko's second car. A pristine and armored black Ford Explorer. "This is all your parents'?" Kontrolyor might have been dazzled, but it was only momentarily. His eyes scanned the property, the neighbors, the street, looking for threats.

"Yes." I swallowed hard. Flynn's red Ford F-150 and Rory's black Cadillac CTS were parked in the driveway.

Kon pulled into the gate. "What is code?"

To his dismay, I hopped out of the car, typed in the code, and directed him to park off to the expansive extra parking side of the driveway. Kon opened the door and I stopped him before he got out. "Listen. You see those cars?"

He nodded.

"They are police. *Politsii.*" I held up four fingers. "Brothers. Father. Not good for them to see you. Not good for Stannis."

His chin raised, eyes narrowed. "Lot of house for *politsii.*"

"Yes," I agreed.

He tipped his head from side to side, weighing the odds of crooked cops being able to protect me. He found in my favor.

I jogged up to the front door and went inside. I locked my bedroom door and called Edward Dunne at the BOC.

"Hullo, lass. How goes it?"

I flopped in one of the taupe microfiber armchairs. *Where do I start?* "Stannislav's decided I'm the reincarnation of his murdered little sister."

"How do you feel about that?"

"Tugged the heartstrings. Until I saw that he'd turned electronic monitoring on when he left." Edward sucked in his breath. "Easy. Everything's copacetic. I'm calling from my parents'. But my ability to check in is over. Stannis twisted Coles's arm. I'm officially on unsigned leave from the Traffic Enforcement Bureau."

"I see." Edward's voice was dour.

"He's also quite insistent I live with him."

"And?"

"I'm in. Yesterday, we watched five double-load semis drop their cargo at CEC Intermodal. We stayed until they were loaded on the trains. Any decisions on the shipment?"

"No. That's up to Walt and Danny to decide how and whether to proceed. What else can I do for you?"

Besides a quick wrapup? "Actually, I need an apartment. Only one that looks like I live there. And fast. Mr. Bannon and I are taking a 'break.' For me to play Stannis's house pet, my family has to believe I'm with Bannon and Stannis has to believe I have my own place. To make this work, I need a secure parking spot to dump my car and an apartment that I can say belongs to me."

"Not a problem," Edward said. "I'll call you back in ten."

I dragged a small carry-on suitcase and duffel bag out of my closet. Makeup, jewelry, hair goo, workout and lounge-y clothes, underwear. I jammed a couple of Brad Thors and Dashiell Hammett's *The Continental Op* in my bag. If yesterday was any indication, I was going to need plenty to read.

Edward called back. "The closest thing I've got to Renko's is eight blocks away. I'll messenger a key and parking card immediately. Third-floor walk-up, 301. Fire escape. Trendy, overpriced. How soon do you plan to visit?"

"I want to drop my car as soon as I can. I won't go into the apartment today, but as soon as Stannislav knows I have a place . . ."

"Okay. It'll be ready," Edward said. "How is he treating you?"

"Too well. I'm having a difficult time reconciling his brutality to others and his sweetness to me."

"Watch yourself, Maisie. Make no mistake. Renko is a killer."

I lugged my stuff downstairs, made a ham sandwich, got a sugar-free Red Bull out of the fridge, and went to find Flynn and Rory. They were in the office, working. Flynn behind the computers, Rory wading through binders of paper at the conference table.

Flynn noticed me first. "Whoa! Your hair!"

Rory went wide-eyed. "What the hell happened to yeh, Snap?"

"Nice to see you guys, too."

"It's nice," Flynn said. "Different."

"I don't like it," Rory said.

"Aren't you sweet?" I said. "I just had it done, so it's gonna stay this way for a couple months."

"Gels and their feckin' hair," Rory said under his breath.

"What are you doing home?" Flynn spun the wheeled desk chair next to him over to me.

I went behind the desk and sat down. "Personal day. Big case?"

"Lake Michigan floater. Not little. About time, too," Flynn said. "We're still waiting on forensics." He shot Rory a look. "Surprised the Matchstick's dragging her feet on our request."

"Don't quit your day job, Flynn," I said. "You'd never make it as a private investigator."

"Huh?"

"Jaysus. He's your brother and partner and you don't notice the St. George medallion's back around his neck?" I smiled at Rory. "How's Dr. Joy?"

"Are you feckin' kidding me?" Flynn said.

Rory glowered at me. I pointed at the case file in front of

Rory. "Want me to take a look, see what else you missed?" I rolled over, grabbed the file, and opened it next to Flynn. "Cause of death?"

"Bullet to the back of the head."

"So?" I opened the folder and looked at the first crime scene photo. A close-up of the gunshot wound in the back the victim's head. He was facedown, a white guy with short brown hair.

"A badass John Doe," Rory said. "Scarred to hell an' back. A couple of gunshots, some blade."

The next photo was a wider shot of the victim's bloated but muscled back and head. His torso was missing everything from the waist down, as well as one arm and the wrist and hand of the other arm. "Whoa. Looks like Jaws had a snack."

"Ship's prop." Rory smirked. "Like the German and the airplane from *Raiders*."

"Nope. *Monty Python and the Holy Grail*." Flynn raised his fist. "For the win!"

God, I miss these guys.

I clapped and Rory grunted his assent. I flipped to the next photo. A strangled squeak slipped from my lips.

Jeff Mant.

Jaysus fecking Christ.

I started coughing. Flynn smacked me between the shoulder blades. "You okay, Snap?"

"Yeah." And I was. Surprisingly relieved to have photographic proof that yesterday's shooter had been a warning for Stannis. Nothing personal.

"He looks pretty good for a floater," Flynn said. "I pushed Dr. Dudek for TOD. His best guess was four or five days. Still, it'll be a tough ID."

I sure as hell hope it's gonna be, seeing as I knew the mad dog and I'm in love with the man who put him down.

I winced inwardly.

Somewhere, somehow, a fundamental shift had occurred in me.

Any of my five brothers would have killed Jeff Mant without a second thought if they'd seen him with the bag over my head, cutting my chest, or even assaulting me on the car.

But they wouldn't have done it a day or even an hour later.
Jeff Mant was an animal. It needed to be done.

Flynn handed me a photo from a separate stack. "Any ideas?"

I looked closely at the flayed bicep that was partially attached to the torso. A tattoo of a skull with part of a beret was still intact.

Shite.

Flynn and Rory weren't just good detectives. They were tigers. As a team, they ranked in the CPD's top five of case closers. And this . . . they'd guard this case like a slab of raw meat.

My blood turned hot and thick.

"Armed Forces, probably. Early to mid-forties—or he'd have more ink." I closed the folder and pushed it away. "Hmmm."

"What?" Rory said.

"Nothing." I fingered the edge of a crime scene photo. "It's just . . . Have you considered he might not be an American citizen?"

Flynn's eyes narrowed. "Why?"

"A lot of immigrants in Chicago. I'd make sure it was an American tattoo, is all."

"Oh?"

I flipped through the photos again. "The vic's scars . . . they don't look like they were attended to by American doctors. Healing's a little rustic."

Flynn scanned the photos again. "And you'd know, Dr. Maisie, because . . ."

"Hank has a lot of scars."

"Jaysus." Rory smacked his hand on the table. "Here we go."

"Hey, you asked. I answered."

"Interesting observation." Flynn pulled my chair into his. "Does our vic appear to be of Eastern European descent to you?"

"Uh . . ."

"Yeh," Rory tagged in. "Tell us about yer fine Mr. Renko. What exactly does he export besides trouble?"

Well, Super Cop, he runs a multimillion-dollar chop-shop operation.

I shrugged. "I'm not sure. Scrap metal, grains. That kind of stuff, I think."

"Are you sleeping with him?" Flynn, who still had my chair by the arms, loomed over me.

My cheeks burned as if they'd been napalmed. "What if I am?"

Ah, the joys of having brothers. They hate Hank and yet, could at this moment, quite possibly hate Stannis more without ever having met him.

"Christ, Snap!" Rory said. "Are you feckin' serious?"

Not like they haven't dated strings of women at the same time.

"Of course not. I'm *friends* with Stannis. I'm dating Hank." I mentally crossed my fingers that Hank and I were still together.

"Rory, help me out here." Flynn ran a hand over the back of his head. "I don't think I've ever met a man who was okay with his girl making out with another guy."

Rory scratched his cheek. "Pimp, mebbe."

Flynn tapped his nose and pointed at Rory.

Dinks.

They'd gotten my ire up, but they'd get no more satisfaction. I had far too much to lose.

The doorbell rang. "I got it." I jumped to my feet and hustled out of the office.

"You're shady as feck, Snap," Rory called after me, laughing.

A young woman in a courier's tee handed me an envelope. I signed her electronic tablet and turned to go back inside.

Kon stood at the car, arm at one side of his body. And while I couldn't see his hand, I was certain it was holding the Glock.

I closed the door behind me, slumped against it, and opened the envelope. Inside was the address, directions, and floor plan of the apartment, the location of the mailboxes, the swipe key to get into the parking garage as well as the front door of the building, and the key to apartment number 301. There was also another $2,500 in Visa cards. I put the cards and keys in my purse, memorized the apartment as best I could, then buried the envelope and floor plan in the kitchen recycle trash.

I climbed onto a bar stool and sat there, knee bouncing,

thinking about things. I knew I should get my car and talk Kon into dropping it off at the apartment before going back to the penthouse, but I was exhausted and wired at the same time.

The house phone rang. I almost let it go, but I was sitting right next to it. I picked it up. "Hello."

"Maisie?" A long pause. Then a raspy groan. "It's Lee."

"Lee? Cash isn't here," I said. "Are you okay? Do you need help?"

"My stomach," he panted.

"Lee, where are you? I'll call nine-one-one."

"Are you my appendix, baby? Because I'm pretty sure I need to take you out."

Oh. My. God.

"You jerk!" A tiny, scoffing giggle popped from my lips. Then I laughed. Really laughed. I couldn't stop. It was like he'd reached inside my head and opened a tension valve. Tears ran down my cheeks. I finally caught my breath. "Rain Man called. He wants his social skills back."

Lee chuckled. "This your first time playing outside?"

"Not gonna happen, cowboy."

I could hear the smile in his voice as he said, "Keep telling yourself that, if it cheers you up. I'll call you later."

Chapter 31

Dropping the Dodge Hellcat in the parking garage went smoother than anticipated. Mostly because I was so preoccupied with how the BOC would take down Stannislav, I didn't have time to get the yips.

I called Hank before I left the parking garage. His overly sexy secretary informed me he was out of country for the next four days, but would I want to see him Tuesday night?

Gee, that'd be a cinch, seeing as I live with Stannis and have a team of bodyguards shadowing me.

I gave the honeypot a restrained and demure, "Hell, yes."

Can't worry about the middle pieces until you have the edges done.

The drive back to the penthouse was spent in a quiet fog of wondering how to come clean with Hank after the chop-shop bust and warn him my brothers were on Mant's case. We rode up the elevator to the penthouse, Kon insisting on carrying both my suitcase and duffel.

Stannis was on the phone. He put his hand over the receiver. "Good, you have suitcase, Maisie. We take trip."

What?

After a stream of Serbian, he hung up, came over, kissed me on both cheeks, took my hand, and led me into his room. He pointed at the bed. "Sit. What I pack, you choose similar."

I gave him a thumbs-up, kicked off my shoes, and flopped down on my stomach.

He came out with a blue-black suit that he laid on the bed. He held up a Charvet shadow-stripe dress shirt. Hanging from one shoulder was a Charvet hairline-stripe silk tie in deep blue. On the other shoulder was a gauze-patterned tie in charcoal silver.

"Mmm. The silver. Definitely the silver," I said. "Bring me your suit bag and I'll pack for you."

He did, flopping down on the bed beside me, watching in delight as I folded his two sets of boxer-briefs, undershirts, and pajamas.

The look in his eyes fairly broke my heart. It was a tragic cocktail of affection, hope, and loneliness. Trouble was, I liked him more every day. The physical contact without any hint of sexual connotation—there was something so safe about his hands on me that wasn't safe at all, like a rabbit with a rattlesnake inside.

Stannis, Kontrolyor, Gorilla, and I flew first-class into JFK at 12:00 p.m. the next day, Stannislav apologizing for flying commercial. A Mercedes limo—not a rental—waited with two men. The driver's copilot took our bags from Kon and Gorilla. The four of us got into the car and drove an hour and thirty-four minutes into Newark. Because, as Stannis pointed out, "A fox never leaves tracks in a straight line."

We parked again on high ground overlooking another CEC Intermodal transport train yard.

Welcome to Newark. The armpit of New Jersey.

Stannis and his men got out of the car. Stannis was wearing black jeans, an Armani jacket, and black jersey tee with steel-toed black work boots. He opened his laptop on the hood of the limo. Kon and Gorilla set up as before.

The driver and the other man remained in the car. I stayed until Stannis signaled me to get out.

Sweet.

We'd parked on a wind plain. It took all of fourteen minutes before my hair was blown to hell and I was freezing.

"Twenty minutes," Kon said, somberly.

"Report says trouble south of Control Point Ten." Stannis

typed on the laptop. "Cars cut loose. Left on stub track, waiting for road train with crew."

Oh shite.

Panic as palpable as bile rose in my throat. My heart beat double-time.

Kon shrugged. "Hot box?"

"Does not say." Stannis frowned.

Hank's Law Number Four: Keep your head.

"What's a hot box?" I asked.

"When the axle get no oil. Fire. Ruins car."

"Twenty-five minutes," Kon said.

The BOC is moving on Renko and his outfit. And I'm here. With him. My hands and the tip of my nose turned to ice.

Stannis reached over and put his hand on mine. "You are cold, yes?"

"I'm fine." *Stay frosty. The endgame won't be here.*

"Train coming now," Gorilla said.

We waited the agonizing half hour for the train to pull in without Stannis's containers. He looked at Kontrolyor. "Call."

Kon dialed. "Is me." He rattled off the numbers of Stannislav's containers. "*Da?* How long? Okey." He smiled at Stannis. "Air brake malfunction. Can occur with five-packer. Repaired and will be picked up by new train. Estimated time, five hours."

Stannis closed the laptop and put his arms around me. "You are my luck, *Vatra Anđeo.* You stay with me always."

Feck. Me.

A tremor of fear wobbled my knees. "Five hours? How 'bout we go get a drink?"

Kon and Gorilla stayed on-site with the chauffeur's partner. Stannis and I drove to the closest bar. A nasty little dive, whose faded and flaking paint spelled out Joshua Johnson's.

Nothing like a country western bar in a union slum.

I glanced at Stannis, looking decidedly upper-crust in his tech-fiber jacket. But he was packing, so it had to stay on.

We walked inside. It smelled like every other dive bar—smoke, stale popcorn, and wet peanut shells. The Boss played on the jukebox.

Yet one more reason to hate Newark.

The regular clientele wasn't exactly thrilled we'd arrived. I told Stannis to choose a table while I got the beer.

Everyone was drinking pitchers of PBR, so we would, too. I ordered a pitcher of beer, chips, and some candy bars from a bartender who thought "the stink-eye" was a hot look for him. I asked for darts. He slapped three pieces of bent plastic onto the counter. I dropped a ten to the twenty I'd laid on the bar. "No change."

He reached beneath the bar, then set a glass with six new darts on the tray.

"Thanks." I waitressed the load over to the low table in between the pool table and the darts where Stannis was sitting. I poured the beers.

He raised his glass. *"Death twitches my ear. 'Live,' he says. . . . 'I am coming.'"*

One of my father's favorites. I clinked my pint glass against his. "To Virgil."

Stannis's eyes danced. "Very good."

Jackson Browne came on, singing about the girl who could sing.

"We have not found shooter yet," Stannis said. "But I promise you there will be much blood."

For the love of Mike. I'm trying to keep my act together here, Bik.

I nodded. "Is Black Hawk hunting for him?"

"No. Only my men." He took a swallow of beer and grimaced. "Tastes like cold piss."

It kinda does. "Isn't he one of your men?"

"No. *Chyornyj Yastreb* is like me, only with smaller team. Very skilled, but does as he chooses." He rapped his knuckles on the table and pointed at me. "You meet him tonight. You like very much, I think."

"Awww. I'll always like you best." I stood up. "Let's play darts."

He beat me handily. Every game. Didn't matter that I was mentally shaken harder than a Bond martini; Stannis was a machine. The more points he spotted me, the more focused he became.

Three florid, beer-glutton local boys moved into the area and started playing pool, making sure to edge a cue into our game every couple of minutes.

We ignored it until the sausage-nosed fire-hydrant ringleader put a cue between my legs.

When it got to mid-thigh, I spun hard left. The cue wrenched out of his grasp and clattered on the dirty cement floor.

A sallow-faced cinder block smacked the ringleader in the chest. "Almost broke it off in the bear trap twat."

The crew laughed.

My fingers curled into fists.

Hank's Law Number Seventeen: De-escalate. The true fight is won without fighting.

I bent and picked the cue up.

The third in their crew, wearing a filthy *Don't Fear the Reefer* T-shirt, jeered, "Yeah, girl. Bend over. That's right. Can't keep your hands off my stick."

I smacked the cue against my palm. "Why don't you have another beer, make another observation."

"My dick in her mouth will shut her up," said Fire Hydrant.

Aren't you a fine, helpful fellow.

There was the smallest hitch in Stannis's step before he came to me, shaking his head. "Maisie, Maisie. You should not provoke."

The crew was so surprised it took almost ten seconds for Cinder Block to grab his crotch and echo, "Provoke this!"

Stannis took the pool cue from me and held it out to the ringleader. "I prefer you play from other side of table, yes?"

The crew laughed. Cinder Block spat. "That's not how it works, asshole."

"Will be challenge then."

The six-foot-two ringleader topped the scales at three bills and change. He gripped the cue and shoved Stannis in the chest at the same time. "Fuck off, Russkie."

Stannis stumbled back two steps.

Reefer laughed. "But leave the muff behind."

Stannis closed his eyes, inhaled a deep breath in his nose, and exhaled it out his mouth.

Uh-oh. "Let's go," I said.

Stannis turned, pulled a S&W .44 short from the holster riding at his lower back and placed it on the table with a *clunk.* Next came a seven-and-a-half-inch folded Buck knife from his front pocket. He cracked his neck and rolled his shoulders.

And we're off.

They never saw it coming. Stannis hit with the ferocity and speed of a mongoose let loose among a nest of sleepy cobras. A throat punch and knee to the groin. Ringleader dropped to his hands and knees, wheezing. Reefer grunted and came at him. Stannis connected with a driving elbow to the eye socket. The gritty sound of breaking bone was unmistakable. Reefer reared back. Stannis whipped a vicious kick into his knee. Reefer stumbled onto a table, upending it. Glasses and bottles shattered against the floor.

Stannis closed in on the last man standing.

Cinder Block drew the pool cue back, tangling it in the bar stools. In a single, smooth motion, Stannis swept up an almost empty pitcher of beer and cracked it against Cinder Block's head.

In broken glass and beer, Cinder Block fell flat-out against the pool table.

Astonishing.

The bar was silent except for the overloud Bon Jovi cranking out "You Give Love a Bad Name."

Wearing a devil's grin, Stannis walked back to the ringleader and kicked him in the face. He followed with a trio of savage rib-cracking punts.

"Stop!" I said. "Enough!"

The bartender racked and aimed a twelve-gauge Mossberg shotgun at Stannis's head.

He stared at the bartender in curiosity. "Is that to scare?"

Without a thought, I raised Stannis's gun to the bartender's head. "Why don't you put that down?"

And because beating the tar out of three guys and sending them to the hospital wasn't enough excitement for us, we went back to the site overlooking the train yard and cooled our heels watching Stannis's recovered five-packer roll in.

The wind hadn't abated. It was cold and boring and I was getting the come-down shakes from the bar.

Jaysus Criminey. The first time I pull a gun on the job I put it to the head of an innocent man. Just call me Super Cop.

I pressed my eyes with the heels of my hands.

That's not how this works. That's not how any of this works.

Kon and Gorilla talked and made notes. Stannis monitored everything on the laptop while the crane hot-loaded the twenty containers onto five double-trailered semis.

"The seals?" Stannis asked, "They appear unbroken?"

Kon looked through the scope. "Clean from here."

Stannis grinned and elbowed me. "A little . . . *hiccup?*" He looked at me to see if the word was correct.

I nodded.

"And still, we have fun, yes?"

Yeah, if you call an armed standoff and the demise of my career as a law enforcement officer fun. "Lots."

We watched the semis exit the CEC train yard, got in the car, and drove back to New York.

Chapter 32

Stannis had a suite at the Baccarat Hotel. A place where swank had to pawn swag just to get in. And like most big shots, Stannislav Renko had no time to enjoy it. Showered and changed, we were back in the limo fighting perpetual Manhattan traffic on our way to the Cetta Brothers' Sparks Steakhouse. The Don Constantino's regular hangout.

Last to arrive, we were escorted through the saloon-like multilevel restaurant to the Violet Room. It resembled a *Downton Abbey* library with one exception: It was topped to the ceiling with shelves of wine instead of leather-bound tomes.

The Don Constantino, Tony "Big Tuna" LoGrasso, and two other heavyweights were smoking cigars. Eddie had brought along his arm candy, Bobby Blaze, the singer from The Storkling. Vi Veteratti and her right hand, Jimmy the Wolf, rounded out the party.

Please, God, don't let them mention Hank.

Stannis and the Italians exchanged boisterous back-slapping greetings.

Vi and Jimmy didn't bat an eye at my introduction.

Maybe the red hair was a blessing after all.

"Mr. Yastreb sent his regrets," said the Don.

"A disappointment, yes." A small frown creased Stannis's brow. He hadn't known. And he especially didn't like hearing it from Constantino.

The Don nodded. "Your man shows respect."

"Yes, he is good. And lucky for me." Stannis raised a hand and stroked my cheek. "I prefer my date not to shave."

That passed for high humor with this group.

Two waiters popped bottles of Dom Pérignon and filled flutes. When everyone had a glass, Big Tuna raised his. "To our continued and profitable partnership."

Everyone drank.

Stannis raised his glass again with a grin. "Or, as we say in my village, one devil does not scratch out another devil's eyes."

Everyone drained their glasses, all wearing the smug smile of *"I am above the law."*

As the waiters refilled, Eddie came over with Bobby Blaze on his arm. He took her glass and set their empties on the waiter's tray. "Bring me a Manhattan."

"Ma'am?" the waiter asked.

"Vodka on the rocks."

"She'll have tea. With honey," Eddie V. snapped. "She has to watch the pipes."

The waiter nodded and left.

Bobby's lip curled. With deliberate motions, she took a long silver cigarette case from her clutch and slipped a cigarette into an ebony holder. Eddie V. frowned, but pulled a book of matches from his pocket and lit one with his thumbnail. "One."

She exhaled a thin wisp of smoke that seemed to last forever. "Naturally."

It should have looked ridiculous. Instead it made me want to start smoking.

Vi Veteratti glad-handed her way over to the Don, past Big Tuna and the heavies. She whispered something in his ear.

Eddie V.'s eyes went flat. He showed Vi his broad back and started talking to Stannis.

Bobby's bright red lips twisted in a friendly sneer. "Who the hell are you?"

"Maisie McGrane." I smiled. "Your stage name is better than mine."

"It's not." Bobby sucked in a lungful of smoke and blew it toward the ceiling. "Eddie made me change it. Legally."

Ouch. Not really much to say to that. "Gee . . ."

"Call me Paulette. Paulette Maslick." She rolled her eyes. "You must be something to land Stannislav Renko."

"I do all right."

Across the room, Vi Veteratti let loose a sensual laugh. Eddie stiffened but didn't turn around.

With a sly smile, Vi snaked her arm through the Don's. Laughing, he kissed her cheek.

"Siblings." Bobby tipped her head back and blew another languid rail of smoke over her shoulder. "You seem like a nice kid, so lemme give you some advice. Watch your toes around Vi. I may be a kitten with a whip, but she's a cat with a chainsaw." She sauntered over to her place at the table.

As women were in short supply, Bobby and I ended up on opposite sides of the table. The Don took the head, Tony "Big Tuna" on his right, and—to Eddie's extreme vexation—Vi on his left. Stannis sat at the opposite end, with a heavy on either side.

Jimmy the Wolf held out my chair, then took his place at my side. "Like the hair. Now you're lookin' like the game you're playin'," he said out of the side of his mouth. "Dangerous."

Less than four hours ago I held a gun to some guy's head.

I opened my mouth.

But then again, maybe you had, too.

"I think you have me confused with someone else," I said.

"Not this time. You like tough guys, dontcha? But maybe you're starting to think you don't wanna play so rough anymore." He reached over and tapped his finger on the handle of my steak knife. "Like that night at The Storkling, am I right?"

I dropped my voice to a whisper. "Are you hitting on me, Jimmy the Wolf?"

"Yeah." He smirked. "I am."

"Well, knock it off."

He laughed. Which earned me a dirty look from Vi.

Terrific.

The Don had ordered in advance. Blasé waiters delivered exquisite lobster, steam-started and broil-finished, and delicately marbled NY strips. Everyone drank the Bordeaux—complex and firm—except Eddie, who poured more Manhattans down his throat than anyone was interested in watching.

It didn't seem to take his cocaine cowboy edge off, either.

My steak was a gift from the gods, seared on the outside, rare on the inside. But as I cut into it, my mind kept flashing on Stannislav's boot breaking the Jersey guy's ribs.

I forced the bite into my mouth. The image disappeared immediately.

Nice to know I'm not squeamish.

Eddie turned to the Don. "Your men get a look at the merchandise?"

Big Tuna answered for Constantino. "We are more than satisfied with Mr. Renko's attention to detail in our dealings."

"Good," Eddie said, twitching and magnanimous. "'Cuz it's time we talk expansion. Renko's working more than this angle and—"

"Now is not the time or the place, Eddie," Vi said.

"Shut your piehole, *sis*. Last time I checked, you couldn't keep your own friggin' house clean."

It was like dropping an electric eel in a puddle. "You dare to—" Violetta started. The Don put his hand on hers and she fell silent.

Don Constantino, Big Tuna, and the heavies showed no emotion. Not even the barest hint of curiosity.

Stannis's voice sliced through the air. "I have no interest in expansion with you."

"Who the fuck are you to tell me no?" Eddie's face darkened.

"I am businessman, Eddie. And we do business," Stannis said. "But I have many interests. I will do as I wish."

"You think you can shit in the nest, then go off on your own? You got another fuckin' think coming."

"Goran Slajic pays much for Don Constantino's protection." Stannis wiped his steak knife off on his napkin. "I do not ask permission."

Eddie's face turned pugnacious. "I friggin' *own* Chicago. You don't do nothing without my say-so. And I say—"

Bobby pulled at Eddie's sleeve. He yanked his arm away and for a split second, I thought he might backhand her. She blanched.

Jimmy the Wolf glared at Eddie and muttered, "Asshole."

"I say 'hop' and you say 'how goddamn high, Mr. Veratti?' Are you friggin' hearing me, you Serbian fuck?"

Stannis tapped the blade of the knife slowly against his palm.

The cachet of having Mobster Paul Castellano gunned down in front of your steak house was one thing, but an eviscerated Eddie Veratti in the Violet Room was something else altogether.

And it wasn't going to happen on my watch. Five Irish brothers gave me the coping skills of Chuck "The Iceman" Liddell.

I picked up a spoon and *tinged* my glass three times.

I wasn't born yesterday, but thank God my parents were.

Everyone turned to me in surprise.

I pushed back my chair, got to my feet, and yawned. Not for effect, but from pure high-octane stress. "Don Constantino, before this becomes a business meeting, Bobby and I would like to thank you for this wonderful meal."

I raised my chin slightly at Bobby and smiled. Feeling a little desperate herself, she stood up.

"Fly me to the moon," I sang. "Let me play among the stars . . ."

Bobby stepped in and took over, slowing it down and torching it up in honeyed tones as she sauntered over to the Don. "Let me see what spring is like on Jupiter and Mars."

A private floor show lasted all of two stanzas before Big Tuna and one of the heavies started belting it out.

Because. Well. Frank Sinatra was a fecking God among men.

Even Eddie was clapping when she finished.

The Don's enchantment with Bobby calmed Eddie, who ordered another Manhattan and started chatting with the heavy on his right.

Stannis cocked his head to one side and shrugged at me.

Not exactly a thank-you. More like a "there's always next time."

Dessert was accompanied by old Mobster stories and easy

banter. As it did with most addicts, Eddie's mercurial anger with Stannis seemed to evaporate into the ether.

Don said something to Big Tuna, who in turn came down to our end of the table and relayed it to us. "Miss McGrane, Mr. Renko? Don Constantino asks you remain at the Baccarat this weekend as his special guests."

Dear Emily Post, is it rude to bang one's head on the table until unconscious?

Chapter 33

I was not a New Yorker. Dealing with the thronging mass of humanity for an entire weekend gave me a certain and desperate ache to move to the Utah Salt Flats and become a prepper.

It was a relief to return to the penthouse. And not just because I was going to see Hank the next day. Although I wasn't sure exactly how I was going to be able to wriggle free of Stannis and his crew.

As the only Russian in Stannis's in-home team, Kontrolyor was an outsider, a perfect mark to befriend. Or so I thought.

He was introducing me to Russian cuisine, and I was somehow choking it down.

This morning, he made me his favorite part of a traditional breakfast. *Kasha,* a sort of porridge made from different grains topped with fruit with *kompot,* a non-alcoholic drink made by boiling fruit in water.

It was beyond dreadful.

Easy to see how Russia produced so many sharp cheek–boned models. They grew up having no interest in food.

A river of furious Serbian spilled out of Stannis's office into the hallway.

Oh God.

I tried not to flinch. My shoulders locked above my ears in a semipermanent cringe.

Had Special Unit moved on the chopped parts?

I pointed my spoon in the direction of the office—miraculously, it didn't shake—and shot Kon a questioning look.

His mouth moued. "Mr. Renko is upset."

"The containers?"

"No. That is very good. The Italians are happy. Mr. Slajic is happy."

"Then what's the trouble?"

Kontrolyor shrugged. "I do not know. Only Russian or English for me."

Stannis strode into the kitchen, back rigid, jaw set.

"Good morning," I said.

"Yes." Stannislav's mouth stretched in an unhappy grimace. He turned to Kon. "Take her out. Get her whatever she wants."

This was what the McGranes called a "defining moment." The moment you either stood your ground or accepted grunt status.

"Hey." I rapped my knuckles on the counter. "Don't do this." I threw Kon the thumb and he lit out of the kitchen.

Sometimes men, like horses, just needed a smack on the nose and to be led back to path.

"C'mon," I said. "Let's go for a run. See if you can keep up."

Stannis folded his arms across his chest.

Jaysus, I sure hope it works this time.

"Please," I said softly. "*Moj đavo.*"

The effect was electric. He threw back his head and laughed. "My devil? Where did you learn this, *Vatra Anđeo?*"

"Gorilla." I winced. "I mean Ivanović."

"No, is okey. He is ape." Stannis touched my cheek. "I change. We run."

Stannis hit the elevator button to the lobby. Only instead of going outside, he turned left and led me down a hallway into a pristine and overequipped workout room.

"But I thought we were going for a run. After I beat you, I was gonna buy you lunch."

He wasn't having any part of it. He grabbed me by the elbow

and marched me to the treadmills. "Are you such . . ." He huffed a breath through his nose. "What is babe?"

"Innocent?"

"Yes." His finger came up in my face. "The shooter. Either you very lucky or he is very bad. He will try again. Or there will be more."

I nodded.

Stannis walked to a table with books and magazines. He picked up the TV remote and handed it to me. "Choose show."

We watched five miles worth of *The Thin Man* on TMC and got off sweating. We walked over to the gym mats.

"What's the trouble?" I asked.

Stannis dropped onto his stomach and knocked out fifty push-ups.

I matched him for thirty, waiting for him to say more.

"Goran asks me for thing I do not like."

I flipped on my back and started doing crunches. "Maybe I can help."

"Maybe." Stannis laughed, rolled, and crunched with me. At 150, he quit, got to his feet, and gave me a hand up. "You know how to steal cars?"

"Doesn't everyone?" I gave him a playful shove.

"New cars?" He pushed back. "Expensive ones?"

I dropped into a boxer's stance. Did a little bob and weave. "I'm sure I could think of something."

Stannis threw a fist at my face. He purposely didn't hit me, but he was so fast I dropped my hands in shock.

"No," he scolded. "Never lower hands." He unleashed a quick, but light, series of six punches. Each one hit me. Toying with me like a cat on a blind baby mouse.

Goddammit.

I pretended to pout. He relaxed. I threw a couple quick jabs. He took my tags with his palms and stepped in with his left foot.

Gotcha.

I threw a left hook and swept his leg out from underneath him.

He stumbled but kept his feet, laughing and shaking his head. "Muy Thai. Did not expect."

"A girl's gotta do . . ."

He grabbed me to him for a hug. "I like. I take you to lunch, yes?"

Driven by Raw Chicken, Stannis and I were accompanied by Kontrolyor, who vanished once we were safely inside Tru. The restaurant, as before, was minimalist wonderfulness, only today it was jam-packed with power-lunchers.

I was more than a little surprised when the maître d' greeted us like old friends and escorted us to a primo table.

Don't let the grass grow beneath your feet, do you, Bik?

Stannis and I chatted about everything that was absolutely nothing during lunch.

It was starting to thicken, the trapped sand in my throat that was Stannis. Slicking over with genuine affection.

It wouldn't be long before I couldn't swallow.

Or breathe.

"The run was good idea," he said.

I gently twisted my wineglass by the stem. *Man up, Maisie.* "What has you in knots?"

He started to speak, frowned, then started again. "Is . . ."

I put up my palm to stop him and said the magic words, "You don't need to tell me. I just thought you might want to talk about it."

The disclaimer, like it had for my mother so many times before, opened the floodgates.

"My uncle, Goran. Now I am *Mesar,* he becomes *Bik.* Charging into new venture. He grows reckless."

And shipping rail containers of chopped auto parts is as safe as a box of methadone in a rehab clinic. "You mean, like stealing new cars?"

"Exactly. New cars not good. A big risk for not-so-good reward." Stannis leaned forward, elbows on the table. "Goran wants a dozen new luxury cars in Juárez next week."

"Juárez, Mexico? Jeez. How?"

"Shipping is no trouble. But I do not like to work with the cartels. Too much drugs make for too little sense, yes?"

I thought of Scarface Junior Eddie Veteratti, and nodded. "Couldn't agree more."

"Exposure at the train yard. Security at the dealership." Stannis leaned his forearm on the table. "How would you do it?"

I chewed that one over. Slowly. Trying to figure a back door for the BOC to walk in. "I'd hit the transport. The cars are at their most vulnerable on the road."

"How?"

There was something in the way those bright blue eyes focused on me. His charisma triggered a need to impress him. Not my usual MO. At all.

I swirled the last of the wine in my glass, watching the liquid move, not thinking of anything in particular. A case of my mother's, distillery tank trucks being robbed, swam up from the bottom of the glass. "Everything is on a shipping schedule. Carmakers can't alter that. Dealers need delivery dates. So do intermodal train yards and truck transport for the last leg."

"Yes." He nodded patiently. "But without prior knowledge, hijack is ineffective."

"Real luxury cars—the kind you're talking about—top-of-the-line BMW, Lexus, Mercedes . . . those cars carry a price tag over 100K. Do you really think the carmakers are gonna risk the final leg in open transport? Where a stray rock or sand could damage the paint job? No way."

"Go on." Stannis rotated his hand in a circle. "From intermodal train yard, semis travel no more than 320 kilometers."

About two hundred miles.

I turned on my iPhone and fired up DuckDuckGo. In less than a minute I had confirmation. "Open transport—cars loaded up on open racks behind semis—constitute ninety percent of all cars shipped. Enclosed transport's ten-percent piece of the pie is divvied up between private individuals and luxury cars. There are only three companies in Chicago with the ability to handle the shipment of multiple luxury cars."

I slid my phone across the table. "That's where I would start."

He barely glanced at the names on the phone. "Next?"

"The trucking company won't let the drivers know until that day," I said. "But Dispatch will. And the more expensive the cars, the better the driver they choose."

"True. And drivers will not be hero when you show them picture of family."

Jaysus, Mary, and Joseph.

Stannis smiled. "What other troubles to forsee?"

"GPS tracker on the transport semi. Radio communication with Dispatch. Armed guard, maybe? Stealing the transport itself would alert law enforcement. Transferring the cars will take time. GPS trackers on the cars themselves." I sat back and pointed at him. "The car keys. Probably in a safe in the cab. Driver may or may not know combination."

"Fast to think." He tapped his finger against his temple. "You know this how?"

"An old smuggling case of my mother's," I said. "She's an attorney."

"A good one?"

"The guy got ten years when he should have gotten twenty. She had him out in thirty months." I shrugged. "What do you think?"

He laughed. "I think I like to know your mother."

Let's hope that day never comes.

"You did very well for start. Not many things you did not consider."

"Oh?" I said. "What'd I miss?"

"The hijack itself. The drivers, the cargo, dispose of transport. Things of this nature."

He hadn't really been asking.

Stannis raised his wineglass. "To live long enough to win many scars."

Chagrined as a piece of burnt toast, I lifted my glass in salute. "To the fut—"

Across the restaurant, I saw the aristocratic, foxy face of Walt Sawyer grinning at . . . *Mom!* He reached across the table and put his hand over hers. She didn't pull away. Instead she flipped hers to hold his.

My lungs compressed.

Stannis scanned the restaurant and saw no threat. "What is it?"

I threw back the rest of my wine and coughed. "My mother is here."

He followed my gaze. Walt was still holding her hand. "Your mother is black?" Stannis asked.

"Yes," I answered mechanically. "My birth mother was killed in an accident. When Mom married Da, she adopted us all."

Stannis put his napkin on the table. "Let us go greet your parents."

"That man is not my father."

He stood up. "Then let us go meet this man."

"Why not," I said and pulled the pin.

Stannis came around to my chair and took my arm. I picked up my purse and forced a smile. Together, we crossed the room.

Walt looked right through me as we approached their table.

"Hi, Mom."

"Maisie," Mom said. Her eyes widened slightly. Lawyer to the core, she doubled down on the hand holding by placing her other hand on top.

The old red-handed trick.

If you're caught in the act, carry on as if you've done no wrong. The longer you delay, the more time you have to construct a reasonable alibi.

"I'd like you to meet my dearest friend." She pulled her hands away, perfectly choreographed to Walt Sawyer raising his to me. "This is Walt Sawyer."

I shook his hand. His face was a polite mask. "Very pleased to meet July's only daughter."

"And who is this?" Mom asked.

"Stannislav Renko."

He shook her hand with a small bow and turned to perform the same with Walt. "Is pleasure."

"Indeed," Walt said. "We haven't ordered yet. Would you care to join us?"

My mother had no physical tells. Which was, in effect, a tell itself. There was nothing she wanted less than for us to join them.

The joke was on her. Walt knew I'd never accept the invitation. "I'm afraid we've just finished," I said.

"Pity." Walt picked up the wine list. "Shall we open a bottle of champagne? Toast to new friends?"

Bastard.

"Walt." Mom laughed. "I'm sure Maisie has to get back to work . . ." She looked at me, full lips crimped in curiosity. "Darling, why aren't you in uniform?"

"She has a meeting with Mayor Coles today," Stannis lied smoothly. "I tell her she is more than parking maid."

The very words my mother was dying to hear.

They seemed to scald her ears.

"So you see," Stannis said, slipping a possessive and casual arm about my waist. "We must go."

Chapter 34

My head was a mess.

Mom and Walt?

Jaysus Fecking Criminey. What the hell?

"You are unhappy?"

"Yeah, Stannis. I think my mom is having an affair, so yeah, I'm pretty feckin' unhappy."

"All from hands together? She showed no concern."

"She doubled down. A trick."

"One I know well," he said. "Very clever, your *majka*." He shook his head and put his arm around me. "Grown, but such child."

I pushed him away from me.

He chuckled. "Maisie." He held up one hand. "Love." Then the other. "Sex." He moved them independently up and down. "Sometime together. Most times not."

"She's married!"

"So attraction is forbidden? Never have . . ." He snapped his fingers looking for the word. "Flirt? Affair?"

"You're not helping."

"Life is too uncertain to forego what makes one alive."

Thanks, Captain Fortune Cookie.

He turned my face to his. "Is wrong to judge your *majka*."

The Range Rover slowed and I looked out the window.

Albany Park. Chicago's Serbian stronghold.

Raw Chicken maneuvered us into an uncomfortably narrow

alley that ran along the side of Christo Keck's Garage, a faded blue and white aluminum-sided building. The SUV barely made a sound as we drove over two separate sets of down in-ground spikes, so Keck's could stop you coming or going.

The alley opened into an enormous eight-foot chain-link, fenced-in yard topped with razor wire. A patchwork of plywood and cheap fiberglass panels kept it private. We stopped right inside the fence, next to a tow truck. The yard was full of cars and junk, impossible to navigate.

Two twenty-foot intermodal containers sat in the rear corner of the yard. A man in filthy coveralls carried a windshield to an open Dumpster at the rear wall of the garage.

How in God's name did they move the containers in and out?

We got out of the car. Kon and I followed Stannis into the garage. The whine of reciprocating saws was punctuated by blasts of acetylene torches, metal clanks, and Serbian shouts.

A pleasant-faced, stocky man with a short beard came around from behind the U-shaped counter in the center of four work bays. "Stannislav." He grabbed him by the shoulders, slapping him heartily on the upper arms. "You are well?"

"Very good, Christo." Stannis removed a single strip of paper from the inside pocket of his suit coat and held it out to the garage owner. A handwritten list of names.

Keck's eyes flickered from me to the list and back to me. "Who is she?"

Stannis opened his fingers. The paper drifted slowly down on to the rubber floor mat.

Keck's cheek twitched. Eyes on Stannis, he bent to retrieve it.

In a blur of motion, Stannis beat him to it. He straightened, the paper impaled on the tip of the Buck knife none of us saw him draw.

Holy cat.

"87. Zed. Plus 8." Stannis extended the knife to Keck, who reached out and pulled the paper from it.

"I meant no insult." The garage owner pulled an ancient Chicago White Pages from 1987 and thunked it onto the counter.

Stannis folded the knife and slipped it into his pants pocket.

The front door buzzed. Keck went behind the counter, hit a button, and the door opened.

Two janky teenagers with the evident markings of meth addicts entered the garage, one carrying a greasy backpack, the other pulling a wagon with a cardboard box inside. They came right up to the counter. The slightly larger one started unloading catalytic converters from the box, while the other, bald with a scabby head, named the vehicles they had been stolen from. "Escalade, Escalade, Ford F-150, Cherokee, Cherokee, Silverado."

Keck opened the drawer and laid eight twenties on the counter.

"Two hundred forty dollars? Shee-it, man!" Scabby scratched his head. "Don't be a fuckin' asshole. Fitty each. Three hunnert."

The garage owner picked up an Escalade converter. "This is worth sixty. The others thirty."

The teens talked it over, took the money, and slunk off, wagon squeaking behind them.

Stannis folded his arms over his chest.

"What?"

"You grow lazy," Stannis said softly. "Foolish. Such risk for little money."

Keck's ears turned red. He held up the paper Stannis had given him. "I get what needs to be gotten."

Stannis turned to Kon. "These mechanics are thirsty. Take them for beers."

Kontrolyor nodded. "Her, too?"

"No."

It took Kon less than three minutes to get the men out of the garage. The automatic door clicked behind them.

The knife was out again. Stannis drew it faster and smoother than a guy on the grift could palm a twenty. "You will not conduct such business inside again." He tapped the blade against his palm.

David Copperfield, the enforcer.

"Yes." Keck's glance flickered between the list and his own fingers, the thin sheen of sweat on his forehead proof he'd heard Stannis's order. He counted backward on his hand, then opened the phone book, tracing down the list to the first name on the paper. He did the same with the next few before raising his head. "When do you need it?"

"Twenty-first. But there is something else," Stannis said. "I need electronic monkeys. Four. Young, fast. Can disable GPS and security quickly."

"Not a chop?" Keck frowned.

Stannis ignored the question. "Rate I pay is one and half. Six-hour notice."

Keck rubbed his forehead. "I can do that."

"I want the one"—Stannis raised a closed fist and waggled his little finger—"the one they call Pug."

Keck opened his mouth to speak, but Stannis spoke first. "He paid the blood price for foolishness. This is his redemption."

The garage owner nodded.

"Good." Stannis said. "Leave us."

Christo Keck grabbed the phone book and paper and disappeared into the back office, closing the door behind him.

Stannis handed me his phone. "Call Black Hawk."

I'll do my best.

Welcome to the Serbian Spelling Bee, where phonics are irrelevant.

I scrolled through the contacts and stopped at the picture of a Sikorsky UH-60 next to the name *Chyornyj Yastreb*. I hit Dial, then Speaker, and set the phone on the counter.

"Go ahead," said a guttural voice with a strange electronic undercurrent. A vox modulator for security.

"I am with *Vatra Anđeo*," Stannis said.

"*Anđeo*," the electronic voice said. "We meet soon, yes?"

Stannis nodded for me to speak.

"I look forward to it," I said.

"The assignment is go," said Stannis. "Tonight I discuss with my men."

"There is still much to be done," Black Hawk said. "We meet tomorrow?"

"Yes."

"Will *Anđeo* be there?"

"No," Stannis said.

"Then let us ask for her blessing."

Stannis winked at me. "What is your wish for our venture?"

Hank's Law Number Seventeen popped into my mind: *The true fight is won without fighting.* I thought for a moment. "I wish for you the blessing of cunning. To take advantage of your target's lack of vigilance."

"*Spasibo,*" Black Hawk said.

Finally, a Russian word I understood. "You're welcome."

"*Andeo* is very wise, Stannis."

"As she is beautiful."

We spent the night at the penthouse, Stannis holed up in his office with three bruisers while Kontrolyor and I played cribbage until he tired of losing.

Kon left me on the white leather sofa binge-watching episodes of *Bosch* on Amazon while he went to work in the kitchen on yet another inedible Russian dish.

I was just starting the fourth episode when Stannis and his men finally said their good-byes. He came back from the elevators, rubbing the blue-black whiskers along his jaw, and sent Kon to clean up his office.

"You look wrecked," I said. "Can I get you anything?"

"No. Am very good." He reached into his pocket and tossed a bank-wrapped stack of fifty-dollar bills onto the coffee table in front of me. "Tomorrow you go to Traffic Enforcement Bureau. Then go shopping or maybe see mother, yes?"

And Hank. "I'd rather stay. Can't I help?"

He bared his lower teeth in a smile. "Your time will come."

Torquing my heart like a rusty lug nut.

I picked up the money and riffled the bills with my thumb. Five thousand dollars. "This is too much."

The smile slid from his face. "How much too much?"

Uh-oh.

I tucked my feet under me. "It's not that."

"A man tries to kill you as warning to me, and you do not demand more? You value yourself so little?" he asked silkily.

"You don't understand."

He squatted down in front of me and put his hands on my knees. "Tell me."

"It feels like I'm taking money for being your friend. And that's not right because"—my voice cracked—"I like you."

Oh God, I really, really do.

"Ah, yes." Stannis laughed and kissed me on each cheek. "And I adore you, *Vatra Andeo*."

Chapter 35

A day without Stannis meant a day without dressing up. Caterpillar work boots, jeans, a black Army Ranger T-shirt, and a black Windbreaker. Gorilla bodyguard or not, I had my Kimber Solo in my bra holster and a Kubotan in my back pocket.

I also had another $1,200 to give Leticia.

Gorilla opened the rear passenger door of the Range Rover. I thought it was ridiculous to ride in the back, but he made it clear that's where I was to be. He crowded me in and out of the car like he was Secret Service, moving from side to side behind me as we entered the Traffic Enforcement Bureau.

"Really, I'm safe here. Why don't you go back to the car?"

Gorilla dug his heels in. "I make certain everything is as it should be."

"Okay-doke." We clipped along to Leticia's open office door. She had her feet on the desk, eating a Taco Bell A.M. Crunchwrap and listening to Rush Limbaugh. "Yo, McGrane! Lookit you, dropping in like an angel of mercy an' shit."

That doesn't sound good.

Gorilla stepped forward and extended a hand. "Lovely to see you again, Miss Jackson."

Check the building, my bare butt.

She extended her hand. He bent and kissed her dimpled knuckles. "I am sure you do not remember me. I am Ivanović."

"I know who you are."

"I have thought of nothing but you for many days."

Leticia actually blushed. "You cupcaking me?"

"Yes?" Gorilla said warily. "If you mean to ask on date?"

Her shoulders began to undulate. "Oh, we'll have us a date." She pulled her hand from his and waved him out the door with a handful of neon lilac square-tipped nails. "You run along now, let me talk to McGrane."

Gorilla left, closing the door behind him.

"I know you be workin' some big chip angle, but you wanna make some serious OT?"

Good Lord, no!

"Doing what?" I asked politely.

"You know how they have all them car shows and auctions at McCormick Place Convention Center?"

"Sure."

"Somethin' went bootsie, cuz now the muscle car guys gonna roll it all outside in a couple weeks. Not sure where yet, but I need some quality peeps who can boot at the ready."

Gee, sorry, Leticia. I think I'll take a pass. I'm trying to stop doing things that make me want to kill myself.

Subject change. I set the envelope of cash onto her desk. "For next week."

"About that . . ." A speculative gleam danced in her eye. "When we tearing this towing op up? It's time for me to go on TV again."

"Uh . . ."

"McGrane. You think they don't got no seat belts on the milk truck? How stupid you think I am? I don't know what shit you got goin' on with that tow truck, but them bonuses are the only thing keeping my retention rate outta the toilet."

"Leticia, I'm sorry I—"

She raised her hands in front of her face. "Don't wanna hear it." She dropped her hands, picked up her drink, and took a slurp. "You give me a week heads-up afore it stops, we take us a field trip, and we be chill as Otter Pops."

"So what's with the uniform?"

Leticia wiggled her brows and pressed the intercom button on the telephone. "Agent Sanchez, please report to my office."

Whiskey Tango Foxtrot?

Leticia stuffed the last bite of Crunchwrap in her mouth, screwed up the wrapper, and tossed it in the trash. "We found 'em."

"Who?" I asked.

"Those Robin McHoodie cart-egging, meter-payin' mother-bitches," Sanchez spat from behind me. "What's *pendeja* doin' here?"

"She can handle." Leticia swung her feet off the desk and stood up. "Plus she all up with the cops 'n' shit."

"Cops?" I said.

"We gonna go all bounty-hunter militia on their ass and citizen's arrest 'em."

Sanchez smacked her fist into her palm. "Can't fuckin' wait." She wore a roll of duct tape around her wrist like a giant bracelet.

A low curtsy to the Queen Mary of all bad ideas.

"Uh, guys. That's not how this works. At all." I rubbed my forehead. "This is breaking and entering, kidnapping, assault."

"We don't need this friggin' pussy-ho," Sanchez said.

"Oh, they're gonna go nice and peaceful-like, won't they, McGrane?"

Cat wrangling at its finest—keeping Leticia and Sanchez out of jail.

Leticia tipped her head to the side, put her hand to her mouth, and yelled, "Ivanovic´!"

Gorilla filled the doorway. "Yes?"

Sanchez pressed her lips tight together. She hadn't forgotten his *Frijolero* comment.

"Us girls," Leticia said. "We're gonna take us a lil' trip. Wanna come?"

"Shit." Sanchez ran her hands along the burled walnut console in between the rear captain's chairs in the Range Rover. "Friggin' car is nicer than my house."

We were back at Ashland and Belmont, home of the unwashed and frowsy.

Leticia put her hand on Ivanovic´'s bicep and squeezed as we neared A Peace of the Sixties. "Slow down. That's it. Their hidey-hole's under The Hemp House."

Gorilla pulled into an alley. "What is tactical plan?"

Leticia and Sanchez looked at each other and shrugged.

Yeah, they have a plan, all right.

"Kick the friggin' door in and bust their asses!" Sanchez said.

"That's it?" I said. *Jaysus Criminey. I'm a fecking cop!*

Leticia nodded. Gorilla shook his head. "That is not a plan." He sighed and pointed at me. "She knocks on door. Asks for help. They open door. We go in, subdue. Call police."

"You know it, Sanch!" Leticia said.

"Why does McGrane get to knock on the door?" Sanchez complained.

"Because she is only one that is not dangerous or in uniform," Ivanovic' said. "You are certain they are there?"

"A safe bet." I glanced at my watch. Eight twenty-five a.m. "Potheads aren't exactly early risers."

No good will come of this.

Hoping to stave off far worse, I got out of the car.

Hank's Law Number Five: Make it look easy.

The others followed, Gorilla keeping them a suitable distance behind me. Cigarette butts, cans, wrappers, and some un-environmentally-conscious plastic bags with *The Hemp House* cluttered the sidewalk. I took the cement stairway to the basement apartment under the store and waited until Gorilla had Leticia and Sanchez in position.

The door was covered in peeling black paint with randomly plastered rainbow-colored *The Hemp House* stickers. I knocked on it, hard.

Nothing.

I turned to the gang and raised my shoulders. Sanchez jabbed a finger at me. I kicked the foot of the door. Hard.

"Maaan, do you know what time it is?" croaked a voice from behind the door. "Step back. So's I can see you."

I stepped into peephole range.

"Uhhh. Girl? Do I know you?"

"Does it matter? I left my cell here like three days ago!" I kicked the door again. "Let me in!"

"Gahhhd. Chill." He unfastened several locks and opened the door.

The first thing that went in was my boot. The smell of wet garbage and pot seeping out of the apartment was eye-watering.

"Ho-there, sister." A skinny white guy with dreads wearing a greasy blanket poncho fingered his goatee. He stood in my way, his foot and leg behind the door. Maybe a weapon, too. This wasn't new to him. "I think you got us confused with somebody else."

I heaved a world-weary sigh. "I just want my damn phone."

"I'm like the resident pot hermit, and I ain't never seen you in—"

Gorilla dropped over the rails and kicked in the door. Dreads hit the floor, wind knocked out of him. We entered, Gorilla with gun drawn. Leticia and Sanchez burst in behind us.

I had my Kubotan out. No fecking way I was pulling my Kimber.

Not yet.

A guy in a dirty Warhol-styled Mao tee struggled to sit up from the couch. Assorted bongs and a vaporizer covered the coffee table.

Leticia fanned a hand in front of her face. "Damn, this place smells like ass!"

Gorilla and I left the two guys to Leticia and Sanchez. We went through the three bedrooms and bathroom, rousting and rounding up three more men.

"On couch!" Ivanovic´ barked, motioning with his gun with one hand, grabbing a guy by the neck and shoving him with the other.

They did as they were told. There'd be no stand for pride. That had been lost long ago.

"Do you know who we are, motherbitches?" Sanchez demanded.

Mao picked up a pair of trendy black-rimmed glasses from a

milk crate end table and put them on. "Oh fuck . . . Meter maids? Hey, how 'bout everybody take it easy." Mao scratched his arm nervously, flashing a Gucci watch and needle tracks. "Smoke a bowl while we talk this shit out, you know? Plenty to go round, man."

His parents supported his major in World Cultural Pluralism. Now they're supporting his heroin habit.

Sanchez got right in his face. "Asswipe! Don't you open your fucking mouth again! You wanna throw eggs at me? You think thas some funny shit?"

Mao curled into the couch arm.

Sanchez kicked Dreads in the shin. "Leticia!" she yelled over her shoulder. "Open that fridge, see if they got any eggs, yo!"

But Leticia had passed through the galley kitchen. "Mc-Grane, get in here!"

I threaded my way through the beyond-disgusting kitchen into a tidy dining nook.

Leticia pointed at the dining nook wall, which held five hooks, each with a green hoodie with red feather. "They think they some mofo superheroes. Stupid-ass suburbials."

The nook held a rectangular dining table and chairs. Plastic bins, neat and orderly, contained checks, money orders, bank receipts, and envelopes at one end. At the other, reams of paper that were actually self-folding envelopes.

The header had a mouse wearing a hoodie beneath a Robin Hood–style hat, holding a bow. Across the page, his arrow was stuck in the coin slot of an expired parking meter. Beneath the cartoon was a message in hokey Ye Olde English type.

> *Greetings Kind Traveler,*
> *Our faire city is rife with rascals out to rob the poor and penitent. But we bow down before no man. We fight not for glory nor wealth, but for freedom alone.*
> *In other words, we saved ye from a vile and unjust parking fine. Huzzah!*
> *Please send us half your parking fine, so we*

can continue to rail against the tyranny and op-
pression of limited parking.
Huzzah!
Robin McHoodie and his Merry Men

Leticia came up behind me and picked up a container of a dozen rubber stamps and ink pads. "Each addressed to different P.O. boxes."

The average expired meter fine was sixty dollars.

This wasn't a little operation. This was thousands of dollars. City dollars.

I pinched the bridge of my nose. *Shite.*

"This ain't little, is it?" Leticia grinned.

"Nope," I said. "Aggravated Battery of Government Employees, Obstruction of Governmental Administration. Class 1 Felony fraud. Class 4 Felony marijuana possession. And more."

Much, much more.

She put an arm around my shoulder. "Here's what we're gonna do, McGrane. You're gonna call your brother, have him come in here, and make the bust. I'm gonna call the local news."

"No media, Leticia. Seriously. I need five minutes, and Ivanović and I can't be here when Cash shows up."

"Thas cool." She gave a shimmy of delight. "Sanchez and I can get our story straight." She leaned away from me. "Yo, Sanchez. Tape 'em up!"

I walked outside, ignoring the whining and moaning of the Robin McHoodies and the unmistakable tearing sound of duct tape.

Cripes. I'm a Chicago police officer.

I called Cash.

He answered on the third ring. "Whassup, Snap?"

"I need a favor."

"How big?"

"Massive." I took a deep breath and explained.

"You'll need me *and* Koji." He snorted. "Jaysus feckin' Christ, how do you—"

"Cash, we're talking five drug addicts duct-taped in an apartment. I don't know how dangerous they are, but they're wily."

"This is gonna cost you . . ."

"I know. I know. I know. Anything."

"No, Maisie," Cash said, ominously. "It's going to cost you *everything*."

Gorilla and I pulled away as Cash and Koji rolled up in separate cars.

He hadn't let me move to the front seat, but he appeared quite chipper. A date with Leticia and scaring the hell out of five spoiled druggies put a spring in his step.

And I was opportunistic enough to take advantage. "Will you please to take me to see my uncle Edward?"

"Why does this Edward not come to see you at Mr. Renko's apartment?"

"He has dementia. Silverthorn Estates is hospital apartment living—doctors and nurses watch over him."

Still in the throes of passion, Gorilla grunted his assent and drove me to the assisted living facility.

He parked in the visitor's lot. "I come with."

I let him shepherd me into the lobby. Instead of taking the private elevator, I went to the reception desk and flashed my Onyx-wing badge. "I was wondering if I could get a pass for my friend, Mr. Ivanović to visit my Uncle Edward Dunne?"

She typed something into the computer. "I'm afraid not. He's had a difficult last two days."

I turned to Gorilla. "I really need to see him."

He gave a heavy sigh and sunk his hands into his pants pockets. "I wait in lobby."

I was inside the elevator, pressing the fourth- and fifth-floor buttons before the doors even opened all the way. Detective/RN Anita Erickson met me. "What gives, Rook?"

"I need Kaplan, Sawyer, and Dunne for a debrief ASAP. I don't know how long my babysitter's gonna wait."

"Sawyer's out. Scorpion's in her office. Head there and I'll see what I can do." She took off in the other direction, talking on her micro headset.

I hustled through *CSI* Central and knocked on Kaplan's door. With a click it sprang ajar. I pushed it open and went to close it. "Leave it," she ordered, coming around the desk in an amber-colored pantsuit. She gestured to the conference table. "Take a seat. Edward will be here momentarily."

Edward bustled into her office before I was able to sit down.

Kaplan opened a folder. "The information we obtained from the train was solid. The VINs on the parts have all been burnt off, which raises evidentiary difficulties. We need a track back to Renko and his men."

I shook my head. "Renko hates computers. He makes a list of parts ordered, disguises them as people's names, and hand-delivers them to the garage. He selects a year for a specific phone book, a single letter and number, neither of which I could discern, and the garage owner opens one of a dozen Chicago phonebooks from the 1980s and deciphers the code."

"Clever and innocuous." Edward chuckled. "Nothing like re-turning to the tried-and-true book cipher secret code of the seventeen hundreds."

"But we have time for that." Kaplan raised a shoulder in un-concern. "The real prize is the evidence we're now tracking. The trailers unloaded at ten different garage and auto parts distribu-tors throughout New Jersey and New York. When we move, that'll take a nice bite of flesh from Don Constantino's working crew."

"Unless, of course, Walt trades it to the Feds," Edward said.

Kaplan looked me straight in the eyes. "Nice work, Agent McGrane."

Whoa! Didn't see that one coming.

"Thank you." I tucked my hair behind my ears. "Stannislav prefers to physically see every aspect possible."

"How so?"

I pulled over the map of the CEC Intermodal train yard and tapped a finger on the bluffs. "We watched his containers load from this mesa top over here."

Edward circled the spot with a highlighter.

"We flew to New York, drove into Newark, and watched them unload there, as well," I said. Kaplan looked at my hands. My fingers were twisting and wringing against each other. I laid my palms on the table. "I'm not here to debrief the chop."

"Oh?" Kaplan said.

"Renko is going to hijack two closed-transport semis loaded with new luxury cars and ship them to Juárez. I don't know the street value, but retail's in the neighborhood of one-point-two million dollars."

Kaplan leaned forward. "Where and when?"

"This week. Friday? Tomorrow? I have no idea."

"Danger to hostages?"

I looked blankly at her.

She gave an irritated shake of her head. "The drivers?"

"Renko may be incredibly violent, but he's equally disciplined. Killing the drivers would force attention on an act that neither the carmakers nor the insurance companies want to go public. I can't guarantee the drivers will be untouched, but they'll be left alive."

"When will you know?"

"I won't." I shook my head.

Kaplan scoffed. "It's your job as a field agent to find out."

"Danny," Edward warned. "Maisie's continued intel is far more valuable to us than a flash-bang collar."

"Besides. If I do find out when and where," I said, "it'll be too late. I'll be with him."

Kaplan sat back and folded her arms across her chest. "HRT?" she asked Edward with a snake-like smile.

Hostage Response Team?

Cripes. The Feds?

"Walt will have to clear it." Edward turned to me. "Best guess, how many would be with you?"

"If he ships them via intermodal rail. If he takes me to watch"—I tapped the circled hill on the map—"we'll be here watching from his Range Rover. Driver, two guards, Renko, and me. Five."

Kaplan nodded. "Doable." She pushed away from the table. "I'll get our freelancer in here ASAP."

We watched her slim, sticklike figure march out of the office. "Blood in the water," Edward said. "She can't help herself."

"Yeah." I cleared my throat. "Blood."

"Master criminals are often extremely charismatic, Maisie. It's human nature to like him."

"I better bounce. Renko's man is waiting."

Edward gave me a sad smile. "Undercover work can leave some sizeable scars."

I'm starting to figure that out.

Chapter 36

My phone rang on the way out of Kaplan's office.

Hank!

I trotted over to an unused glass cubicle and answered the phone.

"You a 'go' tonight, Peaches?" he said.

Abso-firmative-lutely! "You bet."

"Where should I pick you up?"

"Um . . . It'll be easier if I come to you." I crossed my fingers. *I'll think of something.*

There was a long pause.

"Hank?"

"I'm staying at my club."

"Blackie's? Why? Missing me too much?"

"Yeah." He laughed. "That's it."

"What happened? The pipes burst or something?"

He uttered a groan and I could see him dragging his hand over his face. "Wilhelm."

It took a moment to sink in. Hank Bannon, ex–Army Ranger, mercenary—the toughest, coolest, scariest guy I'd ever met—driven from his own home by an OCD butler. "What's he doing?" I somehow managed to ask with a straight face.

"Fussing."

"That's—" I gave a strangled laugh-snort. "Terrib—" And then I started laughing for real. Tears, even. "I'm sorry," I said with a shuddering breath. "Really."

"You through?" he said. "How about you turn up around six?"

"Like a bad penny."

My hair and clothes still reeked of the skunk-weed from the morning takedown. I didn't dare go home. The very last place I wanted to end up was at the dinner table with Cash dragging out that citizen's arrest story. Which left only one place for Gorilla to take me.

The penthouse.

And because I have as much luck as a dog on the wrong side of the door, Stannis was not only home, but he called me into his bedroom.

"How was your day?" he said from the bathroom.

"Interesting." I dropped onto the edge of the bed, trying to figure out how to get the night off. "Gor—eh, Ivanovic´ has a crush on Leticia."

He popped his shaving cream–covered face out of the bathroom, towel around his waist. "What is crush?"

I kissed the air. "New love."

He laughed and disappeared. "My day was very good. I am surprised you are back early."

I sat there, listening to the water run, the *clink* of the razor handle against the sink, and his idle talk, thinking hard. How was I going to get the night off? *I have this date . . .*

Stannislav's phone rang from the nightstand. I flopped across the bed, grabbed it, and read the caller ID. "Coles."

Stannis came out from the bathroom, face clean, still in the towel. He drew a line across his throat.

I swiped the screen and answered, "Mr. Renko's phone."

"Why the fuck are you answering his phone?" Coles snarled. "You're not his goddamn secretary."

"I'm sorry, sir. Mr. Renko is taking a shower. Would you like to leave a message?"

"Tell him I'll see him in an hour." He hung up before I could say, "*Yessir.*"

I winced. "He said he'll see you in an hour."

"Ugh." Stannis rolled his eyes. "Talbott is needy like woman."

"We call that 'clingy' 'round these here parts," I drawled.

"Clingy." Stannis rolled the word around in his mouth, savoring it. "This I like."

Strike while the iron is hot.

I gave him my sweetest smile. "I was thinking I'd spend the night at—"

"No." Stannis said. "Home by one o'clock."

"But—"

"I have meeting in the morning. And I need you, *Vatra Andeo,* my luck."

If Kontrolyor's spade-shaped chin juts any farther forward I might have to sock it back in place.

Kon stomped around the penthouse like a left-winger sentenced to the penalty box.

What he didn't know, couldn't know, was that Stannis chose Gorilla because of his discretion. No one knew of his relationship with Coles except Gorilla and me, so I left Kon to find solace amongst the stove and other appliances.

I showered and dressed, taking my time and ramping it up to the nines, because Blackie's was tony and smart and I hadn't seen Hank in two weeks. I leaned over the sink to put on my mascara. My fingers trembled and I had to stop and take a deep breath.

I missed Hank like the devil. And I was scared as hell to see him.

Lies of omission had settled like a solid steel sable over my shoulders. I wasn't sure who I was anymore. Or who I ever wanted to be.

Shake it off, kid. "Game time."

I strode into the kitchen, where Kon was smearing fuchsia paste on a vile-looking mound.

"What is that?"

"Dinner. *Seledka pod shuboy,*" he said without turning. "Herring under a fur coat."

Wow. That actually sounds as horrific as it looks.

"You will like." He spread the pink shavings like frosting. "The cake is salted herring and vegetables with a 'fur coat' of grated beets and mayonnaise."

Um, yeah . . . that's, ahhh . . . never going to happen, mmm-kay? "Let's go, Kon."

"Where?" He looked up, took in my glam appearance, and shook his head.

"I'll tell you on the way."

Kon braced his hands on the quartz countertop. "No."

"I can either walk the eight blocks to my apartment and drive myself in an unsecure, unprotected vehicle or you can drive me in the light-armored Expedition. Gee"—I tapped a finger against my cheek—"I wonder which Mr. Renko would prefer."

With a grunt, Kon shoved off the countertop. He carefully wrapped the pink mound in aluminum foil and stowed it in the Sub-Zero fridge. "Let's go."

Kontrolyor drove, seething in silence.

Where Gorilla was bodyguard, Kon was Secret Service with threat identified. He jerked to a stop in front of the nondescript limestone building with a black awning and sprang out of the idling SUV, opening my door before the Blackie's valet had even torn the ticket.

Kon escorted me awkwardly to the door, shifting behind me from side to side. The doorman stopped us.

"Maisie McGrane for Hank Bannon."

"A pleasure to see you again, Ms. McGrane." The doorman turned to Kon. "And you are?"

"Not on the list," I said as Kon answered, "Her bodyguard."

The doorman stepped between us. "I'm sorry, sir. I can call Mr. Bannon to see if he'll allow entrance."

"No," I said, "you will not." I put my hand on Kon's chest and backed him up. "This is a private club. A safe and secure building. No one knows I'm here except you, the doorman, and Mr. Bannon."

Outmaneuvered, he nodded. "Twelve forty-five. I come in."

"Deal."

Kon gave the doorman a look so cold he shivered. "I will stay with car, right here."

"Certainly, sir," he said, opening the door and ushering me in.

I took an elevator to an upper floor of the private club. "Tall Dark and Dangerous" was waiting for me in the bar.

Hank whistled. "Hell-o, Firebrand."

My hand flew to my hair. "Better as a blonde?"

"There's no right answer to that question." He closed in and kissed me. Hard and possessive, the way that melted my insides.

Leaving me, as always, behind the count.

We followed a tuxedoed waiter into the mahogany and leather Club Room, Hank's hand at my lower back. The waiter seated us at a quiet table with a panoramic view of the city lights.

Japanese Gin martinis, shrimp cocktails on ice, and Hank Bannon across the table. For the life of me, I couldn't think of a single reason why I was doing anything other than being with him.

I have so much to confess, I don't know where to start or stop.

"What's the grief, Chief?" Hank said.

First things first. "Flynn and Rory got the Mant case."

Not a whisper of worry crossed his face. "Tough hop."

For who?

"They're damn good detectives, Hank. I saw the file. Mant's upper torso survived the shipyard. No hands, but his face is recognizeable. My brothers could—"

"They can't." A comma of iron-dark hair fell across his forehead. "Unless you plan on helping them?"

Mant would have killed me or died trying.

"How can you think that?" My voice cracked. "I would never!"

"Ultimately, I'm to blame. Do what you need to do."

"Hank, I'm serious."

He nodded solemnly. "Maisie. I'm serious-er."

He was actually laughing at me.

"This isn't funny!"

"Even with an ID and solid evidence against me, the state attorney's office will never file."

"Don Constantino," I said softly.

Duh.

"It's the Chicago way, Angel Face." The curve of his superhero mouth was so seductively smug, I couldn't help but smile back.

"I need to be home by one."

"Curfew?" His big hand covered mine. "Square things with your father?"

I shook my head. "A non-starter."

The closest I've ever told to a flat-out lie to Hank. I hadn't even tried to make things right with my dad. How could I?

Hey, Da, guess what? I'm an undercover cop for the BOC's Special Unit and in more trouble minute to minute than I'd have ever been in if you'd have just let me make my own way on the force?

Talk about arguing Sartrean Existentialism with a twelfth-century Crusader.

"Make it liveable," Hank said. "Time's almost up."

I winced inwardly. I had two weeks left of the month he'd given me to square things. "Putting the hammer down?"

"I am the hammer, Sport Shake."

I put my elbow on the table and my chin in my hand and gazed at him dreamily. "God, I love it when you talk like that."

"I'm out of country again this week," Hank said.

"Where?"

"Central America. Anything you want to tell me?"

Yeah. Everything. I gave him my flirtiest, most innocent look. "Can't think of a thing."

It didn't work.

His eyes went flat. He stood up. "Let's go."

My martini was almost full, shrimp cocktail uneaten. I got to my feet and he took me by the arm and hustled me to the elevator.

He was angry. But I wasn't sure why, and I sure as hell wasn't going to start suggesting reasons.

He waited for me to get in the elevator and stepped in behind me. He hit the button to the thirty-second floor. We stood next to each other, not touching. The elevator doors closed.

"Christ, you piss me off," he said in a low voice.

I have a really bad feeling about this.

The doors opened. He exited behind me and turned right. I followed him to the room. He unlocked the door with the key card and pushed it open.

Dark as pitch, I got two steps into the room. He caught my arm and jerked me against the length of him, kicking the door shut. He backed me up hard against the wall, his size and strength dwarfing me, waiting, letting it sink in.

He caught my face and forced it up. I strained on tiptoe to meet his mouth, but all I could reach was the base of his throat. He kept me like that, uncomfortable and fluttery and a little bit scared.

I shivered.

He let go.

Time seemed to stretch. I wasn't scared he would hurt me. I was scared he wouldn't. "Hank?"

"Quiet."

I heard him yank his dress shirt off over his head. A button hit the wall next to me. He stepped in so tight, I could feel the heat of his bare chest through my dress.

His mouth slammed down on mine, fierce and hot. His tongue slicked between my lips, devouring me, sucking the breath from me.

His hands were everywhere, hiking my dress up around my waist, as my underpants hit the floor, the heat between us red-hot. A black haze of love and lust buzzed in my head. My fingers shook as I unfastened his pants and unzipped his fly.

He picked me up. "Leave your shoes on."

I wrapped my legs around his waist, hands sliding over the hard muscled shoulders and ridges of scars across his back.

He carried me to the bed, his mouth never leaving mine. His shins knocked against it. He turned, landing heavily on his back, pulling me down on top of him.

I sat up, straddling him and slowly eased the dress off over my head. He reached up, grabbed the nape of my neck and dragged me down to him.

With an impatient grunt he flipped us over.

He pinned my wrists over my head with one hand, his mouth tight on my throat, jaw rasping against my collarbone, other hand sliding up between my legs. "Maisie . . ."

There is nothing quite as glorious as the ecstasy of pure surrender.

I was a zebra in the maw of a lion. And I loved it.

Faint city lights glowed and blinked from a crack in the curtains. I sat up, hugging my knees to my chest, Hank's warm hand gliding across my skin.

I shivered.

He switched on the lamp.

"Good God." The room looked like a crew of homeless raccoons had had the run of the place for a month. Clothes, books, papers, dirty glasses, empty cans and bottles, capped off by wadded-up towels. Gun oil and brushes and rags covered the small table. "How long have you been here?"

"Three days."

"Gee." I crawled over him and leaned off the bed to pick up a shirt.

"Don't," he said. "I like it this way."

"Only one," I promised, snagging the shirt he'd had on less than an hour ago. I slipped my arms into the sleeves and a goofy grin spread across my face. One of life's most perfect pleasures was wearing a shirt he'd just worn. "Your room is a disaster."

"Exactly." He stared at me for a long while, his eyes the color of shadows on silver.

I got it then. Finally. This room was me.

Hank's Law Number One: You are defined by your disasters.

He poured a large whiskey into a glass. He offered it to me. I shook my head. He took a swallow.

My guts writhed like a snake in hot ashes.

I didn't know where to start. Only that whatever I ended with couldn't be losing him.

Begin at the beginning. Walt Sawyer and the Bureau of Organized Crime.

Instead, I said, "I think my mom's having an affair."

"Oh?" he said blandly.

"She and this guy were holding hands at Tru."

"Who's the guy?"

"Old boyfriend. Well-heeled. Cop." *And my boss.*

"Trust."

"What?"

"You either trust your mom or you don't. Which is it?" His face was clear and resolute and it absolutely infuriated me. Galling, really, his talent for simplifying a situation into a single word.

"It's the guy I don't trust."

"Off point." He leaned back against the pillows. "Either she is or she isn't. There's no halfway affair."

"Well, yeah, but . . ."

"Trust."

Heat crept up my neck. "How can you be so cavalier?"

"I'm not." He set the drink down, pushed a stack of newspapers on the nightstand to the ground, and picked up his iPad. He turned it on, tapped the screen, and turned it to me. Big as life, there I was kissing Stannislav Renko at Tru.

All the blood from my head drained into my stomach. *I'm going to be sick.*

Fecking Facebook.

Hank swiped through a picture of Stannis and I at the Ritz-Carlton to one at The Storkling with Stannis coiled around me like a boa constrictor.

"Do I trust you with a wealthy Serbian exporter with shady connections?" He set the iPad aside.

I wobbled, stunned.

"Yes, Maisie. I trust you."

And like some punch-drunk idiot the words that came out of

my mouth were not connected to any rational thought. "Where did you get those?"

"Flynn sent them my way. Thought I might be interested. I wasn't."

WTH, Flynn? "But that's—it's none of his busine . . ." The words died in my mouth.

Hank picked up the whiskey and handed it to me.

I tossed back a slug.

Why, oh why, hadn't I said yes at the batting cage?

"C'mere, flirt." He put his hand on the nape of my neck and pulled me toward him. "Wanna play rough?"

"Thrill me," I said.

And he did.

"Up and at 'em, Firebrand." Hank yanked back the covers and landed a playful smack on my bare butt. "Trouble's not going to make itself."

Twelve thirty-five. I felt like I'd been with him for five minutes, not five hours.

We took the elevator. Hank kissed me good-bye all the way down to the lobby. "I got your six, Sugar Pop."

I didn't dare answer. I might've started bawling.

I found Kontrolyor outside cooling his heels next to the doorman, who looked extremely uncomfortable.

Kon waited until we were halfway home. He caught my eye in the rearview. "I must tell Mr. Renko where I drove you."

"Yes." A small sigh escaped me.

"But I will not speculate."

I smiled. Awfully sweet, considering I ruined his dinner. "Thank you."

"It is difficult to have relationship with powerful and deadly man, Maisie."

You said a mouthful, pal.

Chapter 37

Hank's Law Number Ten: Keep your mouth shut.

Some of Hank's Laws were tougher to follow than others. This morning, a deep ache had set into my teeth from clenching them shut. A needle and fishing line to sew my lips together would have been less painful.

Raw Chicken drove us down I-290 west.

Stannislav's blue eyes glowed brighter than radioactive polonium. "This is fun, yes? To feel alive."

The heist was happening today. And I had no way of letting the BOC know.

"Adrenaline rush," I said. "You're like a racecar driver." *Or Evel Knievel.*

Stannis chuckled. "Crime is far better than driving fast."

The driver hit the Reagan Memorial Tollway, and exited into the suburb of Downer's Grove. Ten minutes later we turned into the driveway of what looked like an airplane hangar with no runway.

A giant half-barrel building sat atop twelve-foot-high cement walls. Surrounded by chain-link fence, one of Stannislav's men waited where the fence came together, secured with chain and a bolt lock. As we neared, he unfastened the lock and opened the gate.

What is this place?

Stannis said, "That is my lock on city government property. Has been there for two weeks. No one touches it."

"Because of Coles?" I asked.

He threw back his head and laughed. "No. Is just big government. Always lazy. Always incompetent." He winked. "Exactly why I like it."

We drove onto the lot right up to the building. Stannis was already out of the car before the chauffeur got to my door.

Stannis held out his hand to me. "Come, come!"

I took his hand and together we trotted past closed twenty-foot garage doors to a standard office door, where Gorilla waited with a semiautomatic rifle. Nodding at Stannis, he pushed open the door and we entered the half-dome whose ceiling stretched to sixty feet.

It was like nothing I'd ever seen.

Giant white drifts of sparkling snow blanketed one end of the building. Opaque crystals crunched under my feet.

Rock salt.

We were in one of the many of Chicago's Public Works Department's road salt storage facilities. "Brilliant," I whispered.

The Fast and the Furious turns up on the set of *Capricorn One.*

Stannis grinned. "No overhead. No one wants salt until winter. No guards. No troubles. The few people nearby are used to trucks in and out."

"Now what?" I asked.

"We wait." Stannis turned me around. Three of his men, eleven forty-five-foot intermodal shipping containers, and two twenty-foot containers all in rusted shades of red, yellow, and blue were already on wheeled trailers. One container had a ramp leading to its open mouth.

I'd barely gotten a look around when a garage door opened and a closed-transport semitruck drove into the dome and parked up near the trailers. Stannis's men sprang into action, opening the containers, moving the ramps.

A five-foot-six, 140-pound male in his late teens exited from the trailer of the closed transport. He checked the ramps, then raised and rode the electric lift to the upper level of cars in the carrier. Once up, he climbed into the silver Mercedes convertible, backed it onto the lift, and lowered it to the ground.

One of Stannis's men backed the car up the ramp into the rusty red intermodal trailer. The trailer was too narrow to open the car doors. The teen lowered the electric window, climbed out, and sidestepped to the front of the car. He ran down the ramp and backed up the next car.

In less than forty minutes, six Mercedes S-class convertibles and sedans had been unloaded from the semi and loaded and sealed into three of the intermodal containers.

The teen sprinted over to us. "Thank you, Mr. Renko, sir." He had a round face for being such a skinny guy, a short, up-turned nose, and slightly bulging eyes. *Pug.*

"Get plates from Ivanović. Switch on all trucks."

The kid nodded so hard I thought he'd get whiplash. "Yessir." Pug raised his left hand—sans pinkie—in a wave, then ran over to Gorilla, got a set of license plates, zipped back across to the closed-transport truck, and got to work.

I felt surprisingly relaxed.

Maybe those salt mine spas aren't a bunch of hooey, after all.

I wasn't sure if it was gazing upon the swells of sparkling snowy mounds or inhaling the microscopic particles, but I was finding *Halotherapy Heist* far more enjoyable than any of the other generally unpleasant situations I'd been in with Stannislav.

The leader of Stannis's men went and rapped three times on the semitruck driver's door. Kontrolyor was behind the wheel, still recognizable in sunglasses, gloves, and a ball cap. A man wearing a motorcycle helmet with the shield down sat next to him on the passenger seat.

Another man went and opened the garage door. Kon gave a short salute to Stannis and me and then drove away.

"Why is that guy wearing a helmet?" I asked.

"The transport driver? The helmet is secured to his head," Stannis said. "The visor is painted black. He is left blind, deaf, and dumb."

"Why not leave him bound and gagged somewhere?"

Stannis pointed a teasing finger at me. "This is what you do not consider. What if he is needed? For police stop or if something goes wrong with radio, with GPS, with Dispatch? Or what if someone finds him? Or gets brave and tries to escape?" He shook his head. "No. Control him, control situation."

I chewed my lower lip. It was salty. "What happens to him now?"

"He will be left at designated area. His phone turned back on and dialed nine-one-one. They will find him with helmet. He will say nothing."

"Maybe not today," I said.

Stannis laughed. "Not ever. An envelope with one thousand dollars and same picture of family that made him put on helmet arrives in mail. Man still has job. Still has family. And now has story to tell grandchildren."

Another truck entered the dome. The same drill as before, only faster as the closed-transport man from the first semi assisted. Six Lexuses. Four sedans were loaded into two containers as before.

The last two Lexuses were cars I'd only read about. One, a blood-orange RCF sports coupe, carrying a price tag of $180K, was loaded into a yellow twenty-foot container. The other, a chocolate-bronze sedan LS 460 TMG Sports 650 worth at least $250K, was loaded into a more rust-colored than red twenty-footer.

There were still six containers left.

Stannis had told me a dozen cars at lunch. He'd stolen two dozen.

My $1.5M guesstimate to the BOC was at least a million low.

The last two transports arrived and began unloading Cadillacs and BMWs. The shiny reds and blues seemed iridescent against the white mountains of salt. I recognized both drivers from BOC photos of Stannislav's known associates.

An electronic chirp sounded. Stannis pulled a burner cellular out of his jacket pocket. "Hold."

He jerked his head toward a bright orange bulldozer, its nose buried in salt, that sat abandoned in the corner. We climbed up and into the cab.

Stannis hit Speaker. "Go ahead."

"All transports have left?" hummed Black Hawk's electronic voice.

"Last two unloading," Stannis said. "Electronic transponders disabled in closed transports, removed and destroyed from cargo. New plates on trucks."

"Good. Calls were made. Dealerships now expect delivery to be late. A suspicious object at Roseland will pull additional officers south. Unnecessary precaution, I think."

A bomb scare near Chicago State University? Cripes, these guys think of everything.

"Never unnecessary," Stannis said.

"And *Vatra Anđeo?*" Black Hawk's robotic voice asked. "What does she think of my snow palace?"

"Brilliant." Stannis elbowed me. "I have two twenty-foot containers. Deliver yellow one to CEC Intermodal long-term storage under name . . ." He smirked. "Maisie McGrane."

Lovely.

"Okey. My men and I will arrive within thirty minutes to set up perimeter guard," Black Hawk said. "I bring additional driver to take single container and two more. I call with release time."

"Be what will be."

"Yes," Black Hawk said.

Stannis disconnected and turned to me. "Is good, yes?"

I tried to track along. "So the four drivers dump their hostages and transport and come back here?"

He nodded. "Yes."

"Then those drivers and Black Hawk's three more will each drive a truck with two trailers at the same time."

"Is called 'driving bi's'."

"Yes. To the CEC train yard. Tonight?"

Stannis shrugged. "Or later this week. Is up to Black Hawk." He gestured at the men sealing and locking the containers. "Four drivers, four men to disable the electronics systems, plus the four I have here. That is dozen. Add *Chyornyj Yastreb*, who brings six more. Each extra man triples chance of things to go wrong."

And of these, the only one who's going to stab you in the back and cut out your heart is me.

The organization and attention to detail was out of my

league. I folded my arms across my chest. "How do you prevent this?"

"Carry fire in one hand, steel in the other."

Yeah, I pretty much figured you were gonna say something like that.

Back at the penthouse, I brought Stannis a vodka rocks martini from the kitchen. He was behind his desk on the phone, the Serbian flying hot and heavy, punctuated with "Fuck Eddie." He went quiet for a bit, brows knit together. He grunted and said, "*Good bie, Ujka Goran.*"

I set the drink at his right hand, went behind him, put my hands on his shoulders, and began to knead my thumbs into his knotted muscles.

"Is good, Maisie." He took a drink and sighed. "Good day so far." He relaxed into the chair, letting me work the base of his neck. "Later we go to CEC and watch as before. You come with?"

"Do I get my own binoculars this time?" I asked archly.

He laughed. "Yes."

"I'll go change," I said, fishing for a time. "I'm wearing a hat and bringing a jacket this time."

Stannis put his hands on mine. "Not until midnight." He looked up at me, over his shoulder. "We take nap."

And there I was, wrapped in a woobie of Serbian mobster love and undercover guilt, lying on his bed, stroking his hair, wondering how I was going to get a call in to the BOC.

His head rested on my lower abs, his arm possessively tucked around my waist.

Awesome. Because there is nothing like cuddling with a guy you're going to send to prison.

His back rose and fell in even measures. I was just about to wriggle out from beneath him when his phone rang from the office. He jerked awake, rolled off the bed, and trotted out of the bedroom and down the hall, closing the door behind him.

I hit the buttons on my watch and they glowed. The apartment was tracking all electronic signals.

Here's hoping a text slides under the radar.
I hit Text and typed to Edward:

Tonight, I'll dream that we'll go walking with Patsy Cline where we talked about.

Cryptic and eccentric, maybe, but Edward ought to be able to figure it out.
Fingers crossed.

Chapter 38

12:07 a.m. we were back on the bluff overlooking the CEC Intermodal train yard. Everything went as before. Raw Chicken stayed in the car. Kontrolyor manned a night-vision spotter scope, while the rest of us had ATN Night Scout VX night-vision binoculars.

I also had the yips.

Bad.

The really supes-fab thing about the BOC was never knowing if they had your fecking back.

Gorilla checked in with drivers over burner phones with notebook at hand while Stannis oversaw everything with a laptop on the hood. Kon was at the spotter scope. And angry. "Is too much light and dark to read the container numbers."

"Read plates." Stannis unfolded a piece of paper. Kon read off license plates as Stannis read by the light from the computer screen.

I swept the yard with my binoculars, searching for the BOC. They'd had one day and less than a five-hour window to assemble. I scuffed the toe of my boot in the dirt.

Silly rabbit. Panicking for nothi—

Two men in hard hats and reflective jackets pulled up in a golf cart. I recognized one of the BOC's Special Unit Grims.

Edward decoded my crunked-up message after all.

Dammit.

"Hey!" I said. "Who are the guys in the white hard hats?"

Stannis clicked on the computer bringing up a pair of men who waved the crane that had just loaded Stannis's first trailer onto the boxcar.

One for the money, two for the honey, and here we go.

I ran over to Stannis and the computer. One man consulted a clipboard while the other walked back to the golf cart and picked up a bolt cutter.

"We are compromised." Stannis put his phone in my hands. "Get to street. Call *Chyornyj Yastreb* when safe." He took the binocs from my hand and gave me a shove toward the dirt road.

Never look at a free pass to un-ass too closely.

I took off at a sprint.

Even in the dark, the dirt road was easy to navigate. I kept close to the edge so I could hit cover when the BOC's squad drove up.

Ripped off my feet, a heavy hand clamped over my mouth before I could make a sound.

Hank?

"Easy, now. Easy," teased a soft and familiar voice in my ear. "You're okay," Lee Sharpe said. "Except for the fact that your new boyfriend's a POS Serbian enforcer."

My blood was pulsing like a water hammer.

"Cool?" he said. I nodded and he let go. I took a shaky step back. Lee was in full SWAT battle rattle, body armor, face blackened with camo paint.

Holy cat.

Lee Sharpe is the BOC's freelancer?

Just once, could a girl catch a break?

Two human shadows were visible behind Lee. Probably another trio on the other side of the mesa, and a sniper or two.

I didn't know where to start. "Lee—"

"*Tsst!*" He jabbed an index finger at my nose.

The tiniest hum of vibration buzzed no louder than a mosquito. If I hadn't been so hyperaware, I would have missed it.

Lee held up a fist to the men and pressed his finger to the clear plastic piece at his ear. "Copy." He shook his head, dropped his hand, and made a cutting motion across his throat to the two men.

Mission aborted.

The whites of Lee's eyes gleamed iridescent in the moonlight. "I won't tell your brothers, your father, or the assistant state's attorney you were here if you don't tell Stannislav Renko about us."

I nodded furiously, not trusting myself to speak.

He caught me by the chin, leaned in, and said in a low voice, "Tell you what, Bae. When you come to the realization that I am the sexiest motherfucker you've ever met, call me. You got my number."

I turned and he smacked me on the butt.

Cute.

In three strides I was back on the dirt road, heading down the hill. It took a little less than forty minutes to jog the three miles from the overlook to the bus stop near the exit. Which gave me a tension release and time to think.

Something had gone very, very wrong with the stolen cars.

Special Unit didn't know where they were and they weren't going to move on Renko until they did.

And Lee.

Special Unit hadn't told Mr. SWAT-for-Hire I was on the team. Which meant they were trying to keep my cover intact.

I cooled my heels for a solid hour. Bus benches suck. The metal plank had no back and two plastic dividers so I couldn't lie down. *Awesome.* Especially since there'd been no bus in over an hour.

Chicago City Planning Department. Efficiency at its finest.

I dragged my finger across Stannis's contacts again, waffling back and forth over pressing the Sikorsky helicopter. No way I'd call Black Hawk. Not really. Nor would I have called Kon or Gorilla's burners, even if I could.

Hank's Law Number Twenty-Two: When among wolves you must act the wolf.

Xenon LED headlamps temporarily blinded me. The Range Rover stopped. Kontrolyor got out and opened the rear passenger door for me. He gave an almost-imperceptible shake of his head.

Not good.

Stannis stared out the window swearing. Not loud, not soft, just a steady, unbroken stream of cusswords in multiple languages.

I slid in next to him and fastened my seat belt. We hit the freeway and Stannislav's phone rang. He hadn't turned from the window or stopped cursing.

No pressure, no diamonds. Maybe undercover work is a girl's best friend after all.

I answered it. "Hello?"

"*Vatra Andeo?*" hummed the familiar electronic voice. "Mr. Renko, please."

I hit Mute. "It's Black Hawk," I said to Stannis and hit Speaker.

"Where will we celebrate?" Black Hawk said.

Stannis glared at the phone, but his voice was silky. "Where are the cars?"

"On the way to Juárez," answered the robotic voice.

"The containers were stopped at the CEC. No cars."

"Exactly." Black Hawk laughed, jarring and flat. "We owe *Vatra Andeo* a debt beyond measure. Her blessing of cunning was too much like Sun Tzu's *The Art of War.* 'Take advantage of the enemy's unreadiness, make your way by unexpected routes, and attack unguarded spots.' And so I change train."

Stannislav's face was a twisted amalgamation of wronged relief. "Why did you not tell me?"

"I hear the mafiosos sometimes look to take advantage."

"Constantino wants no war with Slajic. Too much money to be made." Stannis's mouth went level with fury. "This is all Veteratti. Eddie Veteratti."

"Inspectors are government," Black Hawk cautioned. "Police informant?"

I jerked upright as if someone had slipped an ice cube down my shirt.

Hank's Law Number Two: Respond to threats with complete confidence.

"No," Stannis said. "But anyone can give tip-off." He rubbed the back of his neck. "How did you switch?"

An electric hiss sounded. "When your drivers returned, I sent them to an alternate site. They picked up the wrong containers and delivered them to CEC. My men moved the containers out of salt storage building. New drivers, unaware of cargo, took the cars to JLB Intermodal."

Black Hawk gave an eerie bark of electronic laughter. "We made money from CEC delivery. Twelve hundred dollars under table."

Stannis chuckled. "Your bonus."

"Already spent." He laughed again. "I used it to attach to Z-train, nonstop to Juárez. Containers will be in Tampico soon. I call with update. When is the party?"

"We celebrate when they are on boat to Lebanon." Stannis's smile was thin and vicious. "At The Storkling."

Chapter 39

When I thought things couldn't get any worse, I hadn't meant it as a karmic challenge.

I spent the next forty-eight hours working out, playing backgammon, and watching Netflix from Stannislav's pocket. The signal tracker was on, the penthouse littered with his men, and he had no inclination to go anywhere.

For some reason known only to him, Kontrolyor thought that sharing yet another tragic Russian breakfast recipe would alleviate my cabin fever. He set a plate in front of me that held a pinkish white slab heavily peppered on coarse rye bread. "*Salo*," he said.

Gorilla and the two other men lounging in the kitchen and eating donuts thought this was hilarious.

"What it is?" I asked.

"Sliced pig lard. Delicious."

Mmm! Nummy! Almost as good as raw bacon.

"Do not eat," Stannis whisper-warned in my ear, before saying in a voice everyone could hear, "We leave in an hour."

I sat at the counter until Kon turned his back, wrapped a sizeable chunk of the *salo* in my napkin, and hid it in the pocket of my robe. "Thanks for breakfast, Kon."

Gorilla leered at me.

"What's that?" I pointed across the room. He turned. I swiped the donut off his plate and trotted down the hall to my room.

I flushed the *salo* down the toilet, took a shower, and got ready. When I came out of the bathroom, a present—my outfit for the day—hung on the closet door hook. A St. John Milano pique-knit fitted blazer and scoop-neck dress in caviar black.

Two thousand dollars of clothes from a brand I thought was too old for me.

I looked like a million bucks in it.

I added a Stephen Webster black diamond bracelet and the Cartier earrings and went out to meet Stannislav Renko.

There is nothing quite as wonderful as flying via private jet. No lines, no security, just a drive right up to the tarmac and a dropoff at the plane.

The Lear 60XR belonged to cartel boss Carlos Grieco. Peerless didn't come close to describing the spacious, stand-up cabin, ebony wood veneers, supple ivory leather seats, Wi-Fi, and every electronic accoutrement known to man.

The flight attendant served us diet Schweppes Tonic Water with lime.

"Eat little. Drink less," Stannis said. "Cartel men are like roosters and mad dogs together."

Awesome possum. Let's do business with Dr. Moreau.

Even with Gorilla and Kontrolyor in tow, we weren't exactly going in heavily armed. The apprehension must have showed on my face.

"I deal with Alfonso Javier Rodriguez," Stannis said. "The bastard son they call 'El Cid.' He is like me. Levelheaded."

Exactly how I think of you, sweet pea. "That's reassuring."

"He is up-and-coming *capo*. Do not trust him."

The lack of alcohol in the tonic water must have gone straight to my head because I blurted, "Aren't you worried about getting the cars through customs?"

His chin dipped in amusement. "There are no customs for things to leave the United States. Only to come in." He smiled. "Again, train cars are mere packages. Not for anyone except sender and receiver."

I know it's true. It just seems so . . . utterly unbelievable.

Stannis set a familiar red box on the table between us.

Cartier.

Hmm. Well. Gosh.

I opened it. A diamond engagement ring.

The Tank de Cartier. A thick white-gold band with a square-cut princess diamond sunk in the center. Designed as the antithesis of showy oversized stones, it could hold no stone larger than 1.15 carats.

Whiskey Tango—Feck!

"Gee . . ." I breathed.

"You like, yes?" Stannis said, nodding. "Is not good to be only girlfriend in Mexico." He took the ring out and put it on the finger of my left hand. A size six, it fit perfectly.

"Yes," I said.

"Good." He sat back in his seat and opened a magazine.

I held my hand out and waggled my fingers, admiring the whiter-than-white sparkler.

Fate's a twisted bastard.

The engagement ring I always wanted. From the man I didn't.

The Lear landed in Tampico in less than six hours. El Cid and his crew met us at the hangar of the private airfield.

Stannis and I descended the stairs to a guy in his late twenties, ringed by a squad of four heavily armed men. Standard Cartel projection—power and muscle. Each wore ballistic vests, Sig P226 handguns, and Ingram MAC 11 spray-and-pray submachine guns.

El Cid was a couple inches shy of six feet. Lean-jawed and hungry-looking, shaved head with reflective sunglasses and an unlit Cubano in his mouth. He was ripped as rock in cargo pants and a black T-shirt.

He gave Stannis a bear hug, then offered his hand to me and said in perfect English, "I am Alfonso Javier Rodriguez. But everyone around here calls me El Cid. And you are?"

I put my hand in his. "Maisie Mc—"

"She is *Vatra Andeo*," Stannis interrupted. "My fiancée."

El Cid's mouth smirked around his cigar. "Nice to meet you, Vatra. Shall we?"

They escorted us out to two armor-plated Lincoln Naviga-
tors, drivers waiting behind the wheel. Gorilla and Kontrolyor
rode in the lead car, while Stannis and El Cid and I were in the
tail SUV.

We passed through miles of *colonias*—Tamaulipas slum
housing—that seemed to stretch forever. El Cid said, "I was surprised to get your call, Renko. Your reluctance to do business
with us is well-known. You do not trust Mexicans?"

Stannis burst into laughter and smacked El Cid in the chest.
"You attend American college, yes?"

"An MBA from UCLA." El Cid rolled the cigar in his mouth.
"What of it?"

"Only college man tries to influence by calling racist."

"Busted." El Cid flashed his palms and chuckled. "So what's
your holdup?"

"Drugs."

"That's not the only area we operate in."

Stannis shook his head. "Interests too often migrate. No drugs
in my shipment. No drugs used by people working for me."

"And if I can guarantee that?" El Cid asked.

Stannis cocked his head. "We wait and see."

The Puerto de Tampico was one of Mexico's busiest and most
important east coast seaports. A small city unto itself, it was the
future of modern port works.

"The Puerto de Tampico is one of the few ports served by
double-railway," El Cid said as we drove into one of the public
terminals. "Your containers are unloaded from the train and directly onto the container ship."

"With correct port-side supervision, yes?" Stannis said.

"It's extremely difficult for any port to ensure one-hundred-
percent accuracy when transporting over nine million tons of
cargo annually." El Cid sighed. "The services Mr. Grieco pro-
vides are unparalleled."

"*Numero cuatro.*" The driver announced our destination as
he put the Navigator in Park.

We got out and walked two city blocks to watch the intermodal crane lift the containers from the Juárez train onto the container ship, while the stink of tar, salt spray, and diesel fuel wafted over us.

"Not that one." Stannis pointed at the twenty-foot rusty red container several containers behind the one the crane had just picked up. "That is gift from Goran Slajic to Carlos Grieco."

El Cid waved over one of his men and rattled off some orders in Spanish. The man took off at a jog to the men working the cranes. El Cid turned to me. "May I inquire?"

Stannis gave me the nod, and I took the key fob out of my purse. "It's a bronze LS 460 TMG Sports 650 sedan. Twin-turbo V8, mind-blowing body kit, fender flares, and stacked exhaust pipes."

"A pretty woman who likes cars." He tipped down his sunglasses, flashing velvety brown eyes. "Hubba-hubba."

That cracked me up. "Get a lot of girls that way?"

"More than I know what to do with." He slid the glasses back up. "What's your story? You a mechanic or a car dealer in your spare time?"

"Neither. With five gearhead older brothers, it was either man up or shut up."

"What rims you rollin' in?"

"Dodge Challenger," I said, not even trying to stop the grin from spreading across my face. "SRT Hellcat."

"No shit?" El Cid tagged me in the shoulder.

God, I miss Hank. "Hey, a girl never knows when she's gonna need to unleash an ungodly hell storm of speed."

"You get that bitch on the track?"

"Not yet." I shook my head. "What do you drive?"

"Aside from being trapped in the Navigator like some prep-school prig?" He spat on the ground. "Only time will tell. I just lost my baby in a race. A '68 Road Runner. I was haulin' the mail, cut a tire, and that was that."

Seriously? "Where are you racing?"

"Autódromo Potosino. Tequila and gasoline, *chica.* Ohhh yeah."

"Don't they run a NASCAR there?"

"A minor one. The track belongs to Carlos Grieco now. My boss is obsessed with Richard Petty and Banjo Matthews. He prefers to settle disputes on the track."

"In hard-to-corner classic muscle cars," I said, shaking my head. *Crazy cartel bastards.* "Talk about nerves of steel."

"That's me." El Cid smiled. "I race myself. Unlike the other lieutenants, who race by proxy. And you're gonna love this— you can race your own or bid to 'rent' one of his, which, if you wreck it, you bought it."

"Wow." I glanced at Stannis, who gave me the frown-shrug of "*are you okay?*"

El Cid caught it. "Tell me, how'd a sweet thing like you hook up with a badass like Renko?"

"Just lucky, I guess." I squinted at him. "You're awfully charming when you don't need to be. What are you after?"

"You."

I rolled my eyes. "Oh, I'm your huckleberry."

He waved his finger at me and quoted *Tombstone* right back. "Oh, you're no daisy. You're no daisy at all." He laughed and stomped his feet in a mini-dance.

"That's right." I smiled.

"Do you have any idea how hard it is to find someone who knows shit worth knowing around here?" El Cid ran a hand over his shaved head. "You're one cool kitty."

"Back at you," I said.

One of his men approached and said something.

El Cid reached into his pocket. "Time to head back to the air-field." He held out his hand to shake and palmed me his business card. "My private number."

"Gee, thanks, Hef."

El Cid grinned around his cigar. "You slay me, *Maisie.*"

Chapter 40

I sank into the leather seat of the jet, exhausted and beyond elated to leave Tampico.

It was a bit of a shocker, however, to find out we were returning to Chicago via Honduras.

"Three days of beach," Stannis said. "I watch the ship load."

I vaguely recall the U.S. government issuing a travel ban.... "I didn't pack anything."

"How much for swimsuit?" Stannis raised a finger. The flight attendant came over. "What can I get you, sir?"

"Vodka. Two glasses. Leave bottle."

She returned after a few moments with a bottle of Chopin on ice and a plate of black bread, caviar, and its accoutrements. We clinked glasses. I struggled to sip it, overcome with the desire to get so hammered I couldn't feel my teeth.

"What think you of El Cid?" Stannis asked.

"I like him," I said noncommittally. "New business partner?"

"Isolated deals, okey. Maybe. Never business."

"Why not?"

"Cartels are empires built on sands of drugs. Greedy, risky money. They destroy everything they touch."

"There's trouble in all business, even legitimate ones," I said.

"No. A drug addict will sell his own child and become whore. The need for drug fuels his animal cunning."

He threw back his drink. I followed suit and poured us another.

"Still," Stannis said, "I like Alfonso Javier Rodriguez. Is clever. Smart."

"He's not that smart," I said.

"Oh?"

I reached in my pocket and took out the business card with no name, only a number and held it up between my fingers. "He believes I'm engaged to you, yet gives me his private number."

Stannis chuckled in pure delight. "You keep safe, *Vatra Anđeo*. He is useful for us."

We landed on Honduras's Roatan Island airstrip and were met by the Mayoka Lodge concierge, who whisked us to French Harbour after Stannis explained I had no luggage.

A sundress, shorts and tee, sunscreen, and two swimsuits later, we were delivered into the lodge's presidential suite. Quiet seclusion with exceptional views, pure rustic luxury. Dark wood, white linens, and Wi-Fi. And, my God, did I have calls to make.

But Stannis, being Stannis, kept me within arm's reach at all times. He was that crushy best friend you love but who never gives you a minute to think, much less a half hour to call your boss to get permission to stab him in the kidneys, making sure to twist the knife on the way out, immobilizing him before slitting his throat in betrayal. The stress was eating me alive. I looked almost gaunt. I hadn't slept in days.

For three days, we snorkeled—poorly, because I was a terrible swimmer—and sunned and shopped and drank.

Sunday, he got the call. The container ship was coming into Port of Puerto Cortes. "You miss Black Hawk again," Stannis said.

"Why?"

"You are unwell, I think," he said. "You stay in room and rest."

"I promise," I said and meant it.

He took Gorilla and Kontrolyor. The second they left, I hit the buttons on my watch. No signal tracking.

I called Edward Dunne.

"Maisie, me gel!" He sighed in relief. "You fair put the heart crossway in us all!"

Nice to know someone cares.

It was good to hear his voice. "I'm on Roatan Island, Honduras. The cars were shipped via another line through Juárez to Tampico, loaded on a container barge, and are entering the Port of Puerto Cortes today. Final destination, somewhere in Lebanon is as close as I can get."

"When can you come in?"

"Soon. I'm hoping we return to Chicago tonight or tomorrow."

"Good," he said. "Good."

"How bad is it?"

"Well, Danny's fit to be tied. Can't blame her, after calling in the Feds only to have it go arseways."

"I couldn't help that—"

"Of course not, lass. Don't fret," Edward said. "Stay safe and come home."

I hung up and called Hank.

"Good afternoon, Miss McGrane," answered the languid drawl of his secretary. "Mr. Bannon is out of country. He won't be available by phone for thirty-four hours and twenty-two minutes. Can I help you?"

Lovely. "Nope. Just checking in." I tapped the red End Call button onscreen.

I dialed home. Because why the hell not?

Mom answered. "Where are you?"

"Hi to you, too, Mom. I'm on a mini-break with Stannis."

"I don't like him."

"That's funny, because I think Walt Sawyer is a prince of a guy."

She gave an inelegant snort. "I know a criminal when I see one, baby."

How does one argue the truth?

"And Hank?" Mom said.

"He knows we're just friends. The thing Hank can't figure out is why Flynn would e-mail him pictures of Stannis and me."

"That was wrong of him. Wrong," she admitted tightly. "You missed the latest on TV, I take it."

Great. Now what?

I fingered the notch at the base of my collarbone. "Oh?"

"Leticia and someone named Sanchez apparently foiled a fraud ring."

Well, this conversation just went to hell faster than a handbasket full of hookers strapped to a Lockheed SR-71 Blackbird.

"And somehow," Mom continued, "Koji and Cash, of all people, ended up with credit for the bust. In fact, they're going to receive a Department Commendation ribbon of merit. From the illustrious Mayor Coles, of course."

Even money that Cash was Googling *Waterboarding: Tips and Techniques.*

"Imagine that." I smiled. "I bet their SWAT teammates will be so jealous."

"When are you coming home? There are some things we need to discuss."

If you only knew.

"As soon as I can."

Chapter 41

We made quite an entrance at The Storkling, Stannis in a black Hugo Boss suit and me in a pale blue and silver Roberto Cavalli dress that made my legs look a mile long. Our backdrop of muscle didn't hurt, either, as three of his guards in dark gray suits with Gorilla and Kontrolyor brought up the rear.

Stannis had reserved the lounge for the celebration. Gorilla texted an invitation to his men moments after we landed. Judging from the overall lack of sobriety, the men and their dates must have left the instant they got it, changing in the car on the way to The Storkling. At the sight of their leader, however, the men instantly straightened up and quieted down. Their dates, less so.

On our arrival, the lounge staff came out with trays of rakija shots.

Stannis raised his glass.

Please don't make it ghastly.

"If you fear the butcher remain out of slaughterhouse," Stanislav said.

His instantly sobered-up men threw back their shots as though they were their last.

That's what us leprechauns call "horrifically delicious."

"Think that was bad?" I held up my left hand with the ring Stannis told me to wear that evening. "You should have heard how we got engaged."

Everyone laughed. The relief washing over the lounge was almost palpable. Including Stannis, who kissed me to cheers.

He and I worked the room, all laughs and smiles and how d'ye dos. The women, unaware of the power he wielded, were far more receptive to our charms.

After a half hour, we left his men and Gorilla and Kon in the bar and walked through the gold curtains into the dining room.

Bobby Blaze was in full swing, singing a buoyant and hip version of "Alright, Okay, You Win."

The Storkling was North Pole kind of chill. How someone as unaware and uncouth as Eddie V. could create this oasis of cool in Chicago was beyond me.

The maître d' led us to Eddie's table, set for six this evening. Zuzu Coles, Eddie, Mayor Coles, and three empty chairs. Zuzu gave a girlish giggle. "We're so very improper around here. But boys will be boys, talking over each other. I find it's easier this way."

Stannis sat next to the mayor. I sat on Stannis's left next to the empty chair between Zuzu and me that I assumed belonged to Bobby Blaze.

"*Chyornyj Yastreb* will not be with us tonight, *Vatra Andeo*," Stannis said softly to me. "He had some difficulties in his travel plans. But you will meet him soon enough."

One less gangster to worry about.

As soon as politely possible, I made a beeline for the restroom and texted Edward.

Ever see The Eagle Has Landed? *Maybe I can come by tomorrow and we'll watch it on Netflix.*

I returned to my seat, only to have Zuzu pat the chair next to her. "Miss McGrane?"

"Yes, ma'am?"

"Zuzu, please." She smiled but her eyes were shrewd. "Why, are you wearing an engagement ring?"

"Yes."

"To Mr. Renko?"

"Yes, ma'am."

"Why, isn't it the sweetest thing you ever heard, Talbott?" Zuzu exclaimed. "Eddie had just told me the terrifying story of how Mr. Renko saved Miss McGrane from a violent assault." She pressed her hand theatrically to her breast. "Have you ever heard of anything so romantic?"

For a split second I actually wondered if steam would shoot out of Talbott Cottle Coles's ears.

Apparently Zuzu did, too. "Eddie, dearest, shall we order champagne for the table?"

Eddie grinned. "Certainly."

Stannis showed no interest in anything or anyone, including me.

"Mr. Veteratti," I said, trying to calm the bizarro love triangle at the table, "you are too kind. While it is so generous of you and Mrs. Coles, Stannis and I are not here as your guests. We came to celebrate a success amidst friends. And as is the Serbian way, rakija is our drink this night."

"What kind of success?" Eddie asked.

Stannis eyed him coldly. "Not yours."

Seriously? WTH?!

Eddie jammed a finger in his ear and shook it. "Oh, I fuckin' know you din't just say that to me."

"My business is not your business."

"You're in my goddamn town, asshole. You think you talk to the Don and everything's copacetic? Is that it?"

"Yes." Stannislav's hand strayed toward his pants pocket.

"Eddie, really!" Zuzu put a hand on his arm.

"Just kidding around, Zuzu baby." Eddie backed down, thinking he had lost a step with Zuzu. He scowled at Stannis. "Renko's the biggest fucking joker of them all. Isn't that right, Miss McGrane?"

Whoa. Definitely put a foot wrong tonight.

I flashed Stannis a love look for Zuzu's benefit. "Oh, he's the king."

Zuzu didn't care either way. "Eddie, let's us toast their future together with your fabulous champagne cocktails."

This perked Eddie up tremendously. He gestured and the waiter was instantly at his side, taking his order. Eddie and Zuzu put their heads together behind the menu in deep discussion.

I stared uncomfortably into space, ignored on both sides.

Talbott tipped his head to Stannis. "Jesus fucking Christ," he said, voice low and forcibly contained. "You know who her fucking family is, don't you?" He sounded eerily like Eddie. "Cops and lawyers."

"Defense attorneys," Stannis said. "I meet her mother last week at Tru. Lovely woman."

That didn't go over well. "Is she your fucking secretary or isn't she?"

"*Vatra Anđeo* is no secretary." Stannis gave him an electric smile with sparks dancing in his eyes to match. "She is my luck."

"Good luck charm? That calamitous bitch?"

Stannis turned slowly to face Coles head-on. "Never call her that."

Coles shook his head, jaw slung forward. He glared at me. "There's a contract in the car I want to show Eddie. Why don't you go fetch it?"

Luckily, Stannis didn't recognize "fetch" as Coles meant it. Any reason to get away from this sniping was good enough for me. I stood up. "I'd be happy to, sir."

Stannis caught my wrist and pulled me down to whisper in my ear, "Take man with you."

I nodded and he let go.

On the way out, I stopped in the lounge to see just who the lucky winner was going to be.

Not Gorilla, who had a girl in a shiny gold dress sitting on his lap. Kontrolyor loomed sullenly in the corner, mouth in a snarl. I signaled him over. "Can you walk me outside but not stay too close?"

"That is not valid protection," Kon said.

I gave him a polite smile. "Fine. I'll ask someone else." I surveyed the lounge full of drunken patrons.

Kon blew out his breath and held out his arm. I took it and he escorted me out of The Storkling and into the night.

Fifty feet ahead of the valet stand, Zuzu's Bentley was parked behind Coles's limo, directly in front of the alley where Jeff Mant had tried to suffocate me.

Ah, the memories.

In full chauffeur regalia, Poppa Dozen leaned against the trunk of the limo, blowing smoke rings.

"How about you wait right there?" I said to Kon and pointed to the mouth of the alley. Better than a kick in the shins, he begrudgingly obliged.

"Hey, Dozen," I said.

Dozen gave me a lecherous once-over, complete with wolf whistle. "Damn! Where you been keepin' your fine self, Bluebird? You out lookin' for a razzle?"

"Uh . . . no," I said. "Coles sent me to retrieve some papers?"

"Man ain't got no papers." Dozen fingered the soul patch on his chin. "He just want you to go away."

Yeah, I figured. I pinched the bridge of my nose. "Well, we better find some. Renko's not going to appreciate him sending me on a fool's errand."

"Girl, where the fuck your head at? Din't you hear me at Impound?"

"I heard you."

"Hell, you did! Look, I ain't gonna bust him out, but you saved my goddamn life. So I'm gonna tell you what I tole him, 'I got no problem merking a mutherfucker. But I got a big problem merking a mutherfucker who done me a solid,' you dig?"

"Coles asked you to kill me?"

"Yeah. But he weren't serious at the time."

Cripes. I ran a hand through my hair.

"Hold up!" Dozen grabbed my left hand, eyes wide.

Kon lunged out of the shadows. "Easy, Kon," I said. "It's cool."

"No, it ain't." Dozen still held my hand. "Who side bustin' our conversation?"

"Renko's man." I freed my hand from his.

"That a fuckin' wedding ring?"

"Engagement," I corrected, "But—"

"We be like . . . friends an' shit, Bluebird, so lemme lay you some. Coles ain't nice, and Renko ain't nicer. Find yourself a new screw, you feel me?"

"Yeah, I feel you."

Bobby Blaze was belting out a sexy, campy version of "My Man." She caught my eye and then looked at an open table near the dance floor.

A return delay to Stannis and Coles's table of strife was A-okay in my book. At that moment I would have happily slipped on an apron and bussed tables.

The torcher ended to healthy applause. The spot went dark and she exited the stage, making the rounds until she finally slid into the seat across from me.

"Hey, kid."

"Hi, Paulette."

She put a finger to pursed lips. "I'm only allowed to be 'Bobby' in the club."

"Sorry."

"Thanks for New York," she said. "I owe you."

"Fuhgeddaboudit. My Mob savvy is a direct result of continued exposure to *The Godfather* and *Goodfellas*."

"You're funny. And fast. I owe you, Maisie."

I tried out my best Cagney. "If youda' left me singin' alone, see, I'd be just another canary wearing a Chicago overcoat."

Paulette was polite enough to laugh. She leaned across the table conspiratorially. "Things haven't been going Eddie's way lately. I'm not saying he's in a jam or anything. But he's a little touchy."

More than a little, at least on Thursday night.

Hank's Law Number Twenty: The most dangerous enemy is the one with nothing left to lose.

I nodded. "This, too, shall pass, yeah?"

Her red lips twisted up at one end. "Eddie may be a hophead asshole, but he's my hophead asshole."

I couldn't help glancing at Eddie V. and Zuzu cozied up at a private back corner table.

"All clear on that front." Bobby swung her curtain of auburn hair over her shoulder. "Gal's got a stick so far up her ass, she never needs a toothpick."

I guess that's one way to put it.

"We oughtta get together, you and me. Have a girls' night. What do you say?"

"That'd be—"

A long, low note played.

Bobby jumped to her feet. "Later. I got another set."

I sat through one more song. But Coles and Stannis didn't look any happier. With a sigh, I forced myself to return to the table. I stopped as I heard their low, angry voices.

"It is business."

"You get engaged in Tampico and don't tell me?" Coles said. "That's monkey business."

Stannis's face was shuttered. "Stop."

"Then you take her to Honduras for four fucking days." Two angry red spots bloomed in Coles's cheeks. "Honduras. And don't bother telling me it wasn't all white sand and sex."

"You make fool of yourself," Stannis said coldly.

If you're trying to turn Coles inside out, you succeeded.

I walked to the table, sans papers.

"Where's the contract?" Coles asked.

Jackhole! Instead I said with a mouthful of honey, "Your driver said an aide picked it up."

A waiter pulled out my chair.

"No." Stannis got to his feet. "We go."

"You're not leaving with her," Coles said.

Stannis took my hand and twined our fingers together. He raised my ringed finger to his mouth and kissed it.

I'd seen the violent side of Stannis before. But never the sadistic one.

We left Coles. Bitter and burning with fever.

Chapter 42

I sat at the kitchen bar, drinking a sugar-free Amp. "Be careful today," I cautioned Stannis, as he slid his Smith & Wesson .44 short into the waistband holster at his back.

He hesitated. "You worry? For me?"

"Of course I do." I *twanged* the metal tab on the top of the can. "Eddie's a loose cannon. When his girlfriend lovingly describes him as a hophead asshole, it's safe to assume he's trouble."

"See? It is as I say. Drugs bad. Drugs scourge of business. Don Constantino would do well to kill him."

Okay-doke. Good talk. "You're not planning to . . ."

He laughed. "Eddie V. is not my trouble."

"He might be."

Stannis came over and kissed my cheek. "I like you to worry." He pinched an inch between his fingers. "Only little."

He left with Kontrolyor, Raw Chicken driving them in the Range Rover to meet Black Hawk. That left me with hungover Gorilla, who was as sick as a small hospital. And about as mobile.

The best liver and onions in town were at Au Cheval. But the lazy bastards didn't open until 11:00 a.m., and honestly, who had that kind of time with a seven o'clock hangover?

I coaxed Gorilla out of the house with a promise of as much as he could eat breakfast at Hollywood Grill on North Avenue. He gorged himself on eggs, pancakes, bacon, sausage, toast, hash browns, coffee, and a milkshake. When we left the restaurant Gorilla looked practically sprightly. Or at least much less green.

"Where do you want to go?" he asked.

"Silverthorn Estates. To see my uncle Edward. Then to my parents' house."

Gorilla grunted and drove us to the assisted living facility.

"I'm going to be a couple hours at least," I said. "He wants to watch a movie. Call you when I'm done?"

"Okey." He drove me to the door, got out, and escorted me to the door.

For once, I didn't feel the slightest guilt at knowing he'd just be waiting around in the car. Nothing like a nap after a big breakfast.

I rode up the elevator, straightening my black suit jacket, smoothing my pants, trying to gear up for a proper ass-chewing.

Anita met me at the doors. "Good morning, Agent McGrane."

Oof. That hurts.

I stiffened to keep my shoulders from sagging. "You, too."

She accompanied me to Danny Kaplan's office, opening the door and closing it behind me.

Not good.

Hank's Law Number Thirteen: Anyone can endure expected pain.

Edward and Kaplan were in position at the conference table. Kaplan wore a pantsuit the color of an editor's red pen, but it was Edward's houndstooth sports coat over a polo shirt that was more damning than Anita's door-to-door service.

Bureaucratic trouble is always accompanied by formality.

"Sit." Danny pointed at the chair with a nail varnished the color of dried blood. "I honestly don't even know where to begin. Edward?"

Edward plucked at a salt-and-pepper brow. "'Twould be only fair to remember this is McGrane's first undercover assignment."

"Horseshit!" Kaplan said. "Anyone savvy enough to ingratiate herself with Stannislav Renko can figure out how to get out and make a goddamn phone call."

Oh yeah? Why don't you try it, sister?

She put her elbows on the table, wrists limp. She resembled nothing so much as a praying mantis spray-painted scarlet. "Do you even realize what a clusterfuck this has become?"

"No, ma'am," I said. "After the shooting, Renko hasn't allowed me anywhere unaccompanied." I tapped the BOC watch they'd given me. "Lights up at the penthouse."

"The shooting?" Kaplan's head twitched from side to side like Netflix with a signal lag.

"Renko's driver and I may have been targets at the Circle K two weeks ago Tuesday."

Edward put his hand on my arm. "Yeh didn't report it, lass."

"No one was injured and it was impossible to know who the actual target was."

"I don't recall receiving the memo that Special Unit had become an EEOE, do you, Edward?" Kaplan said. "But apparently we've hired our own idiot savant."

Aren't you just as compassionate as your average Islamic terrorist?

She ticked off on her fingers. "Unreported shooting. Damaged our relationship with the Feds. Faulty data—"

"My information was solid," I said, unable to stand it. "One of Renko's men transferred the cars to another intermodal train yard. Renko had no idea until your men inspected the containers."

Kaplan and Edward exchanged a look. "Is it possible you've been compromised?" she asked.

"No." I shook my head. "Eddie Veteratti's fallen out of favor with the Don Constantino. And he blames Renko."

She sat back in her chair. Her red suit was so vibrant I saw her negative reflection in green every time I closed my eyes.

Kaplan raised her index finger. "Just for the record, who the hell gave you permission to go to Tampico, much less Honduras?"

"Ma'am?" I asked.

"How could you not consider this would compromise you as an agent? Or worse, compromise Special Unit, or even the BOC?"

"I was in the continued presence of Renko and his men. I called in as soon as possible. The JLB train travelled via Juárez into Tampico, where the containers were shifted to ship."

"That route is well-documented and irrelevant," Kaplan sniped.

Edward gave me a rueful smile. "Once the cars have left US soil, their value is gone."

Jaysus, why not kick me down the stairs and be done with it?

Edward turned to her. "You must admit, her ability to get so close to Renko is remarkable."

Kaplan raised her hands in dismissal. "It's up to Sawyer now."

Feck. I wasn't serious.

Anita had waited for me outside of Kaplan's office.

Terrific. I need a minder now.

She walked me out past the Grims and into the assisted living hall. At her insistence, we stopped in the dining room and had a mini-bottle of water before resuming the march of the condemned. Past the dining room, library, and numerous private rooms.

At the end of the hall, she rapped twice on the door, then twice again.

It buzzed open.

It was an office like any other privately held CEO's. Elegant but utilitarian. I could detect the faint strains of Liszt. Walt Sawyer sat beind a banker's desk of Carpathian Elm Burl, looking as suave and debonair as a Douglas Fairbanks, Jr. "Please, have a seat."

I perched on the edge of a wood-backed upholstered chair. My knee started bouncing. I crossed my legs at the ankles to stop it.

"Last week, two-point-six million dollars' worth of new cars were stolen from the very insurance companies paying Special Unit to take down Stannislav Renko."

I tried to swallow. The muscles in my throat worked, but nothing happened.

"The largest single theft he's pulled off to date. And one of my own agents accompanied him throughout this process." Walt pressed his fingertips down on the black leather desk blotter. "You have proven yourself a brave and resourceful operative. But far too inexperienced for this assignment."

He bowed his flaxen head and said softly, "Patience and caution come with age and experience. I blame myself for allowing this situation to escalate beyond your range as a special agent."

"Sir, while I agree I have become very close to the subject—"

"Your eagerness and inability to maintain boundaries has caused you to compromise the safety of Special Unit, yourself, and your family with the Grieco Cartel."

"What? I met only one of Grieco's lieutenants, Alfonso Javier Rodriguez, in the company of Stannislav Renko."

Walt smiled. "Long enough for El Cid to find you intriguing."

I cocked my head. "I beg your pardon?"

"It has come across our desk that El Cid has been inquiring after you."

Wow. Jaysus. That's really not good.

"I apologize, sir. I think—"

"You will proceed, thus." Walt closed his eyes for a moment. "You will extricate yourself from Stannislav Renko with the barest minimum of strife. Upon satisfactory accounting, you will return to supervising the collection of evidence by your fellow parking enforcement agents."

So that's how it's going to be, huh?

I'll make sure to hustle ass so as not to let the door hit me on the way out.

Or not.

Hank's Law Number Twenty: The most dangerous enemy is the one with nothing left to lose.

I sighed. "Are you having an affair with my mother?"

Walt Sawyer's whiskey-colored eyes met mine. "No." The momentary flicker of longing attested to his truth.

For the moment.

"Any thoughts on how to break up with The Butcher?" I held up my left hand.

Walt's lips thinned. He frowned. "A fake engagement?"

"Yes. But Stannis won't part with me easily. He believes I'm his good luck charm."

Sawyer folded his hands atop his desk. "I have no compunction terminating your employment with Special Unit."

Hardball. In all its badass glory.

I may be a rookie, but you brought me to the big leagues just the same.

"Stannis knows I'm close to my family." I shrugged. "I suppose I could come clean with my mother. Maybe ask her to pretend she's terminally ill."

Walt cupped his chin in his hand, appraising and assessing. "You're exactly like her, you know."

What a lovely thing to say.

I blushed. "Quite a compliment, coming from the man about to terminate my employment."

A slow smile curved up the edges of his mouth. "Perhaps you've been mishandled. A thoroughbred needs a steady hand. To be willfully guided. Danny has a tendency to be choppy at the reins. Yes?"

I nodded.

He changed tack. "Which man of Renko's switched trains?"

"*Chyornyj Yastreb.* Russian for Black Hawk. A Russian hand selected by Goran Slajic for Renko's operation. Stannis treats him as an equal."

"What is he like?"

"I haven't seen him. But he's smart. Cunning. All his conversation is vox modified. He told Stannis he was concerned Eddie Veteratti is out to cause him trouble. Which I think he is. But after Black Hawk switched the trains, he tweaked something I said to give me credit for the heist's success."

Walt straightened. "Black Hawk's either setting him up or trying to move in. Either way, I think perhaps it's time you work directly for me. You need money, equipment? Talk to Edward. Danny's out of the loop for now."

"Yessir."

"Stay close to Stannis. Take no chances. The next move will be ours. And we will manage the situation."

Chapter 43

I left the clean and bright Silverthorn Estates building, feeling relieved and excited and dark and dirty. And sad.

Gorilla idled in the Explorer across the street at the center island. I trotted across the street, trying to shake the guilt raven off my shoulder.

The hulking bodyguard was out of the Explorer and around the hood before I got to the median. "No!" he said. "You were to wait until I came for you. Not safe." He opened the rear passenger-side door. He took my elbow, crowding me as I stepped onto the running board.

I heard a sound like a bare hand slapping a wall.

He fell on top of me, crushing the breath from my lungs and knocking me to the floor of the SUV.

He jerked spasmodically as two more shots struck him.

He wasn't moving. I got one arm free and raised his head.

Gorilla was dead.

I squirmed and wriggled my legs out from under him. A round hit the bulletproof window on the open door and went right through it into the headrest. The Lexan was no match for the high-caliber sniper round. Another came right through the open door into the backseat.

Pinned down.

I couldn't close the rear passenger door. Gorilla was half-in, half-out of the car. I braced my feet, grabbed his suit by the shoulders, and heaved. A bullet tore a hole through the floor inches from my foot.

Holy cat!

Terror pumped strength through me I never knew I had. I adjusted my grip on Gorilla and hurled myself backward, dragging his body into the car. Blood burbled out his mouth, onto my jacket and pants. Crouching, I started forward to pull the door shut.

Bad idea.

I threw myself against the driver's seat.

Hank's Law Number Four: Keep your head.

Duh. There's more than one door in an SUV.

I slipped out the side door, opened the driver's door, and scooted behind the wheel. The key was in the ignition. I turned it, grinding the starter, popped the car in Drive, and stomped on the gas.

Two more shots hit the car as I tore down the street. The interior alarm bells bleeped and pinged like crazy from my lack of seat belt and the still open door. Tires screaming, I took a sharp right at 40 mph, and let gravity close the door for me.

I took a hard left and pumped the gas. Weaving in and out of traffic, head on a swivel, I juiced the gas, my breath coming in short pants.

Hank's Law Number Three: Don't let your lizard brain go rogue.

Gotta calm down. Stay fluid.

I sucked in a deep breath through my nose.

Huge mistake.

My stomach roiled.

Gorilla was dead. The stink of his bodily fluids mingled with blood . . . the stench so heavy it coated the back of my tongue and throat, like gagging up an old penny.

What the hell am I supposed to do now?

Call the BOC? My brothers?

I passed a car on the wrong side and adjusted my grip on the wheel.

The blurp of a siren sounded.

The blue and red lights of the CPD flashed in my rearview mirror. They rolled the siren again.

There's a dead guy in my car.

I pulled over.

Shite! Shite! Shite!

The cop driving lumbered out and cracked his neck before starting toward the Explorer.

No way a cop wouldn't recognize the stink.

Cripes. I scrambled out of the Explorer and took a step toward the officer. At least the blood didn't show on my black suit.

The cop's partner got on the loudspeaker. "Get back in the car, ma'am."

I raised my hands, closed my eyes, and stopped walking.

"Ma-am, please . . ." His voice died away. "Your hair is red?"

Brilliant observation, officer. I opened my eyes and almost closed them again.

Tommy Narkinney.

My arch-rival from the Police Academy and all-around rat bastard who almost got me killed, looking more 'roided-up than ever. "Officer Narkinney." I said.

"Maisie-Daisy McGrane." He waved at his partner to stay in the car and came closer. "You were speeding."

"Yes."

"I'm not going to give you a ticket, but that's it. No more free passes."

Whatever thread of sanity I'd been clinging to snapped inside my brain. I stepped into him, chest-to-chest. "Are you feckin' kidding me?"

"Maisie—" He blanched and rocked back on his heels. "Geez. Never mind. Forget I said anything."

I didn't recognize the voice that came out of me. "The fact that I didn't let Hank kill you makes you my forever-always bitch."

His cheeks quivered.

What in God's name am I doing?

I stepped back. "You better go. Shots fired at Silverthorn Estates." I pointed in the general vicinity.

His face crinkled in confusion.

His partner clicked the loudspeaker twice and hit the lights. Tommy turned to see him furiously waving him to come back to the car.

Tommy looked at me.

"Go," I said.

He jogged back to the car, got in, and took off, siren blaring.

I got back in the Explorer. The smell was overwhelming. I reached back and pulled my purse out from under Gorilla's shoulder. I undid the bloody zipper, got my phone out, and called Hank.

"Mr. Bannon's office," his secretary said, somehow able to make it sound risqué. "Good afternoon, Ms. McGrane. I'm afraid Mr. Bannon's in conference—would you like to leave a message?"

I hung up without speaking. "Siri," I said. "Text Walt. *Okay. Will call.*"

I dialed Stannis. No answer. I called the penthouse.

Kontrolyor answered the phone. "Da?"

"This is Maisie. We have a problem."

"With car?"

Bingo!

"Yes." A giant sigh of relief burst from me. I knew exactly what to do. "Get a message to Stannis. Tell him to meet me at Christo Keck's Garage."

"Da."

"And Kon? Tell Christo I'm coming in hot."

"Hot?" he said in confusion. "I do not understand."

"The car's on fire." I hung up.

The drive was beyond excruciating. I wouldn't let myself even contemplate the corrosive deluge of hydrofluoric acid that would storm down on my family if I got in an accident or, God forbid, got stopped again.

On the plus side, I now knew intimately the nervy adrenaline rush that a killer feels carting a body around.

Finally, I hit Albany Park.

Taking it extra slow, I hit my turn signal well in advance of Keck's alleyway. I pulled in to the narrow passageway, mouth-breathing in short pants.

A man in coveralls unlocked and rolled back the covered chain-link entrance to the rear parking lot. I drove in and he shut and locked the gate behind me.

I got out of the car.

Three men in coveralls glared at me. Keck approached the Explorer, noting the enormous bullet holes in the car. He looked through the broken window and saw Gorilla sprawled between the seats.

In two quick steps he was on me, hand knotted in my hair. He jerked my head back. "Why the fuck do you bring this mess here? To me?" Still holding on to me, he turned to the men. "Wrap him in a tarp. Chop the car."

The men sprang into action, as Keck forced me into the chop shop. He let go with a slight shove toward the counter. He went over to the vending machine, dug out some change, and brought back a Dr Pepper and a Hershey bar.

"No, thanks."

"I may not have a choice over you bringing a fucking dead body into my garage, but you will do as I say until Renko gets here. Eat it."

The soda tasted bitter. The candy bar equally so. I forced them down, eyeing my watch. Within twenty minutes, Christo Keck buzzed Stannis and Kontrolyor into the garage.

Stannis took one look at me and laid his fist over his heart. He rattled off a stream of very pissed-off Serbian at Keck, then, in Russian, snapped an order at Kon, who exited the garage into the rear lot, presumably to check on Gorilla and the Explorer.

Stannis strode up to the counter. He laid a hand on my head and stroked my hair.

"Big holes." Keck tossed a chunk of metal onto the counter. "Went through Ivanovic´'s vest like butter."

"Leave now."

As Keck grabbed his keys and hustled out of the building, Stannis picked up the spent round and examined it. ".308. A pro."

He closed his eyes and took a deep breath, then took out his phone, laid it on the counter, and called *Chyornyj Yastreb.*

"Go ahead."

"New assignment," Stannis said. "Hunting."

"Who?"

"Sniper."

"Importance?" Black Hawk said.

"Critical. Ivanovic̕ is collateral damage."

"Any trail?"

".308 rounds." Stannis set the bullet on the counter. "A pro. Of middling skill."

"You know this how?"

"A hired sniper misses target two occasions," Stannis said. "Should not be difficult to find."

"You?"

"No." Stannislav's hands curled into fists. "*Anđeo.*"

Talk about luck o' the Irish. I'm alive because of the ineptitude of a second-tier hitter.

A high-pitched whine of feedback from Black Hawk's vox creased the air. "Why her?"

"She belongs to me," Stannis said simply.

"Who guards her now?"

"Kontrolyor."

"Is better than Ivanovic̕," Black Hawk said.

"You say because he is Russian."

"No. I say that because he is better." The robotic voice didn't make him sound any sweeter. "Regular rate?"

"Double."

"Done," Black Hawk agreed. "I call you when the job is done."

"No," Stannis said. "Find. Call." He looked at me. "We discuss."

Chapter 44

The Range Rover was running. Kon shielded me into the vehicle. Stannis strode purposely around the rear of the car, scanning the area in defiant anger before getting in.

"The rounds were not slowed by the light armor of Explorer," Kon said from the front seat. ".308?"

Stannislav's eyes filled with tears. "Ivanović." He shook his head. "If only we had taken the Explorer."

Or I had stayed home.

"Where did you go, *Vatra Anđeo?*" Stannis took my hand. "Where did this happen?"

"Ivanović was wrecked from last night. I took him to breakfast at Hollywood Grill." My voice came choppy and short. My breath in short pants. "He drove me to Silverthorn. It happened there."

"What is Silverthorn?"

A slick, clammy sweat coated my entire body.

"Assisted living. Nursing home." Saliva ran down my throat. "See my uncle."

"How long?"

"Two hours."

Kontrolyor glanced back over his shoulder. "Enough time to set up."

Stannis gripped his head with both hands. Kon's unspoken reproof of Ivanović was almost too much for him to take.

If I wasn't such a Grade A screwup, I would have figured out a way to debrief over the phone. To not put a hungover body-guard in the crosshairs.

My crosshairs.

My stomach heaved. "Stop the car."

Raw Chicken didn't flinch. He just kept driving.

I clicked the electric windows. Locked. "Stop! I'm gonna be sick."

"Use floor," Kon said. "Too dangerous to stop."

For feck's sake. Vomit roiled in my throat. I grabbed my purse—with Ivanovic´'s blood still on it—dumped the contents onto the car seat, and threw up in it.

Soda and chocolate. Cold sweat plastered a strand of hair to my cheek.

Dizzy, I zipped the purse and set it on the floor. I leaned my head against the cool bulletproof glass and concentrated on breathing out of my mouth.

Kon made a call as we neared the penthouse. "Okey," he said to Raw Chicken. "Is clear."

We drove into the underground parking garage of Stannis's building. Two of his men were at the entrance, two more inside.

I got out of the Range Rover with my purse full of puke, knees wobbly, sweating ice cubes. Kon took my handbag from me. "I will see—"

"No. For the love of God, throw it away. Please."

A searing hot shower left my skin red, and me still shivering. I put on yoga pants, a T-shirt, a sweatshirt, and wrapped up in a blanket before I went to find Stannis.

He was sitting at the kitchen table, alone. Drinking rakija. The things from my purse were in a ziplock bag on the counter.

"I buy you new handbag," he said and I almost started crying.

"I don't want one." I sat down next to him.

He didn't look at me.

"I'm sorry," I said hoarsely. And I was. Sorry for Ivanovic´, sorry for Stannis, and sorry for my own sorry self.

"You shoulder no blame, *Anđeo*." He swirled the rakija in his glass.

He put his hand over mine. "Look at me." I stared into his pallid face and burning blue eyes. "It is I who is sorry. For my sins to touch you."

"No, *moj davo*," I said softly. "This was not your sins."

"You will be avenged in blood."

I laid my head down on the table and wept.

At Stannislav's insistence, I went to my room to lie down. I still couldn't seem to get warm. The pressure of knowing I needed to talk to Walt Sawyer was like an anchor strapped to my chest.

I needed Hank. Hell bad.

I heard the men arguing in low voices with Kontrolyor over Ivanovic''s death, and a tide of torment broke over me. I couldn't bear another minute in the penthouse.

I put on my shoes and went into the kitchen. "Where's Stannis?"

"His office," someone answered.

The door was slightly ajar. I gave a soft knock and peeked in. Stannis was on the phone. He waved me in.

I stood at the corner of his desk.

He frowned and put his hand over the mic of his phone. "What is it?"

My lower lip trembled. "I want to go home."

"No, no," Stannis said. He removed his hand from the mic. "*Chyornyj Yastreb?* I call you back, yes? *Andeo* is wanting to return home. And this cannot be."

Black Hawk said something.

"Okey," Stannis said and put the phone on speaker.

"*Vatra Andeo?*" said the electronic voice. "You made Stannislav Renko very proud."

"Thank you."

"The gods always smile on brave women."

I hope you're right.

"She has suffered much shock," Black Hawk said. "Perhaps a night with her family is a good idea."

"No. Safer here," Stannis said.

"They will not expect her to move. Let Kontrolyor accompany her."

"Please?" I whispered.

"She is at risk until sniper is caught," Black Hawk said. "I assemble my team, we watch and wait."

Feckin' Black Hawk wants to use me as bait.

"She returns tomorrow." Stannis glanced at his watch. "Kon leaves in one hour." He disconnected and stood up. He put his arm around my shoulder. Together, we walked over to the darkened glass box on the pedestal.

He put his hand on the glass. I put mine next to his. "I promise you, *Vatra Anđeo*. You will be avenged in blood."

My ears were filled with the buzzing and clicking of beetles.

But no noise came from the glass tank.

His phone rang from the desk. He left me and answered it. "Speak." His dark brows knit together as he listened. "Yes, I was pleased with transaction, El Cid."

He waved good-bye to me. "You do not remember our conversation, I think."

I walked to the door in a jerky, lingering stride, desperate to get the hell out of the penthouse but wanting to know what Grieco's lieutenant was after.

"No drugs," Stannis said with finality.

Like the rest of the house, the kitchen was dark, but I knew Cash and Koji were there from his red MDX in the driveway. Twenty to one they were in his room playing video games. Working up my courage to call Walt, I opted for Cash's beat down first.

I knocked on his door, received the expected "no answer" and went in.

They were both sacked out in Cash's beanbags, headsets on, controllers in hand, some version of *Grand Theft Auto* on the television, and dead soldiers scattered all around them.

"Hit me," Koji said.

Cash flipped the lid of a portable Igloo cooler and tossed him another Coors Light.

Koji twisted off the top. "Every frickin' time we're multi-player I get some tweener calling me ghey."

"Or telling you they're banging your mom, amiright?" Cash got out another beer for himself.

"Got one of those for me?" I said, walking over to the TV.

"Nope," Cash said.

Koji frowned. "You totally effed us, Maisie."

"Come on. A departmental commendation's not so bad."

Cash shot me a murderous look. "Oh, look who hasn't heard? Apparently, someone in Coles's office recognized the name Mc-Grane. We're up for a Spirit of Chicago ribbon. And, as the brother to the infamous puking meter maid, Coles's office is pondering some PR brother helping sister nightmare."

Oh shite.

I winced. "I'm sorry. I'll make sure that doesn't happen. I promise."

"Ha! Like you got any pull in this town," Cash said.

"I dunno how long we're gonna be able to take it." Koji shook his head. "The shit we're taking from the team is frickin' brutal."

"I'll talk to Lee."

"Yeah?" Cash's voice went high-pitched and fake-happy. "That'd be, like, sooo cool. Having the squad thinking we tattled. Neato."

Koji giggled.

"Look, I'm sorry," I said, getting nettled.

If he had any idea what had happened to me . . . he would probably act exactly the same way. Or worse.

"Save it. We ain't about to hug this shit out." Cash glared at me. "Your comeuppance is on its way."

"Get over yourself. Cops are supposed to arrest people."

The doorbell rang.

"Oh," Cash said. "It's here now. Why don't you go answer it?"

"On my way," I said. *Jerk.*

* * *

I opened the door.

"Hello, Peaches," Hank said.

"Hi!" I gawped at him.

I've never been so glad to see anyone in my entire life.

"Gonna ask me in?"

"Oh, yeah." I shook off my love haze and swung the door wide. He came in fast, closing it behind him and kissing me.

Gee, I needed that. "How'd you know I'd be home?"

He cocked a brow. "A risk worth taking."

"Want a drink?"

"Sure."

I led him into the den. "Sit," he said.

I went to the couch and turned iTunes onto Da's quiet classical mix. Hank went to the sideboard, browsed the bottles, and decided on Cognac Croizet VSOP. He poured two snifters and brought them over to the couch.

"Thanks," I said.

He sat down next to me and put his arm across the back of the couch. "You're wearing that white-knuckle look."

"Yeah." I swirled the brandy. "I suppose I am."

Hank ran his knuckles against my cheek. "It doesn't suit you."

"Nooo." My voice cracked. "It doesn't."

We drank and listened to the music, Hank steadfast and silent.

The eye of my storm.

"I saw a man I know . . . knew . . . die today." I set my brandy glass down and ran a hand through my hair. "I mean, just living in this house I've seen more crime scene photos than most cops. I've been at murder scenes before, too. I know what death is like." I blew out my breath in a sardonic puff-laugh. "Heck, less than two months ago a dead guy was bleeding on my . . . er . . . your car."

I pressed the middle of forehead. "It's just . . ." My fingers pressed harder, rubbing, trying to force the words from my mouth. "He was shot . . . shot and I couldn't do anything and—" My arm started to shake. "So close. The bullets so close to me."

Hank eased my hand down, wrapped his arms around me,

and held me tight to his chest, his chin on my hair. I didn't cry, didn't make a sound, just trembled like a ribbon tied to a fan.

At some point, in the middle of the shaking, I fell asleep. Hard and dreamless. I jerked awake in his grip.

"You're okay," he said. "And you're going to stay that way."

I nuzzled my face into his chest, breathing in the scent of him. "I believe you."

He kissed the top of my head. "My place?"

I felt so exhausted I could cry. "I . . . can't."

He tipped my chin up and kissed me, sweet and soft-edged with a dark, hot heat. Then he stopped. "You're spent, Slim." He got up and tugged me to my feet. He walked me to the stairway. "I'll call you."

I lay down in my clothes. Too tired to change or even crawl beneath the covers, I pulled part of the duvet over me. My eyes snapped open.

Walt Sawyer.

Dammit.

My phone was downstairs.

Feck me.

I got up, went down, and called in. For a guy who was in love with my mother, he didn't seem particularly bothered that I'd been shot at. Or that Stannis was going to kill whoever did it. He was far more interested in Black Hawk's ID and connections and the call from El Cid.

Chapter 45

I was up before my alarm went off at 5:00 a.m. There was no possible way I was going to fall prey to a parental tag-team interrogation. I changed my clothes, called Kon, and snuck out of the house, down the driveway, and into the Range Rover.

The penthouse night guards were bright-eyed and bushy-tailed. Stannis, however, was sleeping.

Wonderful.

I changed into an oversized tee and went back to bed.

Not everything has to be an ordeal.

I got up around eleven and managed to make a ham sandwich and snag a Coke, while Kon took a smoke break on the balcony.

I lounged on the great room couch, concentrating on the Netflix distraction at hand—Rufus Sewell as Inspector Zen. Dreamy.

With Kon as my new bestie, I wasn't really able to do much except binge-watch episode after episode and swear to him every five minutes that I was perfectly fine and far too full to eat another bite, as he tried to force-feed me more repellent Russian cuisine.

As far as prison went, I'd be hard-pressed to think of a one that suited my design aesthetic any more than Stannis's penthouse. Still, it didn't make it any less agonizing to be feet away from Stannis's office. I had no reason to enter other than to check the progress of the beetles. And that was the kind of mistake that couldn't be unmade.

My phone played the theme music from *Alien*. Unknown number. "Hello?"

A harsh electronic voice said, "This is *Chyornyj Yastreb*. Friend of Stannislav Renko."

Black Hawk. "Yes, hello. I'm sorry, he's not here right now."

"This I know. He is at The Storkling Club. You come for him."

"Is he alright?" I blurted in a rasp. Raw-boned fingers of fear locked around my throat. "What does he need?"

"He needs ride home."

In less than five minutes flat, Kontrolyor and I were speeding to The Storkling in the black-armored Lincoln Continental.

"Do you want me to go in with you?" Kon asked.

"No." I hopped out of the backseat before he'd put the car in Park. "Stay here," I said over my shoulder and sprinted up the stairs.

A thin, nondescript man met me at the door. "This way, please."

I followed him through the main club into a rabbit warren of private rooms and offices. He took me to a padlocked steel door at the end of the hall. He knocked twice, waited, then removed a key from his pocket and unlocked and removed the padlock. He twisted the knob and swung open the door for me but didn't enter.

I stepped across the threshold into a large kitchen storage room and froze. Next to the stainless-steel tables and stools and refrigerator units, stood the six-foot-four bulk of Vi Veteratti's right-hand man, Jimmy the Wolf. Behind him sat Stannis, leg shackled, one wrist handcuffed to the metal arm of the chair. He had a cigarette in his mouth and a glass of what I was rather certain was rakija in his hand. Although his posture was relaxed, his blue eyes were poker hot.

Hank's Law Number Eighteen: Even savage actions have explanations.

The door closed behind me but didn't lock.

A promising sign.

"Hello, boys," I said. "What's the situation?"

Stannis held the cigarette pinched between his thumb and forefinger. He took a deep drag, then flicked the cigarette at Jimmy.

Without a whisper of emotion, the Wolf ground it into the cement floor with his foot. He raised a hand toward the opposite corner of the room. "Please?"

I followed him to the corner.

"We got a problem," he said, brow heavy with concern. "Eddie fucked up. Royally."

"Oookay," I said softly. "Why is Stannis cuffed?"

The Wolf's chin dipped toward his chest. "So he doesn't kill me or start some maniacal crazy shit."

I leaned around one side of Jimmy and glanced at Stannis. He seemed quite calm. "How about we let him go?"

"No." The Wolf took out a cell phone, tapped the keypad, and put it to his ear. "Yes. She's here." He held it out to me. "Vi would like a word."

"This is Maisie," I said.

"I know you were shot at." Violetta Veteratti's nasal tone reverberated in my ear. "And Renko lost one of his crew."

"And Eddie's responsible?"

"Not directly."

"Are you sure about that? He has Mr. Renko chained up like an animal."

"No, he doesn't. I do." Vi sighed. "You have brothers. Five of them. Are there any you wouldn't go to bat for?"

No. But thanks for the implied threat.

"I can understand where you're coming from." I paused. "But the thing is, Ms. Veteratti, I'm not feeling real kindly toward your brother myself, having been shot at twice now."

"I know Renko's man took care of the shooter," Vi said. "I'm offering you and Mr. Renko a debt of honor. You have my word."

Wonder what that's worth on the open market?

I said nothing. Jimmy the Wolf moved in a little closer. I took a step farther into the corner.

"I hear you're the only one able to bring Renko 'round," she pressed. "Are you?"

"Not sure."

"What else can I do to prove I'm sincere?"

My voice dropped to a husky whisper. "What about the lowlife piece of shite who hired the hitter?"

"Eddie finally told me who it was. He'll be delivered to Renko's place within the hour," Vi promised.

Feck. "I didn't ask for that." *The last thing I need to witness is a murder.*

Vi gave a bark of laughter. "Renko did."

"Okay," I said. "I'll do my best." I handed the phone back to the Wolf.

He handed me two sets of keys, all the while keeping one eye on Stannis. "Take your time," he said to me. "Have a drink first."

"Uh, sure."

Knowing what was coming, a drink sounded like a damn fine idea.

I walked over to the counter near Stannis. On the tray were three empty glasses, a bottle of rakija, Marlboro Reds, and matches.

I refilled Stannis's glass, then took an empty one and poured myself a healthy shot. I raised it toward the Wolf, who decided that was close enough to a promise, and left.

"Cigarette," Stannis said.

"I didn't know you smoked." I shook one out, put it between his lips, and lit it.

He blew smoke out of the side of his mouth and raised his cuffed hand. "Only when I wear this."

I laid my hand on his cheek. "You must feel very angry." I took the cigarette from his lips, and he threw back the double shot. "Black Hawk wants you to stay calm." I swapped the empty glass for the smoke. "I want you to stay calm."

"They kill Ivanović. They meant to kill you."

"I'm sorry about Ivanović. He was a good man. He saved my

life." I knelt and unfastened the leg shackles. "Violetta Veteratti has offered you a debt of honor."

"This I know."

I stood up and unlocked the handcuff. "A valuable commodity."

"More than Eddie is worth," Stannis agreed. "She would be better without him."

"The hitter?"

"Black Hawk took care of him. Did Violetta learn the scum who hired shooter?"

"Yes. He's being delivered to the penthouse." I stared into his eyes. "Are you accepting her deal?"

"Of course. Eddie is only small, in the middle." Stannis got to his feet. "Now, let us go see who is to die."

Sweet Christ in a cradle.

Kon kept looking at me in the rearview mirror.

"What?" Stannis barked.

Kon dropped his eyes. "Maisie looks unwell."

Stannis looked at me. "Are you?"

You mean because we're going back to your place to do something unspeakably violent and horrible to a dirtbag who deserves it?

There's not enough Pepto-Bismol on the planet to keep me from hurling up my powerless policeman guts.

"A bit light-headed is all." I tried to smile, but my mouth felt as tight as an old rubber band.

"I tell her to eat—" Kon started to scold and caught himself. "Would you like to stop, Mr. Renko?"

We stopped at Paciugo for gelato. Which was great, because it wouldn't hurt coming back up. I chose vanilla bean. Stannis had lavender and salted caramel.

The first bite was a little closed-throaty and difficult to get down, but it's hard to be freaked out when you're eating frozen angel tears off a spoon surrounded by sleek Italian pastels and terrazzo countertops.

Even if you are eating with *Bik*.

Because I am so never calling you The Butcher. No way. No how.

That misshapen, naïve little thought was a poison blow dart in the chink of my mental armor.

The venom had begun to paralyze and rot, my sense of self bleeding out beneath my skin.

I was lying to everyone I cared about.

Including Stannis.

He stared at me across the table, his electric eye contact unbearable. "What?" I asked. "Do I have something on my face?"

He frowned. "No."

I took the spoon, dragged it across the gelato, and wiped a smudge on my nose. "How about now?"

He blinked. Thinking it over.

And then he laughed, warm and beguiling. His smile baring his slightly crooked, clean teeth.

Disarming. Delightful.

Deadly.

He leaned forward with a napkin and wiped off the gelato. "You are cutup."

Pretty much the last thing in the world a girl wants to hear from The Butcher.

Chapter 46

Ivanovic´'s replacement, a brawny lumberjack of a man with dead eyes and steel wool skin met us at the elevator doors. "He is waiting in library."

Unfathomable, really, how my heels could click against the hardwood, while I was certain I was wading through quicksand.

Stannis paused in front of the closed French doors. "Of grave fortune, yes?"

I'm going to assume you meant of grave importance.

"Are you ready, *Vatra Anđeo?*"

Not one tiny bit.

I nodded.

He threw open the doors. We stared at the man cable-tied to Stannis's desk chair, and then back at each other, our eyes wide.

Whoa.

"It's about goddamn time you showed up!" Talbott Cottle Coles yelled. "Get me outta this fucking chair!"

The pupils in Stannis's electric blue eyes contracted to pinpricks. He laid a gentle hand on my head. "One moment, Maisie." He walked out of the room.

Coles waited until he left. "What the fuck is going on, you treacherous cunt?"

Nothing good, you sonuvabitch.

I took a good long look at Coles behind the empty desk. Wiry, deeply tanned, with a Zoom white Hollywood smile, his salt-and-pepper hair recently darkened. Fear, tinged with the lingering smell of cigarettes, hung around him like a malodorous cloud.

He was wealthy and powerful and the mayor of Chicago. And he had paid someone not to scare or hurt, but to actually fecking kill me.

It wasn't until Stannis reentered the room that I realized Holst's "Mars, the Bringer of War" was now playing quietly in the background. "Close the doors, Maisie."

"Hey. Hey now, Stannis," Coles said. "I don't know what your game is, but let me go and I'll play along."

Stannis slowly shook his dark head. "Your shooter is dead."

"I don't know what you're talking about." Coles's eyes went tight. He tried to spin it, voice dropping into a tease. "You got me how you want me. Get rid of her."

Stannis reached into his suit coat pocket and came out with a full fist. "You think I do not find out?"

He threw the contents hard at the table. Bullets clattered onto the steel desk, bouncing crazily in all directions. Coles cringed, jerking as some hit him.

"Your hitter cost me Ivanović."

"That was Eddie V.'s hitter."

"You work against me?" Stannis raised his palms. "To kill me?"

"No, never! You know I'd never hurt you," Coles said. "He was ordered never to fire when you were there. Never."

"Then who?"

Coles's chin raised, obstinate. "Her."

"Maisie?"

The perverse green monster reared its head. "You are always fucking with her. Always."

Stannis folded his arms across his chest. "I would say you are jealous like woman." He shook his head. "But is insult to Maisie."

He circled behind Coles, opened the lower desk drawer, took out the grisly black ash box, and put it on the desk.

Coles didn't flinch.

He had no idea what was coming. Stannis's legacy, the jar of finger bones, had been moved from the desk to the bookshelf behind him.

Stannis removed the old iron key from his pocket and set it on the desk.

No turning away this time. Not sure I wanted to, anyway.

I stepped forward, picked up the key, and unlocked the box.

Stannis's bright blues filled with emotion. "Claim your place, *Vatra Anđeo.*" He removed the brutal iron cleaver and offered it to me.

Holy Christ.

The skin tightened on the back of my neck.

I laid my hand on top of the blade and gently pushed it down toward the desktop. "No evil is as cruel as hope."

Stannis's eyes sparked with delight.

"You win, all right?" Coles forced out a weak laugh. "I'm sorry I had someone shoot at you. I'll never do it again."

Stannis turned to Coles. "You have choice to make, Talbott. To pay for your betrayal, Maisie will take one finger."

"The fuck she will." He yanked and jerked against the cable ties in impotent fury. "Touch me, bitch, and I'll kill your whole motherfucking family while you watch."

"No," Stannis said flatly. "You will not. I am *mesar*. The Butcher."

Coles stiffened.

"Maisie will take finger or I will take your hand."

The mayor sagged forward, his voice more a moan than a mumble. "Giveherit."

"What?" Stannis asked politely.

"Give her the goddamn knife!"

Stannis offered the cleaver again. I gripped the battered handle and lifted it from his hands.

Oh God.

Stannislav's Buck knife appeared as if by magic. He cut the cable ties holding Coles's left arm.

"I don't think I can do this." I walked to the edge of the desk, as stiff and jerky as a bird.

"Oh, you're going to fucking do it, all right." Coles snorted in disgust, all bravado now.

Stannis moved the box to the edge of the desk. He put Coles's hand up against it. "Choose finger."

"Aren't you the goddamn prince of darkness?" Coles laid his little finger onto the heavily scarred edge. The realization that this was not a onetime thing for Stannis swept across his face. He tried to swallow, couldn't, and cleared his throat.

Coles could die if Stannis took his hand. I squeezed my eyes shut. *You can do this. Just like chopping carrots at home with Thierry.*

"Open your goddamn eyes!" Coles snapped.

I raised the cleaver up past my chin. Stannis reached out, lowered my wrists down to slightly beneath my shoulders, and nodded.

One . . .

Feck it.

I swung the blade down as hard as I could. *It felt like chopping a slab of ballistics gel with a piece of glass in the middle.*

Coles screamed and jerked up his arm, spittle and blood spraying as he cursed. Stannis grabbed his forearm and wrapped his hand in a white cotton towel.

Coles jerked away, his injured hand tight to his belly as he rocked back and forth against the cable ties holding him in the desk chair.

Stannis grinned at me, the enormous close-mouthed smile of a proud parent. He nodded and reached out his hand to my face. "*Vatra Anđeo.*" He wiped his thumb across my cheek, then held his hand away to show me the blood he'd rubbed off.

My vision dimmed at the edges.

I knew what he wanted me to say, so I said it. "*Moj davo.*"

Coles kept swearing. The pristine white towel on his hand was rapidly turning bright red with blood.

"Put your arm above your head, Your Honor," I said.

"What the fuck are you standing there for?" Coles yelled at me, panting and whey-faced. "You've had your fun, you stupid whore. Now go get me a goddamn cup of ice so I can go to the ER and get the fucking thing reattached."

Stannis spun the desk chair to face him. He dropped a heavy hand onto Coles's shoulder and leaned down until their noses were inches apart. "No, Talbott. It no longer belongs to you."

"The fuck it doesn't. It's my goddamn finger!" Coles's cheeks darkened to an apoplectic brick red. "It's my fin—"

A knock sounded. The door opened enough for Kontrolyor to poke his head in. "Boss?"

"Get him out of my sight."

Kon came in, opened a knife, and began cutting through the cable ties.

Stannis put his arm around my shoulders and turned us so our backs were to Coles.

Coles gasped as Kon stood him up.

"Stannislav . . ." Coles said. "Please . . ."

We stayed perfectly still until Coles stumbled from the room, Kontrolyor closing the door behind them.

"He has a vengeful temper," I said.

"Talbott will look at his hand every day and remember. He will do nothing." Stannis walked over to the desk, picked up the little finger, and held it out to me. "Come, Maisie."

I forced myself to take it.

It was still warm.

My head spun. Somehow, I floated over to the plinth with Stannis. He turned on the light beneath the glass cage.

I looked right in, not even minding that I knew the driver's finger had already been removed and placed in the jar on his desk.

I hardly even noticed that the five other fingers were almost ready to join the driver's and that the bones of a man's hand are so very fragile without the sinew and tendons.

"Do not disrupt the Staphylinidae." Stannis slid the lid back. "Slow."

Smooth and unhurried, I lowered my arm into the cage and gently laid the mayor of Chicago's little finger in a nest of wood chips in the rear right corner.

Chapter 47

The kitchen was full of Stannislav's men from last night's wake for Ivanović. "*Vatra Anđeo!*" they stood, toasting me with coffee, juice, and at least a couple of screwdrivers.

I had officially joined the ranks. In what capacity, I wasn't exactly sure. Chopping off Talbott Cottle Coles's finger made me more of a mascot than an equal.

Sweet Jaysus.

I am the rally monkey of the Srpska Mafija cartel.

Kontrolyor was making totally normal American breakfast food: French toast, bacon, and eggs. I stood at the counter eating a piece of bacon, focusing on the crispy, salty goodness, trying to force the latent Coles guilt to the back of my mind.

It wasn't like I had a choice, I kept telling myself.

My conscience has gone deaf to logic.

Stannis came into the kitchen looking like *Vogue*'s idea of a European magnate. He kissed my cheek. "Today, we go to crematorium. Talk of Ivanović." He gave a somber glance at one of the men. "He will take Ivanović home." He raised an apologetic shoulder. "Is not place for you."

Talk about a governor's reprieve.

I nodded. "Are you okay?"

"After today, yes. Slajic will provide for Ivanović's family." He pulled a money clip from his pants pocket and started to thumb through hundreds. "Go shopping. Have nice day."

I stopped his hand with my own. "I only like to shop with you." I pulled a single hundred from between his fingers. "But I will have a nice lunch."

He laughed. "You are good for me."

I was officially off-leash.

And it felt fantastic. I walked with a spring in my step the eight blocks to my dummy apartment's underground parking lot.

I got in the Hellcat Challenger, sucked in a lungful of new car smell, and hit the radio. A clean version of "Damn It Feels Good to Be a Gangsta" started playing. I left the garage, letting my tires squeal a little on the turns. The irony alone had me laughing so hard I stopped the car at the mouth of the garage until I caught my breath.

I put my sunglasses on and told Siri to play The Specials' "Pressure Drop," then took off for Special Unit like a bat with the winning lottery ticket out of hell.

Anita, as usual, met me at the door. "Good to see you, Rook." She gave me a two-finger salute. "You know the way to Sawyer's office."

That I do. That I surely do.

His office door was electronically ajar by the time I reached it. I knock-entered.

Walt's face was as welcoming as a snow bath.

Brrrr.

"What happened?"

"It's been handled, sir." I cringed inwardly as I realized how completely stupid that sounded. "The shooter was after me. Renko's bodyguard was collateral damage."

Jaysus, that sounded harsh.

"Why you?" His voice was as uninterested as if we were talking about how bad the Bears would be this year.

"Eddie's trying to force his way into Renko's operation. Veteratti's in a coke addict's downward spiral. Paranoid, aggressive. Renko figured Eddie tried to take me out to teach him a lesson and hired Black Hawk to hunt the hitter."

Sawyer took a sip of tea, and put the cup back in the saucer. "Go on."

"The next day, Black Hawk calls me to pick up Renko at The Storkling. Violetta Vetterati's right-hand man, Jimmy the Wolf, is holding him. Vi offered up an honor debt to forgive Eddie's participation for brokering the hit."

Walt sighed. "More than enough of an excuse for Constantino to clip him."

"Vi tells us the shooter's been liquidated and his employer would be delivered to Renko's penthouse."

Sawyer's lips twitched. "Are you telling me we have a Murder One on the table?"

"Umm . . . no." I cleared my throat. "This is where things get a little . . . hinky."

"Hinky?"

"Can I go off the record?"

"You do realize, Maisie, that we are the police. Sworn to uphold the law." Sawyer folded his arms across his chest. "There is no 'off the record'."

"Yes sir." I took a deep breath. "Talbott Cottle Coles was who they delivered."

He blinked. "The mayor of Chicago. Hired a hit man to kill you. Why?"

I shrugged. "Jealousy."

"And you yourself do not have a sexual relationship with Stannislav Renko?"

"No sir."

The enormity of the situation fell on me like a piano from a silent movie.

Jaysus. We weren't only talking termination, we were talking serious time. What kind of sentence does an undercover cop get for first-degree assault of a city official?

I must have gone as pale as I felt.

"I take it we're at the hinky part." He sat back in his chair.

I nodded. "Renko's loyalty for Goran Slajic is absolute. He would never kill Coles due to his position."

"And?" Sawyer prompted.

"Coles got to choose. I could take his finger or Renko would take his hand."

Walt Sawyer's face creased in amused disbelief. "And where is the Honorable Mayor Coles now?"

"I'm not sure." My knee started bouncing. "After I chopped off his left pinkie with a sixteenth-century Serbian cleaver, one of Renko's men took him to Northwestern Memorial Emergency Room."

Walt Sawyer raised a palm to me and turned his chair around for a full two minutes. He spun back around. "Upon reevaluation, that conversation was off the record."

Whew.

I nodded so hard my teeth rattled. "Yessir."

"We need to shut Renko down. Now. With the influx of money from the theft of two dozen brand-new luxury cars, Slajic's entry into the arms market is a given." Sawyer rubbed the back of his neck. "Chop shops, the New York Mob, hit men, and kidnapping the mayor are one thing. Gunrunning with the Mexican cartels via Chicago takes precedent. Any ideas?"

"Renko never wanted to heist the new cars," I said. "He thought it a fool's enterprise when chopping is so much safer and cost-effective. He's too clever to use the salt storage facility or hit the closed transports again."

"What if the stolen cars weren't new?" Walt spitballed.

"Chopped, they're worth more than new . . ." I stopped, the pieces of an idea fitting together like parts of a Revell SnapTite model. A slow grin spread across my face. "I need to make a call."

Walt set his desk phone in front of me. "Proceed."

I took out my iPhone. "Would you mind facing the other direction, sir?" I asked Walt Sawyer as my cheeks went fire red. "It's . . . I'm shy."

His eyes widened in disbelief. "Moments ago, you confessed to chopping off the mayor of Chicago's finger, and yet you're embarrassed for me to watch you flirt with a suspect?"

"Exactly."

Walt spun his desk chair toward the wall.

I dialed Alfonso Javier Rodriguez's private number from the card and put it on Speaker.

"Hello?"

"El Cid? This is—"

"Maisie McGrane from Chicago?"

Whoa. He knows my name. That's . . . bad. "Yes, it is."

"What does a girl from a family of cops want with El Cid?"

"Half," I said.

"What?"

"Half my family is police. The other half is defense attorneys."

He laughed politely. "As enticing as the opportunity to be arrested and then defended sounds—"

I'm losing him.

"What can I say?" I paused, then dangled a little *Fight Club.* "You met me at a very strange time in my life."

He hesitated, unsure if I knew what I'd said. He threw back, "And it's ending one minute at a time."

Gotcha!

I spun Walt's chair around and replied to El Cid with a grin, "C'mon, it'll be fun."

"Two things I'm not willing to lose are my freedom and my life," he warned. "You still with Renko?"

"Yes," I said. "Any interest in brokering a deal?"

"I thought you were a smart cookie," he said. "Cutting out your boyfriend isn't clever."

"It'll still be Renko and Grieco's deal. No reason we can't scratch each other's backs. I'm in it for a finder's fee."

El Cid was plenty interested now. "For what?"

"My genius. What kind of interest do you think Carlos would have in two dozen perfectly restored vintage muscle cars?"

"A helluva lot. What's your cut for these raceable dreams?"

"One percent," I said.

"Why so little?"

"A bull and a bear can escape the slaughterhouse, but never the pig."

Jaysus Criminey, I'm starting to sound like Stannis.

"Of course, if you can convince Grieco to ask this of Renko, you, too, deserve a commission," I said, setting the hook. "A car, of your choice, as a gift."

"It can't come with Grieco's containers."

"You'll have to meet it in Juárez," I warned.

"Done." El Cid went silent, considering. "I want a 1971 Chevelle SS 454."

Walt typed the car into his computer and swiveled the screen. A restored model ranged anywhere from $35K to $50K. "Really?" I asked. "That's your choice?"

"I'm no little pig, either. The Chevelle is a workingman's car. Chevy made a lot of them, they're fast as hell, easy to get parts for, and anyone can work on 'em. Even the idiots in my pit crew."

"The show's in a week," I said. "You're gonna have to work fast."

He let his voice go low and husky. "No worries, Maisie baby."

I hung up.

"A non-starter, I thought." Walt tapped his fingertips together. "How did you turn him around?"

"Quotes from the movie *Fight Club*."

He frowned, puzzled.

"With five older brothers, I pretty much know all the words to the Godfathers, *Goodfellas*, *Tombstone*, *Fight Club*, the first three *Star Wars*, and every Tarantino movie."

"It's that easy?"

I didn't think it was that easy. "Pretty much."

Walt leaned back in his chair and tapped a pen against his lower lip. "For Special Unit, forty thousand dollars is a reasonably cost-effective buy-in to the Grieco Cartel."

Chapter 48

It took exactly two days of BFF naps and workouts and shopping and nightclubs with Stannis, for El Cid to ignite Carlos Grieco's fuse. Stannis and I were lying on his bed watching David Niven and Ginger Rogers in *Bachelor Mother*.

His phone chirped from the nightstand. I paused Apple TV.

"El Cid." Stannis frowned. "I am surprised to hear from you."

I could hear Grieco's lieutenant through the phone. "Yes. But there's an opportunity at hand that would be a good test for both of us, I think."

"Oh?"

"There is a muscle car auction in five days. We will pay one-point-five for twenty-four cars."

Depending on age and restoration, two of those cars could easily be worth that.

I popped Stannis in the arm. He looked at me. I shook my head, mouthed "*not enough,*" and held up four fingers.

He sighed. "El Cid. Not enough time. Not enough money. Is no good."

"How much money to make it good?"

"Four. Twenty cars. No specifics."

"Two-point-five."

Stannis looked at me. I gave him a thumbs-up. "I check. See if can happen." He hung up and tossed his phone onto the nightstand, where it landed with a *clunk*. He cuddled up to me and I restarted the movie.

Hank's Law Number Five: Make it look easy.

Either it'd go or it wouldn't.

I ran my fingers through his hair and settled in to enjoy the show. When the credits rolled, so did Stannis, onto his back. "You have muscle car. Tell me about auction."

"Uh, I know a little—a very little—about vintage muscle cars."

"You knew about the money."

"Only because a fully restored Super Bee can run over five hundred fifty thousand dollars. Raceable? A million."

He sat up on his elbows. "And auction?"

"I don't know a thing about that." I hugged my knees to my chest. "I could find out, I suppose."

"How?"

I dropped my chin onto my knees. "Leticia asked me if I wanted to work the auction."

"I do not understand."

"Overtime is big money. I don't know where they're holding the auction, but I know it's not at the usual place because the Traffic Enforcement Bureau is allocating money for additional meter maids and tow trucks. To keep traffic moving. You know, for safety."

His eyes narrowed. "And Leticia has access to how the event is set up."

"You bet. She has to plan the routes, pick out the trouble spots."

"And you would see this if you were working?"

"Ugh." I flopped onto my back. "I don't want to go to work."

He loomed over me. "I want you to. This is significant money."

"How about I stop in and tell her I'll work the overtime as long as I get to choose my route?"

"Oh? No work?" Stannis laughed. "You think you are princess now?"

Just call me Buttercup.

* * *

The next morning, I put on jeans, my steel-toe work boots, an Israel Defense Force T-shirt, and a PEA Windbreaker.

"Kontrolyor will drive you," Stannis said.

"Seriously? Jeff Mant is dead. Vi Veteratti owes us an honor debt, Eddie is scared witless, and Coles? I don't think he'll ever even glance in my direction again." I went over and pulled him up from the table. "C'mon."

"What are we doing?"

"Research."

The Hellcat now resided at the penthouse's underground parking garage. We got in. "A modern-day muscle car," I said.

"Is nice."

Nice? That's it?

I drove us to the freeway, taking it smooth and easy, and pulled into a gas station next to an on-ramp. I looked at him. "You do know how to drive, right?"

"Yes."

"Then get out." He went around while I scooted across into the passenger's seat. He started the car and looked at me for instruction. "Take her on the freeway," I said. He merged on. "Hit it," I said, and boy, he did.

He hit 90 mph out of the chute, the V8 growling, weaving in and out of traffic. "Powerful. Hard to hold back."

"Yeah," I said. "It's a scary feckin' car."

"The traffic is slow," he complained, juicing it as we sliced between two semis. He glanced at me. "I understand now."

"The vintage ones are just as violent and macho. It's Grieco's obsession. Heck, the guy even owns part of a NASCAR track. When his people have a dispute, they race it out."

"Good idea." Stannis nodded, cutting across three lanes of traffic, tires squealing as we hit the off-ramp. "I discuss with Goran." He hit the first turnout, parked, got out of the car, and came around to the passenger side.

I slid behind the wheel. "Forget the way home?"

"No," he said. "I have no license."

"Cute."

"We do deal, yes?" Stannis said.

"The auction's at an abandoned car dealership. I doubt they've laid out for heavy security. I'm guessing a team of guards, maybe? The cars are all covered by the individual owners, and the auction house probably has an umbrella policy. I don't see them taking the necessary precautions for you and yours coming in hard and heavy."

"Okey, yes. We go."

Sweet, no pressure there.

I dropped Stannis outside his penthouse and headed for Silverthorn Estates.

My phone rang. Hank. "Hi."

Gee, I miss you something fierce.

"I'm gonna be on the job the next few days, Angel Face."

Fist pump! No lying! "Aww. That's too bad."

"Moutain cabin or beach house?" he said.

"Cabin."

"Attagirl. How's a month sound?"

"Heavenly."

"Soon," he promised and hung up.

Walt Sawyer looked as natty and fit as the two FBI agents sitting across from him looked rumpled and chunky. They were poring over maps, diagrams, satellite photos. The muscle car auction was taking place in an empty Saab dealership. Price guides and car mags littered the table.

"This is Agent McGrane. Special Unit's youngest and most resourceful. She's gotten closer to Renko than anyone."

"I'll bet," the thinner of the two feebs muttered with a sideways leer.

Dick.

"Why, thank you." I smiled politely. "That's quite a compliment from a real live G-man."

Sawyer's lips twitched. "Renko prefers to keep her close at hand. Her communication ability is severely limited."

"Are there any tall buildings around or parking structures?" I asked. "Renko likes to oversee from off-site."

"Nope," said the better-mannered feeb. "The closest would be another one-story car dealership."

"I need whatever diagrams and maps you can give me," I said, "to add to the standard Traffic Enforcement Bureau request. Stannis meets with his men tonight, and then it's all riding on their evaluation."

"Oh, he'll do it," said Slightly Thinner. "Serbs are greedy bastards."

Go Team Stannis!

The jerkwad feeb has me cheering for the criminal element.

Hank's offer of a month alone in a cabin put the spurs to me. "Walt, how fast can we get El Cid's car to Juárez?"

"There's a burnt-orange metallic 1971 Chevelle SS 454 waiting in a twenty-foot container at the CEC Intermodal yard. The next train to Juárez leaves tonight."

"I'm not sure this is a go for Stannis," I said.

Walt shrugged. "We'd send it either way. Why don't you go ahead and call Carlos Grieco's lieutenant. Let these boys see you work."

Walt was showing me off and I liked it.

I dialed El Cid and hit Speaker. "Hello, handsome."

"I like the sound of that," he said. "Especially since Carlos asked me to personally deliver your finder's fee when the transaction's completed. What do you say to a weekend in LA, my treat?"

"My kind of trouble doesn't take weekends off," I said.

"Riiight," El Cid drew out. "So, tell me. How bad does a good girl get?"

"That's what all the boys want to know," I said with a laugh. "Your cut arrives tomorrow morning. With my own special treat."

"Yeah?" El Cid asked, ready for the tease. "What's that?"

"Papers that'll pass any US DMV."

"No shit?"

"Like you said, I'm one cool kitty." I hung up.

The feebs looked suitably impressed. It's easy to sound tack-sharp when you play with someone who can speak the language of the smack.

The new guy, Steel Wool, came to fetch me. "Mr. Renko would like to see you."

I went alone to Stannislav's office. Kontrolyor and two others surrounded Stannis at his desk, discussing the heist.

"We ignore the entrance and exit. They have only temporary chain-link panels, easy to disable." Kon tapped on the satellite photos of the old Saab dealership. "The trucks enter here, leave here, here, and here."

Exactly as Walt and the feebs had figured they'd do.

"How many drivers in all?" someone asked.

Kon drummed his fingers on the photo. "Two cars can fit in a forty-five-foot container. We have room for driver to piggyback containers. But do we have time?"

"No," Stannis said. "Need ten drivers, I have five. Christo's four electronic monkeys."

"I will not be driving," Kon said. "Black Hawk wants me to secure the hostages."

"Black Hawk's team is five. They will subdue guards, dogs, radio signals, etc.," Stannis said.

"Is not enough," said another Serb.

"Eddie V. is giving us five drivers and three guns." Kon pointed at Stannis's men. "The two of you, our number is twenty-four. Easy to overtake even two crews of guards."

"Twenty-six," Stannis said. "*Vatra Anđeo* and I will be there."

The men left the office.

"You have done very well, Maisie." Stannis stood up and stretched. "Come." He rounded the desk and waved me over to the aquarium. "See progress the beetles make."

Do I have to?

I walked over, a tight smile on my lips. He flipped on the light. Only Coles's finger remained. Almost ready to be taken out.

"A new addition for the jar," I said.

"No. Coles is not my legacy. Is start of yours."

And what the heck am I supposed to do with it?

Aside from the fact that bones are chock-full of DNA, I couldn't have the mayor of Chicago's finger sitting around at home or at Hank's.

I could just imagine the conversation. *"Oh, that? It's nothing. The other day I found a human finger on the subway and just decided to keep it."*

Cripes.

Chapter 49

I fibbed to Stannis that I'd left my jacket in the car, went to the parking garage, and typed a ginormous text to Walt detailing everything I'd seen and heard. The heist would take place tomorrow night at 23:10, a slow time of night for the CPD, when shifts changed over. I warned Walt that Black Hawk would arrange a serious but nonexistent threat to occur across town.

And then I sent him the bad news.

Stannis and I will be on site.
Walt replied: No heroics. Keep your head down and stay out of the fray.

I returned to the penthouse. Stannis was alone in the foyer. "Do you dance, Maisie?"

"About as well as I swim."

Stannis winced and smiled. He clicked a remote and held out his arms. I stepped in to them as the ultra-feminine Kitty LaRoar started singing "Isn't It a Lovely Day." He took it slow, holding me close. "So quickly you change my life."

Unable to respond, I pressed in closer to him.

He leaned away. "What is wrong?"

"Are you sure about this?" I asked. "The cars, the cartel . . . the police?"

"Only worry little for me, remember?" He laughed and spun me in a quick turn. "Laws catch flies but let hornets go free."

* * *

The cars were big, bad, and handsome. Hard-edged and hardass Road Runners, Impalas, and Fairlanes side by side with the coolest of the cool Camaros and Challengers and Mustangs. Most painstakingly restored to factory specs, the rest were Resto-Mods, custom-fit with bigger, brutal engines.

All that is wrong with our country could be summed up in a single word: Prius.

America's downward evolutionary spiral of the tough guy.

Even the name was a derivative of "prissy."

We watched from the Range Rover, counting down the seconds. Stannis cranked the volume on his portable headset and leaned his head to mine, so we both could hear the men.

Three men-sized shadows converged on a squad of two men and a dog. Red gun sights light up the security badges on their chests. The dogless guard's hands shot up to the sky, while the other struggled to restrain the barking canine.

Kon's voice came through the headset. "Quiet the animal or I kill it." The guard uttered a command. The dog fell silent.

At that moment, Stannislav and Eddie's men hit the fence with bolt cutters and wire clippers. Event fencing. Portable chain-link panels bolted and wired together. It took less than three minutes for each pair of men to detach the mobile barrier panels and set them aside.

"Two more guards and another dog are safe in the office," Kon said, giving them a long look at the size of the operation. "Are they paying you enough to lose your life?"

The guards shook their heads.

"Good. We understand each other." Kon and his men escorted the guards into the building. After a minute, Kon came back on. "Men and dogs secure."

There were now four different ingress/egress spaces in the lot fencing.

"We go." Stannis handed me a blackened surgical mask. We got out and ran onto the auction lot, sprinting into the opened door of the dealership. "Find keys."

The rumble of semis started as the first two trucks came onto the lot.

I followed Stannis toward the staff room. He stopped, drew his gun, and said to me, "I threaten. You watch their eyes."

He pushed open the door and we went in. The four guards were wrist and ankle zip tie–shackled. The dogs, locked in a utility closet, were quiet.

Stannis walked in, gun hanging at his side. "Where are keys?"

The guards all looked at the ground. Stannis chose the toughest-looking one and fired at the ground next to him. Linoleum and cement chipped up into the air. He walked to the guard, bent down, and pressed the barrel behind the guard's ear.

"Ergh!" the guard grunted.

"Choose which man will die," Stannis said.

"It doesn't have to be this way," I said. "Where are the keys, guys?"

Two of the three guards pointedly looked at the office area. The third glanced in the opposite direction. The showroom floor.

"Hold up," I said to Stannis. I ran out, and sure enough, there was a valet key panel beneath the receptionist's desk. It didn't even have a lock on it.

Bingo. The keys are even tagged.

"Got 'em!" I yelled at Stannis.

He came into the showroom. "Good." He pressed his headset, said something in Serbian, and one of his men rushed in. Stannis left the showroom to supervise.

The first two container trucks had ramps down in front of the cars. The electronic monkeys checked them with scanners, popped the locks and the hoods, got in, and went to work.

One of Stannis's men and I figured out which were the right keys and he ran them out.

By now, the monkeys had found two of the FBI's super electronic locator tags. The ones they assured Walt Sawyer were undetectable.

They left them and moved on to the next. Everything was moving in rhythm and fast, like the second hand of a stopwatch.

Four cars loaded and gone. The next two semis entered as the others left.

Too fast for my liking.

Semis five and six were setting up to load. I figured the Feds would track the trucks to the CEC Intermodal to bust and recover.

But the men?

Were the Feds going to swoop in or what?

Please don't let us be Chicago's Waco.

The best cars were inside the showroom. Some of them worth over a million apiece. I jogged outside, put my fingers in my mouth, and gave a short whistle.

The men looked at me. I pointed at one of the monkeys and gestured for him to come over. He sprinted to my side.

"Let's see if we can add any of these to the haul," I said.

The cars inside weren't locked. The monkey peeked inside them, passing on a rare Yenko Chevelle and a mint Shelby. "Ravelco plugs." He shook his head. "Can't beat 'em." He skipped the cars in the middle and ran to the opposite end of the room. A 1971 Plymouth Hemi 'Cuda, whose hood was open. He waved a small electronic reader over the car, bit his lip, and flashed me the "metal rock" fingers sign. "Come to Papa, you luscious, race-ready bi-otch."

I opened the showroom doors so he could drive the 'Cuda out.

Stannis came in. "We have trouble." He grabbed me by the arm and we hustled into the small service garage. "Truck One did not arrive at checkpoint." He handed me the burner phone with all the truck driver numbers. "Call Truck Three."

He tapped his headset. "*Chyornyj Yastreb.* We may be compromised . . . Yes . . . *Andeo* is with me. In fallback position."

I called Truck Three and pushed speaker. "Hello?"

"Shit," spat the voice on the other end. "Cops."

"Leave phone on speaker," Stannis ordered the driver. "Put in pocket."

We heard the muffled swipe of fabric on the driver's end. I hit Mute.

"This is the FBI," said Law Enforcement on loudspeaker. "Driver! With your right hand remove the keys from the ignition. Driver! Slowly open the door with your left hand."

Stannis clicked his headset, pacing, speaking staccato Serbian to his team while I listened to the FBI talk the driver to the ground and cuff him.

Stannis reached over to turn off the burner cell.

"Where's the redhead, asshole?" demanded a federal agent.

"Redhead?" the driver asked.

"The girl! Where's the fucking girl?"

Feck me.

Chapter 50

Stannis went stock-still.

The cords in his neck were working hard as he tried to swallow. "*Chyornyj Yastreb* say to me, 'The girl will be trouble. And trouble never comes alone.' It was you. *Vatra Andeo*. My fire angel. You did this."

Hank's Law Number Two: Respond to threats with complete confidence.

I said nothing, doing my best to look confused.

Stannislav's eyes were bleak. "My heart you break. Like no other." He pulled the Smith & Wesson from the holster at his back and pointed it at me.

"What are you doing?" I asked.

Tears coursed down his cheeks. "You destroy me."

There would be no mercy. Stannislav "The Bull" Renko had none.

I took a deep breath.

Better to die on your feet than live on your knees.

The nose of a gun came around the corner of the doorway. "Put the gun down, Stannis," Hank said.

It couldn't be Hank. But it was.

He strode into the room, encased in black bulletproof armor. "Put the gun down."

"*Chyornyj Yastreb,*" Stannis said. "It is over."

What?

Hank is Black Hawk?

WTF?

Stannislav's hand trembled with anger. "She betrayed me. Betrayed us all."

"No." Hank shook his head. "Not her."

"Do not tell me is Veteratti. His men are here."

"Coles," Hank said. "Coles had your place tapped to the gills. He scrambled the SWAT raid."

Stannis lowered his arm. "You come to know this how?"

"He confessed to one of my men. About twenty minutes ago."

"But FBI ask where is redhead."

"She took his finger." Hank gave a bark of laughter. "He may want to tear you down, but he's gunning for her."

The blood drained from Stannislav's face.

Hank had known I was with Stannis all along. All the way back from the day Jeff Mant attacked me . . . Telling Stannis I should live with him. . . .

The gears in my mind were spinning so hard I felt dizzy.

Sirens blared in the distance.

Stannis lowered the gun. "*Vatra Anđeo?*" He took two staggering steps toward me, hand outstretched. "Forgive me," he said hoarsely. "Forgive me."

And because I knew with absolute certainty he would have killed me, I said the single thing that would wound him the most. "I know you'd never hurt me, *moj đavo.*"

He flinched as if struck.

Garbled yelling from outside was broken up by the letters, "FBI!"

Hank was thirty feet away from me, but it might have been thirty miles. He received a message on his headset. "Let's go."

"Is no use." Stannis made an open-palm fist. "We are in the talons."

"Why do you think they call me *Chyornyj Yastreb?*" Hank glanced at the oversized watch on his wrist. "A Sikorsky UH-60 is going to land in two minutes and forty-two seconds. We're going to be on it."

"She comes with us."

Oh no.

Please, no.

"Like hell." Hank's face turned to granite. "She's not a puppy, for chrissakes. Her family has power and money, Stannis. It'll never be over."

Stannis spun, pointing the gun at Hank's chest. "You work for me. She comes."

Hank raised his palms in surrender, lowered his head in acquiescence.

Stannis reached behind his back and put his gun in the holster.

Hank took a single quick step toward me. His right hand whipped forward in an underhand blur.

An icy cold punch hit me in the thigh. I wobbled where I stood and looked down. A thick black handle stuck out of my thigh. I stared at Hank in dumb shock.

You threw a knife at me.

And it hit me.

"No!" Stannis shouted.

"She can't come now," Hank said.

My leg began to throb, my flesh pulsing against the blade. I stumbled backward into the wall. My head felt floaty and light. I slid down to the floor. My fingers twitched and moved toward the handle.

Don't touch it don't touch it don't touch it.

It was the short blade. The one Hank wore on his belt.

You threw a knife at me.

Stannis glared back over his shoulder. "You work for me!"

"No," Hank said. "I work for Goran Slajic. I protect you."

Stannis looked at the knife. He reached into his pocket and pressed a sidewinder key into my palm. "You have trouble? You find Christo." He cupped my face in his hands and kissed my forehead. "You know nothing. No cartel, no Constantino, no Slajic."

The knife in my leg had somehow turned from ice to molten steel. I heard a strange keening sort of whimper.

Oh God. That's me.

"It'll take her a week to remember her own name." Hank

held up a thin silver packet. "Combination of atracurium and ataraxics developed by Mossad."

"Good." Stannis took the key from my hand and slipped it into my jacket pocket. He tapped my temple with his finger. "Fast to think, *Andeo*. You will solve key."

"Jesus fucking Christ!" the room rumbled with a deep voice. "We got full SWAT and Feds out there and those mutherfuckers want to engage, for fuck's sake!" A six-foot-seven Viking in camo paint and full black battle rattle came around the corner. Ragnar. "Are we getting the fuck out of here or what? What's the goddamn holdup?"

Hank jerked his head at Stannis. "Take him."

"Let's move!" Ragnar came over and jerked Stannis to his feet. He spun him toward the door and winked at me, before laying a heavy hand on Stannis's back and hustling him out of the room.

Hank strode over and squatted down on his haunches. "First rule when taking damage?"

"Level head." I tried to smile. "Act quick."

"Clean hit. Fast recovery." He held up the foil packet. "You'll remember everything. Pretend you don't."

"It hurts."

"I know, baby. I'm gonna make you feel better."

I gave him a tight smile. "You're cute."

"You're cute, too." He kissed me.

"The blade." He raised my chin to look at him. His gray eyes had gone as pale as sun-bleached bone. "Remember? Don't touch it."

I remember everything. "Hank, I—"

"Don't get all choked up, Firebrand." He flashed me a wicked grin. "You know I don't mind a reasonable amount of trouble."

He peeled off the wrapper and raised the foil packet to my nose and mouth. It didn't smell like anything.

Everything was dim and blurry and smelled of noxious smoke. The room spun and I closed my eyes. I'm not sure for how long.

My throat and mouth felt like sandpaper. It hurt to breathe.

My leg was on fire, the muscle searing from the inside out. *Of course, I can pull it out. It's already cauterized itself.* My numb fingers twitched against the handle. I gasped.

Don't touch don't touch don't touch.

"Medic!" A loud voice rang in my ears. "One down in here! Knife wound, maybe more."

"Maisie." Gloved hands grasped my chin, turned my face from side to side, patting it none too gently. "Maisie, it's Lee. Lee Sharpe. Can you hear me?"

I forced my eyes to open to slits and tried to point at the foil pouch on the floor. Instead my arm jerked and hung limp. "Drug," I croaked.

"I know. I got you."

"Don't . . . blade."

"No. We'll leave it in. Let the ER docs handle that," Lee said. "You're gonna be fine."

The stink of antiseptic and diesel stung my nose. I lay on my back, slightly elevated on the stretcher's thin mattress. A blond paramedic who looked like he hadn't graduated from junior high yet strapped a non-rebreather oxygen mask to my face.

It resembled the ones that drop from the ceiling of airplanes when you're about to crash so you can suck in a pure oxygen high and enjoy the ride.

"IV of D5w, KVO," Kid Paramedic said into the radio mic on his left lapel, "Patient is alert and oriented." He jabbed the IV needle into my arm and started the glucose drip, then moved on to my leg.

He had me panting and whimpering just from cutting my pants leg up to my hip.

Jaysus Criminey.

"I'm going to pack and stabilize the knife, okay? The ER docs will take it out," Kid Paramedic said. "You may feel a little discomfort."

He packed trauma dressings around the knife. Each bandage press was like another mini-stab.

Oh God.

Tears streamed down my cheeks.

"Maisie? Maisie!" Cash shouted from outside the ambulance.

"Stand down, McGrane." Lee stepped in front of him. "She's going to be okay."

"She's my goddamned sister and I'm going with her."

"Stand. Down."

Cash shuffled in front of Lee, craning over his shoulder to see me. He looked like I felt. I moved my fingers in a slight wave.

Lee climbed into the ambulance.

"Take her to Rush University Hospital," Cash said. "I'll be there as soon as I can, Maisie!"

Lee jerked the doors shut behind him, slamming the metal locks home. "Rush Hospital."

Kid Paramedic nodded. He hit his radio mic and relayed Lee's command to the driver. Lee took a seat on the squad bench. He put his hand on my arm. "You're gonna be fine."

I know.

My leg burned like the devil had laid his tail on it and my arm was refrigerating from the inside out from the IV.

"Is she stabilized?" Lee said.

Kid Paramedic looked at him warily. "Sir?"

"Her vitals. The IV, oxygen. Is her wound packed and stabilized?"

"Yes sir."

"Under any life-threatening emergency?"

"No sir."

"Then get up front. I'll let you know if there's trouble."

Kid Paramedic and the armed and battle-armored Lee were on the same team, but Kid was scared gutless. "Sir, I can't do that—"

"You can and you will." Lee jerked his head toward the door. "Front of the bus. Now."

A thin sheen of sweat broke out on Kid's upper lip. "Miss?"

I nodded weakly at him and slurred, thick-tongued from behind the mask, "Iths aww gud."

"I'm her goddamn partner." Lee raised his hands, fast, open-palmed.

To Kid, they were as threatening as fists. He went through into the cab of the ambulance, leaving the door ajar.

Lee got off the squad bench, smacked the door shut, and planted himself in the jump seat, right behind my head. He dialed his phone and hit speaker. It rang twice. "Sawyer? Sharpe here. Mission failure."

"Score?"

"All cars recovered. Sixteen arrests. Renko, Kontrolyor, and four others slipped the net."

Of course they did. Because: Hank.

"How?" Walt asked.

"They set off a mess of smoke grenades and flashbangs and lit out in a goddamned Sikorsky U-60."

Walt Sawyer gave a bark of laughter and went silent. "Field Agent McGrane?" he asked. "Location? Cover intact?"

"With me." Lee glanced at my leg. "Cover more so than she is."

"Condition?" Sawyer snapped.

"Stable. Stab wound to the leg. Drugged with unknown substance but lucid. We're en route to hospital, alone in the ambulance."

I sucked in a breath. The driver seemed to think it was his mission in life to hit each and every pothole.

Lee put his hand on my shoulder.

"I want to speak with her," Walt said.

"Go ahead," said Lee, holding the phone closer to my ear.

"Well done, Agent McGrane. Well done," Walt said.

"Thank you, sir," I said, through the oxygen mask.

"While losing Renko was unfortunate, Operation Steal-Tow has achieved its intended purpose. The Slajic car theft ring has been virtually eliminated, thanks in no small part to you. We've obtained evidence and insight on Constantino's enterprise, as well as on the Veterattis. And you've managed to ingratiate yourself with a lieutenant of the Grieco Cartel."

When you put it like that, I pretty much kick-ass rock!

"An exemplary effort from our youngest and newest field agent, wouldn't you say, Agent Sharpe?"

"Yes sir," Lee said but he frowned at me.

Walt continued, speaking to me once more. "I'm assuming you haven't established cover with your family?"

"No, sir," I said at the same time Lee said, "She hasn't."

"As of now you are a journalist. Freelancing for Paul Renick at the *Chicago Sentinel*. Credentials will arrive at the hospital within an hour. You'll be debriefed within the next forty-eight."

"Thank you, sir."

"A valiant effort, Maisie. If your family was privy to your heroics, they would be very proud." Sawyer disconnected.

Hank.

My family.

What they don't know won't hurt me.

Maisie McGrane will return in

SHOOT 'EM UP

A Kensington trade paperback and
e-book on sale October 2016.